Redliners

Baen Books by David Drake

The Hammer's Slammers series:
Hammer's Slammers
At Any Price
Counting the Cost
Rolling Hot
The Warrior
The Sharp End

Redliners
Starliner
Ranks of Bronze
Lacey and His Friends
Old Nathan
Mark II: The Military Dimension

The General (with S.M. Stirling):
The Forge
The Hammer
The Anvil
The Steel
The Sword
The Chosen

An Honorable Defense: Crisis of Empire
(with Thomas T. Thomas)
Enemy of My Enemy: Nova Terra
(with Ben Ohlander)
*The Undesired Princess and the Enchanted
Bunny*
(with L. Sprague de Camp)
Lest Darkness Fall and To Bring the Light
(with L. Sprague de Camp)

Redliners

DAVID DRAKE

REDLINERS

This is a work of fiction. All the characters and events portrayed in this book are fictional, and any resemblance to real people or incidents is purely coincidental.

Copyright © 1996 by David Drake

A Baen Books Original

Baen Publishing Enterprises
P.O. Box 1403
Riverdale, NY 10471

ISBN: 0-671-87733-X

Cover art by Gary Ruddell

First printing, August 1996

Distributed by Simon & Schuster
1230 Avenue of the Americas
New York, NY 10020

Library of Congress Cataloging-in-Publication Data

Drake, David.
  Redliners / David Drake
     p. cm.
  ISBN 0-671-87733-X (HC)
  I. Title
PS3554.R196R43 1996
813'.54—dc20   96-17559
                                               CIP

Printed in the United States of America

DEDICATION
To Kay McCauley
For being a great agent and a friend.
Particularly for being a friend.

ACKNOWLEDGMENTS

Help was provided by Dan and Kate Breen, a father-daughter team with a sense of style; Clyde and Carlie Howard; Esther Friesner and Stutzmans of all sizes; and my wife Jo. Thank you all.

Then it's Tommy this, an' Tommy that, an'
  "Tommy, 'ow's yer soul?"
But it's "Thin red line of 'eroes" when the
  drums begin to roll,
The drums begin to roll, my boys, the drums
  begin to roll.

—Rudyard Kipling

PROLOGUE

When I entered Category 4 of the Unity civil service thirty-seven years ago, I gave up my former name and life to become a servant dedicated to all mankind. There are those who say I ceased to be human when as part of the process a computer was embedded in my central nervous system.

I am called John Smith, though my name might as easily have been Xiang Quo or Krishna Singh or Ali Nasr. I am now Chief of Administration, the highest permanent official of the Unity. There are those who say I have the powers of a god and the ruthlessness of an avalanche.

Since I entered Category 4, my only desire has been the long-term good of mankind. Since I became Chief of Administration, my will has been the only will of mankind.

There are those who say I have no more mercy than a surgeon treating cancer.

There are those who say my planning has been mankind's only salvation during these seven years of war with the Kalendru, who understand the concepts of "master" and "slave" but not of "equals".

There are those who say that even such as I must retire, as a blade is retired when grinding use wears it to a sliver—be that sliver ever so sharp.

They say, they say . . .

And they are all of them correct.

1

Operation Active Cloak

—1—

Major Arthur Farrell's bones vibrated to the howls of the generators braking the captured Kalendru starship to a soft landing in the main military port of the world Unity planners had labeled Maxus 377. The engineers hadn't bothered to jury-rig displays after they gutted the ship's hold for the assault force. If the strikers of Company C41 wanted, they could tap visuals from the flight deck onto their helmet visors and look at the warped-looking Spook structures they would attack in the next few seconds.

Farrell didn't bother to watch. Instead he rechecked his stinger. He wore crossed bandoliers of ammo packs and dangling blast rockets; a medical kit; two supplementary communication units; two knives—one of them powered, the other with a shorter fixed blade that could double as a climbing spike; and a packet of emergency rations. The integral canteen of Farrell's back-and-breast armor held two quarts of water, but he carried an additional three gallons in a backpack. The weight slowed him and made his armor sag brutally against his shoulders, but the cost was worth it to him.

When you're pinned down in the hot sun, thirst is the worst torture. Worse than the ripping pain of your wound, worse even than the stench of your friend's half-burned corpse on the ground beside you. Art Farrell knew.

The starship quivered, still twenty feet above the ground though she was nearly in equilibrium with the field her generators had induced in the magnetic mass on which she was landing. *"Wait for it!"* ordered Captain Broz, C41's executive officer, over the command channel.

Nadia Broz was following standard operating procedure, but on this mission there wasn't any risk that a striker would unass early. Normally C41 inserted aboard a purpose-built landing vessel. The hatches opened minutes before contact. For Active Cloak camouflage rather than speed was the requirement. At touchdown the flight crew would blow explosive bolts to separate the outer bulkheads from the skeleton of support members, but until then the freighter's hold was sealed like a prison cell.

"Hey, I think I changed my mind," a striker called over the ship noises. There was brittle laughter.

Kurt Leinsdorf stood stolidly at Farrell's shoulder as he always did during an insertion. On C41's table of organization, Leinsdorf was a communications specialist. In reality he was Farrell's bodyguard, a huge, strong man who carried a single-shot plasma cannon in addition to his other weapons and equipment.

"I wanna be a Strike Force ranger . . ." sang Horgen, a Third Platoon striker. *"I wanna live a life of danger . . ."*

The starship sank the last few feet like a leaking bladder. *Wait for it*, Farrell mouthed, but no sound passed his dry lips.

A locator chart overlaid the upper left quadrant of Farrell's visor: seventy-eight green dots, each one a striker. They were crammed too closely together at the moment for him to count them individually. Every one was a veteran: not only of combat, but veterans of C41 itself.

Strike Force companies were prefixed B, C, or D depending on their size. C-class units had a nominal strength of one hundred personnel. C41 had received eight replacements since the last operation, but Farrell decided not to bring them along on a mission as rough as Active Cloak looked like being. The replacements were good people or they wouldn't have passed Strike Force screening after they volunteered, but they hadn't worked with C41 before. There was no margin here for somebody who misunderstood an order or reacted in an unexpected way.

The Spooks had a civilian colony of five hundred thousand on Maxus 377 in addition to the logistics bases that served their military on fourteen worlds. There was no margin at all when C41 seized the planet's main port ahead of the full-scale Unity invasion.

The tripod landing legs touched the ground in sequence. The freighter rang in three descending notes. "Go!" Farrell shouted, unheard over the clangs of the bolts shearing. He and a dozen other strikers shoved at the toppling bulkhead.

They'd landed just before local noon. Sunlight quivered through heat waves from the port's white concrete surface. Anti-emitter missiles launched in snarling cacophony from the freighter's upper cargo deck, homing on every operating radio-frequency antenna within their ten-mile range.

Major Arthur Farrell hit the ground running,

headed for the port administration building with his headquarters group and two squads of Third Platoon. C41 had begun the invasion.

The rest of the Unity armed forces better follow soon.

The pair of Spooks in the cab of the maintenance vehicle goggled to see the recently-landed freighter fall apart as they drove past. Sergeant Guilio Abbado killed them both with a single burst from his stinger before he jumped to the ground.

"Three-three to the truck!" Abbado shouted. Most of his squad was already running toward the eight-wheeled vehicle. It slowed but still coasted forward after the driver died in a spray of coppery blood. Horgen and Glasebrook leaped aboard, flinging the dead Spooks out of the way. Horgen managed to turn the vehicle before it plunged into an open sump, but she couldn't seem to find the brakes.

One of the Spooks hung out the open door. Abbado kicked the body the rest of the way to the ground as he climbed into the cab beside Flea Glasebrook. The other five strikers of Third Squad, Third Platoon clambered onto the back of the vehicle, shooting at any visible Spook to keep the enemy's panic boiling.

Horgen goosed the throttle. She steered east and accelerated without needing orders.

The truck was a godsend if you believed in God, which Abbado more or less did. The navy flight crew had landed the captured freighter on the magnetic mass nearest the port's northwest corner according to plan. Abbado could see the sense of that, since the port garrison's compound and the administration building were immediately north of the site and the transient military barracks were adjacent on the west.

The trouble was 3-3's objective, the huge maintenance hangar along the east edge of the field, was almost four hundred yards from the ship. That was a hell of a long way to run across bare concrete with a combat load. By the time the exhausted strikers got to the hangar, the Spooks would have had time to wake up.

They were waking up already. A hundred-foot-wide segment of hangar door had been open when C41 appeared. It was closing now, rolling down from the building roof. "Don't stop!" Abbado said, not that there was any likelihood Horgen had planned to.

Abbado hooked his left arm around the frame of the shattered windshield and sprayed a crackling burst from his stinger across the shadowed figures moving within the hangar. Two of them flopped to the ground; one sprang up again and limped out of sight behind his fellows.

The stinger's coils accelerated 15-grain projectiles to 10,000 feet per second. The pellet wasn't effective beyond 500 yards, but the strikers carried rockets to handle the occasional distant target. Stingers had the impact of a grenade on a target at short range. With thousand-round ammo packs containing both pellets and a fresh power supply, they were the weapon of choice for the sudden assaults in which C41 specialized.

The truck had a three-man cab, but the three weren't supposed to be humans in battle gear. The Kalendru were long-limbed, gray-skinned humanoids. From a distance they appeared hairless, but if you looked closely you saw that their skin was covered with fine down.

Kalendru were on average taller, slimmer and significantly quicker than Terrans. Because Spooks weren't as strong, their troops carried lighter, less-powerful weapon loads. A striker learned fast, though, that if you missed your first shot the Spook was going to get in the second one.

Horgen had the truck up to forty miles an hour. Immediately ahead the hangar door closed with a rattle that Abbado hoped meant it was fairly flimsy. "Hang on, boys!" he said as he pulled himself into the cab and crossed his arms over his faceshield. "The party's about to start!"

They hit the quivering door with a crash louder than the battle going on all over the spaceport.

Each of the two 16-round cannisters of plasma cartridges weighed a hair over forty pounds, and there was the weight of the air-cushion dolly besides. Striker Esther Meyer liked to tell herself she was as tough as any man in C41, but right at the moment she was glad Sergeant-Gunner Bloch and Santini, the other loader, had paused to lift her dolly from the hold instead of leaving her to struggle with it alone. Meyer could keep moving despite the heat and constriction of her hard suit as long as anybody, sure; but hefting a full ammo dolly was largely a matter of mass and peak strength.

Stingers and the 4-pound rockets most strikers slung from their belts already raked the port area. Fourth Platoon (Heavy Weapons) was the last out of the ship. With their full armor and bulky loads they'd have needlessly slowed less heavily equipped strikers.

There was no return fire as yet but it'd come soon enough. When it did, the maneuver platoons would be damned glad of 50-pound missile launchers and the plasma cannon.

Sergeant Bloch was a big man who looked gigantic in his polished white armor. His dolly supported the cannon itself and a three-round belt of ready cartridges. Twenty yards to the northeast was a pit holding a transformer beneath surface level where it didn't interfere with starships being hauled across the port in giant cradles. Bloch hunched toward it at a dead run. The pit was the best cover in his sector.

All Fourth Platoon personnel wore hard suits. The crews handling the triple launchers had to worry about the backblast of their own heavy missiles, and a mist of ions as hot as a sun's corona bathed the cannoneers as soon as they began to fire their belt-fed weapons. The armor's protection from enemy counterfire was a secondary concern.

Meyer heard the high-pitched scream of Spook lasers in addition to the snarl of stingers and the *crack*WHAM! of the strikers' rockets. The port's surface flared white at the corner of her eye as a beam burned concrete to glass and quicklime. The Spooks were awake, though for the moment they seemed to be spraying the landscape in panic.

Bloch stepped into the waist-high transformer pit and wrestled the gun onto its bipod in firing position. Santini simply pushed the ammo dolly in ahead of himself. The cannisters were padded against shock, but a direct hit from a laser might penetrate. The best result the crew could hope for then was a low-order explosion that might not kill them. If the bead of deuterium at the heart of each cartridge detonated, hard suits weren't going to make any difference to the resulting thermonuclear explosion.

The captured freighter erupted smoke and another sheaf of anti-emitter missiles. Those were launched automatically when the unit's artificial intelligence sensed Kalendru-type radio frequency emissions. The streak of light that ended in a lightning-sharp explosion in the transient barracks was a missile from one of 4th Platoon's triple launchers. That was fast work, but the team had set up beside the ship because there wasn't any cover in their direction anyway.

Meyer jumped her dolly into the transformer pit and followed it. Bloch fired his ready ammunition in three ravening pulses as fast as the gun would cycle. The ringing air glowed like the heart of a rainbow.

"Feed me!" the sergeant screamed as Santini dragged a 16-round belt from one of his cannisters. "Feed me!"

As she opened a cannister one-handed, Meyer looked over the rim of the pit. She dialed up her visor's magnification. The gun was placed to cover the main highway entering the starport from the north. Seven miles up that road was the planet's largest military base, code-named Active Grid for this operation. That was probably where the tank at which Bloch was hammering had come from.

The plasma bolts had grounded the huge vehicle in an iridescent fireball, but they hadn't destroyed it. Air shimmered in a corona discharge as the tank's generators rebuilt its magnetic shielding.

The Spooks were awake, all right.

The front door of the guard barracks started to open while Striker Caius Blohm was still twenty yards from the building. He fired one of his penetrator grenades through the panel. An instant later the warhead's atomized fuel mixed with the air and detonated, blowing splinters of the door in one direction and the charred fragments of the Spook in the other.

Blohm liked to be on point. In this war the choice was to be quick or dead, and the Spooks were plenty damn quick. Your best chance of survival was the Spook's hesitation, and if *you* hesitated you were handing him your head as well as maybe the heads of the strikers behind you. Technically the building's ground floor wasn't Blohm's responsibility, but this wasn't a time to stand on ceremony.

Blohm trusted himself not to hesitate. Never. Not so much as a heartbeat.

First Platoon's objective was to clear the garrison's three-story barracks. The planners had nixed putting a heavy rocket into the structure because the port command center might be either in the barracks or in the administration building.

The command center would be hardened. Burying it in the rubble of the upper floors wouldn't keep the Spooks in the center from using their outlying gun and missile positions to blow the hell out of first C41, then any Unity vessel that appeared on this hemisphere of the planet.

Blohm and Sergeant Gabrilovitch were C41's scouts. They'd been assigned to lead the four survivors of the platoon's understrength First Squad through the top floor of the barracks while the remainder of the platoon took care of the lower stories. If there *was* a control room in the basement, Lieutenant Kuznetsov wanted to be able to open it without worrying about Spooks coming down the stairs behind her.

At the base of the wall Blohm armed his jump belt. He paused and bent over when he heard the roaring ignition of one of Heavy Weapons' 50-pound rockets. An instant later the transient compound to Blohm's left disintegrated in a green flash and a thunderclap.

The rocket warheads pulsed electricity through an osmium wire whose resistance blew it apart with enormous force. Batteries stored energy more efficiently than chemical high explosives. The bursting wire propagated shockwaves at several times the rate of HE, giving the warheads great shattering force. The blast slapped Blohm hard, but it didn't send him tumbling as it would have done had it hit him while he was airborne on the jump belt.

Blohm looked up the barracks' facade, then triggered his belt. The four self-stabilizing nozzles lifted him vertically at a controllable ten feet per second. He hovered beside the window he'd chosen for entry and fired a penetrator through the pane. The projectiles were fuzed to burst a tenth of a second after impact and spray their filling into the space beyond.

The blast blew the remainder of the pane—clear thermoplastic rather than glass—out past Blohm in a gulp of red flame. He pulled himself through the opening and unlatched the jump belt with his left hand as soon as he was into the smoldering corridor beyond. The belt still had another thirty seconds or so of fuel, but the weight was more of a hindrance than any possible gain it could offer the striker now. The ground wasn't so far away that Blohm couldn't jump down without serious concern.

The bodies in the hallway looked like charred logs. The explosion had destroyed the light fixtures and filled the air with swirling hot smoke. The faceshield of the striker's helmet offered light enhancement and thermal imaging as viewing options, but neither would have helped a great deal under these conditions.

Blohm didn't bother. He had four rounds left in the magazine of his short-barreled grenade launcher.

He ran down the hall, firing one round into each room as he passed. Because the fuze required impact to arm it, Blohm shot through the wall if the door was already open. He had to hope that the internal partitions would be thin enough for the grenade to penetrate.

Blohm compensated reflexively when explosions rocked him from side to side. He wasn't thinking or seeing as a human does. He'd programmed himself like a machine to accomplish a particular task as fast as possible.

"Coming through!" Gabrilovitch shouted. The hall darkened as the sergeant's armored body filled the window sash.

Blohm crouched against the wall as he reloaded. The launcher wasn't a weapon he particularly liked, but he'd spent the voyage out practicing with it until he could perform all the necessary operations instinctively. It was hard to breathe. His helmet filtered toxins, but the fuel-air grenades had used up a lot of the available oxygen.

There were three rooms left on the corridor. The Spook troops in them could have used the pause to ready their own weapons, but there was no time to worry. Just to act.

Blohm straightened. Gabrilovitch's stinger rasped behind him as the sergeant shot a body that was still twitching after the grenade went off.

Blohm lunged forward, firing three times in a single flowing motion. Between the first shot and the second he heard Gabrilovitch scream, "Cease fire! Cease—"

But the words didn't penetrate until Caius Blohm had completed his mission.

"—fire! They're not soldiers, they're kids!"

—2—

Meyer's helmet highlighted movement on the panorama display at the lower edge of her visor. Three Spooks were running toward the rear of the gun position.

She turned, bouncing her armored hip against the transformer as she raised her stinger. Her burst went wildly high. The Spooks dropped into a sunken track twenty feet from the transformer pit. It held one of the cogged tramlines that spiderwebbed the port to haul ships after landing.

Meyer should have been watching the south. The cataclysmic destruction of the tank had drawn her attention three miles down the road in the wrong direction. She didn't know where the Spooks had come—

Two more Spooks ran from the underside of a starship a hundred yards away. They weren't wearing uniforms, but one had a laser, and the bag the other carried probably wasn't full of apples. Their long legs covered ground as fast as a shadow spreads when the sun goes behind a cloud.

Meyer shot the leader with the satchel. The second Spook fired as he ran, but his laser threw up chunks of concrete nearer his own feet than his target. Meyer sighted and sawed the slim body nearly in half. The Spook's corpse hit face down, but his toes pointed in the air.

A 50-pound rocket lit, blasted from its launcher, and banked in a screaming turn that took it southward out of the port area. Meyer could see the target only as a series of dots low in the distant sky. A dot and the missile's tracking flare merged. A flash that grew into a fireball filled several degrees of horizon.

The target was probably a personnel carrier, armored against small-arms fire but still light enough—unlike the hundred-ton tanks—to fly. All the dots vanished. Only one had been destroyed, but the others would have to slow down and hug the ground during the remainder of their approach to the battle.

The visor would magnify by up to a thousand times, but Meyer needed as broad a range of vision as possible to do her own job. She'd almost gotten herself and the rest of the crew killed by looking in the wrong direction.

A Spook threw a grenade out of the tramline. It landed short and went off in a yellow flash. The shock buffeted Meyer; a few fragments cracked against her armor. She fired at the top of the trench, blasting powdered concrete from both sides without harming the Spooks below. One of them popped up ten feet from where Meyer was aiming and fired his laser. If he hadn't been more concerned to duck back to safety than to aim, he'd have burned her head off.

Meyer swung her stinger and shot holes in the air. Two more grenades sailed from separate points along the tramline. The grenadiers weren't showing more than a hand and wrist for a fraction of a second. One grenade landed wide, but the other bounced toward the lip of the transformer pit.

"Down!" Meyer screamed to the gun crew as she hunched low. Fragments of casing and concrete flew in all directions.

The plasma cannon stopped in mid-burst when the grenade exploded. Bloch bellowed a curse. One of the cannon's bipod legs had been blown off. Santini stuck his left forearm under the gunbarrel to support it.

A second tank, starkly terrible in the glow of ions from bolts which its shielding had shrugged off, glided around the wreckage of its sister vehicle.

Meyer jumped out of the transformer pit and ran toward the tramline. Sooner or later the Spooks were going to throw a grenade into the pit. If the blast didn't kill the strikers outright, it would stun them for the fellow with the laser to finish off.

She was ten feet from the tramline when a grenadier raised himself to throw. He saw Meyer's armored figure stumping toward him and dived back with a gobble of horror. The Spook with the laser rose an instant later. Meyer was standing almost on top of him. Her stinger blew him inside out.

Without lifting her finger from the trigger, Meyer hosed the two grenadiers cowering against the cogged track. Sparks, concrete dust, and bits of flesh sprayed from where the pellets hit.

Meyer turned toward the transformer pit. The cannon was firing again. Only a series of plasma bolts in rapid succession could hammer through a tank's magnetic shielding. The tank halted as its fusion powerplant shunted all available power from the lift fans to the shield. It wasn't enough. A moment later Bloch's sixth pulse of thermonuclear energy hit the tank itself.

The shockwave spalled the inner face of the armor across the fighting compartment. The Kalendru crew were all dead before the next round ruptured the powerplant's containment bottle in a greater secondary explosion.

Meyer hadn't noticed her hard suit's weight and chafing when she charged the Spook position. Now she felt drained and dizzy. She sucked at the teat supplying water from the integral canteen as she took a second step toward the pit.

A black spot flecked the sky at the corner of her eye. Meyer threw herself to the ground. She was still falling when the missile launched from Active Grid plunged into the transformer pit.

The concrete rippled, slamming Meyer on the chest. She flipped onto her back like a pancake. The walls of the pit channeled the blast and fragments skyward, but the gun, the crew, and the transformer itself vanished utterly in a white flash.

Where the hell was the rest of the Unity invasion force?

The steps to the admin building's second floor were individually taller and more shallow than those of human structures. The Spook running down them hooting had no trouble until Leinsdorf ripped his white tunic to bloody shreds an instant before Farrell got his stinger on target.

A striker with smoke still curling from the nozzles of her jump belt appeared at the top of the stairs. She shot the Spook again as he toppled forward.

The floor plan of the port administration building was almost circular: almost, because of Kalendru distaste for right angles and constant-radius curves. The ground floor was a bullpen with office cubbies around the outer walls and an open concourse in the center.

Farrell didn't suppose there could be a design that would have provided a better kill zone for the volley of grenades and 4-pound rockets his strikers sent through the clear facade of the building as they charged. There'd been twenty-odd Spooks present, but only one or two had survived long enough to be killed by stinger pellets. The upper story must be broken into smaller spaces.

Strikers now crouched at the side windows and the door to the parking lot behind the building. Farrell's visor overlaid images from the helmets of a guard from each quadrant. The ghost viewpoints were each an eighth-field 30 percent mask across the top. They interfered to a degree with Farrell's normal vision, but he was used to operating that way. He *had* to keep track of everything that was happening or else he'd get his people killed.

The breaching charge went off in the armored stairwell opposite the main doors. The electrically-generated pulse sounded like starships colliding: sharp, metallic, and immensely loud.

The well channeled the backblast upward to tear a ten-foot hole in the bullpen ceiling. Farrell hoped none of the squad clearing the second floor had been standing in the wrong place. A striker with a grenade launcher chugged his entire magazine through the opened door at the bottom of the stairs.

The stairwell belched red flame. Two strikers went in with their stingers pointed. Spooks couldn't carry the weight of armor sturdy enough to survive the grenade blasts, but it was possible that the first door opened onto an anteroom and the real control room was still sealed.

Farrell instinctively started to follow his troops; Leinsdorf blocked him without hesitation. Art Farrell was a big man. Leinsdorf was bigger and even stronger.

Leinsdorf's job was to keep the major alive. When that meant stopping Farrell from doing something stupid, Leinsdorf did whatever had to be done.

Nadia Broz carried a jamming rig instead of extra weapons. While shooting was still going on she'd attached the jammer to an antenna lead from one of the building's wrecked consoles. An anti-emitter missile had cut the roof mast while C41 unassed, but the stump was sufficient for Nadia's purposes.

She glanced up from her display and caught Farrell's eyes on her. "The port defenses shut down when we blew the vault," she said, shouting over the racket instead of using helmet commo to speak to Farrell ten feet away. "The missile batteries at Active Grid are live, though, and the base has links to the sensors here. There's nothing I can do about that."

"We've got support coming," Farrell said, wondering how many of his people were going to die before that support arrived. "They may be hitting Active Grid already."

There were in the order of 50,000 Kalendru troops quartered at Active Grid. The sprawling base was targeted for massive strikes: initially from orbit, followed by dedicated ground-attack vessels making low-level passes. The crucial low-level phase couldn't begin until the Kalendru hemispheric defenses had been knocked out.

It would take the Spooks hours, maybe days, to bypass the control net centered on the vault Farrell's strikers had just opened and destroyed. The missile artillery at Active Grid could pulverize C41, though.

The jammer provided a partial defense. Terminal guidance made artillery accurate to within ten feet. If the missile depended on data loaded into it before launch, accuracy dropped to a Circular Error Probability of sixty-five feet.

The captured freighter erupted when half a dozen

Spook rounds hit it in rapid succession. The starport and military base had been designed and built as a mutually-supporting pair. Buried cables linked sensors in the port area to consoles at Active Grid, allowing the Kalendru gunners to refine their targeting with sensor data. While the result wasn't as good as terminal guidance, it was good enough for targets the size of a starship.

Pretty quick it would dawn on the Spooks they could now shell the port administration building off the map without harming any of their own people.

"The building's secured, sir," reported Sergeant Bastien, the acting commander of Third Platoon. "Shall I shift a squad across to help Abbado?"

A 50-pound rocket slammed from its launcher, supersonic within the first twenty feet of flight. The missile screamed downrange.

C41's plasma cannon were firing also. One of Farrell's overlaid remote images showed a huge explosion in the distance along the highway. The shockwave reached him in two pulses, through the ground and an instant later on the air. Leinsdorf, restive as he looked across the concourse and out the back door, unslung his single-shot plasma weapon. Another Spook tank was maneuvering past the mushrooming tombstone of the first.

"No, withdraw both squads to the warehouses," Farrell ordered. "Abbado has to take his chances. Nobody's going to make it across that bare concrete till the fleet takes care of Active Grid."

He turned. "Nadia," he said, "leave the jammer set up, but we got to get out of here. The—"

Farrell's visor flashed red, indicating a signal from orbital command. One of his supplementary commo units was a dedicated link to the flagship.

"*Primrose Charlie Four-One, this is Primrose,*" an emotionless voice said. *"The operation has been aborted. A large Kalendru fleet is approaching the planet. Can you extract your unit yourself? Over."*

"Primrose, hell no!" Farrell said. At the corner of his eye he saw another missile hit the remains of the freighter. "Primrose, for Chrissake, get us a strike on Active Grid. They've got the port observed. They're chewing us up and you won't be able to get a boat in. Over!"

"*Charlie Four-One, Negative,*" the voice said. Farrell wondered if it was an AI program speaking. No, a computerized voice would have more feeling. This was a human officer who wasn't going to let emotional loading get in the way of precise communication. *"If possible, withdraw your unit to a site out of Kalendru observation and await pickup. Primrose out."*

Out was the operative word. C41 was shit out of luck.

One of the strikers who entered the barracks behind Caius Blohm had clamped a line to the sash for them to leave by. It was about the only useful thing anybody in 1-1 had accomplished during the operation.

Blohm rappelled down the side of the building. First in, last out. The grenade launcher slapped against his breastplate each time he braked with his gloved palms. The weapon was heavy. He'd locked in a fresh magazine to replace the one from which he'd fired three rounds.

His boots hit the ground. The ship that brought C41 was a shattered wreck, the upper half molten. Another missile hit the derelict, lifting a mighty fireball. The Spooks used chemical explosives. The general level of noise was so high that the blast didn't sound particularly loud.

Blohm glanced up the way he'd come. Flames wavered sluggishly from several of the third-floor windows. The fuel-air bombs had ignited fabrics, paper, splintered furniture. Spooks didn't have hair to burn, not really, but the explosions had charred the victims' flesh deeply.

There'd been a lot of them on the top floor of the barracks. Over a hundred, Blohm figured, judging from the one room he'd taken a good look into after Gabrilovitch shouted at him.

Kalendru females were shorter and even slimmer than the males, and they were never members of the fighting forces. Some of the burned corpses were females but most were children. Maybe dependents, maybe overflow from civilian facilities on the south side of the field. Certainly not combatants. But certainly dead.

And very certainly killed by Caius Blohm. He'd completed the job before anybody else arrived. Nothing wrong with his reflexes, no sir.

He ran past the shattered transient compound, following Gabrilovitch. A Spook missile hit twenty yards away and blew a hole in bare concrete. Again a red fireball pulsed upward through sooty black smoke. The air *zing*ed, but none of the fragments hit Blohm.

If a missile went off at his feet, it might burn his shattered body as black as that of the Spook child on the threshold of the room Blohm had looked into.

The good news was that the hangar door ruptured when the truck hit it. Stiffeners sang like guitar strings, parting the welds that anchored them to the edges of the track.

Horgen skidded all eight wheels as she braked. There was nothing to hit in the left bay except bodies and whatever gear the Spook repair staff had dropped when the strikers drove into them shooting.

Abbado's visor reacted automatically to the lower light levels within the structure. He pointed his stinger toward a group of Spooks trying to get behind a large toolcart and held the trigger down. The fishtailing truck ripped the stream of pellets across the Spooks and they all dropped.

The bad news was that a Kalendru corvette filled the hangar's central bay.

This was a land-force logistics base, not a fleet repair facility. There weren't supposed to be naval vessels present, not even relatively small ones with their Tokomak powerplant lifted half out of the cylindrical hull on a gantry. Spooks swarmed up the ramped hatchway. Mostly they were maintenance staffers clothed in motley blues and grays, but a few were mauve-uniformed naval personnel.

An officer with a tuft of black feathers on either epaulet fired a laser pistol at Abbado. The Spook blew two divots from the truck's door before Abbado killed him. Glasebrook leaned through the shattered windshield and fired a rocket into the corvette's airlock, shredding the officer's body and a half dozen other Kalendru. Horgen had dived from the truck, so the backblast didn't fry her.

The hatch rotated closed. The edge mated solidly with the coaming despite the fact that a Spook's arm lay across it.

Abbado jumped. There'd been nearly a hundred Spooks in the hangar when the heavily-armed strikers entered. Now, seconds later, the only Kalendru still visible and moving were those who thrashed in their death throes.

Some Spooks hid beyond the corvette or behind pieces of equipment, but they weren't an immediate concern. The ones still alive aboard the vessel were a real threat.

The corvette's armory probably held enough small arms to outgun all the strikers in C41, but even that was a secondary danger. If the crew got the ship's main battery in operation, it was Katy bar the door for the whole operation.

"Fire control!" Abbado said. The code phrase keyed his words to Lieutenant Whichard of Heavy Weapons Platoon. "Give me a rocket soonest, *mark*!"

He focused his eyes on the ship's closed airlock and blinked twice. That highlighted the image his helmet was transmitting to Whichard and—Abbado prayed—to the sergeant of one of the rocket batteries. "Break, Three-three personnel take cover! Out."

By this time all six heavy rockets might have been launched or destroyed by Spook counterfire. If there was a round left, Abbado couldn't be sure it would bear on the target. At such short range the rockets didn't have much room to maneuver between launch and impact.

The one certain thing was that 3-3 would get the support if it was possible. There wasn't a more important target on the base. Nobody'd dreamed there was going to be a warship in the hangar. The planners might have scrubbed the whole operation if they'd known.

Abbado threw himself on the hangar floor and tugged a personal rocket from his bandolier. He twisted the base cap to extend it and arm the rocket. A 4-pound rocket was unlikely to do serious harm to a starship's hull, but unless Whichard came through they were the best 3-3 had to go on.

A striker threw an electrical grenade into the cab of the travelling hoist above her. The sharp blast flung the operator out in a shower of glass. Both electrical and fuel-air grenades had specific advantages. Electricals offered fragmentation and higher peak impulse, but fuel-air provided incendiary effect and greater total impulse.

Abbado had heard arguments on the subject go on for hours, but the truth of it was that the choice was personal whim. Combat troops like to claim that their decisions are in some objective sense "right," but they know in their hearts of hearts that they'll probably die for no better reason than that they were in the wrong place at the wrong time.

"Three-three," the squad channel warned in a voice that wasn't Whichard's. *"Shot!"*

The eight strikers within the huge hangar crouched in the best shelter they could find. Over the general chaos, Abbado heard the *crack* of a rocket igniting.

The hangar's central door burst inward from the supersonic shockwave and the missile that detonated against the corvette's airlock. The hangar roof billowed up from the joists. Sheared rivets rained onto the floor.

The rocketeers had set the fuzing circuit for point focus because the warship's hull was too thick to be pierced by an omnidirectional blast. The pulse ruptured a cone of wire, forming the electrical equivalent of a chemical shaped charge. The shockwave forged a thin disk of uranium into a molten spear that struck like an asteroid.

The corvette rocked on its landing struts. The heavy-metal spike blew a hole big enough to pass a fully-equipped striker through the center of the hatch. The blast skidded Abbado three feet backward on the smooth floor, and his ears rang despite the cancellation pulse his helmet produced to save his hearing. He scrambled to his feet and ran for the opening, clasping the rocket in his left hand and the stinger in his right with the buttplate against his biceps.

It didn't occur to Guilio Abbado to order his strikers to follow him. It wouldn't have occurred to them to do anything else. If they hadn't been that sort of people, they wouldn't have been in C41.

Two strikers fired rockets through the opening before they charged. Glasebrook threw in a fuel-air grenade. That was useful for the purpose of clearing defenders from the corridors nearest the hatch, but the airlock focused the thumping explosion and knocked Abbado flat on his ass. By the time he got up, Horgen was into the ship ahead of him.

Abbado was on her heels, though he had to shove Jefferson aside. Rank hath its privileges. At a mental level pretty well buried for the moment, Abbado was afraid to die; but he was more afraid that his squad wouldn't follow him the next time if they had the least doubt that he was willing to lead from the front.

The airlock's inner valve had been half open before most of the outer door hit it and tore it off its hinges. Horgen was left-handed so she turned right down the smoky corridor. Abbado went left, sternward.

Although the Kalendru had pulled the main powerplant, the corvette's internal lighting was on. There must be an auxiliary power unit somewhere. If the lights worked, so would the guns and missile launchers.

Abbado swept the corridor with his stinger for the second and a half it took to empty the magazine, then fired the rocket in his left hand. He didn't have a target—any target, though slender bodies writhed on the decking—but he needed his hand free to reload the stinger. Launching the rocket was faster than throwing it away.

As Abbado knelt, Jefferson stepped by him and hurled a grenade into a weapons bay. A Spook jumped from behind the control console and shot the striker in the face. The grenade detonated, blowing the shredded Spook against the ceiling.

Abbado tugged an electrical grenade off his belt left handed and threw it into the compartment's opposite bay. A Spook hopped up from that console also. Abbado and Glasebrook shot him together. As the body fell back, Glasebrook tossed a fuel-air grenade on top of it.

When the bomb blew, the two strikers ran to the last compartment sternward. Neither man sent a grenade ahead to warn the Spooks they were coming. They'd worked together so often in similar situations that they coordinated without overt signals.

The Kalendru repair crew had removed the compartment's upper plating in order to lift out the powerplant. A sailor was trying to climb out of the ship through the large opening. Glasebrook shot him.

An officer's mauve-clad legs lay in the well where the Tokomak had been bolted. Abbado's randomly fired rocket had hit him in the chest.

Two Spooks waited by the bulkhead just inside the corridor hatch. One of them managed to trigger his laser as Abbado's stinger tore them point-blank. The saffron pulse ruptured a pouch of stinger reloads and gouged a collop from the sergeant's breastplate beneath.

Abbado, Glasebrook, and Foyle an instant behind

hosed the lockers and netting-secured bundles that festooned the aft compartment. Stinger pellets hit too hard to ricochet, but the long bursts ripped sparks from the fittings and bulkheads. The compartment roared like a megawatt short circuit, giving the air a lambent neon radiance.

Forward, a pair of fuel-air explosions thumped. There was a sharper blast and the corvette's lighting went off. Horgen or one of the strikers with her had found the APU.

Abbado reloaded. There were no Kalendru alive aboard the ship. The seven pips on the corner of his faceshield indicated that they'd only lost Jefferson in clearing the vessel, better than he'd figured. Last year on Mulholland—two years ago?—Abbado and Jefferson had drunk their way through a case of whiskey they'd stolen from an admiral's private suite.

"Three-three come on, we're not done here," Abbado ordered. "We've still got a hangar full of—"

"*C41, all personnel,*" Major Farrell's voice broke in over the command channel. "*Evacuate the port area soonest and reform in the equipment storage lot behind the warehouses west of the concrete. We'll set up a perimeter there and wait for pickup. Soonest, people, soonest! Out!*"

"What the hell?" said Flea Glasebrook. He'd been counting stinger magazines remaining. His index finger still pointed to the pouch he'd reached when the call came.

Abbado tried to suck a drink of water. He coughed and spewed it across the inside of his faceshield. "Three-three to the truck," he ordered when he got his voice back. "Watch that there's not somebody waiting when we come through the hatch."

He hoped the truck still worked. He really hoped the truck still worked. He was afraid to think any farther ahead than that.

—3—

Blohm lay in the crawlspace beneath a warehouse, ten feet back from the wall. He could see wedges of the port through half a dozen of the open ventilators, but he was practically invisible from the outside.

A pair of Kalendru crouched at the base of a freighter in the middle of the field. They held shoulder-stocked lasers. Blohm aimed his stinger and squeezed twice: separate short bursts rather than a single long one. The projectiles' vaporized driving bands fluoresced in the dimness.

Pellets that missed sparkled like fairy dust against the starship's hull. The Spooks toppled. Blohm scrambled a few feet sideways. Somebody might have noticed the vague flicker from his stinger's muzzle.

You've got to be fast. You've got to act without thinking. Otherwise you're as dead as a child in a fuel-air blast.

On a corner of Blohm's visor was a remote image from Sergeant Gabrilovitch. Gabe had retreated with most of C41 behind the line of warehouses. The lot there was half the size of the huge landing field. It held thousands of vehicles and pieces of heavy equipment in open storage ready for transshipment, but even that quantity of matériel didn't fill the space. The pickup ship could land without scratching its paint on the Spook hardware.

If a ship arrived. If anybody in C41 was alive when it arrived. But worrying about that was somebody else's job.

A vehicle drove through one of the smashed doors of the huge maintenance hangar across the port. Blohm aimed, dialing up the magnification of the stinger's holographic sight while keeping his visor at 1:1 for breadth of field.

No target. It was a Spook truck, all right, but there were three strikers in the battered cab and others clinging to the back. Abbado was bringing his people back, most of them at least. A pair of missiles hit close enough to stagger the vehicle, but it continued to accelerate. Two of the left-side tires were flat, giving the truck a shimmy.

Blohm wished he was alone on a planet. No decisions to make, no responsibilities. Nobody to worry about but himself.

Something rustled; the local equivalent of a rat, or perhaps just leaves blowing. Blohm didn't look away from the ventilators, his firing slits. His helmet would warn him of any infrared source corresponding to a human or a Kalender. Even a Kalender child.

Three Kalendru ran out of the distant hangar. Two had lasers; the Spook in the middle lifted a long launching tube to his shoulder.

Blohm shot the rocketeer first. The Spook dropped his tube and staggered backward, but he stayed on his feet.

This was long range for a stinger. The pellets depended on kinetic energy for their effect, and air resistance scrubbed off velocity. Kalendru lasers had better performance than stingers at ranges of three hundred yards and beyond, but it wasn't often you had to worry about shooting the breadth of a starport.

Blohm raised his point of aim slightly for the second target. The burst hit the Spook in the face and throat. He flung up his hands and fell backward.

The third Spook looked around wildly. Blohm nailed him in the upper chest, then gave him a second burst when he didn't go down. That Spook and the rocketeer collapsed together in a tangle of spindly limbs.

Blohm hoped Abbado made it clear. Well, he'd done what he could.

There was lots of room in the crawlspace. The extruded-metal joists were several feet off the ground across most of the building. A guy could live in a space like this if he had food and everybody left him alone. He'd have no decisions to make at all.

The truck went over a sunken tramline at forty miles an hour. They must have crossed the same trench headed for the hangar, but Abbado didn't remember the jolt being so bad. The present condition of the truck's running gear probably had something to do with it.

Glasebrook bounced high enough to dent the cab roof with his helmet. He shouted a curse.

"Quit bitching, Flea," Abbado said. "There's people who'd pay good money for a ride like this!"

A shell landed where the truck had crossed the tramline seconds before. Horgen dragged the steering yoke to the right, fighting the vehicle's tendency to drift left because of the flat tires on that side.

"They can have my fucking ticket then!" Glasebrook said. He fired at a freighter on which nothing moved but wisps of smoke from all the open hatches.

More shells hit, well behind and this time to the

left of the truck. Horgen continued to steer right. Her elbow rang on Flea's breastplate.

A heavy weapons squad had set up in a pit near where C41 landed. Abbado couldn't tell whether they'd been a rocket or a plasma cannon crew, because a shell had scooped everything out and sprayed it high in the air like ejecta from a volcano.

Bits of hard suit lay in a circle around the pit where they'd fallen. None of the pieces was larger than a gauntlet and half a forearm. One of the strikers lay spreadeagled nearby with a full complement of appendages attached to the armored torso. Blast effects were funny things. Sometimes you'd find a corpse with all his clothes blown off but not a mark on his skin.

"Hang the hell on!" Horgen said as she fought the yoke. She wanted to turn into the alley between the warehouses and the collapsed ruin that had been the big transient compound, but the vehicle wasn't responding the way it should.

The truck was supposed to steer all eight wheels, but there seemed to be more damage than just the flat tires. Glasebrook gripped the right horn of the yoke and forced it down against whatever was dragging.

The truck skidded. Metal shrieked, but they were turning, they were going to make it.

Movement caught the corner of Abbado's eye. He turned his head and looked squarely at the shape waddling into the port from the north.

Abbado pointed his stinger by instinct, but he didn't bother firing. While doing so would definitely get its attention, he could piss out the truck's window and have just as much chance of damaging a Kalendru tank.

"They're eight minutes out," Nadia shouted to Farrell. He'd handed responsibility for orbital communications to her when they left the jammer to automatic operation in the admin building. "They'll be approaching from the west. One vessel."

It'd be a tight squeeze getting C41 aboard a standard landing boat intended for fifty strikers. Of course they didn't have the usual amount of heavy equipment on this extraction.

And again, a fifty-place vessel might be about the right size.

Farrell was in the cab of a construction tanker with plow-like nozzles on the underside to inject plasticizer into the ground. It was in the row nearest the back of the warehouses. Leinsdorf squatted beside Farrell, nursing his plasma tube and looking grim. Captain Broz stood on the tread of the giant earthmover adjacent. Farrell liked having Nadia close because of her electronics skills, though that increased the risk he and his XO would buy it simultaneously.

The rest of the strikers were spread through the ranks of Kalendru vehicles, mostly near the back of the field. The Spook artillery hadn't begun targeting the storage field.

Spook sensor technology was excellent, but the amount of metal and electronics in the park were perfect concealment for the scattering of humans. C41 was going to need all the help it could get to stay alive until the boat arrived.

If the boat wasn't shot down. If Primrose didn't abort the pickup for reasons that a mere striker wouldn't understand. If the boat didn't land on the wrong fucking side of the planet, because that was sure the way C41's luck had been running so far.

If Art Farrell got his people aboard the pickup vessel, his job was over. Even if the ship blew up in the next instant, it was no longer his responsibility.

The Kalendru who'd been in the port area when C41 arrived were either dead or cowed into keeping their heads down. The locals had reacted fast, but they weren't most of them soldiers and they'd been up against the best. The Spooks' quick individual responses meant they'd been mowed down in uncoordinated firefights against humans with better weapons, better armor, and better aim.

The Kalendru whose APCs had landed in the scrub woodland south and west of the port were infantry operating in formed units. There were already several hundred of them and they should have been dangerous, but so far every Spook who reached a firing position had been killed instantly.

The Kalendru infrared signatures made them stand out like flags against the foliage and damp ground. Human troops wouldn't have been any better off. The strikers could track targets crawling forward for hundreds of yards. When a Spook raised his head, several stingers or a 4-pound rocket blew him apart. Sun-heated equipment hid C41 as effectively as absorbent sheeting could have done.

The orange digits 3-3 lit a corner of Farrell's visor indicating a priority report from the squad leader, Sergeant Abbado. *"Six, a tank's entered the field from the north. We're observing, but we don't have shit to stop it. Over."*

Farrell switched to visuals from Abbado on the left side of his visor. The Kalendru tank was an opalescent dome moving onto the field with the care of a blind man. It was too wide to pass through the space between the transient compound and the end warehouse without touching, but the tank's armored sides would simply brush the rubble apart.

"Three-three," Farrell said, "take firing positions but don't do anything till I get there. Out."

He grimaced to Leinsdorf and ordered curtly, "Come on. Nadia, you're in charge."

"Five minutes!" she called back.

C41 didn't have five minutes before the tank had joined them in the storage lot. The pickup boat would have to abort if there was a hundred-megajoule laser waiting for it.

The magnetic shielding that protected the tank against directed-energy weapons was also its main weakness. The flux was so dense that it bent light itself: the driver and gunners looked out through a rainbow curtain as dazzling as the light-shot mist at the base of a waterfall. Inertial guidance took the vehicle over mapped terrain and computer enhancement aided image resolution, but the tank crew still had to grope across the landscape unless it dropped the shield. Besides the blindness, the laser couldn't fire while the shield was in place. The tank was limited to its secondary battery of projectile weapons.

Farrell ran toward the channel he expected the tank to use. The driver might plow directly through the warehouses, but that risked filling the drive fans with debris and immobilizing the vehicle. Though the intake ducts were kinked and protected with several sets of baffles, sand and tiny pebbles showered from a collapsing building could still choke the fans.

Farrell's quartet of 4-pound rockets rattled against his breastplate as he jogged along a line of vehicles. Leinsdorf had a dozen more. The bodyguard almost never fired rockets during an operation, but he carried a triple load on general principles. Even if Abbado and his strikers had used up their rockets in their assault on the hangar, Farrell and Leinsdorf between them carried enough for the purpose.

The magnetic shield didn't affect projectiles—in either direction. The tank's outline quivered within the iridescent dome as an automatic cannon fired at the block of warehouses, perhaps the only target the gunner could make out. Explosions *clock*ed at half-second intervals.

The 4-pound rockets wouldn't do more than scratch the tank's paint. Even a 50-pounder—the last of them had disintegrated an APC that rose to scan the storage field for targets—couldn't have penetrated the tank's armor. A volley of light warheads might cause the Spooks to lower their shielding for a moment to see what was happening, though.

What would be happening then was Leinsdorf nailing the tank with his single-shot plasma weapon.

The roar of the tank's fans staggered Farrell as he stepped into the gap between buildings. The walls channeled sound the way a tidal bore focuses surf. Though the tank was only halfway across the port, its shimmering mass filled the field of view.

Abbado's strikers squatted in the wreckage of the transient compound. They'd slewed a heavy truck across the middle of the open space, but that was more to draw the Spooks' attention than in any hope of blocking the tank.

The tank fired a dozen explosive shells into the truck, which shuddered on its suspension. Tires and upholstery began to burn. Rounds that missed burst among vehicles parked in the field beyond.

Leinsdorf drew Farrell down in a crouch at the corner of the warehouse. He was waiting for the shooting to stop before they darted across the open space. The tankers couldn't see a moving figure through the enveloping rainbow curtain, but Leinsdorf didn't want his major to run into a random shell.

Though Farrell knew he might as well. His plan wasn't going to work. The crew of this tank had seen two of their sister vehicles blasted by the strikers' plasma cannon. They weren't going to risk lowering their shield for even an instant, and not even Art Farrell could blame the pilot of the extraction vessel for refusing to land on top of a Kalendru tank.

No member of C41 was going to survive the operation.

—4—

"C'mon, Meyer, get your ass in gear!" Santini screamed. He was wearing a sweatband and a fatigue shirt with the sleeves cut to fringes, the way he did when he worked out in the weight room on board ship.

Esther Meyer opened her eyes. Had she been drinking? Her head buzzed and the whole universe was a rainbow blur.

"Move it, Meyer!" shouted Sergeant Bloch, gesturing her forward with a sweep of his arm. *"We got a tank to take out!"*

The rainbow was sunlight distorted through the magnetic shielding of a tank. Santini and Bloch were dead, so dead that she'd be breathing bits of them if it weren't for the hard suit's filters.

The tank moved no faster than a blind man walking. A rigid-walled plenum chamber enclosed the air cushion which supported the massive vehicle. Air blasting beneath the skirt's lip skidded Meyer an inch along the concrete, but the tank was going to miss her.

A salvo of 4-pound rockets spat from somewhere the other side of the slagged-down freighter in which C41 had inserted. The warheads twinkled harmlessly on the bow slope. The tank's secondary armament chugged a dozen explosive shells in reply, sending distorted images across the shield's filmy surface.

It'd take a fair-sized meteor to damage a tank's frontal armor with mechanical effect. If strikers were using personal rockets, it meant they didn't have anything better.

We've got a tank to take out.

That was a job for Heavy Weapons, and it looked like the call was for Striker Esther Meyer. Bloch and Santini might be willing to trade. . . .

Meyer rolled into the gutted transformer pit. The plan of action formed in her mind as her muscles acted. The tank didn't shoot at her. She was probably just a shadow through the shimmering distortion.

Darkness, brightening in a microsecond to a quivering ambience like the sun viewed from under water. The circuitry had amplified the apparent view through Meyer's visor. The tank's skirts danced no more than a finger's breadth above the field's surface. Her helmet enhanced to normal viewing levels the light coming through that crack, though objects' edges were slightly fuzzy.

Wind like a tornado's shearing boundary layer pounded Meyer, shaking and bruising her despite her hard suit. Her helmet suppressed as much of the noise as possible, but the low-frequency harmonics made all her muscles quiver.

Air pressurized by four fans supported the vehicle's hundred-plus tons. The forty inch high walls of the plenum chamber held the air in a resilient bubble, spreading the vehicle's weight evenly over the ground. The tank could glide over surfaces in which wheels or treads would have bogged.

The weight didn't go away, though. Meyer's hard suit kept air pressure from crushing her, but the fans' output ducts buffeted her like water from a millrace. Against it, she fought her way from the transformer pit to where she could look up into one of the fans. She still had the pair of 4-pound rockets hanging from her belt.

On the tank's upper surface the inlets to the drive motors were screened and baffled. The output duct into the plenum chamber was angled for protection from mines, but there was only one coarse grating downstream of the nacelle. Scrabbling forward to keep up with the tank's slow advance, Meyer pulled a rocket from her belt and twisted the cap to arm it. She aimed it up the duct, trying to keep the nose straight against the roaring, bone-shaking gale. Strike Force warheads didn't have arming-distance delays: risk was the striker's responsibility.

Ignition and the bang of the warhead blowing apart the grate were lost in the thunder of the fans. Bits of casing cracked against Meyer's armor. She didn't know if any fragments had penetrated.

Meyer armed the second rocket. It was getting harder to fight the wind. She was afraid she wouldn't be able to aim the rocket even the short distance to the nacelle. Her brain responded to crushing fatigue by pulsing waves of color across her vision.

She fired. For an instant she thought the blue glare was another trick of her mind. Her visor muted the light instantaneously. The fan duct was a tube of arcing electricity and reflections as the nacelle destroyed itself. The solid column of air that had rammed Meyer as she squatted in the duct had ceased.

Metal shrieked over the rumble of the remaining fans. The skirt's lip was rubbing against the concrete. Three fans could no longer support the tank when the open duct of the fourth vented the pressurized cushion to the atmosphere.

The tank skidded to a halt, trapping Meyer beneath its armored mass.

The tank settled, closing the gap between skirt and concrete. "But we got the fucker, sarge," she whispered as darkness closed in.

Blohm fired at the twisted image of the tank's main gun, a high-powered Cassegrain laser. The chance of getting a pellet through the tiny objective opening to damage the mirrors within wouldn't have been high even if Blohm had been able to see the target clearly, but it was the best option going.

The magnetic dome in his sight picture changed hue. One of the intake ducts was arcing. The ionized particles couldn't penetrate the magnetic shield, so they swirled around the tank like swarms of angry blue hornets.

The tank slid to a halt. The scream of metal on concrete was so penetrating at close range that for a moment Blohm saw double. A pall of white dust rose around the vehicle, the ejecta of a four-inch trench pulverized from the starport's surface.

Blohm locked a fresh magazine into his stinger's butt well. Instead of firing, he paused to see what the changing situation would bring.

The tank tried to lift on the thrust of three fans. Air backed mournfully through the fourth duct. The shimmer of magnetic shielding vanished. The crew was throwing overload power to the remaining engines in order to get the tank moving again. The power plant didn't have enough headroom to accomplish that and meet the enormous drain of the shield at the same time.

Blohm could *see* the squat laser tube clearly for the first time. He hadn't fired more than a half-second burst into it before the dazzling radiance of a plasma bolt struck the turret. That didn't surprise him. Nobody survived in C41 unless he was fast, and Kurt Leinsdorf was damned near as fast as Blohm himself.

Blohm swapped magazines again. Part of him wondered how many kids Leinsdorf had killed over the years.

The red mask of a priority message flicked three times across Abbado's visor. *"C41, two minutes!"* his helmet ordered. *"All strikers commence withdrawal. Out!"*

"Time to go, kiddies!" Abbado said after he pulled his own boots clear. Rubble shifted when the automatic cannon raked the transient compound, though nobody'd been hit by the shells themselves. He paused an instant to make sure his strikers were all moving.

The tank moved, but it was drifting like a cloud. Its guns were silent. The crater glowing in the turret face was the only exterior sign of damage.

Abbado's legs wobbled for a few steps before he

found the rhythm. He followed Glasebrook, the last of his strikers, toward the pickup point. Two missiles hit the transient compound. A salvo of at least a dozen landed an instant later in a fury of noise, black smoke, and debris.

Major Farrell rose from the shelter of the warehouse. "There's a striker—" he shouted. Abbado looked back.

The tank erupted a hundred feet from where the plasma bolt hit. A white-hot plume ate away the turret, spattering ash and molten metal to all sides. For a moment the huge vehicle continued to drift; then the skirts grounded again. The hull sank slowly as the walls of the plenum chamber softened and collapsed.

A striker in a hard suit climbed from the tramline the tank had crossed just before it stopped. The figure moved toward safety through the fiery drizzle.

Farrell started to go back. Leinsdorf grabbed him.

"We'll cover him!" Abbado called. Glasebrook was with him; the rest of 3-3 had paused among the first line of parked vehicles.

Leinsdorf nodded gratefully. He half-walked, half-carried the major ten strides toward the pickup point before Farrell gave up and jogged willingly on his own. Thunder pulsing intermittently from the west might be the extraction boat.

Abbado sighed and armed his remaining rocket. He and Glasebrook would help the striker from Heavy Weapons—carry him, needs must, because whatever the guy'd done was damned sure the reason that tank wasn't squatting on the pickup point right now. But first the striker had to make his own way through the circle of debris that only a hard suit could survive.

And maybe the boat would still be waiting when the three of them got to the pickup point.

✧   ✧   ✧

The range to the hilltop where the pair of Kalendru were setting up a clip-fed rocket launcher was nearly a thousand yards. Farrell could see them clearly, magnified a hundred times in his stinger's holographic sight, but he either couldn't hit them or the pellets didn't have enough energy at that range to put the targets down.

The extraction boat would land in the center of the storage lot. As strikers withdrew toward that point, C41's base of fire collapsed. Now the Kalendru could raise their heads long enough to observe and engage the strikers.

Farrell lay full-length on the roof of an APC swathed in anti-oxidant fabric. He took a deep breath and squeezed a short burst from the trigger as he breathed out. The stinger's butt was against Farrell's shoulder and he gripped firmly with both hands. Even so the weapon's slight recoil jerked the magnified sight picture up from the target.

A Kalendru shell hit between a pair of tarpaulin-covered trucks and detonated with a bang. The whole line of vehicles shuddered away from the blast. They'd been stored without fuel cells, but fabric and lubricants started to burn. Some of the Spook troops must be observing for the batteries back at Active Grid.

If the extraction boat didn't come soon, there wouldn't be anybody to extract.

Farrell lowered his weapon onto the distant target again. One of the gunners jumped up and clawed at his face. The other Spook was staring behind him at the roaring western sky. Farrell's finger squeezed without his conscious volition. As he did so, another striker's rocket hit the Spook weapon. Gun and crew vanished in a blue-white flash.

The boat came in low. It was a flattened cylinder eighty feet long and twenty wide, with the hatches already open along the rear two-thirds of the hull. Oval intakes sucked air through a fusion torus. The gas—any atmosphere would do—was expelled as high-velocity plasma to drive and support the vessel until it reached an altitude from which its magnetic drive could push against the planetary field. Lasers and light shells sparkled against the boat's blackened armor as it overflew the Kalendru infantry.

"C41, go! Go! Go!" Nadia Broz shouted over the command channel. *"All strikers aboard in sixty seconds!"*

The landing boat hovered, then dropped hard onto the field. The pilot landed with the thrusters shut off to avoid endangering nearby strikers. Three Spook missiles detonated twenty feet above the vessel. Smoke drifted from the point defense turrets in the bow and stern. The triple shockwave rocked the boat but didn't damage it. Strikers started jumping aboard.

Something blew a sullen smoke ring from the Spook-held woods. The fighting had lit several fires. One of them had reached a case of ammunition or grenades.

Farrell looked over his shoulder. Dust and vari-colored smoke rose from beyond the warehouses. Some of the buildings were burning also. Farrell's eyes didn't see any strikers that his visor's location chart had missed.

"For Chrissake come *on*, sir!" Leinsdorf snarled. He gripped Farrell's shoulder and slid him off the APC by main force. Farrell had stopped to provide cover while his strikers withdrew, so he and Leinsdorf still had a hundred yards to run to the boat.

The coil guns in the pickup boat's two lateral blisters raked the Spook positions. The weapons worked by the same principle as stingers but flung half-ounce projectiles. Trees shattered and rock outcrops disintegrated into sparks and lethal fragments.

Salvos of three or four shells each dived on the boat at intervals of a few seconds. Most of the rounds blew up in midair. Clouds of dirty black smoke spread above the vessel. The point defense system cycled flechettes so fast that the mechanisms screamed like saws instead of crackling.

Two of the Spook rounds hit the ground west of the boat. A striker went down; a buddy helped him to his feet. Because the missiles had been badly aimed, the defense system hadn't bothered to engage them. The software targeted only threats to the vessel itself.

Pain crackled along the right side of Farrell's chest. He flipped his visor up so that he could breathe without the constriction of the helmet filters. He should have switched to his oxygen bottle instead. The atmosphere was hot and metallic, sharp with ozone. His legs moved like wooden stumps.

The pickup boat was ten yards away. Strikers in the open bay fired toward the Spook infantry. Abbado and Glasebrook helped the hard-suited striker climb the high step and flop forward on the deck.

Nadia Broz was waiting at the flank of the ship. "Come on!" she screamed. The pilot blipped his air pumps. The thruster inlets honked air and a burp of iridescent plasma seared the ground.

"Go!" Farrell shouted to the pilot on the ground-to-air channel. He turned his head for one last check on any of his people who might be staggering toward pickup without the helmet that ID'd strikers on the locator circuitry. More shells were shrieking down.

Leinsdorf and Broz each grabbed an arm and together hurled their commanding officer aboard the pickup boat. An intense red flash silhouetted them and flung them after Farrell. A shell had landed just short of the vessel.

The boat lifted. The hatches were already closing.

"Medic!" Farrell shouted. He tried to sit up against the weight of Leinsdorf's torso. "Medic!"

The strikers' body armor had performed very well, but there was almost nothing left of either Leinsdorf or Broz below the waist.

"Medic, for the love of God!"

Interlude: Earth

My aide entered the office as I studied the holographic starscape filling the back wall. "I will be retiring soon, Miss Chun," I said.

When I was aide to Chief of Administration Singh thirty-seven years ago, she always called me "Mr. Smith." I have held many positions in the Unity bureaucracy since that time, but my first supervisor marked me more than I realized until I became Chief myself.

"You have several years left, sir," Chun said. She glanced at the starscape. It was a raw blaze of color against blackness, all the stars within the volume the Unity called human space; whether or not the stars had planets, whether or not those planets had life, whether or not there was a permanent human presence in the system.

"I was thinking of Stalleybrass, Miss Chun," I said with a smile. Her implant would have told her if I had careted one of the stars on the display, but even a biocomputer as sophisticated as a Category 4 civil servant cannot read minds.

"Not the choice I would have expected, sir," she said, perfectly deadpan though she knew there must be a joke of sorts somewhere in my statement.

Miss Chun was not afraid of me, but she knew that if I ordered the guards outside to kill her, they would obey me without hesitation. Implants do not rob us Category 4's of personality, but the .8 probability was that Miss Chun would commit suicide if I ordered her to do so. Any decision I made would be, *must* be, for the benefit of mankind.

"The learning curve ensures there will be a dip in the performance of this office when Ivanovitch replaces me as Chief," I said. "Better that the change not occur in two years, after age and stress have made noticeable degradation in my abilities. The Kalendru leave us very little margin."

Instead of repeating her comment about Stalleybrass, Miss Chun looked again at the starscape.

Stalleybrass is a fleet base. It has a permanent cadre of fifty thousand and a transient population of up to three times that number. Those civilians on the planet are as directly concerned with the war effort as the military personnel who outnumber them.

There are plants and shellfish in the seas of Stalleybrass, but the continents are wastes of sand with no indigenous life except lichen. Existence on Stalleybrass is viewed as a penance by all the humans stationed there.

I have been thinking a great deal about penance since I made my decision to retire.

"Not for myself directly," I said. "The Maxus 377 expeditionary force has returned to Stalleybrass."

Chun nodded grimly. "An expensive bit of bad luck for us," she said, "but not nearly as expensive as it would have been if the Kalendru fleet had arrived immediately after our landing instead of immediately before. There would have been tens of thousands of casualties among troops on the ground while Admiral Gage fought off the enemy—if he in fact was able to do that. If the Kalendru had pushed Gage out of the system, the entire landing force would have been lost."

"A .2 probability," I agreed. "Instead we lost only twenty-six personnel."

"Deaths as a result of enemy action," Miss Chun said in the interests of precision. "There were a hundred and five accidental fatalities during the voyage and return, though of course the serious costs were logistical."

"The serious costs to the Unity were logistical," I said, precise in turn. "And our duty is to the Unity. But Miss Chun—have you considered the problem of reintegrating former combat personnel into civilian society?"

Miss Chun stiffened almost imperceptibly. She was wondering if my mental condition hadn't deteriorated abruptly after all. "I'm aware that the problem exists, sir," she said. "It appears to me as inevitable as the danger posed by lightning storms. Neither threatens society as a whole because of the relative rarity of the event."

"They aren't criminals in the normal sense," I said. "The likelihood of a former combat soldier violating laws for the sake of gain is significantly lower than that of a non-veteran doing the same thing. The risk is that they may react with extreme violence to social constraints on their behavior."

Miss Chun walked to her console in the corner. Even with an implant the amount of information one can absorb is limited. Until now Miss Chun had scanned only a summarized report on the Maxus 377 expeditionary force. She called up the full data, from inception to the present.

I had viewed the same file a few minutes before she entered the office.

Interlude: Stalleybrass

Because the driver was afraid of getting into trouble, the surface-effect truck slowed only to about twenty miles an hour. Abbado and his strikers had inserted from vehicles moving a lot faster than that. They unassed from the right-side cargo door, the side opposite the enlisted personnel club, and landed without even bothering to roll.

Methie stumbled because the leg burned at Active Cloak hadn't fully healed on the voyage back. Glasebrook kept him from tumbling.

The driver accelerated, leaving a wake of dust stirred from the barren landscape by the truck's stub wings. He'd tried to argue 3-3 out of hiding in the back as he deadheaded to the port, but he'd given in when Abbado insisted. The driver's kid brother had been a striker in B-4 before he was killed.

"All present and accounted for, Sarge," Horgen said. Abbado waited till the pall of fine red powder had settled a little, then tugged down the kerchief he'd tied over his nose and mouth to filter some of the solids out of the local atmosphere.

Abbado didn't want them to look as though they'd come to stick the place up. They just wanted a beer or two—dozen. He and his six strikers sauntered in line abreast across the "street," a hundred-foot channel between buildings. There wasn't a lot of traffic, but twice they had to wait for a vehicle to pass in the other direction.

The club had been converted from a warehouse like those to either side of it. The unit insignia painted over the door was too dusty to be legible. A Sergeant 4th Class watched through a clear window as 3-3 approached. He looked pissy.

Abbado didn't blame the locals for being in a bad mood. Glasebrook must have been thinking the same thing because he said, "You know, I think I'd eat my gun before I'd let them stick me here in the permanent garrison."

The doorman was in his late thirties, ten years older than Abbado. He wore a dove-gray rear echelon fatigue uniform that was so clean he must have changed into it after he entered the club. Nothing could exist in the open on Stalleybrass without getting a coating of dust.

"Good afternoon, Sergeant," Abbado said. He was a Sgt3 himself, and the one-step difference in rank made no matter off-duty. "What's the beer like on Stalleybrass?"

He pulled at the doorhandle. The door didn't open.

"You're barbs from the fleet, right?" the garrison soldier called through the panel. "Anyway, you're out of uniform for this club. Better get your asses gone before the Shore Police show up to ask what you're doing out of your compound."

"Hey, look, Sarge," Abbado said. He licked his lips. His mouth had a dangerous adrenaline dryness. He didn't like being called a barbarian, especially not through a locked door. "We're Strike Force, yeah, but we just come here for a drink. Our base element got screwed up or something and there's no beer in our assigned compound. We're all the same army, right?"

"I don't know what army you're in, buddy," the older sergeant said. "I just know you're not wearing rank tabs, you're not wearing a uniform prescribed for military personnel on Stalleybrass, and you're not getting into this club."

His hand moved. A buzzer sounded somewhere behind him.

"What is this shit?" Horgen demanded. She tweaked the mandarin collar of her field-service fatigues. "These are the only fucking uniforms we got!"

The fabric blurred like a chameleon's skin, suggesting the color and patterning of its surroundings. For the moment, that meant it was dull, dusty red.

"Then you're in the wrong place, barb, just like I told you before," the doorman said. "Beat it!"

Abbado nodded. He was starting to tremble. "Let's go in, Flea," he said quietly.

Glasebrook put his massive right boot on the doorjamb and gripped the handle with both hands. He pulled. The mortise split and the latchplate pulled completely out of the panel.

"Let's not have a problem, Sarge," Abbado said as he strode past the doorman. "We're just after a—"

Music, a ballad wailed *a cappella* by a trio of androgynes, continued on a holographic stage against the wall opposite the bar. The garrison soldiers inside had formed a rank. They shifted forward. None of the locals was Glasebrook's size, but there were more than a hundred of them in the cavernous hall.

"Three-three!" Abbado shouted as he kicked an oncoming garritrooper in the nuts.

He knew it was all over before it started. The only

reason it took nearly two minutes before Glasebrook flew out into the dust with the rest of them was that the locals were packed too tightly together to use their numbers to full advantage.

The Sgt4 stood in the doorway, panting and livid. The doorpanel had been demolished at some point in the proceedings. The front of the doorman's neat tunic was ripped down to his waistband.

"Go back to the reservation, barbs!" he shouted.

Abbado picked himself up. "Everybody all right?" he murmured. He could feel his cheek swelling. A chair had hit him in the face.

"I'm better than somebody's going to be right soon," Flea Glasebrook said. He started forward again. Abbado caught his arm.

"Go away and stay away!" the doorman said.

"We'll be back," said Guilio Abbado. His throat was as dry as a grindstone. "But we'll be in uniform when we come."

Interlude: Earth

"After all, Miss Chun," I said, "a grenade isn't trying to get rich either."

I smiled.

Interlude: Stalleybrass

"Shit!" Horgen shouted when she realized they were coming in too fast. She goosed both lift fans but the armored personnel carrier still hit like a ton of old iron. They pogoed in the dust cloud before Horgen could chop the throttles, but Abbado and four strikers were already out.

The regular land-force driver had been willing to look the other way while his APC disappeared, but he'd refused to drive 3-3 on the operation. All the strikers knew the basics of an aircar, but they didn't have the trained reflexes. The APC's mass made it react deceptively slowly to control inputs.

Abbado hoped the vehicle was still in shape to extract 3-3 in a few minutes, but that wasn't the first thing on his mind just now.

Methie'd transferred from a mechanized infantry unit to the Strike Force. Because he'd used a coil gun and because of his bum leg, Abbado assigned him to the APC's turret. Methie sawed a line of half-ounce slugs through the club's facade ten feet above the ground. The air cracked like stones shearing.

Somebody had rehung the door in the hours since the strikers had been here previously. The latch was tacked back to the panel with a sheet of brown plastic. Abbado blew the mechanism apart with his stinger and slammed through. A kick would have been quicker, but the weapon made a point he hoped the locals understood.

Some of him hoped the locals understood. The rest was perfectly willing to splatter the guts of any bastard who came for him.

The doorman, the same sergeant who'd been there the first time, bellowed with pain. The stinger pellets along with everything they hit at such short range had disintegrated. The bits the doorman got in the way of had eaten away a chunk of his uniform and the skin beneath. It must have felt like being sandblasted.

Could've been worse, buddy.

The strikers wore helmets and body armor. Abbado hunched so that the point of his shoulder caught the sergeant in the pit of the stomach as he went by.

The visor's capabilities hadn't been much help outside because the swirling dust was opaque across the whole RF spectrum, but enhancement turned the dim interior lighting as bright as a drill field. There were a lot more people present than there had been earlier in the evening. Very few of them even had the sense and reflexes to flatten when coil-gun shot cracked overhead in a shower of splinters from the front wall.

They could scream though. They were doing that even before Abbado's stinger sawed a zigzag in the drop ceiling.

Other strikers were firing. Light enhancement turned the stingers' muzzle aura into flaring brilliance. C41 didn't go in much for non-lethal weaponry, but Matushek had found a crate of riot gas grenades. He lobbed them into the middle of the room.

As ordered, Methie shut down the coil gun after

the initial burst. Abbado'd been afraid Methie would
get overexcited and drop the muzzle with 3-3 in the
club. Besides, the projectiles travelled a hell of a long
way. Even on Stalleybrass there were places Abbado
knew he'd afterwards regret having shot up.

Large chunks of the ceiling came down. Half the
overhead lights were out; flickers showed where
powerlines were arcing.

"Watch it, Sarge!" Glasebrook warned. Abbado
ducked. The doorman flew past and hit the bar with
his arms and legs flailing. Something crunched and
it wasn't the furniture.

The part of the crowd that could still move
stampeded toward the rear of the hall. A place this
big probably had an oversized fire exit with crash bars.
If it didn't, well, safety regulations for rear-echelon
motherfuckers weren't Abbado's concern.

He slapped a fresh magazine in the stinger's butt,
then emptied it into the back ceiling in a single slashing
burst. Flocked insulation swirled down like an explosion
in a pillow factory. Pellets flashed when they hit the
metal stringers. Reloading again, Abbado let the spring-
loaded sling snug the weapon back against his right
armpit as he used both hands to vault the bar.

Gas spread like thin smoke from the middle of the
room where the grenades had landed. Abbado switched
his visor from enhancement to infrared before he bent
and began jerking dispenser trays out of the beer cooler.
The gas scattered light in the visible band, but it didn't
seem to affect the longer IR rays.

His helmet filters were in place but he felt the back
of his hands prickle. He sure hoped the shit wasn't
absorbed through the skin. The gas wasn't supposed
to be fatal. From the look of the REMFs puking their

guts up among the overturned tables, though, some of them wished they were dead.

Abbado slapped trays up on the bar behind him. Matushek was emptying another cooler. Two of the bartenders huddled at the far end, their hands clasped over the back of their necks. The remainder of 3-3 was hauling the loot outside or chewing more of the building apart with their stingers. One good thing about a rear-echelon base was you could count on weapons being locked in armories. Even strike companies had to turn in their hardware.

Some of their hardware.

Abbado jerked the last tray out of the cooler and shouted, "Let's go!"

He grunted as he rolled himself back over the bar. Enough of the hormones had worn off that he was aware of his armor's weight again.

One-handed, Abbado tugged down his stinger and put half a magazine into coolers there hadn't been time to empty. Chrome-faced doors flew apart. At the other end of the bar Matushek paused to pat the upraised fanny of one of the bartenders, an even better way to increase the REMFs' demoralization.

Abbado ran for the door. Glasebrook was ahead of him with a stack of dispenser trays so high that the transom scraped the top one off. Abbado caught it as it fell without really thinking about what he was doing. He dived with his burden into the waiting APC.

"Go!" Methie yelled, keeping count from the turret as 3-3 reboarded. The coil gun put another twenty rounds into the bar ceiling. The burst must have severed a major beam because a quarter of the roof twisted and sagged with a tortured moan.

The APC lifted. The side panels were still lowered.

Abbado saw movement—an aircar with a pulsing red light closing fast from the west.

"Goose it, Horgen!" he said. "The Shore Police's woke up!"

There was a *bang* from above him. Abbado thought for an instant that the SPs were shooting; then he saw a spark curving in the direction of the cops' flashing party hat. "What the fuck was that?" he demanded.

Methie looked down from the cupola. "We got two anti-emitter missiles with the bus," he said. "I figured this was a good time to use one."

The red light spun like a flipped coin and vanished from the sky. Abbado didn't see the flash of an explosion. He felt the future opening before him like a black cone: a complete absence of experience, stretching on forever.

"You blew up a carload of cops?" Caldwell said. "Ah, they'll *shoot* us for that."

She didn't sound excited. They were all too flat after the operation to be excited.

Horgen kept the APC low so it would be harder to track if anybody was trying. They were flying fast enough to keep ahead of the dust they raised. The compound was still a few minutes out.

"Hey, I'm an expert, remember?" Methie said. "I tuned it to home on the RF signals from their front fan, not the radio in the cab. I didn't even arm the warhead! They just had an engine failure."

Glasebrook laughed in a deep rumble.

"They may still have broke their necks when they went down, you know," Abbado said.

"Hey, they took that risk when they got out of bed in the morning," Methie replied.

Abbado'd been sitting on the floor. Now he swung down a seat from the central spine.

"Somebody pass me a beer, will you?" Horgen called from the cockpit. "You got the beer, right?"

"You bet your ass," Glasebrook said with deep satisfaction. He pulled one of the dispensers apart and began tossing cans to the other strikers.

Abbado looked out into the night and sipped his beer. There wasn't a lot to see as the APC roared across a darkened waste of stone and lichen.

There'd be hell to pay in a couple hours, Abbado knew from experience. But for the moment, he was home.

Interlude: Earth

Miss Chun's eyes were slightly crossed while she took the data dump. They focused again. "I see what you mean, sir," she said. "I'd expected that the psychological casualties would have been reported."

She shook her head in amazement that formal reports had been faked. Real information on C41 had to be extracted from second-order effects.

"The entire strike company engaged on the ground has redlined," Miss Chun continued. "We may be able to return some of the personnel to combat duties in the future, but frankly I don't regard that as more than a .3 probability."

"Acceptable parameters for strike force personnel are looser than regulations might suggest," I said. "Sergeant Third Class Guilio Abbado has been broken to Basic twice already in the past six years for conduct like this most recent incident. Broken to Striker, I should say, since he's remained in the Strike Force throughout the period."

"Then you believe these personnel are still functional, sir?" Miss Chun said. She spoke in a perfectly flat voice. If there had been any tone coloring the words, the question would have become an insult.

"I believe that personnel who remain in a Strike Force company for more than one operation are almost by definition unsuitable for other duties," I explained. "Officers higher in the organizational chain know that and make allowances for behavior that would be unacceptable in other units. The strikers avoid psychological support between missions because they believe—correctly—that they're at great risk of being redlined if they do seek help."

My aide watched me, assimilating what was only data to her. Miss Chun was highly intelligent or she would not have been accepted for Category 4, and her implant gave her access to more information than a thousand unaugmented geniuses could have absorbed; but she was twenty-five Earth years old.

There aren't enough human beings in the universe for statistical techniques suitable for, say, gas diffusion analysis to predict low-order behavior; nor was twenty-five years long enough to gain an intuitive feel for all of those behavioral patterns.

"But you're quite right, Miss Chun," I said. "Strike Force Company C41 has to be treated as having crossed the red line. The fifty-four personnel who came back from Maxus 377 in adequate physical condition are as useless to the Unity armed forces as the twenty-six who died or were permanently disabled in the operation."

Miss Chun nodded. "I'll give the order," she said, reaching for the console. "Separated from service with full pensions, I assume, rather than merely assigned to rear echelon duties?"

"No," I said.

And I told her what I proposed to do.

My aide's left eyelid quivered, her only failure of control over her body. "Sir," she said calmly. "You can't do that. You must rethink your proposition."

" 'The word must is not to be used to princes,' Miss Chun," I quoted. "If ever there was a prince in the sense Queen Elizabeth meant the word, I am he. Until I retire, I have any power I choose to exercise. This is the course I choose."

"Sir," said Miss Chun, "if you believe this is the proper way to deal with the redlined military personnel, I defer to your greater experience. But I don't see how the involvement of civilians in this fashion can be consistent with our duty to the Unity."

I stood up slowly. My implant gives me great knowledge and control over my body and its processes. It also provides a harsh record of the degree to which stress and age have ground away at my health.

"Do you believe that the Unity owes its soldiers nothing but burial or a pension, Miss Chun?" I said. My voice didn't rise, but it had less give than the face of an anvil. "Do you think it is to the long-term benefit of the Unity that our citizens regard discharged soldiers as trash that litters our streets and occasionally explodes lethally? Do you?"

Miss Chun's face tightened into marble smoothness. I was angry at myself, at what I had been and still was. She misunderstood, and I could not explain in a way she could understand. She was only twenty-five.

"I regret the necessity of many things I have done for the Unity, Miss Chun," I said more softly. "I regret the cost this colony draft will pay. The cost these *people*, these civilian human beings who are drafted into this colonization project, will pay. Nonetheless I see it as necessary."

Miss Chun nodded; acknowledgment that she heard me, not that she agreed.

"I will give the operation a top project manager," I added.

Miss Chun stood perfectly still, her head and torso framed by the starscape. She understood: not *why*, but what I intended.

"Yes," she said. "We will."

A Place Out of Time

Farrell's strikers clustered about him on a bare concrete plain. He watched the shell for the whole course of its flight. The gun crew weren't Kalendru, weren't human. They were just figures, and he couldn't understand where they were or why he could see them.

"Major, you've got to get us out of here!" Nadia said. All of them were watching him, every striker who'd served in C41 since Major Arthur Farrell was appointed to command.

The shell hit and exploded. Farrell didn't hear the blast, only the screams of his dying strikers. There was no cover, nowhere to run or hide.

"They're going to kill us all, sir!" Leinsdorf said. He didn't have any legs but he was standing anyway, staring with accusing eyes at the commander who let him die.

Another shell approached. It moved as slowly as a tachometer needle rising to redline.

Nowhere to run. All around the plain stood figures watching. They were not involved in any way; just watching.

The shell hit. Another silent blast and the screams. The screams came in pulses, pausing and then vibrating again through Farrell's mind. He looked at blood and body parts and the staring faces of the betrayed.

"Major, why don't you get us out? We trusted you!"

He heard the sound of a last shell diving toward him. All his strikers were dead. Everyone but Arthur Farrell was dead, and he had killed them.

The shriek of the incoming round was louder, closer. The shell throbbed with red light, again and again.

Farrell bellowed as he awakened. The room was dark except for the incoming message light on the communications set beside the bed.

He lifted the handset. "C41, Farrell," he said. His throat was raw from shouting in his sleep. He heard the identifying background hiss of Dirac communication.

An interstellar message was so unlikely that Farrell wondered if he were still dreaming. He lay back on the bed and closed his eyes. The sheets were sweat-soaked and wrapped around his waist.

"Major Farrell," said the female voice on the other end of a line light-years long, *"this is Department One, 701st Regimental Command."*

Earth, operations office. For administrative purposes the Strike Force was listed on the Table of Organization as the 701st Regiment of the Unity Military Establishment. Operations were always conducted at company strength and tasked through theater commands, however. Nothing came from Earth HQ except pay, supply vouchers, and personnel assignments.

"This is a warning order," the voice said.

Though the signals were relayed by a constellation of ordinary geosynchronous comsats, the interstellar transceiver itself was a satellite the size of a planetoid. It trailed Stalleybrass by three light-seconds in heliocentric orbit. The construction was so complex and expensive that only a dozen of the hundred-plus human-settled worlds had Dirac installations.

"Warning order?" Farrell repeated. The dream had disoriented him. Whenever he opened his eyes, the room spun. "Sir, there must be a mistake. C41 is on stand-down."

"Major Farrell, there is no mistake," the voice said. *"Have your unit prepared for operational deployment in twenty-four hours. Hard copy will follow through Theater Base Headquarters."*

"Sir!" Farrell said. "We aren't ready for action. We won't be ready for, for . . ."

This was insane. Farrell's head buzzed. He didn't know if he was awake or dreaming. If he turned the lights on, would he find himself standing on a plain with the bodies of his people around him?

"Major Farrell," the voice said, *"I suggest you recall that in the Strike Force our tradition is to carry out orders, not to argue against them. Transmission ends."*

The hiss stopped. The air was dead, as dead as Nadia Broz.

Our tradition. You rear-echelon bitch.

Farrell felt the handset squirm in his grip. He cradled it. That was only an illusion, a part of his nightmare.

Farrell got up. The sheets dragged after him. He jerked them from the bed and hurled them into a corner of the room. He needed to put a uniform on. Then he had to go to the dayroom to tell whoever was on duty as Charge of Quarters to start alerting people.

Life was a nightmare.

Earth: The Next Step on the Road

As soon as C41's command group got out at what was supposed to be a major starport on Earth, the aircar lifted again with a spray of gritty soil. The pilot hadn't said a word to the three strikers during the flight from Oakland District to Emigration Port 10 on the Balcones Escarpment. Farrell wondered if the fellow had dropped them at the wrong place.

The hull of automated transport 10-1442 was complete. From inside, the whining of power wrenches, the angrier howl of saws, and extrusion equipment that sounded like lions vomiting indicated that construction continued. Sixteen similar vessels were spaced a quarter mile apart at decreasing levels of completion. The monorail that joined the sites in a racetrack pattern brought materials graduated by the stage of construction.

An empty eighteenth site waited immediately west of where Farrell stood with his patched-together command group. The prickly nut grass crawling across the ground there was yellowed. The roots had been cooked by eddy currents between the buried magnetic mass and the starship launched a few days before.

"I don't remember the last time I was in a civilian port," said Lieutenant Marina Kuznetsov. She'd been CO of First Platoon. By virtue of being the only other officer who survived Active Cloak, she was now Farrell's XO. "This isn't much like I expected, though."

Sgt5 Daye, C41's First Sergeant, said, "Active Cloak was a civilian port. Part civilian, anyhow."

"It wasn't a lot noisier when we were there either," Kuznetsov agreed.

Pallets just unloaded from a ten-car train were being gobbled by construction crews. The port's only permanent buildings were five-story rammed-earth barracks, one per site. Every room had a balcony, and the walls' basic dirty-yellow hue was overpainted in garish patterns. Farrell found the result attractive if not in any sense of the word beautiful.

Even when the facilities are the same, civilians live better than soldiers. Well, they've got something to live for.

Farrell would have tried to find a reporting office in the nearest barracks except for the high fence which surrounded the building. There was an eyeprint lock on the gate, and the sign said SITE PERSONNEL ONLY.

It was hot and dry. Mesquite and prickly pear cactus ten feet high grew between the sites. The strikers didn't have helmets or other equipment, just battledress uniforms so new they had a chemical odor. Farrell felt naked and angry and very, very tired.

"Come on," he said. "Let's see if there's anybody in charge in the ship. If there's no billets for our people . . ."

He didn't finish the sentence. There was no finish. The rest of his strikers were scheduled to arrive in forty-seven minutes. If nobody'd arranged for C41's housing and rations, if they'd been sent to the wrong place, if they had to spend the night in a fucking scrub desert with no gear at all . . .

What else was new?

10-1442 was constructed with the extreme simplicity of an object which would be used once and then scrapped. The entrance hold was the entire bottom deck. For the moment it was bare of everything except grime and cryptic symbols chalked on the plates around the support pillars. Inside a workman in blue coveralls was fitting a fresh bottle of insulating foam to his spray head.

"Hey, buddy," Farrell said. "We're looking for the project manager, Jafar al-Ibrahimi. Got any notion where he'd be?"

"Nope," said the workman. He pulled down a clear mask to cover his face and began spraying the bulkhead. The foam went on a dull white but darkened to gray in seconds. The smell made Farrell sneeze; his eyes watered.

Daye switched off the sprayer.

Kuznetsov lifted the man's mask away and tossed it behind her. "Do better," she said. Her voice had sounded like a crow's ever since she took a bullet through the throat.

"Hey, I got a deadline!" the workman said.

"So do we," said Farrell. "Forty-three minutes. Where do we find the project manager?"

"The upper decks got finished first," the workman said. "I'd guess he was up in the nose, somewhere around there. But look, I don't know. Can I do my job now?"

"Maybe in a bit," said Daye. "How do we get to the nose?"

The workman grimaced and pointed toward the pillar along the axis of the ship. "The lifts are that way," he said. "Three and Four work, the others I don't know about. They didn't this morning."

"Thank you, Citizen," Farrell said. "Marina, would you wait by the hatch? I don't know how long this'll take, and I don't want our people to arrive and not have anybody meet them."

"Yeah," rasped the lieutenant. "They might get the idea that nobody gives a shit about strikers." She walked back outside, whistling a snatch of Tchaikovsky.

There were eight lift shafts in a central rotunda, but hoses and power cables snaked into five of them. The door of the sixth was open into an empty cage. Busy workmen in blue, puce, or orange ignored not only the strikers but anybody wearing a uniform of a different color. They shouted to their fellows or into epaulet communicators.

Lift Four arrived as Farrell and Daye entered the rotunda. Three workmen, one of them carrying a powered jack as long as her arm, pushed aboard with the strikers. The cage would easily have held twenty.

There wasn't a call button inside, nor had Farrell noticed one in the rotunda. The cage paused twenty seconds at each deck with the door open, then rose again without command. A workman hopped off at the next stop. Three more got on two decks above.

Farrell frowned. He hadn't realized the degree to which the transport was automated. He'd thought the term applied only to the navigation system. It looked like the passengers would be treated as canned goods in all fashions.

Well, at least the strikers were used to that.

"Sir," Daye said, "what the *fuck* are we doing here?"

"All I know is that C41 is the security element for a new colony," Farrell said. "The planet's BZ 459, and I haven't gotten to a database that has anything to add to the bare listing."

Daye frowned. "External security, sir?" he asked. "Or police for the folks themselves?"

"I don't know," Farrell said. He stared at the door, wishing there were answers written there instead of the stencilled notice MOUNT THIS DIRECTION with an arrow up.

"We're not cops, sir," Daye said. "Shit-fire, they wouldn't be that dumb, would they?"

"I don't know," Farrell repeated. Though the real answer was: that dumb, no; that callous, maybe.

"Shit-fire," Daye repeated softly.

For the first half dozen times the door opened, racket from the deck beyond made the cage vibrate. The last workman got out on Deck 10; above that the pauses were quiet. Only occasionally did Farrell glimpse somebody in the corridor. It occurred to Farrell that he didn't know how many levels the ship had.

When the lift reached Deck 25, Farrell heard angry voices. He nodded to Daye and the pair of them stepped out of the cage just before the door closed. Insulation covered the floor as well as bulkheads and ceiling. It was as soft as a deep-pile carpet. Foot traffic had already dented it.

A young woman stood at the door of an austerely furnished office/conference room. She nodded as they approached and called, "Major Farrell and Sergeant Daye have arrived, sir."

Farrell had no idea who she was.

A man in his sixties sat behind an electronic desk which was welded to the floor. Like the woman he wore loose, many-pocketed clothing that would have been battledress if there'd been any badge or patch on it.

The cloth was brown rather than chameleon-dyed,

but it was still the same synthetic that went into the strikers' uniforms. The fabric was tough and breathed even better than natural fibers, but it was harsh enough to take your skin off when pressed against you by armor and equipment. Maybe these civilians wore underwear.

The three other civilians—a man of thirty, a woman in her fifties, and another man who was probably as old as the fellow at the desk—turned when the strikers entered. All of them wore ordinary business clothes of excellent quality, though the older man's socks were mismatched.

The younger man had been shouting in a resonant tenor voice. The three were standing, though the bulkheads had fold-down seats. Two short benches could also have been pulled up from the floor to face the desk.

"Gentlemen," the young woman said, "this is Project Manager Jafar al-Ibrahimi. I'm his assistant, Tamara Lundie—"

Farrell saw a thought flick behind Lundie's eyes, though she didn't blink physically.

"I'm a Manager 3, that's the equivalent of a senior lieutenant," Lundie continued. "Manager al-Ibrahimi is the equivalent of a full colonel and is in sole charge of the project."

Farrell felt his mouth smile. Did she think strikers were so rank-conscious that they needed to have civilian pecking orders explained to them? Oh, God, his poor strikers, being dropped into another ratfuck . . .

"Major," al-Ibrahimi said, "is the remainder of your unit on schedule?"

The project manager was a slight man who appeared brittle, an appearance Farrell decided was false as soon as he heard the man speak. Al-Ibrahimi wasn't going to break, and Farrell didn't think he'd be easy to grind down either. What surprised Farrell was the degree to which something had already ground al-Ibrahimi down.

There was plenty of steel left, though.

"Yes sir," Farrell said. If there'd been a problem, somebody would have reported through the finger-sized communicator he carried in his pocket in lieu of the helmet he was used to. This wasn't a combat operation where no news might mean—usually meant—that everybody in the silent unit had been killed instantly.

"Good," said al-Ibrahimi. "Major, Ms. Susannah Reitz is president of the building council and therefore *de facto* leader of the colony. Dr. Joao Suares—"

He nodded toward the older man. Suares looked surprised.

"—and Mr. Matthew Lock are her co-councillors. Madame, gentlemen, Major Farrell is head of our security element, and Sergeant Daye is his ranking enlisted man. We'll be working closely together after landfall."

"Mr. al-Ibrahimi," Lock said, "I *demand* that you halt this process until my request for an injunction can be heard. The very idea of assigning the residents of an urban apartment building as the initial colony on a totally unsettled planet is insane!"

Farrell didn't let his face show surprise, but that was at least one thing he and the councillor could agree on.

Lock was in good shape. He must keep fit with sports and exercise equipment. It was a civilian sort of "good condition" though, and it looked soft to eyes like Farrell's. He was used to strikers whose flesh had been pared off by discomfort, stress, and the lack of appetite caused by exhaustion.

Farrell found it odd to look at civilians close up. Real civilians, not Unity bureaucrats providing support to the armed forces. Farrell hadn't been on leave in a real rear area during the past five years, and civilians sure as hell didn't show up in the places he *did* go.

"Tamara," al-Ibrahimi said, "brief Major Farrell on his unit's billets, supplies, and duties during the voyage. The remainder of C41 can be expected in thirty-nine minutes."

The project manager hadn't checked either a clock or a schedule, so far as Farrell could see.

Lundie turned on her heel. She was pretty enough but not Farrell's type. Farrell's type was a woman who didn't look at him as if he were a pallet of rations—and an equally unlikely love object.

"As for you, Councillor Lock," al-Ibrahimi continued as the strikers followed Lundie out of the office, "I will carry out Unity policy as it devolves on me, and you will do the same. Failure to comply with a Colonization Order means loss of citizenship—"

"I know that!" Lock said. "But—"

"—and a life sentence to a labor camp," the manager continued. Lundie had led the strikers back to the rotunda, but her chief's crisp voice was still perfectly clear. "Now, during the voyage each two decks of colonists will be separated by a deck of supplies and . . ."

A lift cage arrived. The strikers stepped aboard in unison with Lundie. Daye looked as worried as Farrell had ever seen him.

The only thing that kept Daye going was the hope that his CO had the situation in hand. Farrell knew that was a vain hope if ever there'd been one.

Lundie led them off on the next deck down. "Your quarters are here on Twenty-four," she said, the first words she'd spoken directly to the strikers since introducing them. "Your rations and equipment will be stored with you. The remaining volume on this deck will store colony supplies that won't be needed until after landing on Bezant 459."

She led Farrell and Daye down a corridor. The doors to either side were ajar. The rooms had eight pull-down bunks, a shower stall, a double washstand, and a latrine. The space and amenities were better than those of a troopship and enormously better than an assault vessel's, but Farrell didn't imagine the civilian colonists were going to be happy.

"Ma'am," said Sergeant Daye. "Ah, can I ask a question?"

"Yes, of course," Lundie said. "And please refer to me as you would refer to one of your own officers."

"Yes ma'am," Daye said. Farrell wondered if he was having as much trouble as Farrell himself was imagining the young woman in C41. "What that fellow said about a whole building being turned into a colony—is that true?"

"Yes," said Lundie. "Horizon Towers in the Central Chicago District. Every resident of Earth is subject to Colonization Orders, but this particular technique has never been used before."

"Did some computer blow a fuse?" Farrell asked. "Or did some dickheaded human really think this was a good idea?"

"I can't answer that," Lundie said. When she spoke on most subjects, her voice had the false rhythms of an AI program forming words. This was so flat that perversely it indicated real feeling.

"Rations and other consumables for your company have already been loaded into these two compartments," Lundie continued. "And there's a large compartment here—"

"C41 bunks aboard while the ship's being finished, you mean?" Daye interjected.

Lundie looked at him. "The ship will be finished very shortly," she said. "Liftoff is in six hours, twelve minutes."

She opened the door as she'd started to do. There was nothing to be seen but an empty room. Throughout the vessel, ringbolts on all flat surfaces provided anchors for cargo nets and tie-downs.

"—for your personal stores and equipment. There's a separate compartment for use as an armory."

"We keep our hardware with us in C41," Farrell said flatly. "Is that going to be a problem?"

Lundie's face was still. "That isn't necessary on the voyage," she said carefully.

"It's necessary if I'm going to sleep," Daye said. "I'm itchy right now, ma'am."

"C41's pretty stressed," Farrell said. He didn't know how to explain to a civilian. "I know there's a risk, but I think the risk is worse if I, if we . . ."

Daye grimaced. "Look, ma'am, if you can get us reassigned to something we know how to do, that'd be great. We're strikers, we're not, we're . . ."

"Arrangements for security personnel are yours to determine, major," Lundie said. "Assignments to the Bezant 459 project are of course from higher levels of the government."

She cleared her throat as a period, then continued, "The colonists will be arriving in three hours. Since your helmets have full communications and mapping capacity, we'll use your personnel as guides for corridor assignments. Initially only the upper seventeen decks will be complete, so . . ."

Farrell continued to listen to the young woman. From long experience he'd be able to reel off her statements word perfect when he assigned individual missions to his people.

But Farrell's heart was in a dark place of its own, and his soul was as dead as the strikers C41 had left scattered across a galaxy at war.

The landscape of spiky trees and spiky grass, scattered sparsely over gritty dirt, could easily have been a frontier planet. Abbado hadn't known there were parts of Earth that looked like this.

It was probably news to the colonists being herded off the train by uniformed police, too. The largest expanse of vegetation most of the civilians would have seen before was their apartment building's roof garden.

The poor bastards stared at their surroundings with shell-shocked expressions. "They better get used to it," Abbado said aloud. "I don't know about Bezant, but I've seen a lot of planets that make this look like an R&R base."

The police carried shock batons. They weren't hitting people with them that Abbado saw, but they chivied the civilians with their free hands while the batons waved.

"This ain't right," Glasebrook muttered. "I don't like us being mixed up with it."

"Cheer up, Flea," Abbado said. "This assignment got us off Stalleybrass fast. I wasn't much looking forward to answering questions about a little problem there at a cadre bar."

Abbado had been more relieved than he would admit to his strikers. The morning after they'd shot up the REMFs he'd been asking himself how the *hell* he'd let himself do that; but at the time, at the time . . .

The police wore riot helmets and breastplates, not a patch on Strike Force equipment for weight but not particularly comfortable in this climate either. That was probably part of the reason they were treating the civilians like animals.

Already some strikers were shepherding ragged columns of civilians toward the starship. *"Sarge, we've found ours,"* Horgen called over the squad push. *"We'll see you at the billet. Out."*

"The ones we're looking for are going to be the batch that caught the wrong train," Abbado grumbled to Glasebrook. Matushek, the third member of the group, was scanning civilians to match the holographic portraits downloaded into his helmet database.

For the loading, Top Daye had broken 3-3 into fire teams under Horgen and Abbado to get colonists to decks 18 and 19 respectively. Methie and Foley were detached to help the two survivors of Heavy Weapons guide the building support staff.

The apartment block from which the colonists came had eight stories. For the voyage the residents were split into east and west corridors and each group was supposed to be on a single car of the train. If there'd been a little coordination back when the train was loaded the strikers would know exactly which carload went to which deck, but of course that hadn't happened.

"Don't see why civilians can't count the decks up to nineteen themselves," Glasebrook muttered.

"Buck up, Flea," said Abbado. "Nobody's shooting at us, right?"

The monorail shivered for its full length as current to the magnets raised the hangers a hair's breadth from the elevated track. The train accelerated slowly, but it was up to ninety miles an hour by the time the last car whipped past Abbado and his strikers. Suction dragged at them, but the only sound the train made was a hiss and the faint click of couplers.

"Sarge, got them!" Matushek reported. He was standing twenty feet from the others, so he used helmet commo to speak over the nervous chatter of a thousand colonists and their guides. *"They were on the other side of the track! Over."*

"Fucking typical," Abbado said as he strode toward the clump of fifty-odd stunned-looking civilians. In a louder voice he shouted, "Six West! Form on me!"

The track serving Emigration Port 10 had loading platforms only on one side. Naturally, one of the cars had been misaligned so that its doors were on the wrong side; and naturally, the folks Abbado was looking for were on that car.

The police had noticed the misplaced civilians also. Half a dozen of the nearest strode under the support rail ahead of the strikers. A tall, badly overweight cop bellowed, "Hey you assholes! What're you doing over there? Move it!"

He grabbed the nearest civilian by the arm and jerked her in the direction of the starship. She was carrying bulging net bags, far too much of a load for a woman in her sixties. One of them spilled packages onto the ground.

"That's okay, buddy, we'll take care of this!" Abbado said. His voice was thinner than normal because he was going to be reasonable, he wasn't going to do what he wanted to. "Folks, we're your—"

The cop turned and said, "When I want your opinion, dickhead, I'll—"

Abbado kicked him in the balls. Shit, he'd known he was going to do that all the time.

A cop holding a shock rod faced Glasebrook, who took the rod from him and broke it over his knee. The blue sparks snarling against Flea's left palm stopped when the shaft fractured.

"Fellas, we can let this stop right here," Abbado said. The big cop had settled to his knees. His riot helmet had skewed and now hid his eyes, though the faceshield was up. "Let's do that, right?"

"Yeah," said Matushek. "Let's."

He bobbled a grenade in his open right hand. For an instant Abbado was afraid somebody might not believe the grenade was real or that Matushek really would throw it. A grenade wasn't much of a weapon for close enough to spit, not if you cared about surviving yourself.

"Ace, put that fucking thing away," Abbado said as he stepped between his striker and the police. Christ on a crutch! He'd thought this was a cush assignment and he'd be able to keep out of trouble.

Glasebrook helped up the man Abbado had kicked, holding the fellow by collar from behind. "All under control, right?" Abbado said.

A cop looked over her shoulder. Maybe she was expecting to see help coming. What she saw was the rest of C41. There were about as many cops in the escort detail as strikers, but the police didn't have lethal weapons and C41 didn't have anything else. The company's baggage hadn't been delivered yet, but the strikers had been nervous about the screwy situation. Most everybody'd brought a security blanket.

Abbado keyed the unit channel. *"C41, doesn't anybody have a job to do?"* he snarled. *"Come on, there's not a problem! Out!"*

"S'okay, we're going," a policeman said. The group of them moved down the trackway.

"Have a nice trip," Ace Matushek called. He dropped the grenade back into a side pocket.

"Six West!" Abbado called to the civilians staring at him. "We're going to take you folks to Deck 19, but we'll wait a bit to let some of the folks ahead of us clear the lifts, okay? Let's just relax for a bit."

A woman started to cry. A pretty one, too. Jeez, he'd really stepped on his dick this time!

"Can I help you pick those up, ma'am?" he offered brightly. And it wasn't till he knelt to help the old lady with her packages that Abbado realized he was holding his powerknife. The blade trembled like caged lightning in the bright sun.

"Look," Seligman said to Esther Meyer as they waited for a construction crew to lay decking over the maze of conduits in the corridor floor, "the cits who live in the building, if they want to go play colonist, that's fine. But it's not right they take us staff along! I'm a services supervisor, I'm not a fucking farmer."

Seligman was an overweight, middle-aged man with a red face and wavy hair implants that didn't match the fringe remaining around the edges of his scalp. He acted angry because he was scared and ashamed of it.

He ought to be ashamed. Scared of going off-planet!

"You think this was their idea?" Meyer asked. "I heard they got drafted into this, same as you."

Meyer hadn't been drafted. Everybody in the Strike Force was a volunteer. Sometimes she tried to think back to when she took that step forward. Stupid fucking thing to do, but she couldn't imagine an existence in which it hadn't happened. Funny.

"Don't you believe that crap!" Seligman said. "Horizon Towers isn't full of peons, these are cits! They don't get orders they don't want. Or if they do, they call somebody so high in the Unity you and I couldn't breathe there, and the order gets cancelled. If they're going off-planet, it's because that's what they decided. And they're dragging me along, just like I was their pet dog."

The service personnel were supposed to operate the colony's heavy equipment and provide the sort of support that they'd given the building residents, the citizens, on Earth. The Population Directorate was like a hog processing plant: it used every part of the pig except the oink.

"Life's tough all over," Meyer said. Two workmen held plating in place as a third drove a welder down the seams. As soon as the deck was complete, she could deliver Seligman to the storeroom where he'd wait the arrival of the on-voyage consumables for which he'd be responsible.

The welding trolley reached the end and turned around. With the other two workmen jogging behind, it whined toward Meyer and Seligman. One was talking into a lapel microphone.

"Hey, is this safe to walk over?" Seligman asked as the crew came past. They ignored him.

"They're walking on it, aren't they?" Meyer said as she started down the corridor. She'd be glad to see the back of Seligman. Civilians had to be told every fucking thing. It gave her the creeps, being around people who didn't know how to react.

"All right, this is where you go," Meyer said, opening

the door. "It'll be keyed to your palm-print after the goods arrive."

They stepped inside. Meyer bumped the doorframe. She'd projected a corridor map on her helmet visor with a sidebar giving specs of the storeroom and its contents. She was used to looking through a thirty-percent mask, but she moved awkwardly because normally Heavy Weapons set up in open terrain. Working in a ship was a new experience.

The volume was empty except for the omnipresent tie-down anchors. The strip lighting in the moldings flickered; somebody in the construction crew shouted angrily in the corridor. Seligman chalked his initials, WAS, on the door. He didn't have a helmet database to distinguish between identical panels.

"Ah, hell," Seligman said miserably as he looked at the barren gray cell. "I told my brother-in-law, you know? He's in district government. I figure, he can do something. And you know what he says?"

"Look, I got to get back," Meyer said. She'd done her job.

An insulation sprayer whined in the corridor. Whitish fog entered the room. Seligman sneezed and closed the door.

" 'Too bad,' he tells me," Seligman said. " 'Too bad!' That's all he can say about his brother-in-law being shipped God knows where to be eaten like as not!"

"Nobody's going to eat you—" Meyer said.

The lights went out.

The room was pitch dark. The walls crushed down on Meyer. She was alone and there was only blackness squeezing—

"—you all right?" Seligman cried. He held her arms as she sagged.

Meyer straightened. The lights were on again. She looked at herself through Seligman's horrified eyes. She jerked the door open.

"I'm fine," she said in a whisper. "I think . . . There must have been a short circuit, you know? I got a shock."

She strode down the corridor, bumping her right shoulder on the bulkhead at every other step. A workman called to her.

"Fuck off," she said without turning her head.

Alone.

The doors of Lifts Four and Six opened. Faces staring from the packed cages matched those projected on Caius Blohm's visor.

"Come on," he ordered, grabbing the nearer door with his hand to keep it from closing automatically. Nobody in the cages moved. A baby was wailing.

"Come on, Four East, this is your deck!"

The other door started to close. An older woman reached an arm past the people in front of her and blocked it. "This is where our quarters will be," she called in a clear voice. "Quickly, now. Let's clear the lift for the others."

Blohm's helmet AI identified the woman as Seraphina Suares. She looked alert if not cheerful. Most of the other civilians had the appearance of the human prisoners Blohm saw in the camp C41 had liberated a year and a half before.

People moved out of the cages. One of the men held the door so that Blohm could step away. "Where do we go?" asked a woman holding an infant. A man with a toddler in either hand stood beside her in the rotunda, looking gray.

Blohm shrugged. "There's rooms," he said. "They bunk eight."

He didn't know what to say. He didn't have any connection with these people. They were a different species with their worried faces and their children. God, how many of them had children!

Another lift opened. "Here's our deck, folks," Sergeant Gabrilovitch called from the cage. "Everybody out for Deck Nine, that's home till we get to Bezant."

This duty didn't bother Gabe. "Hey, I ran a restaurant on Verugia before I enlisted," he'd said when Blohm complained. "What's so hard about showing people to their stalls?"

"All right," Suares said, "we'll group ourselves to minimize difficulty on the voyage. Will all the families with children under ten please step this way."

The words were a question, but the tone wasn't. People began sorting themselves obediently. The lifts emptied and closed.

Gabrilovitch stepped close to Blohm. "Guess she's got things under control," the sergeant murmured. "Her husband's a building councillor, but it looks to me like it's her who calls the shots."

Blohm didn't speak. Gabe frowned, waited a moment more, and said, "Hey Blohm! You okay?"

"Yeah, I'm fine," the striker said. He was watching the crowd of frightened civilians. The children clutched toys and extra clothing, looking around in wonder as their parents were directed to rooms.

So many children.

Day One

"Your personnel have settled in, Major?" al-Ibrahimi said. He was looking in Farrell's direction, but his eyes were focused on the holographic display before him. Because the interference patterns were aligned toward the manager's side of the desk, Farrell saw only an occasional shimmer like cobwebs drifting through a sunbeam.

"We've spent our share of time on troopships, sir," Farrell said. "This is better than the usual. I'm not used to traveling without flight crew, but it seems to be working well enough."

The ship trembled every few minutes as it sequenced between bubble universes, navigating by means of the differentials between constants of velocity and momentum from one continuum to the next. To those aboard 10-1442 the sensation was similar to thunder so distant that it was felt, not heard.

"Statistically," al-Ibrahimi said, still watching his display, "fully automated operation is only insignificantly more dangerous than crewed spaceflight."

He looked at Farrell through the holographic curtain and smiled. "I trust I'm as capable of dispassionate analysis as the next man," he added, "but speaking as an individual I'd be just as pleased if the

Population Authority spent a little more on transport costs."

Farrell shrugged. "Life has risks," he said. Some of his people worried more about transport than they did about what the Spooks had waiting at the far end, but it'd never particularly bothered him.

"Tamara's organizing the colonists into skill groups, but she'll be back shortly," the manager said. "I'll have her download full data on BZ 459 so that you and your company will know what you'll be facing after we land. Or I can do that myself, if you'd like?"

"We've got a week and a half," Farrell said. "I don't guess another hour's going to make any difference."

He cleared his throat, wondering how to get out what he'd come to ask. This was the first time he'd talked—really talked—to the manager.

"One advantage of the unusual makeup of the Bezant 459 colony," al-Ibrahimi said, "is that we have four fully-trained MDs. We don't have the equipment that would be available on a developed world, but we're far better off than the normal run of Population Authority initiatives."

"Look, sir," Farrell said abruptly. "You could have C41 relieved immediately as the security detail, right? You've got that power?"

"Yes I do," al-Ibrahimi said. "I could send a message capsule to the base at Varnum, approximately a day and a half from BZ 459. I would expect it to take the base commander a day to arrange for the personnel and transport, then three days for a full-sized vessel to make the return trip."

Al-Ibrahimi touched a control on his desk and nodded approval at whatever the database told him. He returned his attention to Farrell, smiled mildly, and said, "I have no intention of doing anything of the sort, however. I'm extremely pleased with the way your company has performed."

Al-Ibrahimi's eyes were an unusually deep blue. Farrell had found it disquieting when the manager watched the display while looking toward him. The weight of al-Ibrahimi's direct gaze was uncomfortable, though the fellow was perfectly calm.

"Sir, I appreciate you saying that," Farrell said. Only as the words came out did he appreciate how true they were.

Mostly in the Strike Force—in life, Farrell suspected, though life wasn't something he claimed to be an authority on—praise was a gruff, "Nice job!" Followed with a tougher mission the next time to prove the statement was sincere. Al-Ibrahimi sounded like he meant it, and it was important to him that Farrell knew he meant it.

"The thing is, sir," Farrell said, "we really need a stand-down. I suppose somebody at Regiment thought that's what he was doing, pulling C41 out of combat and letting my people, you know, relax."

"I don't think BZ 459 is going to be very relaxing, Major," al-Ibrahimi said. In a funny way, the manager struck Farrell as having a striker's personality. The man looking over that desk had the right focus on mission, the willingness to do whatever it took to achieve the objective. "Compared to one of your normal insertions, perhaps; but that's a relatively short period of time, whereas you'll be on BZ 459 for at least six months."

"Sir," Farrell said. Al-Ibrahimi hadn't gone through the roof when Farrell made the request, but Farrell no longer thought there was a snowball's chance in hell that the manager was going to pull C41 from the project. He hoped he wasn't whining, but he *had* to make this cold man understand. "It's not us I'm worried about, it's your people."

He shook his head and continued, "Look, I—shit, I love my strikers if the word means anything at all. But they're tight, really tight since the last mission. I'm afraid something's going to happen, somebody's going to nut and, you know, hurt a bunch of civilians. Hurt them bad."

He rubbed his forehead with the tips of all eight fingers. He could see it like it had already happened: a striker standing over a dozen bodies sprawled in a circle of guts and blood and scraps of bone. The only thing the image lacked was the striker's face. It could be anybody, God help them all. Up to and including the company commander.

"We shouldn't be around where people don't . . . understand what we're like, sir," Farrell said. He met al-Ibrahimi's still blue eyes. "We're not, not the way civilians mean it. We're not really human anymore."

"I'm also concerned about my people, as you put it, Major," al-Ibrahimi said calmly. "I appreciate the risks to all concerned rather better than you think I do. If I didn't believe that the risks were justified by the benefits of the colony having C41 as its security element, I wouldn't have accepted your assignment in the first place."

Farrell braced to attention. "Yessir," he said to a point beyond the manager's right ear. "I'll return to my strikers then, sir. You'll find C41 ready to carry out its responsibilities insofar as humanly possible."

He turned on heel and toe to the door. It was a parade-ground movement that strikers had little call for, but which al-Ibrahimi's glacial calm seemed to require.

"Major?" al-Ibrahimi said. Farrell glanced back over his shoulder.

"Please recall that I am the *project* manager, Arthur," al-Ibrahimi said. "You and your strikers are as surely my people as the civilians they guard."

He smiled. The manager's tone and expression were as sad as anything Farrell had seen at a funeral.

"Krishna!" said Caldwell as she watched the projected display. "They're going to put humans here?"

"They're going to put us here, Josie," Ace Matushek said. "I've never been sure we qualified as human."

Bipedal herbivores spread across the holographic landscape, killing everything in sight. "They weigh about forty pounds apiece," Abbado said, quoting the figure from the database. The creatures' forelimbs were modified into either horn-edged cutting blades or bulbous tanks of caustic which the creatures could spray a distance of several yards.

Individually the creatures weren't particularly imposing, but the image taken from a survey ship orbiting Bezant showed tens of thousands in the swarm.

"Like locusts," Foyle said. "Only they suck the plants dry instead of chewing the leaves off."

3-3 had a compartment to itself, so Abbado had the squad view the mission background as a unit. Strikers would repeatedly go over the data as individuals during the voyage, but Abbado knew that mission success depended not only on good personnel but on their ability to work together.

He'd have been more comfortable if the major had been able to brief all C41 together, but the transport wasn't configured to allow that. The major'd given C41 a pep talk in the rotunda of their deck, the only space available that held everybody—barely. The lifts kept opening, and there wasn't a large-scale holographic projector. Projection from a striker's helmet worked for one squad in its compartment, but you couldn't enlarge the image enough for the entire company to see details.

"These things don't fly," Abbado said. "Locusts don't bash farmers over the head if they're in the field when the swarm lands, though."

The creatures spooked an animal from its burrow. The solitary animal was an armored quadruped whose stubby limbs bore long claws. Half a dozen young clung to knobs on the adult's back. The adult bobbed forward awkwardly, handicapped by its rigid carapace.

"What're these bastards called, do we know?" Glasebrook asked.

"Anything you like, Flea," Abbado said. "Or anything the cits like, I suppose. There isn't anybody on Bezant to name them till we get there."

Dozens of bipeds stopped feeding and jogged ahead of the main swarm, moving to either side of the quadruped's track. The quadruped lurched to the right. A biped sprayed a cloud of white vapor over the quadruped's head and forequarters.

The victim rose on its hind legs, clawing furiously with both forelimbs. Two of the young lost their grip and rolled to the ground. Bipeds chopped at them and the adult indiscriminately. The victim's claws raked open several of the attackers and flung the bodies a dozen yards away, but the site crawled with more bipeds joining the fray.

A caustic fog covered the climax. Abbado didn't

have any difficulty imagining what was going on.

The viewpoint panned upward. Individual creatures lost definition against the background. A wedge of landscape, broadening as it advanced, showed the ashen gray of vegetation from which all life had been sucked. Another scar, similar but for the moment smaller, appeared hundreds of miles west of the first as the image area expanded still further.

"The analysts figure broods hatch, go on for a while, and die," Abbado said, reading from a sidebar focused for his eyes only. "The critters *must* die or there wouldn't be anything left but bare rock."

"Can we spray the eggs before they hatch, Sarge?" Foley asked.

"Hell, Analysis doesn't know for sure they come from eggs," Abbado said. "Maybe, but for now we've got to figure on eliminating a swarm when they're looking pretty much the way that one was."

He didn't even try to keep the disgust out of his tone. Everything on Bezant in the database had come from orbital imagery and a few automated probes to sample the microbiota. Nobody'd bothered to put scouts on the ground. C41 had gotten a lot of tough missions, but Abbado had never before been handed one where he'd had so little hard data to go on.

"Do we have electric fencing?" Horgen asked. "Only it'd take a hell of a lot of fence if the whole settlement area's going to be covered."

"That's one problem," said Abbado, "but they don't think fences would stop them—"

He ran the chip back to a close-up of the swarm's advancing front.

"—and there I got to agree with Analysis. These things dam creeks so they can cross and weave rafts to get over rivers. A fence isn't even going to slow them down."

"So what is?" Methie asked.

"We are," said Abbado. "With our stingers. They can't run as fast as a man, and they can't even squirt you without you let them get inside ten feet or so. In broken terrain it'll be a problem, and they come by the righteous shitload. Fifty, sixty thousand Analysis figures. If a swarm heads in the direction of the settlement, we get in front of them and shoot every mother's son."

"*Krish*na," Caldwell repeated.

"Now, the chance of a swarm of those critters being in the wrong place may not be very high," Abbado continued as he indexed to the next set of images. "The large carnivores have overlapping territories, and it'll be a while before we stop having to kill the ones that replaced the ones we killed the week before."

An animal with four legs, a short body, and a whip-thin neck appeared in the projection area.

"These're ambush hunters," Abbado said, "and they charge at *at least* 65 miles an hour because that's what the one they spotted here was doing."

"Shit," muttered Matushek. "Shit, shit, shit."

Esther Meyer sat on her bunk with her helmet on. She viewed the Bezant data at 100 percent on her visor, completely blocking her sight of the compartment around her. Several strikers played cards on a footlocker elsewhere in the room. She was aware of their voices, but the words didn't impinge on a consciousness focused on the vessel's destination.

"Hey Essie."

"Besides being toxic at least to native lifeforms," said a voiceover from the database as a vine uncoiled in Meyer's apparent field of view, *"this species appears to digest animal carcasses through rootlets—"*

"Meyer! You there?" Knuckles rapped on her helmet.

Meyer flipped up the visor. "Nessman, you got a problem?" she snapped. She didn't like having her concentration broken, and she was plenty willing to revert relations with the willowy blond striker to their old hostile footing.

"Aw, Essie, I'm sorry," Nessman said, looking and sounding contrite. "I just wanted to know what you think about this place. Did you see what it said about disease? The colonists all need immune boosters!"

"Yeah, I saw," Meyer said. She ducked forward to lift off her helmet so that she wouldn't bang it against the upper bunk. "What's the big deal? We've all got boosters since basic training."

The booster was a porous ceramic shell the size of a little finger implanted in the user's left hip. It was a biofactory that cleaned the user's body of everything from viruses to parasites that were almost big enough to see with the naked eye.

The tradeoff for this protection was that each booster cost as much as a mid-quality aircar. For the military, that expense was reasonable. There was no point in training and transporting troops to a distant planet only to have them die of disease even before they closed with the Kalendru.

Colonists were another matter. Planets were scouted thoroughly before settlement, a luxury that an invasion force didn't have. If the microbiota was too dangerous, the Population Authority could simply pick another world. The number of nearby Standard Planets—

Earthlike within tight parameters—was in the tens of thousands.

"But colonists?" Nessman said.

Meyer rubbed her scalp. Nessman looked like he was going to say something he shouldn't, like, "You want me to do that?" But he shut his mouth again and raised his right palm in a peace sign.

"I can't figure out what Military Command thinks it's doing," Meyer said. "Don't ask me to figure out the Pop Authority."

Nessman had been a rocketeer on Maxus. His crew had launched two of their rounds when a Spook lasered the third. Nessman came out of it okay because he happened to be squatting on the other side of his sergeant when the missile blew up in the cradle. He and Meyer were all C41 had left from Heavy Weapons; though Bateson had survived without his legs and when the strikers left Stalleybrass the medics still thought they might save Lieutenant Whichard.

Steve Nessman was a handsome fellow who liked women, or at any rate liked screwing them. He'd made a pass at Meyer a couple days after she was posted to C41.

Meyer turned him down flat. She'd met the type before. They were too full of themselves to be any damned good, and she wasn't naive enough any more to believe they actually meant any of the things they said before they got into your pants.

A few days after that, she'd been checking inventory alone when Nessman entered and closed the storehouse door behind him. He wouldn't take no, so she clawed for his eyes instead.

Nessman was stronger and he'd obviously had experience with this sort of thing before. He wasn't enough stronger that he'd be able to rape her without killing her first, though, and after thirty seconds or so he realized that was the choice. Nessman had banged her head against the floor, but although Meyer was groggy she came close to biting his nose off a moment later.

He'd gotten up then, dabbing at his scratches as he backed out of the storeroom. They hadn't spoken about the incident afterwards, neither between themselves nor to anyone else. In fact, they'd kept as wide a berth from one another as a unit the size of C41 permitted.

Active Cloak gave them a shared bond. The operation had been tough for everybody, sure, but it was damned near suicidal for Heavy Weapons Platoon. Meyer and Nessman hadn't become friends, but they were colleagues for the first time. Meyer hadn't asked to transfer to a different compartment when Kuznetsov automatically billeted her with Nessman and 1-1.

"I dunno, Essie," Nessman said. "There's a fuckup somewhere, and we all know where that leaves strikers. Swinging in the breeze. I don't like it."

"I'm not saying you're wrong, Nessman," Meyer said. "But if you want to know the truth, I'm looking forward to a place that doesn't have Spooks in it. Especially I'm looking forward to a place that doesn't have Spook tanks."

She glanced sharply at the other striker. Nessman was the closest thing Meyer had to a friend in this universe, and even on his best day she couldn't convince herself that she much liked him.

She chuckled at the irony. Nessman raised an eyebrow.

✧   ✧   ✧

Blohm and Gabrilovitch watched as the image of a white mass launched itself from the top of a tree, expanding into a sticky sheet as it fell. It splashed onto one of a herd of small quadrupeds rooting for nuts among the tree roots. A thin umbilicus still tethered the sheet to the high branch.

The victim thrashed wildly. The net grew tighter, constricting as it congealed. The umbilicus began to retract.

"Hell, the animals are bad and the plants are worse," Gabrilovitch muttered. "This is going to be a bitch for you and me, snake."

The projected scene was a computer creation based on vertical imaging. You could never be sure how accurate a construct like this was. It was extremely dangerous because it *looked* perfectly real even though it wasn't. The virtual run-throughs of Active Cloak had all three floors of the garrison barracks occupied by Kalendru soldiers, for example.

"I don't see what's so bad about it," Blohm said. "Watch what trees you walk under, sure. But they'll have cleared a hundred square miles to prep for the colony, won't they? We won't see anything green till the crops start coming in."

Blohm liked the sergeant better than anybody else who'd commanded a scout section Blohm was in. Gabe knew that Blohm was quicker and had better instincts than he did. He didn't let it bother him. Gabrilovitch let Blohm set the agenda for the scouts and used his rank to put that agenda across in command group meetings.

Besides that, Gabe was as good a choice to cover Blohm's back as Blohm figured he'd find until they cloned Blohm himself.

"Negative on the site prep," Gabrilovitch said, shaking his head. "The only thing they did was plant a couple of message capsules and a landing grid for us to put down on. There's a pair of bulldozers with land-clearing blades on Deck One, but nothing in the way of herbicide like you'd figure. It's going to be a lot of work, and a lot of *hand* work, to open the settlement."

On the display the umbilicus continued to shorten, dragging the captured browser toward the treetop. The victim had ceased to struggle. It looked like a gigantic cocoon. Its body would feed the tree for the next several weeks.

"They going to expect us to do it, you mean?" Blohm said. "Hell, Gabe, before I transferred to the Strike Force, they had me burning shit on Christophe where the water table at the base was too high for septic tanks. I guess I can handle a saw if that's what it comes to."

"No way C41's going to be doing the labor, snake," Gabrilovitch said. "The cits are going to have to handle that while the strikers *guard* them. Look at how dangerous this place is! The work's going to have to be done, and the cits are going to be lucky if half of them don't get eaten by things like that—"

He gestured at the holographic image, by now no more than a normal-looking tree with a white lump perhaps of fungus among the leaves of its peak.

"—for all C41 can do to save them."

The display blacked out and segued into the next potential danger. For the moment the image looked like an ordinary bramble bush, but Blohm knew that would change shortly.

"Well," he said thoughtfully, "I don't know it's going

to be that hard. We've got the database loaded in our helmets. The visor'll cue us if we come on one of these. Or whatever."

His finger prodded the image, scattering it into discordant shimmers until he withdrew and permitted the interference patterns to reform. An animal the size of a pig appeared, cropping shoots several yards away from the bush.

"And we'll, we'll clear it with a grenade or whatever."

"Some stuff isn't going to be in the database," Gabe said.

"That's so," Blohm agreed. "Especially at first. Sure, we'll have to be careful, but we're used to that, Gabe. Are you going to tell me this is as bad as a drifting minefield like we had to walk through on Kwam III?"

"There's something else you're not thinking about, snake," Gabrilovitch said. "The rest of the people may stick close to base, but the major's going to want you and me out in the boonies scouting. For things like those swarms and maybe worse stuff coming in. Tough as Kwam III, you say? Tougher, I'll bet you, and we're going to be out there pretty much the whole time C41's on planet."

"They'll scout in aircars," Blohm said, frowning.

"They got one, count them, *one* aircar on Deck One," Gabrilovitch said. "How long do you figure that's going to last with no more maintenance than a bunch of janitors can give it? It's not like this colony's got a real support echelon, you know."

The browser suddenly stiffened, kicking violently with all four feet. Its square head remained close to the ground. A close-up showed that a shoot had sprung open like an explosive harpoon when the animal bit down on it. Petals held the browser as if it was chewing a mouthful of fish-hooks. The bramble bush hunched forward to engulf the browser held by the barbed root tip.

"I guess you might be right, Gabe," Blohm said slowly.

"I'm going to go talk to the major," Gabrilovitch continued, "but I know what he's going to say. 'You volunteered for this unit, and by God you'll do the job I give you now that you're here.' *That's* what he'll say."

"I guess you're right, Gabe," Blohm said.

Blohm imagined himself in the jungle with nobody else around. It'd be like being alone on a planet. No responsibilities, letting his helmet report conditions. No decisions to make that affected anybody else, just following a patrol route.

"I'll see what I can do, snake," Gabe said as he rose. He shook his head. "But I figure we're fucked, you and me."

The situation Gabrilovitch described was what Caius Blohm had wanted since he killed a floorful of civilians during Active Cloak. Maybe there was a God after all.

Getting to Know You

"A different kind of architecture from what I'm used to," Councillor Suares said with a faint smile as he viewed the settlement plan projected over al-Ibrahimi's desk. He glanced toward Farrell and explained, "I've been in industrial design, you see. I suppose the challenge will be good for me. I don't suppose anyone has computed moduli of strength for the local woods?"

"Not in that precise form, Mr. Suares," said Tamara Lundie. She was operating the hologram projector at a console folded down from the end of the desk. "I can compute approximations based on the span and thickness of branches, if you like."

"Oh, that would be excellent!" Suares said. "Of course initially we'll be limited to walls of stabilized clay with sheet-stock floors and roofs. But we'll move on."

The colonists had reacted remarkably well to their enforced circumstances. Farrell supposed that was an advantage to drafting an elite group—as the residents of Horizon Towers clearly were. It seemed a waste of talented people, but a soldier gets used to that sort of thing.

"Not the sort of law I'm used to either, Jafar," Matthew Lock said, "but I'll go over the proposed codes tonight and make a recommendation tomorrow.

I'd advise you to create a proper committee for the purpose, though, to avoid recriminations afterwards. You realize that there are at least thirty attorneys in the vessel, don't you?"

Farrell wasn't sure whether Lock had calmed down since the two of them first met, or if the apparent shouting anger had been merely a ploy the lawyer had dropped when it failed to have a useful effect. He was clearly an ambitious man. A raw colony was probably a small pond compared to the scope of Lock's ambitions back on Earth, but he was making the best—the most, at any rate—of his present circumstances.

"There are fifty-four persons aboard who hold law degrees," Lundie said. "Not all of them were licensed or in active practice."

Even Lock looked surprised. It struck Farrell that there was exactly one lawyer per striker with the colony. Given the situation on the ground on Bezant, Farrell would've recommended more guns and fewer mouths.

"Your peers elected you to represent them, Mr. Lock," al-Ibrahimi said. The contrast with Lock's appropriation of the project manager's first name was evident and therefore, from a man like al-Ibrahimi, pointed. "Based on that election, I'm delegating to you the task of making a recommendation in your field of expertise. The decision will be mine."

Al-Ibrahimi smiled the way a striker might when talking about dismemberment. "If necessary," he added, "I'll handle any complaints that arise from your fifty-three fellows."

"It seems to me that we're a small enough group for true democracy to apply," President Reitz said. "Even for matters like trials. A thousand people can run themselves without an institutional structure."

Tamara Lundie looked up sharply from her console. Al-Ibrahimi nodded minusculy to his aide.

"Ms. Reitz," Lundie said, "for the next six months and subject to extension, the structure of Colony BZ 459 is that of a Population Authority project under the sole control of the project manager which the Authority has appointed. We are not a democracy."

"Technically yes—" Reitz began, her argument cloaked as agreement by the use of the limiting adverb.

"And in practice as well, madam," al-Ibrahimi said. "A colony at its inception is too delicate for any government but tyranny. That's more true of this colony than most, perhaps more than any other before it. And I am that tyrant."

Reitz gave the manager a level glance and spread her hands on her lap. "I see," she said.

Farrell was impressed by the president's calm. He'd gathered that Susannah Reitz's wealth came from inherited investments. She'd taken the presidency of Horizon Towers to occupy her time, and the changed circumstances might have left her completely out of her depth.

That hadn't happened. Reitz had a cool appreciation of the realities of power. She might or might not use wisely what she had, but she didn't bluster when the authority was elsewhere.

"Major Farrell, do you have any concerns about your company's role that you'd like to raise here?" the project manager asked.

"I have one thing, sir," Farrell said, a little surprised to hear himself speak. "I don't worry about my people being able to operate on Bezant. Also we understand that our mission, our sole mission, is to protect your colonists."

He looked around the room. The three colonists watched the striker with concern, more or less well concealed. Al-Ibrahimi was calm; Farrell had never seen him any other way. Lundie kept her eyes on her console, but a hint of stiffness in her shoulders indicated she was intent on what he was going to say.

"C41 will do its best," Farrell said. "I've never known my strikers to do anything else on an operation. But I want to be clear this is on-the-job training for us and there's going to be a learning curve. We've never had to protect civilians before."

Suares blinked; Lock grimaced; and President Reitz's expression had a hard stillness to it that Farrell had seen all too often on the face of a wounded striker.

"I appreciate your concern, Major," al-Ibrahimi said. "There will be problems because this is new for all of us. There will be mistakes, and there will very likely be deaths that could have been prevented if we were all inhumanly perfect. That is understood."

The project manager glanced from one colonist to the next to focus their attention, then looked back at Farrell. "Before I end this meeting, Major, I need to correct one misstatement," he said. "You and your strikers have been protecting civilians throughout your military careers. The only difference on Bezant is that for the first time we civilians will be watching as that occurs."

Meyer entered the armory to check the plasma cannon and its ten cases of ammunition. In a manner of speaking it didn't matter: either the cargo locker had the correct contents or it didn't. The ship wasn't going back to Earth for a replacement if there'd been a screw-up during loading. Meyer had decided to look for want of anything better to do.

C41's weaponry didn't fill the compartment, so the strikers had shifted much of their personal gear here from the sleeping compartments. Strikers accumulated a surprising amount of entertainment electronics, souvenirs, and just plain junk. C41's deployment was categorized as a permanent change of base, so the clutter moved with the unit in 3-cubic foot shipping containers.

Professionals at Emigration Port 10 had struck the lockers of weapons and munitions neatly down around the bulkheads. Meyer climbed over a waist-high wall of containers stowed more haphazardly in the center of the compartment.

Nobody else was in the armory. That both bothered and calmed her.

Since Active Cloak Meyer was uncomfortable being around other people, even strikers. It was as though there was one-way glass between her and everybody else. They didn't see her, and she had no contact with them. She was afraid to be alone, but it made things worse to be in the presence of others and *still* be alone.

Meyer's boots hit the deck. There was a gasp and a muffled curse from beside the cannon locker. Nessman's head and shoulders rose from behind another stack of containers.

"What the hell—" he started.

"Is somebody there?" a female—a girl's—voice trilled. "Steve, is—"

An elfin face framed by blonde hair in a perfect halo appeared beside the striker's. "Omigod, Steve! Omigod, Momma will kill me!"

The blonde ducked down. Her elbows knocked

against containers as she scrabbled to put clothes on in the tight space.

"Hey, it's okay, sweetheart, nobody's going to tell Momma," Nessman soothed. He looked up at Meyer again.

"I was going to check the gun," Meyer said. "Ah, I didn't know anybody was here."

"Steve, please, make her go away so I can get dressed," the concealed voice pleaded. Meyer's first thought had been that the girl was barely sixteen, but she guessed that was wrong by a few years. Civilians looked younger than the people Meyer was used to being around.

"Look, Essie, give us five, okay?" Nessman said. A bare knee lifted beside him. He put his hand on the girl's hands to prevent her from tugging up panties of rose-pink lace. "Now, sweetheart, don't worry about that just yet." He forced a smile at Meyer again. "Okay, Essie?"

"Yeah, sure," Meyer said, backing away. "I wasn't—hell, there's no need to look at the stuff. I won't, I won't be back, you know."

As she reached the armory door, she heard Nessman saying, "Now, sweetheart, it's okay. Nothing's going to happen, you see? I told you I'd take care—"

Meyer closed the door.

Christ!

There was absolutely no reason Nessman shouldn't be doing exactly what he was. The kid's mother might go off like a bomb—would go off, from what the kid had said—but that was no concern for Meyer or Major Farrell. There wasn't any regulation against contact with the civilians.

Actually, there'd never been regs against contact

with civilians. For all practical purposes strikers didn't come in contact with real civilians except on leave— if then. If God up on Deck 25 had a problem with Steve Nessman doing what came naturally, he should have said so earlier.

Meyer walked down the corridor to her compartment. Some strikers had started going down to the civilian decks for a change of scenery. Nessman probably wasn't alone.

Good for you, Nessman, she thought. At least one member of Heavy Weapons was fitting in.

Deck 8 was only partly filled with cargo. Parents had turned the empty remainder of the volume into a playground, creating slides and a jungle gym with construction materials from the cargo. Glasebrook stood arms akimbo, staring with satisfaction as kids crossed the horizontal ladder the rest of 3-3 had helped him build.

"Wish we could build a decent rope swing," Glasebrook said. "The ceilings just aren't high enough."

Adult civilians, not only parents, and a dozen or more strikers stood around the edges of the common space watching. Star travel—the mass version common to troopships and colony vessels, at any rate—was dead boring. You could only study your destination for so long at a time. Besides, Abbado wouldn't be surprised if a lot of the civilians refused to look into the database again once they'd gotten a taste of how bad Bezant was going to be.

"We might be able to rig something in the lift shafts," Abbado said after thinking about the problem. "Disconnect two cages, drop them to the bottom, and take out the partition between shafts."

Glasebrook frowned. "Jeez, Sarge, I dunno," he said. "I think that'd be pretty dangerous."

"Have you taken a good look at Bezant, Flea?" Abbado said. "But yeah, I know what you mean. Well, it's just another week anyway."

A heavy-set man of forty with coarse, intensely black hair walked over to the strikers. He looked vaguely familiar.

Glasebrook took his hands off his hips; Abbado changed his stance slightly. The civilian had something on his mind. Until the strikers were sure what it was, they remained wary.

"Gentleman," the fellow said, "I am Dr. Ahmed Ciler."

He held out his hand. Abbado shook it, then Glasebrook. "I believe you were the soldiers who guided us to our deck, were you not? I'd like to thank you for your support when we were being mistreated."

"Yeah, us and Ace Matushek," Abbado said. "Sure, I thought I'd seen you before. And no big deal with the cops. We've had our own problems with cops."

Most strikers had. In not a few cases, that was the reason they'd enlisted in the first place.

"This is enough of an injustice," Ciler said. "They didn't need to add pointless brutality. I—all of us— appreciate it very much."

"If they want to knock somebody around so bad," Flea said, "there's plenty of Spooks out there they can go after before they get down to old ladies."

"Can I ask you about the place we're going?" Ciler said. "BZ 459. Do you know of any military reason a colony should be sent there?"

Children at the top of the slide started pushing their fellows in front of them. Parents called nervously and stepped over to intervene.

Abbado looked at Ciler. He wondered if "doctor" meant Ciler was a medic. Seemed like half the adults on this ship were a doctor of one kind or another, though not many were the sort you'd want around to sew up the after-action damage.

"Look, doc," he said, "we're just strikers. You probably know more about this business than we do. Even the major, he just does what he's told. We stopped being subject to the Pop Authority when we enlisted."

"I thought as much," Ciler said. "Still, I hoped someone might have some insight. Manager al-Ibrahimi merely says that it's his duty to set up a viable colony, and the reasons behind the decision are no proper concern for him or us."

The doctor shook his head. "There are eighty-four children under the age of twelve on this vessel," he said. "I'm a pediatrician, you see. And that pig on Deck 25 tells me that I shouldn't be concerned about why those children are being sent to Hell."

Ciler glared at the strikers, his dark eyes full of grim fury. "This is *not* a normal Population Authority initiative. The team that surveyed the planet listed it as WHOLLY UNSUITED FOR COLONIZATION, did you know? Officially it's BZ 459, but if you look into the Survey Team's notes you'll find that among themselves they called it Hell. And that's where these children are going!"

"Now, doc," Abbado said. He'd had the same thought, but it wouldn't do any good to say so. "Don't let what some jerk-off who never got out of orbit says get to you."

"Yeah, I figure the sarge is right," Glasebrook said. "I mean, they wouldn't really put civilians on a place that bad."

Abbado nodded with false enthusiasm. "I guess there's about a hundred planets somebody or other called Hell," he said. "It's about as common as Paradise and I tell you, I've been on some of both. There's not that much to choose between them once you been there a while. It's not going to be Hell."

Caius Blohm was standing a few feet away from the other strikers, apparently watching the playing children. He turned to Abbado and said, "You got that right, sarge. Hell isn't a planet."

Blohm saluted with a wry smile and walked off toward the lifts.

Sergeant Gabrilovitch got up from the poker game with Second Platoon strikers when Blohm reentered the compartment. "I'm out," he said, putting the remainder of his stake in his pocket. "Maybe I ought to check out the civvie decks and see if I'm lucky in love."

They were playing for military scrip. Since C41 wouldn't be near a place where scrip (or for that matter, Unity Credit Chips) bought anything for at least six months, the plastic bills were just easier to count than toothpicks or beans.

"Want to sit in, Blohm?" a striker asked.

"Naw," Blohm said. "Maybe tonight. You'll still be playing."

"Hey, you got something better to do?" said the striker who was shuffling the deck.

"You been below?" Gabrilovitch asked. "Have any luck?"

Blohm shrugged. "I was just looking around," he said. His helmet hung from the end of his bunk. He held it, working the visor up and down a couple times.

He looked at his sergeant. "It's funny being around civilians like this, you know?"

Gabrilovitch nodded. The poker game resumed behind the two scouts. It would continue until the ship was in the final stages of landing.

The game didn't keep the others in the compartment awake. If anybody cared he could crawl into his null sack and cut himself off completely from the outside world, card games and all. That wasn't really necessary, though, because for a striker in the field sleeping was something you did when you got a chance. "The right conditions" might include shellfire, four inches of water where you lay, and drenching rain—all at the same time.

"I was thinking about that," Gabrilovitch said. "You and me, we've been a lot of exotic places, right? We all have."

Blohm blinked. "Yeah, I guess," he said. "You mean like Glove White, where the plants were clear till they caught the sun and then it was like you never saw so many colors?"

"Yeah, that sort of thing," Gabe agreed, nodding his bullet-shaped head. A wedge of white hair marked a scar along the suture line on the top of his skull. "Or on Case Lion, where those bugs hung in the air and sang sweet as sweet?"

"The hummers," Blohm said. "The size of my finger. They'd come around like they liked having us to sing to."

"I brought a branch back from Glove White. It turned gray and went to dust in a couple weeks," Gabrilovitch said. He grimaced. "Don't know what I thought I was going to do with it anyway."

"That's not where they put base camps, though," Blohm said. "Remember Kaunitz?"

Gabrilovitch nodded vigorously. "And Stalleybrass," he said. "Or any other damn place, mud or dust, that's the choice. Sometimes I think there's a Directorate of Mud on Earth to make sure military bases never run out. But you know, snake?"

He turned his gaze directly onto Blohm. "If they'd built a base on Case Lion, it'd have been all mud in no time. And Glove White would have got just as dusty as Stalleybrass."

"Might be," Blohm said. The thought made him uncomfortable, though he didn't see why it should. It wasn't any of his doing, it was just nature. A hundred thousand troops in one place gave you a mud pit or a dust bowl, take your choice.

"The places that're kind of neat to look back at," Gabrilovitch said, "there wasn't time to think about it when we were there. They pulled us out of Case Lion as soon as we'd cleared the Spook command and control unit. What, six hours?"

"I sure didn't want to stay longer," Blohm agreed. "That tunnel complex went thirty miles in every direction, and that's just as far as we could trust the echo mapper. There might have been a million Spooks down there. It wasn't going to be long before they got their shit together and came for us."

"Sure, I know," Gabrilovitch said. "But sometimes I think it's a shame that we got to shoot first and ask questions later, so to speak."

Blohm's expression froze. He stared toward his reflection in his visor's outer surface, but his mind was on the children playing on Deck 8.

"Just shoot first, Gabe," he said. "Better not to ask questions at all. The answers'll confuse you."

Landing

"Now for God's sake remember it's not a real combat drop!" Farrell ordered. He spoke slowly and distinctly, because the magnetic flux bringing the ship to a soft landing played hell with radio transmission despite enhancement by the strikers' helmet AIs. "Wild shooting is going to scare the civilians. Six out."

10-1442's every plate and stringer vibrated at a different frequency. This single-use Pop Authority ship hadn't been built to the standards of the transports C41 was used to. Farrell didn't consider the situation worse, just different. Military transports, torqued by hundreds of liftoffs and landings, often clanged a single bell note that meant sympathetic vibration was doing its best to hammer to death the vessel and everyone aboard her.

"One minute to landing," Lieutenant Kuznetsov reported in a distorted voice.

Kuznetsov was at Hatch C with her former First Platoon; Farrell himself had Hatch A with most of Second Platoon. Sergeant Bastien had commanded Third Platoon at Active Cloak. He'd survived so he now had them at Hatch B. A scratch group of Heavy Weapons, the scouts, and four orphan strikers of line squads were under Sergeant Daye at Hatch D. It didn't bother Farrell that C41 was so far down on officers from its Table of Organization strength, but he sure

113

wished he had more stingers and grenade launchers ready for the next few moments.

"Welcome to the pastoral beauties of Bezant," called Sergeant Kristal. "No expense has been spared to make your stay a pleasant one."

Second Platoon strikers close enough to hear her laughed. C41 was loose for this landing. Nobody was careless. The strikers were poised with their weapons aimed, reloads and backups ready . . . but nobody really believed the wildlife was a danger on the same scale as Kalendru troops.

It wasn't, of course. Art Farrell's real concern was what came next, guarding a thousand civilians from that wildlife.

"Thirty seconds to landing," Kuznetsov said.

The trouble with the transport's automatic operation wasn't the voyage, which had gone as smoothly as any similar period Farrell had spent on a starship, but right now: the landing. 10-1442 was a can of meat until the four bottom-deck hatches opened—which they would do whether or not anybody aboard wanted them to, and before the human cargo had the slightest view of what was waiting for them outside.

A Population Authority advance team had fabricated a landing grid from the system's asteroid belt, then used a robot lander to drop the mass to the colony site. The actual location might be miles away from the one planners on Earth had penciled in. That could be a problem anywhere; on Bezant, 10-1442 might land right in front of a swarm of murderous herbivores. Deck 1 was for C41 alone until Farrell was very damned sure the site was as safe as his strikers could make it.

"Five seconds to landing," Kuznetsov said.

The vibration rose to a roar so loud that Farrell's

helmet had to filter it. The transport generated identical magnetic polarities in its own lower hull and the upper surface of the grid. The charges repelled one another. The transport settled to the grid, slowing progressively because magnetic effect increased as the cubed reciprocal of the distance.

The transport touched down, its seams wheezing and groaning. Huge bolts withdrew, unlocking the upper edge of the hatches. Farrell winced at themechanism's *bangbang/bangbang/bangbang/bangbang*. The only thing he'd heard that sounded quite like that was the hull of an assault boat taking fire, and he'd heard that often enough.

"Careful, people," Farrell ordered as the hydraulic rams whined in the relative silence. "Nobody gets more than twenty feet from the ship until I—"

The transport slid with a grinding of metal, then began slowly to topple.

"Watch out for the cargo!" Farrell shouted. "If those bulldozers shift—"

The hatches, three-quarters of the way down, continued to open outward. A green wall of vegetation towered in the middle distance.

Farrell let the sling snatch his weapon and gripped the hatch coaming with both hands. His boots slipped on the deck; the ship tilted farther.

The ship was falling more or less away from Farrell at Hatch A. Metal screamed; the hull was taking stresses at angles where it wasn't braced. He heard the seam between the transoms of Holds C and D fold inward and tear.

When the deck was at a 30-degree angle, Farrell waited for the accelerating rush whose momentum would flatten the fat cylinder against the ground. The starship halted. The reason it stopped didn't matter any more than the reason it had tilted in the first place.

"Out of here, strikers!" Farrell cried as he got a boot onto the coaming and launched himself from the vessel. He pulled his stinger into firing position before he hit the ground twenty feet below, tucked into a roll, and came to his feet ready for whatever Bezant wanted to throw at him.

They'd landed in the middle of deep forest, but the vegetation within forty feet of the hold was yellowing. The flux which braked thousands of tons of starship generated enormous waste heat in the magnetic mass. That soaked into the soil and killed the roots of the surrounding plants.

Farrell was familiar with the process: he'd seen the same thing when he boarded at Emigration Port 10. But to have yellowed and dried to their present condition these trees had to have been cooked weeks ago, not in the past few minutes as the transport landed.

Until he got clear, Farrell had guessed the ship slid because the grid was misaligned. In fact there wasn't a landing grid at all. They'd braked against a nickel-iron asteroid which had been dropped to the planet unformed.

The asteroid made a perfectly satisfactory magnetic mass, but its domed, pitted upper surface wasn't even notionally flat. 10-1442 had lowered itself into contact, then slipped sideways until it overbalanced. The only reason they hadn't gone completely over was that the open hatches braced them.

Temporarily. The starship creaked as it wobbled. A gust of wind, subsoil cracking under the strain, or the collapse of Hatch D's hydraulic rams could finish the job at any moment.

C41 was out of the vessel, even the two strikers per hatch wearing full hard suits because Farrell hadn't known what to expect. "C41, perimeter a hundred feet out!" he ordered. "Nobody in the footprint where the ship's going to fall. Out."

He stayed where he was while his strikers, laden with weapons and equipment, lumbered away from the ship. Farrell needed to be central because he didn't know where the threat would be coming from.

He knew for certain that there was a threat, though.

He manually keyed the liaison channel. "Farrell to Ibrahimi," he said. "Get your civilians out immediately, but for God's sake keep them close to the ship. Farrell out!"

If the chunk of nickel-iron had been a natural meteor moving at orbital velocity, it would have blasted a crater the size of Emigration Port 10. Only droplets would remain on the site. The bulk of the projectile would have splashed through the stratosphere and rained down in a circle thousands of miles across.

This mass had been dropped at deliberate speed with braking rockets like those which slowed the grid where the transport had been intended to land. A raw asteroid wasn't suitable to land a human transport, but Kalendru military vessels used outriggers of variable length to permit them to come down safely on crude surfaces.

"C41, watch out for company," Farrell said. He tried to watch both his strikers and the masked schematic of their deployment on his visor. "This is a Spook site, and they're going to be coming for us. Six out."

When 10-1442 started to slide, Esther Meyer's first flashing thought was that the planet had opened its green maw and was swallowing them. She hadn't seen much of Bezant yet, but she'd seen enough to dislike it.

Meyer was in her hard suit, ready to push her dolly of cannon shells down the ramp to wherever Top or the major decided they wanted the weapon emplaced. Now she jerked the two heavy cannisters out of their clamp restraints and let the little support device bound off one side of the lowering ramp.

The gun was dollied-up also. Nessman switched his lift fan off, collapsing the air cushion. The dolly continued to slide down the increasing slope. Nessman jammed a boot in the crack between the hull proper and the lowering hatch. With that purchase he was able to keep the heavy gun from spilling wildly out of the ship.

Meyer tried to drag her cannisters up the deck to where she could hook an arm through a cargo strap. When that didn't work she sat down. Her boots had non-slip soles, but the seat of Meyer's ceramic armor was close to being a frictionless surface. It still seemed like the natural thing to do when she was trying to keep from falling out of a starship that was about to topple on whatever was below it.

"C41, watch for cargo shifting," the major's voice warned. This boarding deck had no partitions, just stanchions and the lift shafts which acted as structural columns. The circumference of the deck was open. Items too large for the lifts to carry to higher levels were secured in the remaining volume.

It was possible that one of the vehicles was going to break loose, but that wasn't Meyer's first concern. She'd chance having a bulldozer land on her and hope it wouldn't crush the hard suit. The entire mass of

10-1442 was something else. She'd never be found.

The ship stopped tilting. "Everybody out!" Sergeant Daye ordered, pausing at the edge of the hatch to make sure his people were clear before he jumped. Daye gripped the jamb with one hand and bent to help Nessman with the cannon's weight.

"Fuck it I'm caught!" Nessman shouted. He thrashed his right leg. The hatch had flexed. It pinched his left boot.

Meyer let one of the ammo cans go. Daye tried to pull Nessman free. Meyer judged the distance and swung her remaining can against the back of Nessman's armored foot. The shock sprang him loose.

Meyer and Nessman, clumsy with their hard suits and the equipment they still clung to, tumbled down the ramp to ground only marginally softer than the steel deck. Sergeant Daye grabbed both of them by an arm to help them up. "Set it where the bitch won't fall on you!" he said, pointing vaguely to the right. "*Christ* what a ratfuck!"

Meyer scooped up the handle of the second can and moved, using the ammo's momentum to swing her body for each next step. Nessman cradled the gun in both arms and waddled forward as though he was carrying an anvil. A good-sized anvil wouldn't have been any heavier or more awkward that the load he did have.

Trees a hundred and fifty feet high formed the main wall of the forest, swathed in vines and curtainlike mosses. For a hundred feet out from where 10-1442 now teetered, retro rockets had seared to death the larger trees; the asteroid's final impact shattered the boles to blazing splinters. Brush had already grown twenty feet high, but the leaves of the nearer shrubs were curled.

The lesser ground cover, mostly plants with claw-tipped leaves the size of a man's hand, was dead and gray. Stems crumbled under Meyer's armor. Even strikers in ordinary boots and battledress strode through the shrivelled tracery without noticing. The only green near the ship were vines growing inward along the ground from the edge of the blasted area. They looked like the spokes of a gigantic wire wheel.

There wasn't a good field of fire anywhere. Nessman picked a stump uprooted when the magnetic mass hit and laid the barrel of the plasma cannon across it. He was only ten feet from where Hatch A wiggled in the air, no part of it touching the ground. The weapon was too awkward and heavy to carry any farther.

Meyer, bent like a knuckle-walking ape, dropped the ammo cannisters beside the gunner and gasped with relief. They were probably clear of the ship when it went over, but if they weren't she was too wrung out to care.

She'd heard the warning about Spooks, though she didn't understand it. She switched her sensors to high sensitivity. The immediate blur of warning signals—movement, vibration, and IR sources, all careted in different colors on her visor—virtually blinded her.

Fuck it. She'd rather be able to see a Spook if he hopped up in front of her than hope to identify him before he was close enough to be a danger. Meyer cut back immediately on all inputs except electronic. The AI notched striker gear out of the search spectrum unless the user deliberately entered friendly signatures, so that wasn't a problem.

The ground was coarse red limestone that scuffed to gritty dust beneath the strikers' feet. The thin topsoil didn't look sufficient to sustain trees the size of those surrounding the site. Obviously it was, but Meyer could see why the impact of the magnetic mass had so thoroughly cleared the area.

Civilians poured out of the ship like ants from an overturned hill. Crying and shouting, they stumbled to the ground. Almost all of them came from Hatch D, the only one whose ramp reached the ground. The risk that the ship would fall in that direction didn't seem to affect them if they even noticed it.

"Hey, keep clear!" Nessman shouted. A dozen people, at least three generations of a single family, ran in front of the plasma cannon. They held hands as they headed toward the living forest.

Maybe they thought the starship was going to explode. They could be correct, but Meyer remembered the briefing information on Bezant. If 10-1442's powerplant blew, it couldn't kill those idiots any deader than the local wildlife would.

Strikers shouted at the running civilians. Lieutenant Kuznetsov tried to head them off, but they had a lead and no equipment to weigh them down.

Meyer aimed her stinger and raked the ground ten feet in front of the adult male who was more or less leading the conga line. Ash and wood spurted several feet in the air. Where the pellets hit quartz in the soil, there were satisfactory sparks as well. The civilians threw themselves flat weeping and hugging one another.

Meyer reloaded her weapon. She'd only fired off a hundred or so pellets, but this wasn't a place to trust ninety percent readiness.

She hadn't realized how simple life had been on C41's normal insertions. She could almost wish that the problem on Bezant *was* Kalendru troops rather than human civilians.

✧   ✧   ✧

"Gee but I want to go home," somebody hummed on the squad push as 3-3 advanced toward the unbroken forest wall. *"I'm tired and I—"*

"Horgen, shut the fuck up!" Abbado said.

Insects were buzzing around them. That was unusual in an environment to which humans hadn't brought their own bugs. Mostly people were different enough chemically that the local insect-equivalents didn't recognize them as possible dinner.

Larger carnivores were generally less picky, of course.

"Sorry, Sarge," Horgen muttered.

They were all jumpy, and not just because the landing was so awful. Abbado and three members of his present squad once had crawled from a boat that spread itself across half a mile of prairie when Spook gunfire had knocked out the braking nozzles on final approach. The problem was that the whole mission had been unfamiliar, and now all the planning was down the tubes besides.

"Sarge, I've got something," Methie said in a whisper. He echoed a pink highlight to the lower, panoramic view on Abbado's visor.

"Methie, switch places with me," Abbado said. He eased to his right.

The squad froze in place. There was ten feet between strikers to give 3-3 a respectable frontage. Abbado wasn't willing to increase the interval any further, though his flank personnel were already a hundred feet from the nearest support.

The major was pushing a squad out to each cardinal point, probing the landing site. C41 didn't have the troops to secure the entire treeline. Matushek and

Glasebrook wore hard suits, so Abbado'd put them on the ends of his skirmish line. He didn't know if that was the right decision or not. He didn't have a clue as to what 3-3 was getting into.

Abbado reached Methie's slot, twenty feet to the right of his own. The visor indicated there was an object with straight lines lying at the base of a sapling whose branches were spiked clubs. It was twenty feet beyond the strikers, on the edge of the circle cleansed when flux baked the soil to coarse stone.

How the artificial intelligence knew whatever it was had straight lines was beyond Abbado. Ground cover and leaves that had yellowed and fallen from the tree when its roots were cooked hid everything but a lump so far as the human eye could tell. Well, that was why strikers' helmets had sensors and internal data processing.

"I had a little drink—" A pause. *"Sorry, sarge."*

"Okay, we're going to move up all together," Abbado said. The squad's helmets were locked on 3-3's separate channel—actually a pattern of frequency hopping rather than a frequency in itself. Abbado wanted to be able to talk normally to his strikers even though they were spread out to shouting range. "Very slow, straight forward, and remember, it could be a mine."

"It could be a rock with a smooth fracture," Foyle said. He must have remoted a close-up of Methie's view to his own visor.

"The AI didn't say it was a rock," Abbado said. "The AI said it was a thing, and the AI doesn't make mistakes like strikers do."

Civilians were leaving the starship the way milk gurgles from a dropped jug. They pooled around the vessel in clothing that they'd doubtless brought because they thought it was suitable for a frontier. The brightly colored garments quivering on Abbado's panorama display struck him as incongruous, but the civilians might be right. It wouldn't take long to get tired of the grays and drabness of the immediate surroundings. Didn't plants on Bezant have flowers?

"Okay, everybody hold up," Abbado said. "Methie, you slide back behind me."

Abbado knelt. He could see that the object beneath the seared vegetation was flat and angular if not square. The AI didn't warn of a booby trap. He extended his stinger toward the mound, using the fat barrel as a probe.

Maybe he ought to have one of the hard suits do this. Their gauntlets weren't as delicate as Abbado's bare hands, though; and besides, he was squad leader.

He prodded the object. Dead leaves rustled bitterly. Nothing exploded. The AI was right. It wasn't a bomb. Abbado picked the thing up in his left hand.

It was a fabric pouch with individual cells for three batteries. Two batteries were in place. They were of a type familiar to Abbado: they would fit into the butt compartment of a shoulder-fired Kalendru laser.

"Six from Three-three," Abbado said, still kneeling. He used the identifier to key his transmission to Farrell rather than switching his helmet manually. "I've got a Spook ammo pouch here with two batteries in place. It doesn't look too weathered. Over."

He tried to scan the treeline. IR told him there were no large animals but as for the rest, while none of the saplings in the intermediate zone was more than an inch and a half in diameter, there were enough of them that they concealed the details beyond them as effectively as a gauze curtain.

"Three-three, understood," the major's voice said. *"Break, C41, we've got recent Spook equipment north of the ship. Patrol leaders continue to advance to the forest edge but hold there. Look particularly for any sign of a trail. Out."*

"You heard him, people," Abbado muttered as he rose. He ducked around another grim tree that looked like a stick figure wearing spiked boxing gloves. This one still had its leaves. "Keep your eyes open and—"

He heard a *crack*swish behind him. He didn't have any idea what it meant—except it meant Guilio Abbado had fucked up.

"Watch—" he shouted as his instincts tried to throw him to the ground. Something whacked him in the middle of the back and hurled him twenty feet without his boots touching the ground.

Abbado's nose rapped the inside of his visor, bloodying it. His ribs ached. His body armor had stopped the blow and spread it evenly across the whole surface of his backplate, but it had still been one hell of a wallop.

"Sarge, the tree hit you!" Caldwell said. *"The tree!"*

The ground cover where Abbado landed was still alive. Thorns were tearing the backs of his wrists and hands. He swore and pulled himself loose. Pain stabbed up and down his sides, but that was stressed muscle. He knew the feeling of a broken rib stabbing splinters toward a lung.

"C41," he said, unable to prevent his voice from wheezing. "The trees that have spikes on the branch tips, *mark*—"

He blinked to load the image of the sapling he was looking at. The ground cover at Abbado's feet still waved leaves toward him like the paws of a rending beast. Drops of his blood splashed the shiny surfaces.

"—can bash you like you wouldn't believe if you come close. And watch the fucking ivy, too, it moves and it bites. Three-three out."

Abbado scuffed his boot across the vegetation, tearing stems from the roots. Leaves caressed his legs to mid-shin, but the barbs couldn't penetrate the boots or tough battle dress leggings.

The sapling that he'd stepped close to had three branches spaced equidistant around the slim trunk. Two of them were still cocked up at about a forty-five degree angle skyward as they had been. The third now lay flaccidly against the trunk. Some of the thorns had broken off when the knobby end smacked Abbado's backplate.

Stinger pellets didn't ricochet at short range—they were moving way too fast. They and generally whatever they hit disintegrated. Abbado still aimed deliberately because the starship was downrange.

He triggered a ten-round burst, blasting the tree apart at the roots as effectively as a charge of explosive could have done. The sapling toppled toward him as though it was trying to get in one last blow. It wasn't tall enough by a foot or two to reach.

"Three-three, let's go," Abbado said.

There hadn't been any real point to chopping the tree down: there were hundreds more just like it in the immediate area that the strikers would just have to avoid. It was the only thing Abbado could do to solace the ache in his ribs, though.

Caius Blohm squatted among uprooted trees which lay against their living brethren like strikers flung dying into the arms of their fellows. Blohm touched nothing but the ground. Leaves brushed his shanks and boot tops with the dry sound of snake scales. He ignored them as he merged himself with the forest beyond.

"Do you see anything, snake?" Gabrilovitch asked. He knelt, fidgety, a dozen feet from Blohm. The sergeant wore gloves. He'd cleared his immediate surroundings with his powerknife, but the sight of leaves groping vainly toward him seemed to get on his nerves.

"Shut up, Gabe," Blohm whispered.

He wasn't being insubordinate. He didn't have enough conscious intellect left at the moment to be polite. Blohm was coming to an understanding with the forest.

The forest wanted to kill him. Wanted to kill all humans. Wanted to kill everything alive that wasn't forest.

Blohm raised his visor so that he could breathe the still air pulled from the trees when the sun's heat created an updraft from the clearing.

A powerful motor whined to life in the ship's hold. Treads clattered on the decking: somebody was driving one of the bulldozers out. Blohm couldn't have seen 10-1442 even if he'd turned around. There were too many small trees, living and dead, in the way.

The noise didn't break Blohm's concentration. It was just an element of his surroundings, like the booming call from somewhere to the west. Low frequency sounds travelled for amazing distances through a forest because the sound waves were too long for even tall trees to act as effective baffles.

Though at first glance the forest appeared uniform, Blohm's AI had differentiated a hundred and thirty-five species of trees. Only three of them were noted in the database, which put survey information about on a par with what strikers learned to expect from military intelligence.

Vines hung from the tallest nearby trees. In some cases Blohm could see the vine's own leaves flaring in the canopy, seemingly having forced aside the foliage of the host tree.

One species had striations like braided cable. It rooted at the base of the tree it climbed but also sent a tendril toward the landing site with the determination of water sliding down a chute. Surface roots anchored the tendrils, but there were no leaves or other apparent reason for the plant's expenditure of energy.

Blohm wasn't trying to make sense of the forest's individual elements. He was forming a gestalt of the whole. Everything the forest did was hostile to foreign life. Therefore the tendrils were a threat. Eventually Blohm would figure out how—the why didn't matter— but the method of the threat was less important than knowledge of the threat's existence.

No decisions to make. No noncombatants. The whole forest was Blohm's enemy. He felt his lips spreading in a smile.

The second bulldozer clanked out of the ship. The track plates had deep cleats that rang and squealed on the hard surfaces. These tractors were solely for use in wild terrain. They'd tear up any pavement with which they came in contact.

The tracks were of monobelt construction. Miniature clutches in the track pins locked the lower surface of each tread into a single rigid beam, spreading the load to greatest efficiency. The massive vehicles could cross ground too boggy to support a man walking. At the end of the run the pins declutched so that the take-up roller could lift the plates.

Blohm hadn't been sure they—the others, the civilians—would be able to get the bulldozers clear before 10-1442 fell. The air was almost dead still and the soil had baked to rock when the vegetation was cleared. Maybe the ship would remain upright for centuries.

The others were going to need the bulldozers if they were to survive any time in this place. Caius Blohm thought that he might have been able to come to an accommodation with the forest if he'd been alone.

He locked his visor down to check by technology what his instinct told him. "Gabe," he said, "there's something funny just ahead there. You see those three trees, *mark*?"

"I see the trees," Gabrilovitch said doubtfully. If he'd completed the thought, it would have been, "But there's nothing funny about them."

The trees were fat and grew in a triangle with eight or ten feet between trunks. Their gray bark was smooth except for a single vertical slit running the length of each bole. The triplet was only a dozen yards out in the undamaged forest, but Blohm couldn't see through the intervening barrier of saplings and shrubs to be sure what the lower twenty feet of the boles looked like.

The tops stood only a hundred feet in the air and should have been shaded by the taller trees. Instead, the luxuriant fronds spread beneath a sky as open as that of an apartment building's airshaft.

"See how the trunks split?" Blohm said. "The splits line up with a common axis."

The odd pattern wasn't what had drawn his attention.

Blohm had noticed it after he got the feeling to begin with.

"There ought to be undergrowth between the trees," he went on. "There's not, but there's something below the level we can see because the IR reading's a fraction higher than it is a few feet either way."

"Okay, snake," Gabrilovitch said. "What do you figure?"

"I'm going to take a look," Blohm said. He held the curtain of moss aside with the barrel of his stinger and slipped past. His knife was in his left hand but he hadn't switched on the blade.

"Ah, shit, snake," Gabrilovitch said. He didn't waste his breath ordering Blohm to return.

The forest murmured. Blohm felt he'd stepped into a dark cave and heard a beast breathing somewhere in the twisted grottos beyond; waiting, considering its options.

Saplings and the boles of full-grown trees were planted more thickly than Blohm had learned to expect in other jungles. Normally, except where streams and clearings permit light to reach the ground, the foliage of the monster trees forms a canopy hundreds of feet in the air and starves lesser growth.

Seeds sprout on stored energy and die as pale wraiths of their hope unless one of the neighboring giants falls during the sapling's brief window of opportunity. In this forest, chinks in the canopy permitted young trees to continue to grow if not exactly to flourish. They'd be ready to replace their forebears immediately.

Blohm moved without haste, like a shopper moving down a store aisle. His helmet scanned in all directions for sudden movements. Blohm kept not only his eyes but his whole mind open against danger.

Particularly he watched the treetops and higher branches. Moving through this forest was like city fighting: the real dangers lurked in the upper stories.

Fans set up an echoing howl in the clearing behind him. They were flying the expedition's sole aircar out of the hold. The starship and those around it existed in a world with only peripheral connection to Blohm's.

He didn't touch any tree. He always looked before he placed his foot for the next step. And he moved with a ghost's effortless silence, wrapped in a shroud of total awareness.

The pair of Kalendru soldiers hadn't been so careful. They'd run through the little clearing bounded by the triplet of trees and now stood in contorted poses.

Sap had sprayed simultaneously from the ruptured bark of the three trees. Blohm judged it had started as an aerosol, but it must have set instantly because the weapons the Spooks dropped in their terror hadn't reached the ground.

The sap dried clear, though air bubbles and ripples in the surface distorted images in the hardened mass. Blohm thought refraction explained the corpses' blurred outlines, but when he switched his visor to microwave imaging he realized his mistake.

The sap had been intensely corrosive as well as entombing its victims in mid-stride. The Spooks looked fuzzy because their bodies had started to dissolve in the instant they were caught. Even the metal and plastic of their equipment was pitted.

"C41," Blohm reported, "*mark*. The Spooks got here ahead of us, but I don't think they're our main problem. The forest doesn't like them any better than it does us. And people, it doesn't like us even a little bit."

Survival, Considered as an Option

"Is everybody out of the ship?" Farrell asked al-Ibrahimi, shouting because of the aircar idling beside them. Even feathered, the lift fans moaned as they dragged air down the filtered inlet ducts.

"There are *mumble-mumble*—" Lundie said.

"Shut your fucking motors off!" Farrell shouted at the building staffer driving the eight-place open car.

"Who do you think you are?" she shouted back. Farrell knew she was just nervous; and she wasn't in the military, much less under his command, but his anger spiked in a way that made everything but the driver's red face fade to the fringes of his awareness.

Lieutenant Kuznetsov, looking toward the tree line, reached into the vehicle and threw the main circuit breaker. The twin fans wound down with a last whisper of despair. Kuznetsov stepped away from the car, talking to one of the squads placed at the edge of the jungle.

"There are ninety-two colonists still on the ship," Lundie repeated. Her expression hadn't changed during the "discussion," but that in itself was a remark. "Most of them refuse to leave of their own will, but on Deck 13 the monitors failed to account for the residents before they left the vessel. The six persons missing from that deck may include some injured."

Lundie and her boss wore skeletonized headsets. The rigs had the same projection and communication abilities as the strikers' helmets, though they didn't protect the wearer. Al-Ibrahimi spoke in a quick, calm voice to someone. Farrell glimpsed a montage of twelve images when the project manager turned his head and the hologram aligned almost subliminally for Farrell as well.

Farrell ran his fingers over the pouches of his crossed bandoliers. He had four squads on the perimeter, a terrible deployment. The squads couldn't support one another because of the dead and fallen trees throughout the landing site. Besides, he didn't have any particular reason to assume the Spooks would attack at those particular segments of a perimeter over a mile around.

There was no doubt of the Kalendru presence. Quite apart from the bodies Blohm found, the Spooks had abandoned so much equipment that strikers turned up dozens of items while moving through the area.

Farrell had retained just under half his force near the ship as a reserve. If he'd concentrated all of C41 here any Kalendru attack, even a single sniper, might slaughter scores of civilians before strikers could get into position to stop them.

There were too fucking many civilians for C41 to draw a close cordon around them. If the strikers were to provide a forward defense, Farrell needed to know where *forward* pointed.

President Reitz and Councillor Suares had joined al-Ibrahimi. Farrell didn't see Lock, but the other councillor might be anywhere in the mass of civilians. Some of them now wanted to go back into the ship to get additional belongings. Lundie had asked Farrell to prevent that: the elected monitors, two per deck, were busy organizing the people for whom they were responsible, and the building staffers were emptying heavy cargo despite the threat of 10-1442 going over.

Farrell didn't much like putting his people on what amounted to crowd-control duties, but he didn't see a better solution. Sergeant Daye chose ten strikers for the job.

"Major?" al-Ibrahimi called. Ms. Reitz broke off whatever she'd been saying to the manager.

"Sir?" said Farrell as he moved a step closer. His visor's upper range echoed in miniature the view from the four perimeter squads. There was no reason he shouldn't talk to his superior until something popped.

"We've landed one hundred and twelve miles east of the intended site," al-Ibrahimi said, speaking to Farrell and the civilian officials together. "The asteroid the Kalendru placed was more massive than the grid that the Population Authority intended for us."

Al-Ibrahimi smiled. His thin, swarthy face was capable of humor all the more remarkable for flashing from his usual expression of reposed detachment.

"The degree to which these transports are automated," he added, "is a matter I'll take up with the relevant bureaux when we reach the correct site and the communications capsule prepositioned there."

"Aside from their active hostility our surroundings bear no resemblance to those the briefing chips led me to expect," Suares said. "Have we perhaps landed on the wrong planet, Mr. Ibrahimi?"

"No, though I'm afraid it's a particularly insalubrious region of the correct one," the manager said. "We're in a large crater which orbital imaging showed to have uniquely dense vegetation. Unfortunately, the attack and defense mechanisms so notable in vegetation elsewhere on BZ 459 are abnormally developed here as well."

Farrell nodded, thinking of Blohm's Spooks. He wondered if the managers' headsets received military transmissions. All Farrell had reported was the fact of the Spook bodies.

"The crater walls separate the local biota from the remainder of the planet," Lundie said. "The population pressures appear to have increased the rate of adaptation."

"What about the animals?" Suares asked. "Are they different as well?"

"The survey didn't use techniques that would penetrate the jungle canopy," Lundie said. "The probability is that the same pressures affected the zoobiota as well as the phytobiota. Perhaps more so."

Her words were chillingly emotionless.

"If the Kalendru landed here by chance," al-Ibrahimi said, "they were remarkably unlucky. As we most certainly are."

"We've got to begin ferrying people to the correct place at once," Reitz said. "We won't be able to complete the job before dark, but if this is as dangerous a place as you say we need to begin."

"Ma'am, you're right," said Farrell, "but I don't want to risk our only aircar until we know what the Spooks, sorry, the Kalendru, are up to. If the car overflies them, they'll shoot it down."

"Why are Kalendru here?" Reitz demanded. "Is the Unity sending colonies to the war zone? Is that it?"

"No," al-Ibrahimi said flatly. "The Spooks—"

He looked deliberately at Farrell and nodded.

"—shouldn't be here. A probe this far into human-settled space is risky, and that they chose to land on BZ 459 would be unthinkable had they not done so."

"A crash landing, perhaps?" Suares said. "Castaways?"

"No," said Lundie. "A prepared landing, on a magnetic mass placed with considerable effort."

"I just want to avoid them," said Farrell. "When we make it to the commo capsule, I'll call in a proper force to deal with them."

"That shouldn't be difficult," Lundie said. "I'll be on the aircar—with your agreement, sir?"

"You or me," al-Ibrahimi said. "I haven't decided yet."

Lundie's face went still in a fashion Farrell had learned was equivalent to another person's scowl. "There will be strikers in the car as guards," she resumed. "The military sensors in the helmets are capable of identifying Kalendru equipment at ranges beyond risk to us in this dense vegetation."

"Not really," Farrell explained. "We can only use high gain in a virtually sterile environment. The signatures of an aircar in operation swamp the signal from, say, a Spook laser's cooling mechanism."

"I can discriminate," Lundie said flatly. "My headset, cued to the helmets, can discriminate. The guards can filter their inputs as they desire. I'll use their passive sensors at maximum sensitivity."

She looked at the project manager. There was steel in her expression and flint in his.

Al-Ibrahimi smiled minusculy. "Yes," he said. "The initial flight to the grid will involve minimal personnel— my aide, the pilot, and however many personnel you choose to attach, Major."

"I'll go also," Suares said. He seemed surprised when everyone stared at him.

"For site planning," he explained, as if it should have

been obvious. "As an architect, not because I'm a . . ." He waggled his hands to indicate the slight significance of his position as building councillor.

"We won't be able to ferry the heavy equipment and materials on the vehicle available," Suares added. "I need to plan housing construction as quickly as possible. Do we have an inventory of hand tools?"

"Yes," said Lundie.

"I'll ride along, sir," Kuznetsov said. "I've used commo capsules before."

"Who do you want to take with you?" Farrell asked.

Kuznetsov shrugged. "If we can really dodge the Spooks," she said, "I'm fine by myself. You need all the strikers here."

Farrell grimaced. "You got that right," he agreed. This balls-up could be straightened out inside of a week; but keeping the civilians alive for that week wasn't a job Art Farrell looked forward to.

"All right, Mr. Suares," al-Ibrahimi said. "I take your point. And as the sooner we start, the better, I—"

"*Contact!*" Farrell's helmet warned. "*Contact!*"

Flashes and explosions in series wracked the northern treeline.

"Don't touch that," Blohm warned. "It's sticky and I think the sap'll burn you."

Gabrilovitch turned with a sour expression toward the tree an inch or two from his elbow. The bark had the sheen of wet rubber. Now that the sergeant looked carefully, he noticed that bits of leaves and other detritus of the sort that falls from the canopy stuck out of the bole here and there. Not only were pieces being absorbed into the tree, the visible portions had a seared, shrivelled texture.

"Shit," he muttered. "Let's get back into the clearing. Those guys—"

He nodded toward the pair of Kalendru frozen in their death throes.

"—aren't going to tell us much."

"Yeah, all right," Blohm said. "You're the boss."

He hadn't called Gabe through the forest wall in the first place. Having the sergeant present was one more thing for Blohm to worry about in an environment that had plenty along those lines to begin with. Gabe wasn't careless, but he didn't understand yet that this forest was as dangerous as the jaws of a shark.

The major had attached Blohm and Gabrilovitch to Squad 2-1 to watch the northern perimeter, but Sergeant Kristal hadn't expected them to stick close. Her squad was used to working as a unit, just as the scouts were used to working with each other or alone. It made sense for Gabe to position himself and Blohm a hundred feet east of the nearest member of 2-1. That way the intervening vegetation would stop anything which reflex aimed before the shooter's consciousness worried about who else might be standing in that direction.

Gabrilovitch started under a sapling. Since he'd passed by it to join Blohm, the slender bole had kinked. Sprays of leaves now dangled where they would inevitably brush his helmet and back.

"Wait," said Blohm. He reached past the sergeant and severed the sapling near the ground with his powerknife. The foliage writhed as it fell.

"Fuck this fucking place!" Gabrilovitch whispered.

"Look, why don't I lead?" Blohm said. He stepped around the sergeant, choosing a course at an angle to the one he'd taken on the way in. Gabe nodded agreement, but he ground his boot heel onto the sapling before he followed.

Blohm wasn't echoing information from the helmet of any other striker. He needed to concentrate entirely on what he was doing. The hell with what was happening to somebody else.

The scouts would pass near the bole of a tree large even in this forest of giants, an emergent whose peak lifted a good fifty feet above the canopy. There was movement in the topmost branches. The helmet AI thought it was caused by a breeze that didn't reach the forest floor, but Blohm shifted his line on instinct. The tension squeezing his ribs eased, though nothing he could have pointed to had changed.

Blohm made two quick cuts with his knife. Branches twisted toward the incisions on their upper surfaces. The scouts stepped through the sudden gap in the forest wall, back to the area devastated by shock.

"I'm glad—" Gabrilovitch said.

Blohm signaled silence with his left hand. He flipped up his visor again and drew in a deep, slow breath. "Spooks," he said, his lips barely moving. "I smell them."

Gabe switched his visor display with his tongue, then said, "Breeze is at three-thirty degrees to your heading. Are you sure?"

He released his stinger. It *clock*ed against the take-up reel under his arm. In its stead Gabe aimed the grenade launcher he carried clipped to his breastplate.

"I'm sure," Blohm said.

Gabrilovitch aimed the grenade launcher up at a sixty-degree angle so that its projectile would clear the saplings and windwrack. He fired twice. At the second *choonk*, brush crashed as if a herd of cattle just out of sight was charging the starship.

"Contact!" the sergeant cried. He emptied his magazine with four quick triggerpulls, turning as he fired so that by the time the high-trajectory projectiles fell they would intersect the invisible running figures. "Contact!"

Caius Blohm knelt, saying nothing. When a wraith-like Kalender suddenly rose behind a fallen tree only ten feet from Gabe struggling to reload, Blohm's stinger cut the Spook in half.

"Thought I'd broke it," Nessman said, probing the heel of his right foot gingerly with the fingers of both hands. The boot and his armored gauntlets lay beside him, but he wore the rest of his hard suit.

"It's okay, then?" Meyer said, holding the butt of the plasma cannon against her shoulder so that it wouldn't slip off the log. She peered at Nessman's foot by rotating the view on the lower range of her visor. She couldn't turn her head because her suit was buttoned up. The gorget locked her helmet to the back- and breast-armor.

"Damn thing's swelling," Nessman said. "I don't think it's broke, though." He tilted back so that she could see his grin through his open visor. "Beats hell out of hanging in the door till the ship fell over on me, though. Thanks, snake."

A creature the size of Meyer's middle finger hopped out of a hole in the log and stared at her with four eyes. It squeaked. The creature was bright green and stood on two legs, though when it hopped down the log it used all four.

"If it's swelling, you ought to get it looked at," Meyer said, peering through the plasma cannon's sight. She wondered if the little animal was poisonous. Most anything here was likely to be, from the quick warning the major had given C41 when he explained where screwed-up navigation had landed them.

Meyer was glad she was wearing a hard suit. She'd been antsy ever since Active Cloak. She was okay, though.

"Aw, the docs have got enough on their plates," Nessman said as he picked up his boot. "I'll just get this back on while I still can. Maybe when things settle down."

"That'll be a while," Meyer said.

Civilians trilled and hooted like swarms of birds. There wasn't a single open space large enough to hold all of 10-1442's passengers, not that half of them wouldn't have wandered somewhere else anyway. Deck monitors were trying to organize them, but the forest's shattered remains broke the landscape into sections as discrete as the partitioned cubicles of a hangar-sized office. The barrier distorted speech, and you couldn't see twenty feet in any direction.

A lot of civilians had been banged around when the transport skidded. Meyer couldn't imagine that as many as were shouting for doctors really had anything more wrong with them than bruises; but hell, she didn't know.

Meyer crouched, lowering the gun butt so that the muzzle pointed above the brush and fallen trees. Unbroken forest filled the projection sight. It was like staring at an oncoming tank, huge and implacable.

Nessman clamped his boot shut and gave a sigh of relief. "Goddam but it hurts when I squeeze it!" he said. "I sprayed it, so I figure I can walk all right till it wears off."

"Then we find you a doc," Meyer said.

All the strikers got first aid training and carried a

basic medical kit. There were normally two specialist
medics with a C-class company. C41 had gone into
Active Cloak with only one. He, Hung Sen, was working
on the legless sergeant of Gun 1 when a follow-up
shell minced him and his patient together.

"Aw, I'm all right," Nessman said without a lot of
emphasis. He reached for his gauntlets.

There wasn't a good field of fire for a stinger on this
landing site, much less a plasma cannon. Any striker
wearing a helmet in the line of fire would appear as a
caret in the cannon's sight, but there was no way to
tell if some civilians had walked behind a fallen thicket
downrange to take a dump in privacy. You'd think people
would worry more about having their asses blown away
than they did about who might see that ass bare, but it
wasn't true. Wasn't always true of strikers, either.

"Want me to—" Nessman said, rising to his feet.

"Contact!" the helmet warned. *"Contact!"*

Meyer pulled back the lever on the side of the
guntube and let it go, switching power to the trigger
mechanism. Launcher-fired grenades, two and then
four more, went off near the perimeter to the northeast.
One of them speared a branch skyward on a burp of
orange flame.

Meyer horsed the weapon around to point in the
direction of the blasts. The trunk slanted and the tree
had been dead long enough that the bark fell away in
large flakes under the gun's weight. The barrel wanted
to slip down the log.

There were strikers a hundred yards away to the
right of the weapon's current heading: two warning
icons had flashed on the sight as it swung across them.
Ten feet before the cannon's muzzle was a tangle of
sapling and vines, knitted together in a gray and brown

fabric. In a moment or two a company of Kalendru might come leaping over the barrier with their lasers ready and their inhumanly quick reactions. For now Meyer didn't have anything to shoot at.

Nessman, moving with care because he knew the hard suit made him clumsy, climbed onto the root ball beside Meyer. His visor was locked down. He pulled himself up hand over hand, kicking footholds in the mass of hardened clay. If his foot hurt, he didn't let it slow him.

Strikers chattered with excitement on the general push, but nobody had a better target than Meyer did. Another grenade went off, this time a hand-flung electric. It wasn't anywhere close to where Meyer expected the Spooks to be. She waited for her partner to cue her, working to control her breathing.

Nessman stood, balancing on the slippery trunk and six feet higher than before. *"Vector, mark,"* he said, using the Heavy Weapons channel that only the two of them shared.

A vertical red line appeared on Meyer's faceshield display. It was about ten degrees left of where the gun pointed. She pivoted, bringing the sight pipper into line with the vector her partner transmitted. She was still aiming into the long pile of debris.

"Three Spooks," Nessman reported. *"Four—"*

A pair of pale saffron laser pulses stabbed for him. One turned a dead limb into a puff of smoke and splinters. The other hit Nessman's helmet with a flash and a *crack* like heartbreak.

Meyer squeezed the trigger. The barrier exploded into a fireball flinging detritus in all directions. The point-blank destruction shoved her as her body recovered from the cannon's recoil.

Plasma-scoured pits fogged the face of her visor. The vector line was brilliant against the muted background. Nessman was down.

Meyer realigned the cannon and fired again. Fifty yards downrange a treetrunk as thick as the one she used for a gun rest blew apart. The ends of the log lurched high; the twenty feet closest to the point of impact vanished in iridescent hellfire.

Kalendru—she couldn't tell how many, didn't care—had been just the other side of the log. The blast knocked them flat, but she saw movement. Meyer fired a third round along the channel she'd blown through the knotted wasteland, then a fourth on top of it.

Dead wood—dry, shattered, and heated to temperatures near those of a star's corona—bellowed upward in an inferno. Everything in front of Meyer was aflame. The tree on which the plasma cannon rested was beginning to smoke from the nearby blaze. Meyer's suit protected her from the heat.

She lowered the weapon's butt to the ground on her side of the log and staggered around the roots to find her partner or his body. From training she kept her stinger ready, but she didn't expect to need it.

Spooks didn't wear body armor. Meyer didn't think even she in a hard suit would have survived the fires of Gehenna she'd ignited to engulf these attackers.

"Watch this bastard," Abbado warned. He held the prisoner's right elbow; Methie held the left. Now that they'd dragged the grenade-stunned Spook all the way to Major Farrell near the ship, Abbado wished he'd brought Flea instead of leaving him with Horgen and the rest of the squad. "He bites."

The sergeant was barechested. His bloody tunic

was draped over the Kalender's head for a makeshift hood.

Colonists crowded toward the command group with a rising murmur. It struck Abbado that in all likelihood no civilian on Bezant had ever seen a living Spook. "Give us some room, please!" said Top Daye.

Of course under normal circumstances, strikers didn't see living Spooks for very long either.

"Bites?" said Farrell. "Is he wounded?"

"Just knocked silly by a grenade," Abbado said. "I grabbed him and he bit the shit out of me. I, ah . . . I thought he might be rabid or something and the docs could . . ."

His wrist throbbed and was noticeably swollen. The Kalender's teeth, though delicate and smaller than a human's, were hell for sharp. The wound still oozed blood.

"Christ, yes!" Farrell said. He took the prisoner's arm himself. "Doctor! We need a medic here!"

"Yes, I am here," said Ahmed Ciler, the doctor Abbado'd met before. He wore a cleverly designed chest pack that folded down into a waist-level tray to display its contents. "Sergeant Abbado? Sit down and I'll look at that."

"I think he's got a bug or something, doc," Abbado said. He swallowed. His throat felt dry and he imagined he could feel it swelling shut. "He fought us all the way. Spooks aren't like that."

No concept of honor required Kalendru to continue fighting when resistance was useless. Spooks weren't cowards. They'd risk their lives on a chance just as readily as humans would. Where there was no reason to struggle—no main body for a rear guard to protect, no greater good to be purchased at the cost of an individual's life—overwhelmed Kalendru lapsed into perfect docility.

"He fought like an animal as soon as he came to, doc," Abbado said. Ciler teased a little serum onto the tip of a probe, then stuck the probe into the analysis port on the edge of his kit. "He kicked and twisted all the way back and he *knew* he couldn't get away. But he'd had a laser, it's not like he didn't have any mind left."

"It'll be a minute or two before the analysis is complete," Ciler said in a pleasant, soothing tone. "I added a military database when I learned where I was being sent. It's very unlikely that any Kalendru disease would affect a human being, and of course your immune booster is proof against such an event anyway. I'm going to clean and cover the wound. This may sting slightly."

Four strikers held the Spook spreadeagled. Daye pulled off the shirt Abbado'd thrown over the bastard's head to keep him from biting anybody else. Abbado felt like a damn fool, coming in to have his "wound" treated. Plenty of times he'd hurt himself worse and never even noticed it till he sobered up the next morning.

The way the Spook acted had scared Abbado. It was like having your pet goldfish try to take your finger off. There wasn't any real danger, but something was bad wrong for such a thing to happen.

Horgen could handle 3-3. It took two strikers to get this prisoner back to the command group. Abbado would have made the bite victim one of those escorts without even thinking about it if it'd been another squad member.

There was no doubt about any of that. But the truth was, Abbado'd been scared.

"There, that should do," Ciler said. He nestled the spray can back in its niche on the tray. The sealant tingled as it dried to a flexible, transparent scab over the toothmarks.

A chime sounded melodiously. Ciler touched a button that projected a dust-mote twinkle of holographic information. He smiled.

"Everything is perfectly normal," Ciler explained to the sergeant. "Any sensations you may have are merely the result of mechanical trauma, the bite."

His smile expanded. "Or imagination, of course," he said. "And you'll be pleased to know that based on the saliva sample, your prisoner is in good health also. Though suffering from deficiency in a few dietary proteins."

"Thanks, doc," Abbado said. He stood, feeling a relief greater even than sexual climax. He could handle the things he understood. It was the shit that came out of left field that made him shiver.

Lieutenant Kuznetsov was trotting down the ramp with the interrogation kit that they'd left in storage with the rest of the gear they weren't going to need at the landing. Who the hell expected there'd be Spooks here? The prisoner might be screwy, but screwy or not, electronic interrogation would let the strikers know what they were up against from that quarter.

Dr. Ciler looked toward the crowd around the prisoner, then grimaced and gave up the obvious thought. Abbado could have watched the interrogation by echoing the image from one of the officers, but Ciler didn't have that option.

"Let's see what's happening, doc," Abbado said, putting his arm through the crook of Ciler's. "Let us through, please!"

Civilians made way without complaint. C41 didn't know diddly squat about what was going on, but the strikers were used to being in life-and-death situations with no picture bigger than that of their gunsight images. For the colonists, being dropped into the shit without a clue must be terrifying. They were ready to defer to anybody who acted like he knew what he was doing.

Which Abbado did. Abbado knew he was leading Ciler to a place where the doctor could watch a Spook being interrogated.

The prisoner was now bound and gagged with lengths of the tape used to lock pallets into a starship's hold. 3-3 didn't have anything suitable for immobilizing captives, so they'd tied the Spook's wrists with a sleeve of the same tunic they'd used for a hood.

Abbado's back itched from ash and debris clinging to his sweaty skin. Insects kept lighting on him too. He needed to get another tunic from the ship. He looked up at 10-1442, wondering if the sucker was ever going to fall the rest of the way.

The prisoner thrashed his head from side to side and tried to kick. Methie sat on the Spook's bound ankles; Daye immobilized the head so that the major could fit the electrodes to the smooth scalp.

"What's this?" Farrell said. "Turn him face down. What the *hell* is this?"

The strikers flipped the Kalender on his belly. The big boss, al-Ibrahimi, and his aide watched with no more expression than a pair of lizards. Other civilians pressed closer by a process as gradual as a glacier sagging downslope.

There was a sac or cyst the size of a walnut at the base of the prisoner's skull. It was a darker, purplish gray than the skin around it. It looked obvious enough now, but Abbado and his strikers hadn't noticed anything when they were struggling with the Spook.

"Let me see that," said Dr. Ciler in a tone of sharp command. "Give me space, if you please!"

Ciler flopped his kit open and withdrew a probe. He held the sac steady with one hand and inserted the point with the other.

The doctor wasn't wearing gloves. Abbado felt himself twitch. There were more kinds of unthinking courage than what it took to unass an assault boat on a hot landing zone.

Ciler withdrew the probe and slid it into the analysis port. The prisoner's muscles tensed like the springs of a strain gauge. Abbado distinctly heard ribs crack in the instant before the spasm ended in death. The Spook's slim body relaxed like a slit bladder.

The kit chimed. Ciler frowned at the result; everyone who could see him waited. "It's Kalender nerve tissue," the doctor said. "But so thin an intrusion into the cyst shouldn't have caused such a reaction."

"Whatever it is, doc," the major said, "it's not a cyst."

He pointed. The lump had fallen away from the Kalender's flaccid corpse. The skin it had clung to was pale, almost white, but unmarked except for a puncture over the brain stem.

The lump lay on its back. Abbado saw eight tiny legs and, he supposed, a proboscis sticking from a body as swollen as the skin of a grape.

"Everyone check the back of your necks," Manager al-Ibrahimi said. "Immediately." His voice rang like wood blocks clapping.

Abbado patted his neck. The overhang of his helmet covered and protected him, the way it was intended to do against shrapnel from air bursts.

Dr. Ciler reached back with blunt, sensitive fingertips. "Oh God, the great and the merciful!" he cried in a despairing voice.

Abbado, acting with the killer's reflex that speed is life, brushed the doctor's hand aside. He caught the insect, for the moment no bigger than a rice grain, between his thumbnail and the callused pad of his trigger finger.

He squeezed. The insect burst with a spray of amber juice.

Ciler turned, his eyes full of wonder and relief. The striker grinned. "Favor for favor, doc," he said. "Get them quick before they grow."

More insects buzzed nearby. Abbado snatched another out of the air one-handed and crushed it, still smiling.

Simple Problems

The woman was in her sixties, though you had to look into her eyes to be sure. A lot of money had been spent to hide the fact. Her hair was a lustrous black which by its very perfection proved that science had augmented nature.

"Now just bend over and throw your hair forward, ma'am," Abbado said. "And hold still. Before we can put the patch on, I got to shave you with this."

He gestured with his 8-inch powerknife. The blade was dull gray except for the wickedly sparkling edges of synthetic diamond. When the knife was switched live, the paired edges sawed their microserrations against one another. The half-millimeter oscillations occurred hundreds of times a second and would slice through just about anything.

"Omigod, no," the woman said, shrinking back against the man standing next in line. She covered her face with her hands.

Abbado opened his mouth to snarl a curse. "Hey, ma'am," Glasebrook said. "Look here at me. It's no sweat, right?"

He lifted his helmet and rotated so that all the nearby civilians could see the patch of cargo tape he, like the rest of the strikers, wore where their spine entered the skull's foramen magnum. The helmets kept the bugs from lighting, but it'd be a bitch having to sleep with your helmet on. The major wasn't taking chances.

"Let the sarge shave you and you can look as pretty as me," Flea added, turning again and giving the woman a smile so broad he looked like a finback whale.

The aircar fifty feet away ran up its fans, lifted, and settled back in place. Abbado didn't try to shout over the induction howl. When it ceased, he said, "We need to shave the hair so the tape seals right, is the thing. You don't want to be like that Spook we caught, believe me."

He was glad he was working with Glasebrook. He'd never seen the Flea lose his temper. Abbado's own disposition—usually balanced enough when he was sober—had gotten pretty frayed since the Spook bit him.

As soon as the strikers near the ship had their brainstems taped, Major Farrell had swapped them with the squads on the perimeter. When all the strikers were protected, the ones now with the ship had been tasked to take care of the civilians. They worked in pairs: one with the knife, the other to hold the civilian's head still during the rough-and-ready barbering. A twitch at the wrong time and a powerknife could take a head off as easy as it did the hair.

The woman moaned softly and obeyed, sweeping her hair in front of her face in a veil of the greatest delicacy. An insect sat like a tiny scab at the base of her skull.

The civilian behind her gasped and felt his own neck again. Abbado held his finger across his lips and scowled to keep the fellow from blurting something. He thumbed the powerknife live. Glasebrook took the woman's head between spread fingers that could crush walnuts.

Abbado sheared the back of the woman's scalp and

the bug lurking there in the same swift, smooth motion. Severed hair trailed away as black gossamer. Abbado rubbed the shaven area with the edge of his right hand to smear off any remnants of the insect, then put the prepared square of cargo tape over it.

"There you go, ma'am," Glasebrook said as he raised the woman to meet his bright smile. "When we get where it's safe, you can take the tape off and your hair'll be just as pretty as ever in no time."

"Yeah," said Abbado. "The adhesive dissolves in alcohol and the tape falls off without you feeling it a bit."

And if you believe that, I'll try you on "I won't come in your mouth."

Aloud he said to the following man, "Next?"

Abbado would have liked to hurry things because the line was still damned long, but he knew that wouldn't work with civilians. He only hoped that the bugs took longer to get dug in than the strikers did to cover the brainstems. He didn't want some pretty girl to nut on him the way that Spook had.

A pair of fuel-air grenades went off fifty yards away. Strikers were blowing a firebreak to keep the plasma-lighted blaze from spreading toward the ship. A pebble thrown from the explosions bounced off Farrell's helmet, sounding like a gunshot. It didn't hurt him, but even Lundie and the manager started at the noise.

"We're going to get a storm," Top said, looking southward past the transport's nose. "Well, maybe it'll cool things down. Not that I'm counting on it."

Kuznetsov stood beside the staffer flying the aircar and called, "Everything checks out. Sir, are we clear to go?"

"When Mr. al-Ibrahimi gives you clearance," Farrell said. Strike Force companies were used to operating as a law unto themselves. Farrell didn't usually have a superior on the ground; but this time he did, and his strikers shouldn't imply that nothing a civilian said mattered.

"Sir, perhaps you should go instead of me," Lundie said. "The danger here probably *is* greater than—"

"There's more than enough danger for everyone on BZ 459, Tamara," al-Ibrahimi said. The tight-lipped blonde flinched as though al-Ibrahimi had whipped her across the face. It was the first time Farrell had heard him interrupt his aide. "The sooner the expedition removes to the proper site, the better off we'll be. Please proceed with your duties."

"Yes sir," Lundie said. She turned to Suares and added in a louder but still wooden voice, "Councillor, we're going now."

Suares stood hand in hand with a plumpish woman of his own age, shorter than the councillor by ten inches as well as being soft in contrast to his gaunt angularity. They looked as though they belonged together nonetheless.

Councillor Suares bent and pecked a kiss on the woman's cheek. "Be careful while I'm gone, my dear," he said.

She patted the back of his hand. "*You* be careful, Joao," she said. "Don't forget where you are and go wandering around by yourself."

"Sir?" said Top Daye. "The building superintendent wants to know if we can give her some strikers to manhandle heavy gear out of the ship. She doesn't have the people to do it, not with it tilting like it is."

The super, a stout woman with hairy arms named

Rifkind, glared at Farrell in gloomy irritation. Two of her staffers watched from the hatchway.

Al-Ibrahimi heard the exchange. "No," he said. "The colonists will supply the manpower. Major Farrell and his personnel are here for what we can't provide for ourselves, protection."

The aircar lifted into a hover, then turned and headed north in a gradual climb. Lieutenant Kuznetsov waved back to the strikers on the ground.

"Boy, I hope the Loot gets us some support damn quick," Top said. "Not that I'm counting on it."

Lightning flashed in the distant clouds.

Meyer twisted. The second leg piece separated and fell away. Sweat tacked the pants legs to her thighs.

"Bet you're glad to be out of that suit," said Methie. His visor was raised. His partner, another Third Platoon striker named Caldwell, wiped ash and grit from the belt of shells which hung from the cannon's loading port.

"It's okay," Meyer said. She felt more comfortable in a hard suit than not, but if she said that they'd think she was losing her nerve. She was fine, pretty much. "You know how to handle that thing?"

Caldwell was the same size and build as Meyer, but she kept her scalp shaved so the tattoos could be seen clearly when she wasn't wearing a helmet. She looked up and said, "I guess we can manage. We've got the specialty endorsement in our personnel jackets, if that's what you mean."

"Hey, sorry," Meyer said. "It's a hot day, okay?"

She gathered up the pieces of her hard suit. The arms, legs, and connectors seemed to weigh more in her hands than they did a moment before when she was wearing them.

"Hey, snake?" Methie said. "You and Nessman really waxed them bastards. Nice work."

Meyer smiled and walked toward the command group with her gear. The aircar rose in a test run. Meyer closed her eyes so that the trash thrown up by the drive fans wouldn't blind her. With her arms full, she couldn't flip down her visor to cover her face.

She wondered if the aircar was going to hold out long enough to transfer all C41's equipment to the new site or if the strikers would wind up humping it through the forest. Top Daye'd said something about bringing in another starship with more transport. That'd be nice. Strikers didn't live very long if they thought the high command was going to make things easy for them, though.

Nessman was seated on the ground, removing the upper sections of his hard suit while a medic looked at his foot. He waved at Meyer. Half a dozen small fires still burned from the recent battle. Ash and bitter smoke drifted through the site.

"Meyer!" Sergeant Daye called. He waved her over.

Top stood with the major, God, and a group of civilians who looked as though they thought they should be in charge of something. A good-looking man was saying to the project manager, "It's important than Margaret not feel she's being pressured to leave the compartment. She'll realize the necessity on her own, but we have to give her time."

"Councillor Lock," God replied in a voice that was either coldly hostile or just cold, "the ship is not a safe refuge. I suggest that you convince your wife to leave promptly, because I won't authorize a search for her body if the vessel collapses and she's still inside."

"Meyer," said Daye, "you haven't had your neck taped, right?"

"I had my suit on the whole time, Top," she said. She hadn't followed what the flap about bugs was, since she and Nessman continued to crew the plasma cannon until they were relieved minutes ago.

"Well you don't now," Daye said. "Some of these bugs, they dig through the back of your neck into your brain and you go crazy. Have—"

The aircar lifted again, this time with Lieutenant Kuznetsov and three civilians aboard. It rose twenty feet vertically to keep from sucking in debris its own fans kicked from the ground, then headed north in a gentle climb.

"Have Abbado fit you with tape like this," Daye resumed as the whine faded. "If he's turned over the spool to some—"

The aircar made a sound like a double hiccup. It flipped end over end before it crashed into the jungle just beyond the landing site.

Blohm was only a hundred feet farther from the crash, but the car came down just beyond 3-1. Sergeant Bastien shouted, "Come on! There may be somebody alive!" to his squad and pushed into a stand of finger-thick shoots growing from a fallen log.

The shoots bent like strands of putty until the sergeant was halfway through. Then they snapped vertical again, squeezing his waist tighter than that of a nineteenth-century belle wearing stays. He screamed on a rising note.

"Three-one, watch overhead!" Blohm called. He dodged a bush he could have jumped over or plowed through. He just didn't trust the look of it. As he passed, he saw the woody stem was bent like a bowstaff and quivering with tension.

Two strikers cut the shoots with their knives. The severed ends flew apart like released springs. Bastien fell to the ground and lay moaning. Another striker glanced upward in response to Blohm's warning, but he didn't see that a section high on the trunk of the emergent at the clearing's edge was expanding visibly.

"Mark!" Blohm called desperately. "Three-one, get the fuck out from there! The tree's going to burst! Over!"

Two strikers bent over their platoon sergeant. The others peered into the foliage overhead, combing through their helmets' vision options. They still didn't see any reason for concern.

Blohm slashed a burst from his stinger toward the treetop. A few pellets chipped bark, but the bole continued to swell. It was twice its diameter of a minute before.

Gabrilovitch was running behind Blohm. His grenade launcher chugged five times. The 4-ounce projectiles were easily visible throughout their flight. The first blew the swelling apart with a blue-white flash: Gabe had loaded with electricals.

A mass of thick white liquid slurped from the ruptured bole. The second grenade burst in the middle of it. The syrup ignited in a *whuff* of smoky orange flame.

All of Gabe's well-aimed salvo was in the air before the first grenade hit. The remaining rounds blew fiery bubbles that vanished instantly as traceries of soot.

The flaming mass crawled slowly down the trunk. 3-1 scrambled back, two of them carrying their sergeant, but the immediate danger was past. If the tree had expelled the sticky fluid under pressure, it would have engulfed the whole squad.

Blohm drew his powerknife but he kept the stinger in a one-hand grip. He paused at the forest's edge to slow his breathing, then stepped through the opening cut to free Bastien. Sergeant Gabrilovitch locked a fresh magazine into his grenade launcher's butt-well and glanced up at the gooey flame devouring the tree from which it had come.

Strikers from 3-1 hesitated, then followed the scouts into the forest. "For God's sake, step where I do!" Blohm snarled.

Blohm heard a stinger fire in the wreck as soon as he was past the forest margin. Somebody was alive. Probably the Loot, but one of the civilians conceivably knew how to pull a trigger.

Ahead he saw a swatch of blue plastic, the aircar's hull. The vegetation between looked at first to be a stand of wrist-thick saplings. The "trunks" merged twenty feet in the air and from there spread into dark-leafed branches. They were air roots like those of terrestrial mangroves.

And what do you *do to people, tree?* Blohm wondered with a slight smile. He stuck the barrel of his stinger between a pair of roots and shot into the spherical mass joining roots and branches in an hourglass shape.

Bark and wood the color of a drowned man's skin flew into the air. Clear sap dripped from the cup-sized wound and evaporated as quickly as methanol on a hotplate. Filters clicked over Blohm's nostrils.

"Three-one, visors down," Blohm said in satisfaction. There was no caret on his display to indicate he was in danger of absorbing the gas through the skin. "Gabe, wait for me to cross."

The tree's poisonous breath would be a danger for civilians, but the strikers were equipped for it. Blohm cut a pair of roots, severing them first at arm's length above him, then flush with the moist ground as the ends wobbled. The gap was eighteen inches wide.

Blohm slid through without touching the supports to either side, crossed the circular clearing beneath the tree, and cut through the arched roots on the other side. Pores in the bark spread like eyelids opening. The air beneath the tree became faintly misty.

The aircar lay tilted to the right. Its underside was toward the rescue party. The stinger had stopped firing, but Blohm heard a powerknife from the passenger bay.

A vine as thick as an anchor cable hung onto the crashed vehicle from a branch of one of the neighboring trees. Ten feet above the ground, the vine's tip flared into scores of tendrils. They moved in the still air. Stinger pellets had chewed the tip nodule, sawing off a number of tendrils but not destroying the spongy nodule itself. Kuznetsov had been forced to fire straight up.

Blohm's stinger tore the vine for half a second before a grenade from Gabrilovitch shredded a two-foot length in a spray of juice and white fibers. The sergeant's shoulder steadied Blohm from the blast.

The severed nodule swung outward. Tendrils twisted like a Gorgon's hair. Blohm let his stinger go and gripped the car's quarter panel with his right hand. He pulled himself halfway onto the vehicle. Gabrilovitch knelt to provide his shoulder as a step. Blohm rotated his legs over the side of the car and slashed through the tendril groping toward his thigh.

The old civilian and the driver had hurtled from the front seats when the aircar hit. Vine tendrils curled around their necks and snaked under their cuffs. The victims' skin was sallow and the tension of their muscles bent the corpses into rigid bows.

The blonde woman hadn't bounced out of the central compartment, probably because the Loot had judged the angle of impact and braced the both of them against it. Now Kuznetsov held the blonde pressed against the tilted car so that what had been the floor of the central compartment protected their backs.

"Get her out of here!" Kuznetsov shouted as her powerknife cut a tendril reaching around her for the blonde. She ignored the tip probing where the cuff of her battle dress bloused into the top of her right boot. The tendrils might have slowed when the strikers' fire severed the supporting vine, but for the time being they retained life and motion.

Blohm gripped the blonde's coveralls at waist level and heaved upward. She had enough presence of mind to grab his shoulder. For an instant Blohm thought they were going to overbalance and land face first in the nodule, but a striker caught his equipment belt from behind and anchored him.

Kuznetsov bent and sawed through the tendril. Its tip had disappeared beneath her boot top. The severed end writhed. It continued to writhe as the lieutenant's body arched backward and her limbs spasmed. The powerknife flew aside, still whirring.

Blohm tried to throw the blonde onto the ground behind him, the fastest way to put a barrier between her and the remaining tendrils. She misunderstood and continued to cling to his arm. The tip of a tendril brushed Blohm's breastplate and curled onto the civilian's bare wrist.

Instead of cutting the plant, Blohm slid his knife between the tendril and the blonde's arm, shaving flesh and the tip of a wrist bone. The blade's vibration spit blood in all directions.

The civilian gasped but didn't scream. Blohm rolled himself backward, taking her with him in a somersault. Gabe ducked aside, dodging Blohm's knife.

Blohm hit on his shoulders and tucked by reflex. He managed not to fall on the blonde, but the breastplate she slammed against was a lot harder than the ground beneath him.

A striker from 3-1 leaned over the tilted aircar, stepping on the laced hands of one of her fellows. "Blast that—" Blohm wheezed.

A gush of dazzling white fire spewed from the muzzle of the striker's weapon. She carried a flame gun using high pressure oxygen to throw a jet of metal-enriched fuel. It carved the vegetation with a ferocity only a plasma bolt could have bettered.

"Striker Blohm, I think you'd better get me to medical help," said the blonde civilian. She'd clamped her right palm over the wound, but blood and serum leaked around the edges. "Or your courage will have been for nothing. Some of the toxins have already entered my system."

The forest gave an angry sigh. Perhaps the sound was air rushing to feed the blaze the flame gun had ignited.

Simple Wrong Answers

"I knew Daniello, jeez, must be five years," Seligman said. "He was flying the car. Did you know that?"

"I didn't know any of the civilians," Meyer said without emphasis. She paused to check the diagram on her visor again. A sidebar provided the compartment manifests. "We need the next door, not this one."

Lieutenant Kuznetsov had been all right. Meyer had never served directly under her, but C41 was a small world. Kuznetsov looked out for her people.

"I don't see why the hell they need building supplies anyway," Seligman complained. "They ought to be thinking about getting us where we're supposed to be instead. You know, if they'd carried a couple more aircars, we'd be a damn sight better off!"

Meyer wondered if Top had picked her to guide Seligman because she'd worked with the staffer before. She didn't like being inside the ship, knowing that if it fell she might be trapped in the crumpled hull.

"The First Sergeant said we'd be using rolls of roofing to sleep on at night," she said aloud. The sooner she completed her job, the sooner she'd be able to get out of this metal tomb. "I guess they're afraid that if we lie right on the ground, something might come up out of it while we're sleeping."

She patted the hatch with the flat of her hand. "Try this one."

You'd have thought the support staff would have their own way to navigate around 10-1442. Would have drawn maps, at least, during the voyage. Nope. And Meyer wasn't counting on cargo being stowed where the manifest showed it, either.

Seligman opened the hatch with the electronic key for all the locks on Deck 17. The air had a chemical odor. The compartment had probably been closed since the cargo was stowed.

"It don't make *any* damn sense all of us having to hike through the jungle," he said. "They ought to, well, send a few of you guys to the right place and bring in aircars in another ship. You guys hike a lot, right?"

"Not a lot, no," Meyer said. "Mostly we ride."

By assault boat. But Seligman wouldn't get the point even if she said that.

Seligman knelt and checked code tags with an electronic reader. "Yeah, this is it," he said. He looked over his shoulder at the striker. "I still think some of you soldiers ought to fetch help. It's what makes sense to me."

Right, divide your force when you know there's a shipload of Kalendru troops in the immediate vicinity. Meyer shrugged. She said, "I just follow orders, buddy. The decisions come from the manager, not me."

She stepped back into the corridor. "I'll leave you to it, then," she said without turning her head. "You can bring the labor crew up when you're ready to."

"Hey, I'm coming!" Seligman said. "I tell you, this damned planet isn't someplace I want to be alone."

You don't know what alone is, buddy, the striker thought, but she didn't say anything aloud.

✧   ✧   ✧

Patches of forest still smoldered despite the afternoon downpour. The smoke tended to hang on the nearby foliage the way rival groups at a party refuse to mix. At the edge of the clearing Blohm smelled the damp, chalky odor of clay turned by the tracks of the bulldozer as it dragged the aircar free.

Superintendent Rifkind wasn't really examining the wreckage. Technical experts had done that while it was still daylight, even carrying pieces back to study in the ship despite the risk. Rifkind ran her gloved hand over the nacelle. It had warped when the fanblades sheared and let the motor spin ungoverned.

The sky was clear and brilliant with stars. Blohm wondered if the colonists would name the constellations to their children, the way adults on Earth had done. He couldn't guess how many different night skies he'd seen since he enlisted, but he'd never learned what to call those new stars.

"I don't see how it happened," Rifkind said. "We tested it, Daniello did. I watched him test it."

Bonfires burned near the ship. Blohm supposed the fires were for the civilians' mental comfort. Somebody hoped it would help, anyway.

Rifkind fingered the intake housing. The screen was intended to filter incoming air so that chunks of debris wouldn't damage the fan blades.

A flashlight bobbed out of the encampment. Blohm increased his visor's magnification. An older civilian woman was coming up the trail one of the bulldozer's treads had crushed in the soil. The striker didn't recognize her, but there were limits to the detail you could expect from even Strike Force optics at night.

The manager and several civilian specialists carried

off the aircar's front screen for examination. A resilient, airtight sheet of cloudy substance filled the meshes.

Their rear intake was the same. When the fans couldn't pull air through the blockage, the car had dropped like a brick.

"Ma'am?" Blohm called. "You're not supposed to be here. Go back to the others, please."

Half the strikers were on watch at intervals all around the perimeter of the clearing. The other half were off-duty unless needed as a reaction force. The major'd ordered that nobody should take his helmet off.

Blohm didn't know about the Spooks, but the forest at least seemed quiescent since the sun had set. The scout no longer had the feeling that something large and hungry was watching him from behind.

The woman reached them and stood diffidently. "I'm Seraphina Suares," she said. "My husband was killed in the crash. I came to see him one last time. His grave."

Suares had kept the flashlight aimed down so that it wouldn't overload the image intensifier in Blohm's visor. When she was within ten feet and sure of the track before her, she switched it off entirely.

"Ah," said Blohm. "They're on the other side of the car, ma'am."

"Yes," said Suares. She added softly, "His real monument was his work, of course. We never had children of our own."

They'd recovered the bodies, but there was nothing to do then except bury them in a trench the bulldozer gouged for the purpose. Bastien was buried close to the ship. He'd bled out internally by the time his strikers had gotten him to doctors. Jagged fragments of the sergeant's pelvis had severed two of the arteries in his groin.

"It shouldn't have gotten into the air with the ducts plugged," Rifkind said. "I don't see how it *happened*."

The widow traced her husband's name with her finger. They'd used a rocker panel for a marker because the plastic wouldn't decay like wood or the site's coarse limy shale. It was the major's idea.

Mrs. Suares turned. "The screens were covered by a bacterium," she said. "It's common in the air here." She waved her hand.

"Yeah, but how could they take off?" Rifkind demanded. "There's more to it than that."

"The bacterium multiplies explosively in a high-velocity airstream," Suares said. She spoke with the dispassion of an engineer discussing structural failure. Maybe she was. "It coated the tractor's heat exchanger when the cooling fan ran for a few minutes also. There the immediate consequences were merely a loss of efficiency in the working fluid rather than catastrophic failure."

Suares touched the grave marker again. "A low-level electrical charge prevents the bacteria from forming," she added. "A very simple protection. Now that we recognize the problem. Joao always said that recognizing a problem was far more difficult than solving one."

"Shit," Rifkind said. She rubbed a fist into the opposite palm. "I'm going to go get some sleep."

"Yes, I'll go back also," Suares said. Her lips smiled. "I'm not sure how much sleep I'll get."

The two civilians started toward the bonfires. Blohm heard Rifkind say, "This *damned* planet."

"I'm not sure that it's the planet that is damned," Mrs. Suares replied in the starlit darkness.

❖   ❖   ❖

The command group gathered fifty feet from the nearest bonfire. A tiny glowlamp burned in the center of the circle in consideration of Reitz and Lock who didn't wear image intensifiers. Colonists spoke and sang to crying babies, but the crackle of burning wood was generally the loudest sound in the background.

"We'll set out at mid-morning," al-Ibrahimi said. "I'd like to leave at dawn, but it'll be very difficult to get the civilians moving at all for the first few days."

"How will we limit the amount of baggage?" Tamara Lundie asked. "They'll almost certainly want to bring more than they can carry."

The manager's aide wore a bandage of plastic film to protect the antiseptic sealant sprayed over her wound. Her face looked drawn, but she spoke in the even tones that Farrell had come to associate with her.

"Major Farrell, do you have suggestions?" al-Ibrahimi asked.

Farrell shrugged. "Warn people but let them bring what they want," he said. "They'll throw it away themselves after an hour or two."

"I'm worried about food," President Reitz said. She snorted a tiny laugh as she thought about what she'd just said. "Among other things. But I don't see how we can carry enough supplies to last until the relief ship arrives, even with both bulldozers pulling trailers."

Farrell wondered if he should speak. He looked at al-Ibrahimi.

The project manager nodded awareness. To Reitz he said, "We won't be carrying any food or water, madam. Our Strike Force guards are equipped with field converters which process any form of carbohydrate into edible rations. Pure water is one of the waste products.

The colonists will operate the converters throughout the day as we march. That should provide a more than adequate volume."

Farrell felt his fingers checking the magazine of his stinger. He forced himself to stop. "People won't eat as much as you think, ma'am," he said.

They wouldn't eat as much as they ought to. Field rations when you're exhausted were as attractive as wet sawdust. Swallowing them down was one more job for a body already overloaded by effort.

"Both tractors will retain their clearing blades," Lundie said, correcting a false implication in Reitz's question. "The tractor in operation at the head of the column won't be able pull a load at the same time. The tractor out of service will pull two trailers with munitions for the Strike Force and ground sheets. Nothing more."

"No," said Councillor Lock. "No. With all due respect, Manager al-Ibrahimi, this is absurd. When the citizens understand what's involved, they'll refuse to go, and they'll be right to refuse. The fact that a half dozen diseased aliens wandered toward the ship— it needn't have been an attack, you know—"

"It was an attack," Farrell said. "I know an attack."

His voice was a harsh buzz, more like a bee's wings than human speech. He stood, then turned away from the gathering. His muscles were trembling.

"Sit down, Major Farrell," al-Ibrahimi said.

"Yessir, sorry," Farrell whispered. He nodded an apology to Councillor Lock, though the civilian didn't understand what had almost happened.

Christ, they should have redlined me. If I'm going to come that close to killing a civilian who can't be expected to know what's going on, what am I going to do the next time I hear a rear-echelon colonel spouting bullshit?

"Councillor Lock," the manager said in a tone with no more anger than the blade of a guillotine, "you are not a stupid man. Do not permit your concern for your wife's neurotic behavior to cause you to say stupid things. Our margin for survival is very slight."

Lock nodded. "Major Farrell," he said, "I apologize for intruding on an area outside my competence. It won't happen again."

Indeed, he wasn't stupid. It'd only taken Lock thirty seconds to put the pieces together.

"I'm wound too tight," Farrell said. He forced a smile to make a joke of what was the truth if it had ever been spoken. "Sorry."

"Apart from the probability that 10-1442 will fall over within the next thirty days, sooner if the rain we experienced is a daily occurrence," Lundie said, looking at Lock, "the danger from the Kalendru is incalculable. We have to assume that whatever forces they have in the area will be drawn to the ship."

"I'm also concerned about the natural environment," al-Ibrahimi added. "While BZ 459 was clearly going to be a difficult location for a colony, the biota we've encountered in this crater is far more dangerous than survey data suggested for the planet as a whole. I believe the risk of waiting here until a rescue vessel arrives is greater than the risk of cutting our way out of the crater as quickly as possible."

"Better to stay a moving target," Farrell said before he remembered that he wasn't talking to other strikers. He cleared his throat and went on, "My lead scout says the whole jungle's alive and gunning for us."

"Of course it's—" Reitz said. "Oh. Consciously alive."

Farrell shrugged, wishing that he'd kept his mouth shut. "Blohm's been pretty close to the edge since the last operation. He's, I mean, I trust him, but I don't say his head's in a good place."

"There are twenty-seven colonists who refuse to leave the ship," Lundie said, looking unblinkingly at Lock.

"I'm going to talk to Margaret," Lock said abruptly. He stood and walked away from the group. "This is my problem to solve."

"Sir?" Farrell said to the project manager. "Do you have any idea what the Spooks are doing here? I never heard of them planting a base this far inside the human sphere."

There were a lot of things the Unity command didn't tell strikers. Spook soldiers in places the Unity couldn't afford Spooks to be, though—that was something the Strike Force was going to hear about pretty damn quick.

Lundie and al-Ibrahimi exchanged glances. "That isn't information which would be available to the Population Authority," the aide said. "I don't believe that the highest levels of the Unity administration would have authorized this colony had there been any knowledge of Kalendru penetration of this region."

Manager al-Ibrahimi nodded. "President Reitz," he said. "Councillor Lock is right that there will be objections to leaving. Please gather your deck monitors tonight and emphasize to them that no one will be permitted to remain behind. Our only chance of survival is to march to safety."

"I'll tell them," Reitz said. "We understand this isn't a democracy. But there'll be a lot of anger. And perhaps some rebellion."

"Rebellion will be ended by force if necessary," Lundie said. "They must understand that."

"They should be angry," al-Ibrahimi said. "They've been treated very unjustly. The citizens and your personnel both, Major Farrell. But we are going to act in the fashion that gives us the best chance of survival in the situation where we find ourselves."

"It's no use arguing with facts," Farrell said. "Sir, do you need me further just now? I'd like to check with my first sergeant on the munitions we're loading. I want to be ready to go in the morning."

"Of course," al-Ibrahimi said. "And see to it that you get some sleep yourself. We'll need you as alert as possible if we're to survive."

"I'll go with you, Major," Lundie said. She stood, then wobbled before catching her balance. "I want to discuss the alert system with you and Sergeant Daye, since I'll be monitoring the sensors of your personnel."

They walked toward the tandem-hitched trailers near the ship. Too near the ship, Farrell thought, because the hull might kick back if the ship fell. Still, it eased loading the heavy cases of ammo and explosives.

Life was a series of tradeoffs. Until you died.

Lundie stumbled again. "Are you going to be all right, ma'am?" Farrell asked. "That's a pretty bad wound, and . . ."

"The wound itself isn't serious, except that it handicaps me when using a keyboard," Lundie said. "Unfortunately the vine was covered with fine hairs, some of which broke off in the skin all over my arm. They're too small to remove. As they dissolve they release psychoactive chemicals."

She looked at Farrell and went on, "Generally this

is a low-order problem, but I'm concerned that I might have a psychotic episode at any time. It gives you and me something in common, I suppose."

Farrell blinked at what she'd just said. Then he laughed harder than he remembered doing in years.

"Ma'am," he said at last. "You know, you're screwy enough to be a striker? But I think you're too fucking smart."

A civilian walked toward the plastic sheet on which 3-3 sat in darkness. Horgen hissed a warning. Abbado took the bladder of whiskey from Glasebrook and put it under the tunic lying beside him. If there was a problem, it was his squad and his problem.

"Excuse me?" said Dr. Ciler's familiar voice. "I'm looking for Striker Methie in the Third Squad?"

"Hey Doc," Abbado said. "Come sit down. What do you need with the Methman?"

"Aw, I was supposed to come by so he could look at my leg," Methie said. "I'm okay, Doc. Really."

"If you are," the doctor said, "then ligaments have miraculously healed themselves in the past twenty-four hours."

"I just need to watch how quick I turn, is all," Methie muttered, but he pulled up his left trouser leg. The strikers still wore their boots, but they'd released the closure clamps for comfort.

Ciler squatted down on the sheet. Thirty feet away a gas pocket in a burning log ruptured. It shot blue flame with a banshee shriek for several seconds. The doctor tensed, then steadied. "Might I turn on a light, please?" he asked.

"Oh, sure," Abbado said. "We didn't want to get too much attention, you know. There's some cargo we thought we'd use up since it don't look like we'll be back here any time soon."

Ciler switched on the minilight clipped to his collar. He bent so that it bore on Methie's knee as he probed with the blunt fingers of both hands. "You think anything we abandon will be lost forever, then?" he said while keeping his eyes on his work.

"Usually it's just REMFs in base camps who steal your shit," Horgen said. "The way this jungle grows, there'll be a big green hill in no time. And I'm thirsty now."

"Ah, would you like a drink, Doc?" the sergeant offered. "It's whiskey from Earth, not something run through a heat exchanger while the tractor was shut down."

"We wouldn't be drinking it right now," Matushek said, "except it's that or leave it behind, you know?"

Ciler turned off the light. "I'd like a drink, yes," he said. "Though I think you men and women need it worse than I do."

Abbado handed him the bladder. "All told we got three gallons, Doc," he said. "More than we'll need if we're going to march in the morning. I'd offer it around pretty generally, but that'd mean Top hears and comes down with both boots."

The doctor drank deeply from the mouthpiece and lowered the bladder. Caldwell took it from him and drank in turn.

"Mr. Methie," Ciler said, "the swelling hasn't increased. I'm afraid that a pressure bandage would do more harm by cutting circulation than the support will benefit you, so I'm going to leave you as you are. I want you to come to me tomorrow after you've been walking on it. Do you understand?"

"Sure, Doc," Methie said in embarrassment. "Sorry."

"How long are we on point tomorrow, sarge?" Horgen asked. "All day?"

Abbado shook his head. "Till the major shifts us, I guess," he said. "Anyway, we're not really point, the bulldozer is. With luck it'll just be a walk through the woods, not even much exercise."

"With luck I'll wake up and find I'm in bed with my girlfriend on Verdant," Matushek said. "But I'm not holding my breath."

The bladder came around to him. He finished it and added, "Time to open the next one, Foley."

Dr. Ciler put his face in his hands. "This isn't right," he said hoarsely. "All these children . . . And half of you, you should be in hospital yourselves. You know that. Methie, you should have had surgery on that knee."

"Aw, Doc, they'd have held me on Stalleybrass or some pisspot like that," Methie muttered. "And then reassigned me God knows where. I'd never have got back to C41."

"It's not *right*," the doctor repeated. Caldwell handed him the fresh bladder of whiskey.

"No, it's not, Doc," Abbado said softly. "But that doesn't matter. It's never right, and it never matters."

Another log shrilled in the night. Ciler froze, then sucked in more liquor.

Preparations

Blohm watched Sergeant Gabrilovitch pause, then take a second pouch of magazines for his backup weapon, the grenade launcher. They didn't intend to fight anybody. The plan was that the pair of scouts would slip three miles through the jungle to the site of a magnetic anomaly the major wanted checked out, report, and rejoin the column without firing a round.

The rest of the universe, the Spooks and in particular the forest itself, might have different plans. Blohm clipped another fuel-air grenade to his equipment belt. If he and Gabe stepped in shit, they were a whole lifetime away from resupply.

The encampment was waking up. There were sizzles and cooking odors from the last proper meal the column would have until a relief ship arrived with replacement ranges and prepared food. Children called in shrill voices, angry at being roused before dawn.

Blohm looked toward the sky, pale enough to hint at colors in the forest. "Ready to go, snake?" he asked.

Gabe laughed without humor. "Not as ready as you are. But yeah, let's do it. You lead?"

C41 was marshalling near the ship. The major and Sergeant Daye made sure the strikers knew their placements in the column. Sergeant Kristal saw the scouts standing apart and walked toward them.

"Hey, you two," she called. "You've still got your converters. Bring them over to the cit woman at the trailers. The president. She'll take care of them from here out."

"Who died and made you God, Kristal?" Blohm said. He and 2-1's sergeant had rubbed each other wrong since she transferred to C41 from a line battalion.

"It happens that Top tasked me to help with administration since we're short of officers," Kristal said in a hard, pale voice. "But for a pissant like you, Blohm, all that matters is I'm a sergeant and you're a striker."

"Major Farrell wants us to check something magnetic out in the jungle, Sue," Sergeant Gabrilovitch said. "We need the converters. We're headed out right now."

"Come on, Gabe," Blohm said. He wasn't going to give up his converter. Not if the major himself ordered it.

"Well, hell, nobody told me," Kristal muttered. She knew she'd stepped on her dick by trying to pull rank. She turned to go back to the main body. Over her shoulder she added, "When you get back, then. The cits are taking care of catering."

"No," Blohm said. "I need my converter. I might be out there—"

He nodded.

"—any time."

So long as Caius Blohm had a converter and a knife, he was independent of every other human being on Bezant. He could pretend, *believe*, he was completely alone.

Both sergeants looked at Blohm with carefully blank-faced concern. They'd seen redliners plenty of times before. There wasn't a psych wing to bundle people off to here; and besides, even Kristal would have admitted the expedition needed Blohm just now.

"Look, Sue," Gabrilovitch said, speaking more to Blohm than to Kristal. "When we're in camp, Blohm'll run his converter for any cits that need it, right? He'll do it himself. Top can't complain about that, right?"

Kristal shrugged. "Yeah, sure," she said, watching Blohm the way she'd have watched a cobra; only she knew the scout was faster than a cobra. "Have a nice hike through the park, why don't you?"

"Come on, snake," Gabrilovitch said in an urgent whisper. "We got a job to do, right?"

"Right," Blohm growled. He twitched his whole body to settle his pack, then strode toward the edge of the unbroken forest.

Kristal watched the scouts disappear. Blohm entered the jungle like a fish diving home in the sea.

The civilians' faces were sullen over layers of fear, anger, and uncertainty; but mostly fear. Abbado walked down the line of the two deckloads who'd start at the head of the column and were therefore 3-3's primary responsibility. He reminded himself that they *were* civilians; and he tried to remember to smile.

The civilians had been told to prepare to colonize a planet, not for route marching. They didn't have load-bearing equipment. Many of them carried bundles in their arms. Others had travel cases with handles and sophisticated support devices on the underside, a dead weight over the bulldozed terrain between here and the proper site.

Strikers were talking to the civilians about their baggage, helping them sort and toss items aside. Abbado noticed Glasebrook was checking everybody's neck patch. Flea seemed to have made that a crusade, which was fine with his sergeant. Abbado's wrist still ached where the crazy Spook had bitten him.

A few civilians had tried to manufacture their own packs. Lack of proper materials handicapped them, but Abbado nodded approval at the initiative. Half a dozen adults carried their loads balanced on lengths of plastic pipe. That was probably the most efficient technique, though it'd be awkward in tight places.

Abbado didn't worry about the marchers crowding together. This mob was going to straggle from the first step, and he only hoped nobody thought it was the job of his strikers to close them up. Trying to protect the poor bastards was going to be problem enough.

Dr. Ciler bobbed his head silently to Abbado. The sergeant lifted a hand in response. He recognized a number of the faces, though he couldn't have put names to them. People from the batch he'd guided aboard the ship. "Hey, it's homecoming, right, folks?" he said.

Jeez, these poor bastards are meat on the table unless we stay razor sharp, Abbado thought as his lips smiled.

The tractors were turning over as staffers checked the prime mover and ancillary motors. The drives were electric, generated by fusion-heated steam in a light-metal working fluid.

The tractor cabs were covered on the top and three sides. The staffers driving would wear hard suits from C41's stores, most of which had to be abandoned at the ship. The major had decided to put a striker in full armor on the platform behind the cab for additional protection. They couldn't afford to lose the tractors.

Abbado stopped beside a woman in her forties. Most of the civilians stood in small groups, families or

neighbors together, but she was alone. She wore a
tailored pants suit and what looked to the sergeant
like slippers.

"Ma'am, do you have other shoes than these?" he
asked. The beige suit was probably all right, loose
enough to be comfortable and of a synthetic that was
tough though diaphanous. "Or boots, maybe?"

The woman covered her face and began to cry. She
started to fold at the knees.

"Ma'am?" Abbado said. He reached out but he was
afraid to touch her. He looked desperately at the
nearest civilians.

A father took the hand of a six-year-old so that his
wife could put her arms around the crying woman.
"It's all right, Mrs. Florescu," the mother said. "I've
got an extra pair that I don't want to carry. What size
are you?"

"One-sixty-five," Florescu said, trying to control her
sobbing. "I'd just moved in. A new life after the divorce.
And then *this*. I didn't know what to do. I couldn't
get anything ready, I just couldn't!"

"I'm one-fifty-five," the other woman said. She
looked at Abbado with a worried expression. "Do you
think that's too small, captain?"

"Shit, I'm a one-sixty-five and I've got a pair in my
hold baggage that was just going to feed mice,"
Caldwell said. "Cover for me while I get them, Sarge?
They're up on Deck 24."

Abbado nodded. "Don't let Top see you going back
aboard," he said. "And don't waste time."

Caldwell put a bulldozed line of brush between her
and the command group as she trotted toward the
ship.

"You're going to be the envy of all your friends, Mrs.

Florescu," Abbado said. "Genuine Strike Force boots, guaranteed to outlast the wearer. Now, let's take a look at your bag, here."

He knelt and turned over a suitcase that probably weighed pretty close to what the owner herself did. It had a built-in air cushion lift similar to that of a Heavy Weapons dolly—and here as useless as tits on a boar.

One of the bulldozers squealed as it raised its blade from resting position on the ground. Whining and clanking, the massive vehicle started toward the edge of the forest.

These poor bastard civilians.

The second bulldozer backed slowly toward the trailer's tow-bar. The drive started out at a high-pitched whine, but the sound lowered as torque overcame the vehicle's initial static resistance.

"There are still ten adults and two children on the transport," Tamara Lundie said—ostensibly to the project manager but loud enough that Farrell would be sure to hear over the tractor's squeals and clangor. "Councillor Lock's wife and child are among them. I believe the councillor has gone back aboard also."

"That's under control," Farrell said wearily. He hadn't slept worth a damn. Dreaming about the extraction from Active Cloak, and he'd have thought his subconscious could have found more pressing concerns. "I've got four strikers chivying people out."

Farrell tried to visualize the column stretching through the jungle. Half a mile long, and that was if the civilians kept together better than he had any expectation that they would. How the hell was C41 going to protect them?

"I've placed the second tractor in the center of the column as you requested, Major," al-Ibrahimi said. "Because it's as large as the path the leading vehicle cuts, it divides the column . . . which it would not do if it were at the rear or front."

The tractor backed over the tow-bar. The two staffers holding the bar ready had to jump aside, shouting curses at the driver.

The driver lifted her helmet visor. "It's this fucking spacesuit!" she shouted back. "You try to do better wearing one, Biggs!"

She closed the visor. The bulldozer whined forward a foot and a half and halted while the other staffers gingerly returned to lift the bar.

"I want resupply in the middle of the column," Farrell said. "My people are carrying double their usual ammo loads—"

Which were about double what Logistics thought a striker's basic load should be to begin with.

"—but we don't know what we're going to run into. The only way we've got to cover the civilians is to lay down enough fire to chew this jungle to a golf green at the first sign of trouble. The dozer can cut its own way off the path if we need to get by it."

Susannah Reitz broke from a group of floor monitors and strode toward the project manager. "Manager al-Ibrahimi," she said in a voice with a shrill edge, "I've taken a look at some of the citizens you claim are fit to march. We have a woman from Three West who's eight and a half months pregnant! We have fourteen residents over seventy years old, and we have an asthmatic for whom a walk of as much as half a block in this heat and humidity will mean a life-threatening attack."

The building president stopped in front of al-Ibrahimi, ignoring Farrell and Lundie. Her face was flushed both with heat and anger. "What I want to know, Mr. Manager," she said in a lower voice that cut like a hacksaw, "is do you expect to treat people the way you treat the excess luggage? Throw them into the jungle when they get to be a burden?"

"*No,*" said Farrell. He'd heard dogs snarling that sounded more human than he did. "We're not abandoning anybody alive, Ms. Reitz. Other folks'll carry them or they'll ride the trailers. The dead I don't care."

"The ground pressure of the trailer wheels—" Lundie began.

"Fuck the ground pressure!" Farrell said. "We'll throw out ammo before we leave people behind."

"I don't think that will be necessary, Major," al-Ibrahimi said with a faint smile. "Not at the rate I fear you'll be using that ammunition. Ms. Reitz, why don't you and I discuss the matter with our less healthy fellows and see what can be arranged."

He offered Reitz his arm. The gesture obviously surprised her, but she accepted it.

Farrell's eyes were closed. He felt his stinger's magazine click as he reseated it in the butt-well.

"Major Farrell?" said Tamara Lundie in a quiet voice beside him. "You're correct, of course. The human considerations are the only considerations that are really pragmatic."

The nearby tractor whined like a giant hornet. It was starting forward against its own mass and that of the two loaded trailers.

"We don't leave anybody behind," Farrell whispered to his ghosts.

❖   ❖   ❖

The doors to the living compartments on 10-1442 didn't lock, but 2A was closed unlike any of the others on the corridor. Meyer checked the name on a sidebar, then raised her visor to look less threatening. Top said not to scare the cits and not to use any more force than necessary.

"Margaret Lock?" she called and started to push the door open.

"No!" a woman shouted from inside. The door slammed against its jamb. A child began to shriek.

The sound of the door threw a switch in the striker's mind. It was shutting her out, not in, but all Meyer's nightmare reflex heard was the closure. She hit the panel with her right shoulder and pivoted in. Her finger was within the trigger guard of her stinger. The muzzle swept the room.

Male and female, not obviously armed. Child of three or four, female, screaming like a steam vent. The parents were around thirty, the man trying to view both Meyer and the woman Meyer'd flung across the compartment with the door. The woman looked like a harpy's corpse, but she'd probably be all right when her face wasn't distorted with fear, anger and a day of hysterics.

"I'll take care of this, soldier!" the man said. "I'm Councillor Matthew Lock and this is my wife."

"Get your little girl out, sir," Meyer said, breathing hard. She let the sling snap her weapon back under her arm. Christ, what had she been thinking of? "Don't threaten them," Top had said. "I'll guide your wife."

Meyer reached for the child's arm. The child screamed, "Help, Mommie!" and dodged back.

"Get away from her, you filthy whore!" cried the woman. She launched herself at Meyer.

Meyer kicked the woman in the crotch, a bar-fight reflex that was about as effective on one sex as the other. The compartment was too small. Filters of memory darkened it in the striker's mind. She was back on Active Cloak.

"I'll have you—" Councillor Lock said as he grabbed Meyer by the shoulders. Meyer slammed her stinger's barrel into the pit of Lock's stomach.

He doubled up, still clinging to her. Meyer's intellect caught her instinct just before she butt-stroked him in the face. She batted the insides of Lock's elbows to break his grip, then stepped away.

Both civilian adults were on their knees. The woman made wet sobbing sounds. The kid's mouth and eyes were wide open, but for a wonder she'd stopped screeching.

"Coming through!" Steve Nessman warned. He entered in a crouch with his stinger ready, then straightened uncertainly.

"My people went out on their own," Nessman said as he eyed Meyer. "Figured I'd stop off on Two and see how you were doing, Essie."

"Yeah," Meyer said hoarsely. "Help me get these guys to the lifts, will you?"

Councillor Lock put his arms around his wife and stood, helping her up with him. "Alison, come along at once," he said to his daughter in a breathy voice. "We'll get the luggage later."

Lock walked the woman out of the compartment, holding her to hide her face against his chest. He kept his eyes straight ahead. The child caught the slack of her father's trouser leg and followed. Unlike the adults, she stared at Meyer while leaving, turning her head like an owl.

Nessman stepped into the doorway to separate the parties. "You all right, snake?" he asked.

"Yeah," said Meyer. "We'll just wait till they're on the lift, okay?"

Her eyes were aware of the compartment's normal lighting, but the lonely darkness squeezed tight on her mind.

Responses

Blohm stopped at the edge of a creek or elongated pond. The water seemed to be a sheet of black glass. Leaves and what looked like a berry floated on the surface. There was no discernible current.

Gabe picked up a pebble. "Don't," Blohm said, but the pebble was already in the air, flipped from the back of the sergeant's thumb.

It plopped into the water. Ripples spread evenly.

"What was wrong with that?" Gabrilovitch said in a wounded tone. He didn't object to his nominal subordinate being in charge whenever the two of them were alone on a mission, but he didn't like being treated like a half-witted child.

"Maybe nothing," Blohm said. "Look, just . . . I want to sit and look things over, Gabe. I don't want . . . if you touch something, make something happen . . . look, I want to understand this, do you see?"

Gabe didn't understand that there was anything *to* understand. The trees were dangerous—so far in over fifty different ways only a quarter mile into the forest. There were probably animals—otherwise how explain the berserk vegetation?—and they'd be dangerous too, though large predators weren't likely in the apparent absence of large prey animals. The sergeant didn't believe that there was anything to know, however; as

187

opposed to things to avoid, to destroy and to survive.

"There's something moving on the trunk of that tree across the creek," Gabrilovitch said. *"Mark."*

"I got it," Blohm said.

He'd seen the movement already. A creeper was unwinding from the smooth black bark of a tree ten feet in diameter above the buttress roots. As plants move the activity was blindingly fast, but it would still be minutes before the vine had completely straightened from its original helical grip on the tree.

At that point, Blohm guessed the upper end of the vine would come spearing down in his direction like a snake's head. Caius Blohm had no intention of being in the target area long enough for that to happen.

"Look, I got a bad feeling about it," Gabrilovitch said. "I don't think we ought to be standing around waiting for something to whack us. This place is bad news, snake."

"Gabe," Blohm said softly. Frustration at being interrupted was a raging red glow in his mind, but his voice was mild and colorless. "Why don't you get into your null sack for a bit. Leave the RF port open and you can watch everything through my helmet. You'll be as safe as if you were back on Stalleybrass."

"Shitfire, Blohm," the sergeant said. "I just thought you ought to know about that thing across the creek. Who the hell do you think you are?"

"Gabe . . ." Blohm said. "If you don't get into your sack and let me concentrate on this, I'll drop a stitch and the forest'll grease me sure. If that happens, you may as well eat your stinger right now, because I tell you, snake, you don't have a snowball's chance in hell of making it back to the clearing without me."

Blohm's visor was set on panorama with movements highlighted. Twenty yards back in the direction the scouts had come, the upper half of a tree with a coarse, scaly surface was rotating. The entire bole moved. It was visible only through a notch between the interlaced branches of two nearer trees.

"Yeah, sure, snake," Gabrilovitch said. He pulled the tube-shaped roll of his null sack from its pouch. "The place gets on my nerves, that's all."

Blohm shifted his position a step and a half to the left so that another treetrunk separated him from the one in motion. He had no idea what would have happened if he'd remained where he was; just that it would have been fatal.

Plants don't chase down prey. Neither do web spiders. But spiders grow fat on animals which move without thinking.

Gabe stepped into the mouth of his null sack, pulled the sides over his head, and lay down. There was a faint sigh as he operated the closures; then nothing. Absolutely nothing.

The sack's outer surface was the black of powdered carbon, not shadow. Shadow has color and shows the outline of the surface on which it lies. The null sack absorbed energy right across the spectrum from heat to microwave. The inner and outer surfaces were of identical material, but the layer between was a high-efficiency heat sink that expanded slightly as it stored energy.

Micropores in the sack passed oxygen molecules through to the interior. The slightly larger carbon dioxide molecules filtered through the inner surface but were trapped in the middle layer until flushed when the sack was serviced after use.

A man inside a null sack could breathe normally for a day and a half without changing the CO_2 balance of the air around him. He had no heat signature and active electro-optical sensors would not show his outline. The sack blurred but couldn't completely defeat sound ranging, but that was almost valueless in a breathable atmosphere to begin with.

The sacks could be operated in either completely buttoned-up mode, or with a one-way RF window that permitted a striker to receive data from an external source. That could be a spy cell clipped to a tree, for example; or in this case, the helmet of a striker who wasn't in a null sack himself.

Blohm sighed and let the soul of the forest sweep around him like slow green surf. Water reflected the canopy in near perfection. The ripples from Gabe's stone had died away, but here and there insects skated in dimples of surface tension.

The scouts had come this far without cutting or blowing the jungle out of their way. That was partly standard operating procedure—you didn't want to leave a trail for enemy patrols to track you by—but Blohm had carried it to an extreme his sergeant found unreasonable. He'd even insisted that they go around the curtain of moss tendrils hanging from a branch instead of shearing through with their knives.

There was a slap and patter in the foliage nearby. A broad leaf had suddenly everted, dumping a pint of water stored from the evening's rain. The dripping continued almost a minute, from one layer to another and finally to the soil.

None of the drops landed directly on the surface of the pond. It was a pond. It had no current at all. The ends were concealed in forest, the banks only six feet apart—not quite close enough for a burdened striker to leap.

But it had to be a pond; or a moat. A moat only inches deep, because Blohm could see the pebble bottom through the black water. There were no twigs or decaying leaves among the stones, and no animal life.

The broad, round plants floating on the surface looked like water lilies, but flat stems anchored them to the bank. A flying insect buzzed to the miniature pink flowers, then dipped to the pond. Its wings riffled the water as it drank through its proboscis before flying off.

Blohm chuckled softly. There were two ways to deal with this forest. Brute force would work if you had enough force. Perhaps two bulldozers and the firepower of C41 were enough.

The other method was to treat the contest as a chess game. Blohm wasn't sure he was going to win the game; but he might, he just might.

He walked to a tree five yards from the edge of the pond. Thorns as long as a man's hand lay flat in recesses along the trunk, almost invisible against the speckled bark. Blohm switched on his powerknife. He advanced the point cautiously and cut off a thorn at the base.

As the spike dropped away, a hydrostatic mechanism in the wood snapped viciously, rotating the base. Body heat would have released every spike within range to rip like tiger claws if the scouts had brushed the trunk as they passed.

Blohm's left hand was gloved. The garment was part of the body sock worn with a hard suit in extreme temperatures. He carried the thorn with that hand to the edge of the pond where he probed at the bottom, shifting pebbles. There was a stiff surface beneath; perhaps clay, perhaps some rubbery plant excretion.

"Okay, Gabe," Blohm said. "We've got to go around this pond. We'll try the right side. Watch out for the white-barked tree twenty feet on. It's got seeds that look like spears up where the fronds flare, and they weigh a couple pounds each."

Gabrilovitch slipped out of his null sack with itchy speed. "Why don't we just cross?" he asked, not arguing. "Afraid of getting your feet wet?"

"The top inch or two is water," Blohm said, holding up the thorn. The point was black and already shrivelling. "Underneath it's something else heavy enough that the water just floats on it. Concentrated sulfuric acid is my guess, but I don't suppose we need to know for sure."

Gabrilovitch stared at the black water. "God *damn*," he whispered.

"Come on, Gabe," Blohm said mildly. "That vine you saw across the pond's going to have us for breakfast if we stay much longer. You did a good job to notice it."

The rain had brought out fresh foliage on the young trees growing in place of the giants killed when the asteroid hit. The leaf flushes were of brilliant hues: reds, maroons, and poisonous, metallic greens which seemed to have nothing to do with life or growing things.

A civilian started to cry. He was a middle-aged man whose tight, youthful face had profited from cosmetic shaping and whose pudgy body had not. "They're going to kill us," he whimpered. "They hate us and they're going to kill us all."

Abbado cleared his throat. He'd been about to give the civilians a pep talk before the lead tractor moved past and took a bite out of the jungle, but he thought he ought to do something about the crying man first.

Glasebrook walked over to the fellow and hugged him one-armed against a torso lumpy with crossed bandoliers and a waist belt whose every slot held munitions. Four-pound rockets waggled like tassels, rattling against other gear.

"Don't you worry, Mr. Bledsoe," the Flea said. "We're not going to let them kill you. We're going to kill them first."

"Bedsoe," said the civilian. "My name is *Bed*soe." He straightened. "I'm so very sorry," he said with a dip of his head to Abbado.

Abbado cleared his throat again. "The dozer's going to cut us a twenty-foot trail through the woods there," he said in a deliberately cheerful voice to the watching civilians. "That sounds like a lot and it is, but I don't want anybody getting careless. God and his pretty blonde—"

He grinned and thumbed toward the mass of people with Manager al-Ibrahimi at the heart of it.

"—assistant say six feet is as close as you're to get to the sides of the cut. Does everybody hear me?"

There were nods and murmurs, mostly nods. The civilians looked scared, clutching their baggage or family members to them. They watched Abbado with wide eyes.

"Right," said Abbado. "Now, it's important that you stay closed up. Help your neighbors if they aren't keeping up. People are more important than any of the other shit we're carrying. If the column straggles, it'll take us twice as long to get out of these fucking trees and I tell you, people, I don't even a little bit like their company. Understood?"

This time at least a dozen civilians spoke in agreement. Ace Matushek said, "Too fucking right!" from the back of the assembly. He faced outward, bouncing a grenade on his palm, just in case the Spooks or the forest wanted to start something early.

"Now folks, listen," Abbado said. "There's over a hundred of you. I'll have two or three people in front, backing up the dozer, and there'll be two or three on each side of the column. Because we're at the front, that's better protection than most of the other folks are going to get; but it's pretty damn little even so."

He took off his helmet and looked at the outer surface of his visor because it was an excuse to avoid all those frightened, trusting eyes for a moment. He raised his eyes again.

"Folks," he concluded, "you got to be careful, you got to help each other as much as you can. My strikers and me, we'll do our best. But that's all I can promise. That we'll do our best."

The civilians gave a collective sigh. They seemed to be trying to stand straight.

Abbado smiled with wry affection. He eyed the regrown forest beyond the assembly. Some of the young trees looked like misshapen men carrying torches.

And Bedsoe was probably right. They *did* hate people.

The bulldozer squealed ahead ten feet, just enough to take the strain off the right track. The left track, turning at three times the speed of the other, broke up the thin soil and the harder substrate as it rotated the vehicle in the direction where it was to attack the forest.

Esther Meyer wore a hard suit with her visor locked down. She walked stiffly toward the bulldozer. The cab, a tightish fit for a driver in full armor, had heavy frames and an armored roof. Meyer's position was on the non-skid deck around the cab's sides and open rear.

"Hey Meyer," somebody called. She ignored the voice. The bulldozer was making enough noise that she could pretend not to hear a bomb going off if she wanted to.

Besides the weight of the hard suit, Meyer carried her stinger, a grenade launcher, and a dispenser pouch of hand-thrown grenades of both styles. All that was fine, but Top had insisted she have a flame gun as well. Meyer hated flame guns. She'd never used one except in training, seven years before.

The choice was carry the flame gun or give somebody else the station on the tailboard. Since the strikers on guard with the tractors were the only ones who'd be wearing armor, she'd agreed. The tank of pressurized fuel on her back still gave her the willies.

"Meyer, this is Top," the command channel snapped. *"I'm at the plasma cannon. Come here for a moment, I've got a job for you. Over."*

"Top, you gave me a job," Meyer protested. "I'm with the dozer, remember? Over."

"Meyer, first I want you to burn off the ammo, all right?" Daye said. She could see him waving from the log where the gun still rested. *"We can't afford the weight, but I don't want to leave the gun and ammo both. The Spooks may not be so tight for transport. Over."*

"Top, I'm coming," Meyer said wearily. "Out."

She raised her visor and clumped to the first sergeant, feeling like a rock trying to roll uphill. Her load was one thing if the tractor was carrying it, another when she had to.

It wasn't worth dumping the gear and then draping herself with it again, though. And she understood Top's idea—you didn't fire a plasma cannon except with a hard suit on. That meant her or Pressley on the other tractor, and she was closer.

"I thought what we'd do," Daye said when she reached him, "was save the lead dozer some work. I want you to blast a hole right through the trees on the vector we'll be taking out of here. Just keep shooting till all the ammo's gone, right? We'll kill two birds with one stone that way."

He looked pleased with himself. Well, he had a right to be. Meyer just wished it hadn't meant her hiking an extra fifty yards, kitted out like a whole weapons locker.

"Okay," she said. She dropped her visor again to get the vector, then checked it against the position of everything that she *didn't* want bathed in plasma.

Bolts dispersed to a degree in an atmosphere. If one hit a solid object, even something as slight as a finger-thick sapling, the stream flared widely. Meyer didn't want anybody, strikers or civilians, within fifty feet of her sight line.

The main body was behind the gun position, in the area the bulldozers had cleared west of the ship. The colonists' section leaders were sorting them out, trying to anyway. C41 stood on guard around the mass though occasionally a striker got involved helping or explaining something. They were all well clear of the plasma cannon.

Sergeant Abbado had his squad and the leading company of civilians on Meyer's left, well away from the main body. They were in an open area formed by the asteroid's shockwave, large enough for the number involved. Although they were a trifle forward of the cannon's muzzle, they were well to the side and protected by a wall of logs and brush.

"Five, this is Four-four-three," Meyer said formally, using call signs as if C41 was at full strength and she was loader on the fourth squad of heavy weapons platoon. "Request permission to fire. Over."

"C41, this is Five," Top said on the general push. *"The plasma cannon will burn off twenty-six rounds. Inform colonists that this is not an emergency. Over."*

Top had moved a safe twenty feet back from Meyer's position. He turned to watch strikers talking to the nearest civilians. When he decided that enough of them had gotten the word, he said, *"Four-four-three, you are clear to shoot. Over."*

Meyer squeezed the trigger. The butt was solid against her armored shoulder, so her whole body rocked back. The hundred feet directly in front of the muzzle was a blackened waste from the fires set during the Kalendru attack, but sprigs of new growth were already probing from it. They shriveled as the plasma flashed a dazzling track above them.

Brush and fallen trees were tangled on the edge of the unbroken forest. The bolt hit a giant tilted against a trio of its upright fellows. A fireball of gas and blazing wood engulfed the base of the dead tree. The trunk lifted on the shockwave and had just started to drop when the second round hit.

Meyer kept the trigger back. The weapon cycled at sixty rounds per minute, an artificially low rate to permit the osmium bore to cool between thermonuclear explosions. All that remained of the target was a pillar of flame gushing through the foliage of the trees with which its branches were twined.

The gun stopped firing when the belt ended. Thunderclaps from the burst continued to echo from the edges of the forest for a second or two more. Meyer opened the lid of the remaining cannister, then lifted the cannon's loading gate. The air around her fluoresced as ions snatched electrons to balance their charge.

She knew everybody in the landing zone was looking at her. The attention made her feel oddly more human. She locked the fresh belt into the gun and settled the butt against her shoulder again.

Though the leading bulldozer would now have the fire to contend with, the plasma bolts were a great morale booster for the cits. Green trees wouldn't burn with anything like the enthusiasm of wood drying for weeks or months, but the moisture in the living cells disintegrated the boles in flashes of steam. That should be at least as spectacular.

Meyer aimed a little right of center of the tree filling the left half of the bulldozer's initial course. She squeezed off a single bolt. The base exploded, lifting and shoving the rest of the trunk into the forest. The tree fell with a rippling crash that seemed remarkably sustained in contrast to the weapon's lightning-like *CRACK*.

She shifted her aim slightly. A squat tree with a trunk three feet thick grew near the smoldering roots of the monster Meyer's previous round had blown clear. The trunk spread at the top like a mushroom; branches sprouted above it, all of them coming from a common center like the fronds of a palm tree.

Let's see if I can punt this one completely out of sight to the right, Meyer thought as she squeezed the trigger.

The jet of plasma hit exactly where she wanted it, a little left of center of the tree's base, destroying it with fiery enthusiasm. The oddly-shaped bulge on top ruptured simultaneously.

An eight-inch spike of wood with enough intracellular silica to scratch porcelain whanged off Meyer's breastplate and flung her backward. Similar spikes drove through the log where the plasma cannon rested, knocked the gun itself away spinning butt over muzzle, and snatched the flame gun from its crossbelt.

Hundreds of people were screaming. Meyer rolled to her feet, gasping for breath. Her armor had saved her life, but the shock nonetheless punched all the air from her lungs.

She looked behind her. A spike had ripped apart the flame gun's tank and sprayed the fuel in a cloud across the landscape. Sergeant Daye was trying to run out of it. He'd almost made it to safety when the plasma cannon took a hop that thrust its white-hot muzzle into the atomized fuel.

The explosion was a *whoomp* rather than a sharper sound, but the blast hurled Meyer, armor and all, back over the log.

As she somersaulted, Meyer caught her last glimpse of Sergeant Daye: his helmet, at least, spinning a hundred feet in the air.

"There's a band of the same species all around the edge of the clearing," Tamara Lundie said. "I've reviewed recordings made by the helmets of the scouts

as they moved out of the area. They show none of
the species more than forty yards out."

"Doesn't surprise me," Farrell said. "And the tree
shoots back at the shooter only?"

He couldn't logically justify his confidence in
Lundie's ability to synthesize information from the
helmet sensors. Maybe he trusted her because he didn't
have any choice.

"That's correct," Lundie said, raising her voice to
be heard clearly. The wounded were either calm or
sedated, but children wailed in helpless terror in the
background. Some were now orphans. "The head is
armed in all directions, but it discharges only in the
direction from which the plant's integrity is breached."

"All right," Farrell said. "I'll send the pair in hard
suits ahead to blow the trees with grenades from the
back sides before the dozer starts." He shook his head
and added, "What a *bloody* damned planet."

The medics—the *doctors*—had the wounded
under control. The project manager was organizing
stretcher parties, which meant a number of the
civilians would have to leave their personal luggage
behind. Al-Ibrahimi didn't seem to be getting near
the argument he would have before the tree's
projectiles raked the crowd.

Eight dead, twenty-three wounded. Civilians, that
was. Sergeant Daye had gone the way most strikers
did, quick. Velasquez had a clean through-wound to
the right thigh. She claimed she was fit for duty,
marching included. As short-handed as Farrell was
he didn't intend to argue with her, but he'd make sure
Top put Velasquez on the rotation to ride the dozers.

Shit. He'd tell Kristal to put Velasquez on the
rotation.

He'd recalled the scouts when the tree ripped the column, figuring at this moment he needed their expertise more than he needed to know about the magnetic source deeper in the forest. He thought about warning them specifically about the shooting trees, then decided against it.

When Farrell figured out what had happened— initially he'd thought the cannon had exploded—he'd radioed a general warning that covered everyone on C41's net, the scouts included. Gabrilovitch stayed alert, and Blohm didn't miss any damned thing that might mean his neck. No point in breaking their concentration again at what might be a bad time.

There weren't any good times on Bezant.

"I said 'plant' and 'species' rather than tree, Major," Lundie said, "because it appears to be a very fast-growing fungus rather than a woody plant. The band of them sprang up after the asteroid impact."

Farrell looked at her. "Planted by somebody, is that what you mean?" he said. "Do you think the Spooks put them there for a minefield?"

Ordinary mines were of little use against strikers. The helmet sensors sniffed explosives at distances of up to a half mile depending on the breeze. Trees mixed with a million other trees, though . . .

"I don't believe the Kalendru had anything to do with the occurrence," Lundie said. "I can't speculate as to what other directing intelligence might be involved. This particular species fits the pattern of hostility shown by almost all the other life in the crater, do you not think?"

"Yeah, I guess," Farrell said. It wasn't an assessment that particularly pleased him to hear, but it seemed accurate enough. He shifted his left bandolier to prevent it from rubbing. "I'm going to organize the clearance team," he said.

He nodded toward the colonists constructing stretchers of fabric and plastic tubing from the building supplies. "They'll be ready to go in ten minutes or so."

"Major?" the aide said. Farrell turned back to face her. "You and your *strikers*," slight emphasis on a technical term, "reacted as if you'd planned on the explosion occurring. I was struck by your professionalism."

"We've been ambushed before, ma'am," Farrell said, trying not to smile. "There's an SOP for this sort of thing."

"I understand," Lundie said. "I would have expected a more emotional response nonetheless. Because of the casualties, if nothing else."

Look who's talking about emotions, Farrell thought. Aloud he said, "We've seen dead people before too." He cleared his throat and added, "Tamara."

The "ma'am" of a moment before had been an unintentional insult, the expert sneering at the layperson.

"We've got jobs to do," he said. "When things settle down, we'll, you know, think about Top. I'd known him three years, closer than any of my kin."

He smiled tightly, then went off to brief 3-3 and the strikers in hard suits for the clearing operation.

Farrell knew he'd be seeing Sergeant Daye again soon. Just as soon as he next went to sleep.

Brute Force

Esther Meyer wasn't sure she'd have noticed the tree if her helmet hadn't highlighted it. It was amazing. You wouldn't think something three feet thick and forty feet high could stay hidden when you were almost on top of it. If she'd been trying to watch everything instead of cueing her helmet to shooting trees specifically, the alert would have come from the sheaf of projectiles slashing at her and the column of civilians behind.

She skirted the trunk carefully. They weren't sure what it took to trigger the head. Maybe bumping the tree with an armored elbow would be enough. The spike that hit Meyer the first time hadn't penetrated, but that could have been luck and the extra fifty yards. She planned to get behind something big and lob a grenade to set this one off.

Pressley was somewhere off to Meyer's right, dealing with another tree. The major wanted a wide enough swath cleared of the damned things that if the second tractor had to divert in an emergency, the driver wouldn't set one of the bitches off. God's blonde aide had marked a total of six shooting trees on the helmet displays, though how she knew that was beyond Meyer's guessing.

The forest was huge and dark and as merciless as a

Kalendru tank. Meyer didn't like, she *really* didn't like, being out here twenty feet ahead of her backup, but she didn't dare say anything about it. Besides, it was her job. She didn't need a superior to tell her that.

Branches swung lazily in the canopy a hundred feet above Meyer's head. Patches of unfiltered sunlight flickered across lower foliage like diaphanous butterflies. Anywhere else, Meyer would have guessed the wind was blowing higher up, but not in *this* jungle.

In her hurry to avoid whatever was being prepared above, Meyer stepped into a thicket of thin, pale leaves growing directly from the soil. The individual strands were a yard long and no more than an inch and a half across. They wound among the trees in a thick line instead of springing from a common center like the terrestrial grasses. She'd brushed against similar stands before, but this was the first time she'd pushed her way through them.

The leaves wrapped around her armored thighs, exuding sticky fluid along the stems. She swore, stamped her bootheel twice and pulled with all her strength. The leaves clung like cargo tape.

Meyer was holding the electrical grenade she'd planned to use to trigger the shooting tree. She shouted, "Fire in the hole!" armed the grenade and hurled it into the forest ahead to clear her hands for her stinger. She had a sudden unreasoning fear that if she'd merely dropped the grenade at her feet, the vegetation would manage to throw the arming switch and blow her legs off.

The icons of strikers from 3-3 converged from behind on her visor overlay. "Stay clear!" Meyer shouted. They didn't have armor and she didn't want to be responsible for them.

She squeezed the stinger's trigger, guiding its fire along the ground like a plowshare. Pellets ripped the roots in a spray of mold and pebbles. The leaves' grip lessened. Meyer tore herself clear and fell backward. The grenade burst with a nearby *crack!* and a gulp of cell tissue minced by the shrapnel.

A fruit the size of a pumpkin sailed from the tip of a high branch across twenty feet of horizontal distance. It burst like a water balloon on the ground where Meyer had been held a moment before. Everything organic, even the rich layer of topsoil, smoldered as juice from the ruptured fruit splashed over it.

Meyer scrambled to her feet. "Get clear!" she snarled to the pair of strikers with powerknives and stingers ready to cut her loose. "Can't you fucking hear! Get clear!"

She pulled a fuel-air grenade from her belt and armed it. "Fire in the hole!" she repeated as she threw the grenade into the undergrowth

Meyer crouched. The shockwave rolled her over, but the hard suit protected her against injury from the non-fragmentation blast. A hundred square feet of vegetation, including another stand of grass, vanished in an orange fireball.

Meyer trotted into the middle of the patch she'd just cleared, arming an electrical grenade. She wasn't going to take any chance of the ground cover grabbing her this time.

Blohm eyed the six lumps on the obvious path. Each was mottled gray and about the size of a soccer ball. Except for their slightly elevated infrared signatures, they might have been stones. "I don't trust those," he said.

"I don't trust any damned thing in this jungle," Gabrilovitch said sourly. "We go around?"

Blohm scanned a two-hundred-seventy-degree panorama of forest. The scouts were returning by a route that never crossed, much less followed, their original track. It looked to Blohm that despite that precaution the landscape had them neatly blocked unless they wanted to pass the "stones."

The bushes to the right had sword-shaped leaves that you'd want to avoid on any planet. The emergent whose branches overhung the lesser trees to the left was laden with bulbous fruit which could be anything, but was certainly dangerous.

"Got your nose filters in place, Gabe?" Blohm said as he aimed his stinger. A treetrunk in the middle distance concealed all but his helmet and gun hand from the target.

"Roger," said Gabrilovitch, turning to face their backtrail.

Blohm fired a single pellet into the most distant of the lumps, thirty feet away. It was a toadstool. The casing ruptured in a geyser of spores.

"We'll let those settle—" he began.

A blue spark snapped at the base of the toadstool, detonating the spore cloud. The shockwave swept away the other lumps as sheets of pale dust.

"I guess that wouldn't have killed us if we'd been walking down the trail," Blohm said softly, "but it sure would have pushed us to one side or the other in no shape for quick thinking."

"I'd rather be in a tunnel on Case Lion," Gabrilovitch said. "I swear to God I would, snake. I'm a city boy."

"Come on, Gabe," Blohm said. "We'll be with the company in an hour and you can relax."

For his own part, Caius Blohm was as relaxed as he'd been since Active Cloak.

Brush and trees eight inches in diameter cascaded off the side of the land-clearing blade as the bulldozer advanced. The driver made a minute adjustment to center the point at the lower left corner of the blade— "stinger" to the operators, though the term made Abbado blink every time he heard it—on a monster five feet in diameter. There were larger trees in the forest, but this one was bigger than Abbado would have tangled with if he'd been driving the vehicle.

Because the tractor's transmission was a torque converter, the thrumming engine note remained constant though the chink of the treads slowed. Topsoil, clay, and finally crumbling laterite lifted from beneath the tracks as the bulldozer's mass tried to anchor it to attack the even greater mass of the tree.

"Take back your gold . . ." Horgen sang under her breath, *"for gold can never buy me . . ."*

Wood cracked like the fire of an automatic cannon. Pressley, riding the platform behind the cab, bobbed as the vehicle jerked and attempted to go forward.

"Horgen, shut the *fuck* up, will you?" Abbado said gloomily.

Horgen raised her left hand and nodded an apology.

The driver shifted to neutral, then reversed. The treads ground backward over the piles they'd dug. The double trench was six inches deep and layered, black over yellow over deep ochre that would harden to rusty brown in the air and sun.

The colonists were twenty feet behind, watching the big vehicle work. The strikers were doing pretty much the same thing, which was natural but'd get them all killed if something came from the side. "Three-three," Abbado ordered. "Watch your flanks and watch the canopy. That's where the trouble's going to come from, not from the tractor. Over."

The tree had a ropy, almost braided-looking, surface. The blade's stinger had started a vertical split which trailed ten or twelve feet up the trunk. As the driver maneuvered to hit the tree again at a slightly different angle, the crack lengthened. A parallel crack opened a few inches to the left and raced upward also.

"Give me the love, the love that you'd deny me . . ."

The lower end of the strip of bark lifted. For an instant Abbado thought the bulldozer had severed it. Several finger-like fibers waggled from the tip as it squirmed over the blade's grated upper portion and caressed the front of the cab.

"Hey!" Abbado shouted. "Pressley, watch—"

The end fibers tugged at the mesh protecting the cab window, then released and flowed over the top of the cab. More strips, *ropes*, of bark split away to either side of the first one.

Pressley aimed his flame gun. The jet of white-hot fuel caught the tip and spattered in brilliance over the front of the tractor. Another bark tendril snaked around the side of the cab toward Pressley. Abbado and Horgen ripped it with their stingers as they ran forward. Pellets that missed sparkled from the armored motor housing and the back of the blade.

There were scores of wobbling tendrils now. The tree's core was the silvery white of a rapier's blade in sunlight. Pressley jerked to the right. His flame gun slashed a line of radiance across the edge of the cab, momentarily splashing him and the armored driver.

Horgen shouted. The fibers at the tip of a tendril

gripped her waist, almost spanning it. She blasted the tentacle point-blank. Though the pellets shredded their target, the bark was a fibrous mat that retained its integrity.

Pressley lifted suddenly into the air. Civilians screamed and ran backward as the flame rod twitched toward them. A snap of the tentacle flung the weapon from the striker's hand and shut off the flame.

Abbado let his stinger go and drew his powerknife. The tendril that first gripped Horgen was a rag clinging without force, but a second had caught her left arm as she tried to insert a fresh magazine in the stinger.

Abbado clamped the squirming rope with one hand and pulled the powerknife across with all his strength. The bark had a dry, quivering feel to it like the body of a powerful snake. Fibers frayed to either side of Abbado's cut. It was like trying to shear steel cable.

Horgen's stinger cracked like a miniature bullwhip, forty times a second. Other strikers were firing. Abbado heard the *chunkWHACK*! of a grenade launcher.

Something grabbed his right ankle. He kicked. Another something caught the left calf. The tendrils lifted him, pulling in opposite directions.

"Shit!" shouted Sergeant Guilio Abbado. "Shit!"

A part of his mind wished that he'd come up with something better for what were probably his last words.

Like the mouth of a tunnel, Farrell thought as he walked with the project manager toward where the dozer was starting its cut. Colonists made way for them with a mixture of curiosity and concern. Not the hostility Farrell expected from civilians, though. That surprised him, especially after he'd screwed up and gotten so many of them dead or wounded.

The air was smoky with a touch of ozone sharpness, the latter from either the plasma bolts or the tractor's electric drive. The tree the gunner punted to the left with her first bolt smoldered, but only the shattered portions of the dense green wood could sustain combustion on their own. The dozer had grubbed out or crushed down what remained where the tree stood. Fresh clay clung to roots twisting from the wrack shoved aside by the broad blade.

Like snow melting in the sun, the shooting tree had shrunk to barely twenty percent of its original volume. Unfired spearheads now protruded through what remained of the head. The support fibers were less spongy than most of the plant's tissues. They stood out like the sinews of a man straining at too great a burden.

The dozer spiked a large tree and started to lug. Farrell eyed the wobbling canopy with concern, but his helmet AI didn't warn him of anything about to drop on the vehicle. Besides the armored striker behind the cab, Sergeant Abbado and one of his people followed the dozer closely. The other five squad members flanked the civilians, a little back of Farrell himself.

"Clearing the road is going to be a slow process," al-Ibrahimi said as he watched the dozer struggling against the forest giant. "Though most of the larger trees can be avoided, I hope."

"Slow is a good thing," Farrell said, though his attention was concentrated on the forest. "The civilians aren't going to be able to move fast, and we don't dare let the dozers get too far out ahead. We can't afford to lose—"

A tentacle of bark detached itself from the bole and

trembled across the tractor. White wood gleamed for a hundred and fifty feet up the side of the tree.

The driver was either too busy with his controls to notice or saw so little through his grilled windows that he didn't realize anything more was happening than a piece of debris flying up. He shifted from reverse to neutral, preparing to hit the tree again.

"Get those civilians back before they're fucking killed!" Farrell said, aiming at the tentacles. He wasn't sure himself if he was speaking to his strikers or to al-Ibrahimi, but it was God's truth that he wanted the manager out of the way also.

He fired at the target quivering twenty feet in the air. Things were bad enough without a stray round hitting one of his strikers.

Two more, twelve more, tentacles separated as the first one had. The entire bark sheath squirmed toward the bulldozer. Pressley's flame gun carbonized the end of a tentacle. The portion above the flame's destruction could no longer reach the dozer, but the brown serpent continued to twist and strain like a vicious dog on its chain.

The driver realized his danger and shifted into reverse. Tendrils gripped the blade and clogged the drive gears. The tree swayed like a fishpole bound to its catch by a score of cable-thick lines.

Pressley's armored body flew in a parabola that ended when he slammed the trunk of another tree, fifty feet in the air. The tentacle released him. The striker fell, tumbling like a mannequin. The hard suit was undamaged, but the body within had been crushed despite the padding.

Farrell unhooked a 4-pound rocket and armed it by twisting open the launch tube. He checked behind him, turning his head rather than trusting the panorama display. Civilians were still too close though they surged backward under the lash of fear. Manager al-Ibrahimi shouted orders in a voice like dry thunder.

Farrell stepped to the side so that the backblast would singe forest, not the colonists his life was pledged to protect. Something nuzzled his left leg. He ignored the touch and squeezed the bar trigger.

The rocket snarled away, the motor a white glare in the half second before burnout. The last of the exhaust gases batted Farrell like a huge, hot cotton swab. Thrust against the sides of the tube rocked him back a step. The tentacle closed around Farrell's ankle, two ropy tendrils to either side of his boot.

Farrell's rocket hit the central pole of the tree a hundred feet in the air and blew it to toothpicks in a thunderclap. The peak and all the bark tentacles tumbled down like the head of Medusa.

The grip on Farrell's ankle tightened, then relaxed. He'd been straining against the tree's pull and fell backward when the tension released.

Flaccid tentacles slid from the bulldozer's cab and blade. The vehicle began moving. Other ropes still clogged the tracks and drive gears, but vegetable fibers flattened beneath density-enhanced metal.

The tracks accelerated slowly. The driver struggled with the lifeless tentacles choking his cab, oblivious of the fact that he was clanking backward toward the mob of civilians.

Farrell staggered to his feet. Sergeant Abbado was already trotting alongside the cab with Horgen. Abbado gave her a lift onto the platform. Brown fragments of a tentacle still dangled from Horgen's waist. Whatever she said to the driver was sufficient, because the bulldozer immediately shuddered to a stop.

Farrell looked around. The colonists had halted a hundred feet back. Strikers from the lead squad were in position nearby, reloading weapons. Some of them had raised their visors. They looked shaken. Farrell damned well *felt* shaken.

His visor overlay showed that C41 had held position pretty well, though there'd been a little easing forward. Fighting drew the strikers even though they knew there was more risk of an attack from the sides or rear than there was of the tree pulling up its roots and charging down the column.

Not that Farrell was ready to count that possibility out completely.

One of the bark tentacles slowly uncoiled on the ground. That was gravity, not malevolence. The tree was dead, waiting to be uprooted and flung to the side as soon as the bulldozer got moving again.

"C41, all clear," Farrell ordered. "We'll hold five minutes to get reorganized. Tell your civilians. They're not on the net, so they won't know what's happening. Over."

Manager al-Ibrahimi walked toward him. His aide came from where she'd been in the center of the column, her concern for al-Ibrahimi obvious even though her face was without expression.

Farrell rubbed his right wrist where the backblast had seared him. The manager would probably have to replace the bulldozer's driver until the original staffer had a chance to settle down.

Farrell needed to pick another striker to ride the deck.

He'd been thinking of the march in terms of miles and days. Now he started wondering how long it would be before he ran out of strikers.

Local Visitors

The air was hot and still and humid, but at least the trees towering to either side of the cut shaded the column from direct sun. Abbado noticed Dr. Ciler nearby, helping a woman with a cane. She was tramping along determinedly instead of riding on top of a trailer.

"Hey Doc?" he called. "How long do you think it's going to be before the leaves all go transparent so the sun can shine on us full strength?"

The old woman turned in horror. "Oh, dear heaven," she said. "Is that going to happen next?"

"The sergeant was joking, Mrs. Trescher," Ciler said. "Certainly I would applaud if I thought I'd have nothing worse to treat than sunburns, though."

A stinger fired from the front of the column, just a short burst. When a squad from First Platoon took the lead after four hours, 3-3 and the civilians they guarded let the front half of the column move past them. It didn't seem to Abbado that any location was more dangerous than another, but a lot of people were going to be convinced that wherever they were was the hot seat. God or the major kept the level of bitching down by rotating the order of march.

It had taken the new team about an hour to stop blasting the hell out of anything that looked weird. This whole fucking jungle looked weird. You had to

214

learn to use stingers sparingly, a few pellets here and there to recon by fire. Otherwise you were likely to have half the squad reloading when the shit really hit the fan.

Abbado was responsible for over two hundred colonists in this position. The major'd given his squad leaders the choice of how they deployed their strikers. Abbado split his in pairs at intervals among the civilians. He didn't trust a lone striker when these damned trees were likely to come at you from both sides at once.

Abbado was alone at the head of the section, but what the fuck. That was the sort of decision you made when you let them give you the promotion.

There were still stretches of thirty or forty yards between pairs. The way the trail zigzagged meant sometimes civilians were out of sight of the nearest guards. You couldn't expect people hauling stretchers and too much of the wrong kind of luggage to stay in parade-ground formation. Abbado hadn't thought much about civilians since he enlisted, and what he did think hadn't been very positive. These folks were okay, the most of them.

Mrs. Florescu, the woman wearing Caldwell's extra boots, took the old lady's arm from Dr. Ciler. Florescu was carrying a soft bag in her left hand, dragging the bottom along the bulldozed ground. Abbado wouldn't have bet that either the bag or the woman would last out the day, but he'd sure give her credit for trying.

Meyer sat a little to one side of the track, taking off her hard suit. She looked drawn. Since she was already suited up, she'd moved to the lead dozer when Pressley bought the farm. Meyer kept the slot after 3-3 rotated back in the line. Abbado figured the vibration as the dozer chewed its way forward would have wrung him out in a lot less than four hours.

"Hey, Essie," he said. "Get tired of the scenery up front?"

The sound of a tree falling started and went on for a long time, too loud for conversation in a reasonable tone of voice even this far back in the column. Abbado motioned to the civilians nearest to him. "Take five," he shouted. They were getting too close to the staggering tail of the previous section. Mixing the groups was a worse danger than stringing the whole line out a trifle longer.

Meyer sucked water from her canteen. She shook her head. "The major took me off," she said. "I'm lazy. I'd ride the whole way if he'd let me."

The utter exhaustion in her eyes belied her words. There was no doubt in Abbado's mind that whoever was guarding the lead tractor was an even-money bet to be the next casualty.

After the initial disaster, the dozer hadn't run into anything that posed a danger to the vehicle itself. A stand of jointed, thirty-foot high reeds had bent suddenly from either side of the blade cut and lifted Meyer off the platform not long after she took over the job, though. Glasebrook's flame gun and the stingers of the rest of 3-3 had scythed the gripping reeds down before they proceeded to whatever was next on their agenda.

It had been real close. Meyer's hard suit was scarred by pellets Abbado had fired directly at her because there wasn't any choice.

The major put the scouts out in front when they rejoined. The route had been a lot less straight since then, but there hadn't been any more real problems.

The last civilians had meandered out of sight. Meyer

released the catches of her back and breast, then started working on the leg armor. White-cored speckles with black rims marked where flame had spattered her right thigh piece.

"Well, hang in, snake," Abbado said. He saw the purple dot that marked the major moving rearward in the overlay miniaturized on the upper left corner of his visor. He'd already walked the length of the column, checking on how things were going. He seemed to be making another round. One tough mother, Six was.

Abbado turned and called to his weary civilians, "Mount up, people. We want to get to the barracks before the others use up all the hot water in the showers, right?"

Carrying seventy pounds of weapons and munitions, Sergeant Guilio Abbado started forward. He glanced back to make sure the colonists were following him. They were, many of them doing what they could to help others.

They were a damned good group of people, they were. He was proud of them.

Blohm focused on a tree twenty feet in diameter and said, *"Mark!"* The trunk was as smooth as a lamppost to the peak a hundred and fifty feet in the air. From there branches flared like the leaves of a root vegetable.

Instead of shading out lesser vegetation, the emergent's foliage was almost hidden above the main canopy. Only infrared and the AI's processing capability enabled Blohm to trace the limbs' course over the surrounding jungle.

"What's the problem with it, snake?" Sergeant

Gabrilovitch asked. The scouts stood within arm's length of one another, but Gabe's visor echoed his partner's display. The sergeant didn't see anything exceptional about the tree except its size, and even that wasn't unique.

"The branches are hollow," Blohm explained. "See how thick they are? The AI says they couldn't be that thick if they were solid."

Gabe's expression didn't change as his eyes calculated that the two of them were well within the branches' seventy-five foot radius. The only reason he could imagine for the limbs to be hollow was that something poured out of them like beer from a spigot.

More likely, like fire from a flame gun.

"It's not meant for us," Blohm said quietly. "We're moving with the forest, not against it. But before the bulldozer gets close, somebody better cut the top off."

"Us?" Gabrilovitch asked. He carried a pair of 4-pound rockets taped to his thigh so that they didn't dangle.

Blohm shook his head. "That's not what we do, snake," he said. "That's for the other guys. I marked it for them."

"I—" Gabrilovitch said.

Blohm, suddenly tense, hushed him with a quick gesture. The environment had changed, subtly but suddenly. It felt like it'd begun to rain, though the drops wouldn't penetrate the leaves of the canopy for minutes more.

Blohm didn't know what was really happening. The only change you could expect from this forest was a change for the worse, though.

"Six," he said to key his transmission to the major,

"this is Six-six-two. There's something going on. I don't
know what it is, but keep your head up. Over."

Sergeant Gabrilovitch eyed the forest beyond and
behind his partner. Gabe's mouth pursed stiffly, but
you had to know him well to recognize that as a sign
of tension.

"Six-six-two, this is Six," Major Farrell's voice replied.
*"Do you have a vector, Blohm? There's nothing showing
up on the helmet sensors, yours included. Over."*

"Six, negative," said Blohm. "It's—sir, like the sun
came up or the wind started to blow. It's just a feeling.
Maybe nothing. Over."

The branches of a nearby sapling were drawing
noticeably closer to the trunk. Blohm didn't know what
that meant, but he wanted to be some distance away
within the next minute or so.

*"Six-six-two, yeah, maybe there's nothing to it, and
maybe I'm going to be elected to the Grand Council
of the Unity,"* the major said. *"Break. Six-six-one—"*
Gabrilovitch, the titular patrol commander *"—come
on in. It's getting late enough that we'll camp before
we've gotten any farther than you are now. And if
something pops, I want all the help I can get back here.
Six out."*

"Six, roger," Gabrilovitch said. Blohm was already
indicating the start of their route to join the column.

Still seated, Esther Meyer detached the stinger's
take-up spool from the stud on her breastplate and
reattached it to her right shoulder where it was ready
for use. She'd left most of the extra weapons and gear
on the cab platform for Velasquez who took over for
her.

She paused. The next part of the program was to

walk forward, carrying the pieces of armor to the trailers by now well ahead in the column. Every moment she sat here the walk got longer and the job harder. *Christ*, she was wrung out.

"Hey, Essie," said Tomaczek as he trudged past. They'd trained together as recruits. Years later they both wound up in C41. Despite that they'd never had a lot to do with one another. "You all right?"

"Yeah, I just need to get moving," she said. She thought of asking Tomaczek to give her a hand with the gear, but he was already bent beneath enough weaponry to anchor a ship. Typical little-guy stuff . . . But who was Striker Esther Meyer to talk?

Tomaczek wasn't really interested in anything but putting one foot in front of the other. He vanished behind a screen of brush where the trail kinked just beyond where Meyer rested. Meyer hoped he'd notice if his helmet flashed a warning caret.

There hadn't been much trouble back of the lead squad thus far. Every once in a while motion in the canopy would draw a grenade or rocket. A pair of teenagers had slipped off the trail together. The strikers responding to the screams thirty seconds later found broad leaves unfolding from bodies already black and swollen. No problems other than that.

Meyer stared in the direction of the passing colonists without seeing them as she prepared to stand up. She suddenly realized that she was glaring toward (if not at) Councillor Matthew Lock, his wife and daughter.

Meyer and the adult Locks looked away in mutual embarrassment. She heard the little girl squeal, "Mommie! Mommie! It's the nasty lady!"

Fucking wonderful. At least the kid thought she was

human, which is more credit than Meyer was ready to give herself.

Meyer put the leg pieces, the last bits of her hard suit, in the net bag. She stood, swaying slightly. Now she was going to have to pass the Locks again. If she'd just gotten her ass in gear when she should, she might never have had to see them again.

Ahead: screams, a stinger firing, and a *whock-whock-whock* that could have been several people chopping wood simultaneously.

Screams like large animals being disemboweled, probably an accurate description of what was going on.

Meyer dropped the bag and ran forward. "Get back!" she screamed to civilians who'd frozen on the trail. She rounded the corner.

The natives were humanoid and man-sized, brown-beige-green in color. Their skin had the waxy gloss of a healthy leaf. Tomaczek had killed at least one. His stinger ripped another standing over a civilian with a bloody club. The native lurched backward, spraying white ichor from the chest wounds.

Two more hacked Tomaczek from opposite sides. A third squirted the striker with thick liquid from a tube projecting above its forehead. Tomaczek's battle dress turned black where the fluid touched. He tried to aim his stinger but the pellets merely cratered the ground he fell on.

Meyer killed the pair continuing to chop at Tomaczek. There was blood, human blood, spattering everything. The barbed clubs slung it in all directions.

She jerked a civilian backward by the collar. The native striking down at the civilian hit the top of Meyer's helmet instead.

Meyer's knees buckled. Her vision reduced to black and white for an instant. She didn't have time to wonder if the problem was in the visor's electronics or her own optic nerves. Her stinger was almost in contact with the native as she fired, scooping his chest out like a shucked oyster.

Natives converged on her, still slashing at any unarmed civilians within reach. She shot one in the upper chest. He spun and went down, hacking at the body of a decapitated woman.

Short bursts because there wasn't going to be time to reload. She was alone.

Meyer squeezed off a head shot but let the stinger rise on recoil so that the pellets also shattered the raised right club arm. He was holding Matthew Lock by the hair with the other hand. The native's smooth skin *broke* instead of puckering like a human's. The native weapons looked like plastic extrusions.

The native with the tube on his head sprayed Meyer in the face. The visor saved her eyes, but the brown sludge was opaque on the outer surface. Her hands burned. She fired in the direction of the natives she'd seen coming for her when she shot the one with Lock instead.

A pair of clubs hit her helmet like trip hammers. She tried to squeeze the stinger's trigger but she had no feeling in her hands.

She felt the shock between her shoulder blades. There was no pain, only a flash of light that expanded into burning darkness.

"Medic!" Farrell shouted as he came around the angle in the trail. The colony's doctors weren't on the commo net but maybe a striker would relay the message.

The native's face was slimly oval. Its coloration would have been attractive on the outside of a house in a wooded setting. The black-throated tube projecting above the forehead looked like a cyclops' eye in the instant before Farrell's stinger blew the skull to white mush.

Farrell stepped aside or the civilian running in a crouch would have collided with him. Farrell body-checked the native chasing the civilian and groped left-handed to hold the club arm. His stinger snarled a hundred pellets across and into the pair twenty feet distant hammering a fallen striker.

The native was stronger and heavier than its size suggested. The forest-toned body must not carry any significant amount of fat. Farrell's fingers slipped on the slick skin. The club struck awkwardly at his back, gouging stinger magazines in the crossed bandoliers. Farrell put his weapon against the native's neck and decapitated him with a short burst.

The body spasmed. Farrell flung it away and killed two natives still standing. Nessman came up the trail from the other direction and knocked the last one down with the butt of his stinger. He put half a magazine into the creature as it tried to rise. Nessman hadn't fired immediately because the native was slashing in the midst of a group of civilians trying to shield their offspring.

"Med—" Farrell said.

Dr. Ciler ran past and knelt. Dr. Weisshampl, eighty if she was a day, arrived literally in the arms of a pair of younger women. Four 2nd Platoon strikers were with her. Glasebrook, Methie, and a moment later Sergeant Abbado appeared behind Farrell. They turned to cover the jungle in all directions.

"Horgen's got our cits bundled together up the trail, sir," Abbado muttered without keying his helmet.

"C41," Farrell ordered. "Hold in place. Ten—*twelve* humanoids attacked section five with swords and acid sprays. The initial attackers have been eliminated. Echo my display but *don't* fucking interrupt unless there's an attack. Six out."

Farrell had left Tamara Lundie with the second tractor, fifty yards up the trail. The aide joined him, breathing hard. Her eyes had the open horror of a victim saved from drowning.

"How did it happen?" she asked in a husky whisper.

"Are the rest of the medics—the doctors—are they alerted?" Farrell said. He wasn't going to release his strikers to carry out first aid until he was damned sure there wasn't going to be a follow-up attack.

"Yes, they're coming," Lundie said. "Jafar has halted the column awaiting your instructions."

There were two strikers down. Tomaczek was dead. From helmet readouts the other, Meyer, was only stunned, bruised and burned. An edged club had hacked through a bandolier in the middle of her back. Farrell began to regret leaving the body armor behind except for a handful of suits for special purposes. But weight considerations meant it was armor or ammo, and they *had* to have the ammo . . .

Nessman was putting analgesic and counterirritant onto the backs of Meyer's hands where the native had squirted her. Farrell squatted to look at the first native he'd shot. Most of the face was missing, but Farrell could see that the acid spray was a hollow channel in the skull rather than being a manufactured weapon like the barbed clubs.

"They came out of the trees," Farrell said; still

squatting, finally answering the aide's initial question. His hands trembled as he swapped his stinger's magazine for a full one. "They didn't make a fucking sound. Jesus, how many did we lose?"

Now that Farrell had the leisure, he heard the screams of the wounded and terrified. A four-year-old gripped her mother's hand and cried her heart out. The woman's body lay some distance away. The arm the child held had been hacked off at the shoulder, and the child had never released it.

The other two doctors and a man who'd risen to Director of Nursing but hadn't forgotten the basics reached the twenty-yard stretch where the slaughter occurred. There were speckles of blood everywhere.

Farrell fingered the weapon of the native with whom he'd grappled. The edge was more like that of a saw than a sword, but the scores of individual points were as sharp as broken glass. The material had a massy, slick feel. Flakes had spalled away in a few places, leaving conchoidal fractures in the surface.

"Seven adults and one child are dead," Lundie said with a precision Farrell supposed he should have been expecting. "Twelve adults and four children have been injured. I'm not an expert, but it appears to me that three adults and a child may not survive given the present conditions."

She swallowed and added, "I include your strikers in the two categories."

Farrell rose and looked at her. "Why didn't you pick them up?" he asked. "Was there something wrong with the sensors?"

"There was nothing wrong with the helmet sensors," the aide replied evenly. At this moment her eyes had no more depth than a reflection of the gray sky. "I've reanalyzed the data. There were no sound and vibration anomalies. The humanoids' movements were entirely within the normal parameters of the forest."

Farrell unhooked the damaged bandolier and removed the magazine that had taken the club stroke. Three teeth had penetrated the dense plastic; pellets dribbled out onto the bulldozed soil. "I don't understand," he said.

"Any forest moves," Lundie said. She was looking at the sprawled bodies, not in fascination but with the rock-jawed rigidity of someone forcing a memory on herself. "Everything living moves. The ground trembles when branches sway and even when roots take up water from the soil. Your sensors can feel that, Major."

Farrell grimaced. It was a joke in the Strike Force that you could hear a gnat fart if you cranked up your helmet high enough. Lundie really meant it, though. More to the point, she meant that she could discriminate among microsounds despite the hugely-greater background of human feet, voices, and equipment.

"Why *didn't* you hear them, then?" he said. There'd been one blessing. The dozer blade raised a four- to eight-foot row of brush and scraped topsoil on the left, the side opposite the direction of the attack. None of the civilians had time to climb off the cleared path. That would have been as quick a death as the natives' weapons.

"Because their movements were within parameters," Lundie repeated. "Major, at any possible level of detail, those humanoids didn't come through the forest. They *were* the forest."

Meyer sat up, flexing her arms to make sure no ribs

had been broken. Her partner Nessman watched anxiously. Councillor Lock knelt nearby. Blood splashed his head and torso, but none of it seemed to be his. Lock cradled a child's head in his lap. The body lay behind him, under that of its mother.

"In the future," Lundie said, "I'll use carbon dioxide levels. The humanoids are animate. They give off CO_2 as a waste product. The range isn't as long as vibration sensing should have been, but I'll be able to provide some warning. They won't surprise us the same way again."

Major Arthur Farrell scanned at the jungle. If there were a button he could push to turn this whole crater into a glassy desert, he'd do it in an eyeblink.

Night Sounds

"Mr. Blohm?" Seraphina Suares, leading a train of children, said to Sergeant Gabrilovitch.

"That's him," Gabe said, nodding across the mini-lantern's circle of light. "What is it you need, ma'am?"

Blohm rolled down the sleeve of his tunic without speaking. There was a line of tiny ulcers across the inside of his elbow, but they'd been shrinking in the past hour. His immune booster was handling the microorganisms.

Blohm's body temperature had been elevated by about half a degree ever since 10-1442's hatches opened. His augmented system was fighting off local diseases. The slight fever didn't seem to affect his judgment dangerously. He hoped the same was true for everybody in the expedition, but that wasn't something he could do much about.

The woman met Blohm's eyes. She was too old for any of the six children to be her own. The eldest was probably ten, the youngest no more than two and carried in her arms. She smiled. "Sergeant Kristal said that Mr. Blohm would be responsible for feeding me and the children. She directed us here."

"Oh," Blohm said. He'd removed his equipment belt, but the converter was still in its pouch. "Okay, that was the deal. I . . . What is it you want to eat? Not that you're going to tell much difference."

"I think it's best that we try whatever you planned for yourself," the woman said. "Sit down, children, and be sure to stay on the plastic. Mirica, dear? Won't you sit down?"

A four-year-old with bangs and short dark hair remained standing. Her eyes had the thousand-yard stare that Blohm had seen often enough before—on redlined veterans. None of the kids looked *right*.

Gabrilovitch looked over the gathering and rose. "Guess you've got it under control, snake," he said. "I'll see you after my guard shift."

Blohm drew on his left-hand glove as he walked to the brush piled at the edge of the clearing the bulldozers had cut for the night. The ground was covered with quarter-inch roofing plastic. It was temperature-stable—bonfires burned in several parts of the camp—and too tough for anything to penetrate overnight, though there was still a danger of shoots or roots coming up between the edges of sheets.

God or the colonist brain trust said that the forest wouldn't be as active after the sun set. Blohm was willing to believe that; but he didn't expect to sleep very soundly the first night, even during the hours he didn't have guard.

"I wasn't expecting, ah, kids," Blohm said. He worked loose a four-foot length of root and sawed it off with his knife. Any organic would work so long as it fit the mouth of the converter. He wasn't sure how much he'd need, but this was a start.

"We're the widow and orphans brigade," the woman said. Her voice was too even for the soul behind it to be calm. "I'm Seraphina Suares. I said I'd look after children who'd been, who'd, you know. I lost my husband when the aircar crashed."

"Ah," Blohm said. He extended the converter's doubly-telescoping base and opened the top flap, focusing on the task with needless concentration. He didn't know why he felt embarrassed. Hell, he'd been an orphan himself; raised by the state in Montreal District.

Mrs. Suares checked the feet of one of the younger boys for blisters. The ten-year-old was changing the infant's diaper. Several of the kids were bandaged though the silent one, Mirica, didn't seem to have received any physical injury. She was about the age of the Spook he'd killed in the doorway at Active Cloak.

Blohm stuck one end of the root into the converter; the box began to hum. He steadied the root with his gloved hand, feeling a faint vibration. Converters dissociated organic material at the molecular level, not by grinding or other mechanical means, but it was as fast a process as combustion.

"I've got it set for chicken and rice," Blohm said. "That seems to do as well as anything. Do you have something to put this in, ah, ma'am?"

"Children, take out your cups and spoons," Mrs. Suares said. "And Mr. Blohm, please call me Seraphina if you can. Is your nickname Snake?"

The children were taking a variety of containers from their little packs. A six-year-old raised an ornate metal mug that had set somebody back in the order of a year's pay for a striker. The mug and the clothes on the kid's back were the only things remaining of his family.

"Hold it here," Blohm said, drawing a cup down to the output spigot. A gush of thick gruel spurted until the child drew back. "Next one, step up. It's not that bad and it's got all the vitamins and whatever."

The bad light was actually an advantage. The flavor of food from the converter could be varied somewhat, but the color was always gray. In daylight, you had to remind yourself you weren't eating wet cement.

Another kid stuck her cup under the spigot. Others were staring at the first one as he dug his spoon doubtfully into the glop. Mirica was as still as a stump, but at least she'd taken out an eared mug in the shape of a grinning face.

"Ah, snake's not a nickname, ma'am," Blohm said. "Not exactly."

It's what veterans call each other instead of miss and mister, which we're not . . .

Rather than say that aloud, Blohm muttered, "My name's Caius, ma'am. I guess it doesn't matter a hoot what you want to call me."

"Caius, then," Mrs. Suares said with satisfaction. Blohm didn't remember anybody calling him by his given name before.

They got through five of the kids without a problem. Two ate with something like enthusiasm, which said more for their appetite than the meal. Mrs. Suares was feeding the two-year-old from her own bowl.

Mirica took the filled cup and even tasted a spoonful. After a moment she cradled her head in her arms and began to sob. The mug slipped from her hand and oozed its contents onto the ground.

"Oh, sweetheart, darling," Mrs. Suares said with sad concern. "Please, darling, you've got to eat. We all have to keep our strength up so that we aren't a burden on people like Caius here. Please, Mirica. Please sweetheart?"

Blohm detached his mess can from the bottom of the converter. "I know how she feels," he said to Mrs.

Suares. "They had a hell of a time getting me to eat at the creche when I was a kid too."

He didn't think about the creche much, but it wasn't that he'd had a bad time there. It was a lot like the army. Not great but mostly okay; and anyway you better get used to it because that was what life was going to be until you died.

"Are you all right, Caius?" Mrs. Suares said.

"Sorry," Blohm muttered. He must have been staring at her or some damned thing. "Sorry.

"But you know, thinking back . . . Hey," he said. "Mirica? Do you like tapioca pudding? That was the only thing they could get me to eat."

Blohm carried the converter over to the berm and dumped its contents onto the wrack from which it had come. Kneeling in the lanternlight, he reset the output and fed an additional length of root into the system. "I never thought of doing this myself, you know? Shit, it must be fifteen years since I had tapioca pudding."

The converter's holding tank had a non-stick surface that wouldn't even raise a meniscus if filled with water. The kid's mug would have to be washed to get the "chicken and rice" out of it, so Blohm ran the new batch into his own can.

They all watched him as he put his finger into the can and tasted it. Even Mirica turned her head, though she didn't lift it from her arms. "Goddam," Blohm said in surprise. "It tastes like tapioca pudding."

He looked at Mrs. Suares. "Ma'am," he said, "this is the first fucking thing I've had through this bitch that tastes like it ought to. It's *good*. Here kid, you try it."

Mirica stuck her finger out. Mrs. Suares started to say something but caught herself.

Staring solemnly at Blohm, the child licked the goo off her finger, then straightened into a sitting position. He and she each took another fingerful of the sticky mass.

Blohm shook his head. "Fuck if I know why I never thought of doing this before, ma'am," he said. He suddenly realized he wasn't speaking to another striker. "Oh, Christ," he muttered. "Ma'am, I'm sorry about my language. With the kids and all."

"You have nothing at all to be sorry for, Caius," Mrs. Suares said with a smile warmer than the still night air. "And it's Seraphina, please."

Esther Meyer heard somebody talking in a low voice to the doctor who'd just checked her over, but she didn't open her eyes. Kristal had told her she was off the guard rotation tonight. Meyer didn't think she was hurt that bad, but she wasn't going to argue with the decision.

She was okay. She just felt like she'd been dragged all day behind the tractor instead of riding on it. She was face down, her cheek against the cool plastic. Her back hurt like hell whichever way she lay, though the doc said nothing was broken. He'd injected an enzyme to reabsorb the swelling by morning.

The plastic sheeting was fairly stiff, but it creaked and rippled when someone walked on it. Meyer felt somebody stop and kneel on the other side of her. "Yeah?" she muttered. Best guess was she was about to learn she was on guard after all.

"Striker Meyer?" said an unfamiliar voice. "I'm Councillor Matthew Lock. I came to apologize."

Meyer tried to turn over. She gasped and swore with pain. Relaxing, she took a deep breath.

"Striker Meyer?" the voice repeated in concern. "Please don't—"

"Can it!" Meyer wheezed. "Just give me a sec—"

She lurched into a sitting position. Her muscles relaxed into patterns that didn't stress bruised and knotted tissue. The relative lack of pain was sudden pleasure.

Meyer smiled into the citizen's worried face. "It's just getting from one posture to the other that's a problem," she said, wiping her brow absently. "They couldn't give me the stuff they would've done in a base hospital because then somebody'd have to carry me, right?"

Lock swallowed and nodded. He looked like he'd lost ten pounds since she'd seen him in the ship. After that—all Meyer remembered was a flash of Lock's face as the native convulsed away. It'd been as much luck as Meyer's skill that she hadn't blown the cit's head off with the same burst, but there hadn't been a lot of time.

"Striker Meyer," Lock said formally. Fire lit half his face; the other side was sketched by the fainter, even glow of an electric lamp. "I've already withdrawn my complaint to the project manager about your conduct. I want to apologize to you personally as well."

He cleared his throat. "I told Manager al-Ibrahimi that I'd first acted like a fool in the ship, then compounded my error by complaining like a fool to him. He assures me that no disciplinary action had been contemplated in any case."

Lock gave her a wry smile. "So you don't have to worry about fools running the expedition, just fools among the civilians you guard."

"That's okay," Meyer said. She tried to shift her

weight sideways. Staying in the same position gradually hurt worse than moving to a new one. The choice of when to move was a bitch, though. She grimaced. "I'm sorry it happened. I screwed up."

Meyer thought of saying it was the compartment that got to her rather than the woman and the screaming kid, but that didn't matter now. It hadn't much mattered before either. You either fuck up or you do your job. She'd fucked up.

"I didn't understand how quick you had to be to survive," Lock said softly. He turned his face from Meyer. His eyes were on the forest, but she wasn't sure they were focusing.

"When the savages came out of the trees I just looked at them," Lock said to the forest. "And one of them grabbed Alison. And I said, I *said*, 'What are you doing?' and he cut her head off. Like that. And he grabbed me and you killed him."

The civilian stared at his hands, washed clean of his daughter's blood. He began to cry. "You were trying to keep us alive and I didn't understand," he said through the tears. "I'm a lawyer, Ms. Meyer. I don't belong here, and I didn't understand."

Meyer turned her head. "Nobody belongs here," she said. "Human beings don't. The jungle doesn't like us."

She cleared her throat. Lock wiped his eyes with his sleeve, angry at the weakness but not attempting to disguise it.

"Well, it'll be okay soon," Meyer said. "It's not as though we were planning to stay."

Esther Meyer tried to remember when was the last time she'd thought she belonged anywhere.

✧   ✧   ✧

When the bonfires flickered, branches beyond the cleared margin looked as though they were moving, but Farrell's helmet knew better. Though—

The natives had fooled the helmets once. Fooled Tamara Lundie on the vibration sensors, and not enough infrared signature to give Tomaczek more than a heartbeat's warning.

Farrell smiled tightly toward the project manager and his aide. Neither of them reacted, but President Reitz paused in mid-breath.

"I was just thinking," Farrell said. "You can't live without trusting something. Even if you can't trust it."

"I consider the day's progress very satisfactory," al-Ibrahimi said, either because he didn't understand what Farrell meant or more probably because he did. "The humanoid attack was unexpected and costly, but C41's speed and skill limited the scope of the catastrophe. Tamara assures me that in the future we'll have at least some warning."

"Yes," said Lundie, a syllable edged with cold anger.

"I wonder if the Kalendru ship crashed and they've been looting it," Farrell said. "I've been thinking about those clubs. They're plastic, not stone or wood or something."

"According to analysis by Professors Gefayal and Bronski," al-Ibrahimi said, "the clubs are a complex folded protein, stiffened and hardened with silica. The professors don't believe the clubs could have been cast. They suggest that they must have been grown."

"But they were *animals*," Reitz objected. "They didn't have any technology. Only the weapons, and those so simple."

"A culture can have biological sophistication while

remaining very simple in the mechanical realm, madam," Lundie said.

"Which is true but doesn't answer the question of how the bodies of three of the twelve humanoids were themselves modified to spray caustic," the manager said. "The sophistication is undeniable, but I remain doubtful that the humanoids themselves are more than agents. We'll have to wait to gather more data before we determine who is the principal."

Farrell thought about the Spooks who'd attacked the expedition the day before. They were already brain dead. Whoever was in charge didn't like Kalendru any better than it did human beings.

"We're closer to the magnetic anomaly now," he said. "I'm going to send a scout to check it tomorrow." He played with his stinger. "If you approve."

"You're in tactical command," al-Ibrahimi said. "If there are more Kalendru on BZ 459, we need to know it."

"None of the species we're encountering is in the database," Tamara Lundie said. She didn't seem to be speaking to anyone in particular. "The survey wasn't exhaustive, but it *had* to have been thorough. It would have taken more effort to invent so large a self-consistent database than it would to orbit the planet a few times gathering imagery."

The sentence ended with the closest approach to an exclamation point that Farrell had yet heard in the aide's voice.

"Tamara, I believe you're reacting to toxins from your injury," al-Ibrahimi said. "I'll monitor the sensors for you. Go to one of the doctors and direct him or her to sedate you for a three-hour period. After that we'll examine your condition."

"I can't," Lundie said. She gripped the bandaged wrist with her good hand and squeezed until tears sprang from her eyes. "Sir, you need your sleep. I'll carry out my duties."

Farrell stood with a poker face to conceal his aches and the patches of skin rubbed raw by his equipment. "Sir," he said to the project manager, "I need to make the rounds of my duty section. I know where Doc Ciler is. I'll take her by. Miss?"

"I'd appreciate that, Major," al-Ibrahimi said. "Tamara, analyze the probable result of having a psychotic overseeing our sensor data."

"I'm not . . ." Lundie said, but she rose to her feet at Farrell's gentle pressure.

"You're perilously close or you wouldn't suggest that you'll carry out your duties when you're obviously incapable of doing so," her superior said. He spoke with the emotionless impact of so many hammer blows.

"Yes sir," Lundie said. "Major Farrell, I believe I'm able to walk unaided. I'd appreciate being able to hold your arm."

"Sure," Farrell said. "We'll find the doc and he'll fix you up fine."

He remembered the time he'd screamed that he was still in command, that he was still capable of leading C41, as Leinsdorf held him down for a medic to sedate. He'd been seeing double images from the knock on the head and giving orders to dead people, some of them dead for years.

Farrell led Lundie through groups of colonists sleeping or trying to ready themselves for tomorrow's march. She closed her eyes. Children were crying; children, and a few adults.

"The biota of this crater bear only a family resemblance to what the survey ship reported for the planet as a whole," Lundie said in tones of flat despair. "And that was bad enough. Without data, Major, what chance do we have?"

"You've got us," Farrell said. "For what it's worth, ma'am, you've got us."

Guilio Abbado walked among the sleeping colonists, not in a hurry and taking no particular course. The roof sheets unrolled to eight by twenty feet each. They were laid with a slight overlap. People were supposed to stay a foot back from the seams. Mostly they did, but folks moved in their sleep.

And some of them were sloppy, strikers as well as cits. Abbado hadn't found any rootlets quivering murderously around the edges, but his boot had prodded a few legs and butts until they moved someplace safer.

Caius Blohm sat beside his unrolled null sack, closer to the berm than most folks wanted to sleep. The scout had finished his guard shift twenty minutes before, when 3-3 came on duty. It wasn't always easy to sleep, even after a day of exhausting strain.

"Hey, Blohm," Abbado whispered in greeting. "Looks like the brain trust was right about things settling down after dark."

"Hey, Sarge," the scout said. "So far, so good."

The null sack murmured. Abbado looked at it, the visual equivalent of trying to grab a handful of jelly.

"It's one of the orphans," Blohm muttered. "She was having trouble sleeping. Ms. Suares and me thought . . ."

"Caius?" a little voice said. The child stuck her head out of the sack's mouth. Christ, she was little.

"I'm here, Mirica," Blohm said. A small hand reached out of the sack. He took it in his. "You're all right, honey."

"Hold me, Caius?" the child said.

"Guess I'll get back to work," Abbado said, attempting to keep his tone completely neutral.

"Just a second, honey," Blohm said in a voice gentler than anything Abbado'd ever expected to hear from him. "I gotta talk to the sarge for a minute, that's all."

The scout rose in a motion that would have made a cat look awkward and motioned Abbado with him to touching distance of the berm. "Listen, Abbado," Blohm said. "There's nothing going on. She's scared because her folks got greased and I'm taking care of her. You see?"

"Hey, don't get your knickers in a twist," Abbado said as forcefully as he could in a low voice. He felt like a dog facing a cobra. "I was there, remember? I saw the poor kid with her mom's arm. If she's got nightmares and needs somebody to hold her, what the fuck do you expect?"

"Ah, shit, Sarge," Blohm said, relaxing with a quiver like a released spring. "I forgot you knew. Shit, I thought . . . You know, some of the guys."

"This was a bitch of a place even before the wogs showed up," Abbado said calmly, starting to relax a little himself. "Well, maybe they ate the Spooks before they got around to us, you think?"

"I looked at the recordings of the attack," Blohm said bitterly. He hadn't listened to Abbado. "Those bastards were killing kids because they *wanted* to. The one that chopped her mom, he was going for Mirica when Nessman waxed him."

"Remember to get some sleep yourself, snake,"

Abbado said. He moved away, walking slowly. "The major's got us tapped for your backup tomorrow. I don't want you stepping in shit cause you're tired."

"Roger, Sarge," Blohm whispered. "Sorry for coming down on you like that."

Caldwell was twenty yards distant, standing near the roots of a tree toppled by a dozer. Abbado walked toward her, knowing his helmet would caret anything it saw as a danger. A quiet night thus far.

There were strikers in C41 whose sexual tastes were well outside the mainstream. Sometimes that was why they'd enlisted in the Strike Force to begin with. A guy everybody expected to die was cut slack in other ways. Abbado didn't think that was the case with Blohm, but he'd have kept his mouth shut anyway.

Caius Blohm wasn't somebody he wanted to fuck with. The chances of surviving Bezant were bad enough already.

Partly it was a day's experience for himself and the helmet database, but the main reason Blohm could safely cross a mile of jungle in less than an hour was that he didn't have to nursemaid Sergeant Gabrilovitch. That was a hard way to think of Gabe, but it was the truth.

The shooting tree stood in a grove of tall reeds whose foliage hung down like a fan dancer's props. The sprays of compound leaves were slightly russet, a hue different enough from that of most vegetation to call attention to itself—

And to conceal what was behind it, Blohm assumed. *Exactly* like the dancer's fans.

This was the first shooting tree Blohm had seen since he got beyond the margins of the landing site. As he moved gingerly closer, his helmet located half a dozen more in the immediate vicinity. The AI built swatches of surface or a shape implied by surrounding vegetation into a predicted presence. The largest tree was eight inches in diameter; much smaller than the one that discharged at the landing site, but large enough to be lethal.

Blohm eased a reed stem sideways with his knife. He didn't switch on the blade. Leaf fans rustled against one another.

It was at least possible that the reeds were harmless in themselves, merely screening for the shooting trees. Using the stinger barrel and the silent knife together like a spreader clip, Blohm opened a narrow window to look beyond.

Bingo.

"Six, this is Six-six-two," he whispered. "The anomaly is a Spook ship, all right. But it hasn't landed here, it's crashed. Six-six-two over."

The Kalendru vessel was a globe much smaller than 10-1442. It lay on its side; the bottom and outriggers were only a dozen feet from Blohm's vantage point. Heating in the magnetic eddies of takeoff and landing swirled the plates with color.

The hull maintained its basic shape, but there was some crumpling and a number of seams had started. As Blohm watched, something raised its head from one of the ragged gaps in the metal and looked back at him.

"Why doesn't he shoot?" Tamara Lundie asked, viewing the relayed image of the creature's triangular head. The compound eyes had the soft gleam of faceted amber. The beak was saw-edged and long enough to shear through a human with a single bite.

The column was halted while both bulldozers snarled into a tangle of branching fungi that grew like a wall through the green jungle. Gills flaring fifty feet in the air shook clouds of poisonous spores when any part of the system was touched. Helmet filters protected the strikers, but Manager al-Ibrahimi had ordered clearance of a much wider path than usual to protect the colonists.

"I don't tell Blohm how to do his job," Farrell whispered. He had to force himself to speak at all, though he knew the creature couldn't hear them talk. It raised twin crests of feathery tissue, sensory receptors of some variety. They could be for hearing or scent, or both together.

"Note the coils of vine attached to the outriggers," al-Ibrahimi said. "When the vessel took off, their grip spun it sideways. The pilot wouldn't have had time to respond."

Like the aircar, Farrell thought as he looked at the tight spring of vine. He wouldn't have noticed it without the manager's comment. By timing its attack, the jungle had let the ship's own power effect its destruction.

The beast's crests shrank back against the skull; the head withdrew. Blohm's unseen hands let the reed stems back into their original alignment, closing the realtime image in a blur of vegetation.

"Sir," Farrell said to al-Ibrahimi. "I'm going to send my other scout to guide five strikers to the ship. I want to develop the threat and if possible to clear the vessel. A ship that size could carry five hundred troops and their equipment. Maybe they're all dead, but if there's a couple companies of them holed up in the bow I'd rather know it now."

He half smiled. "Not that I'm sure what I'd do about it."

The administrators' headsets not only received Strike Force transmissions, they projected imagery as air-formed holograms without a combiner field. Al-Ibrahimi nodded as he watched an image that to Farrell was only shimmers.

"You are in tactical command, Major," he repeated. "I myself am less concerned with the threat the Kalendru pose than in the question of what they're doing on BZ 459, but I hope your plan will provide answers to both."

The older man looked directly at Farrell. Even smiling his face was a swordblade. "That shows a foolish lack of pragmatism in me; which would surprise my colleagues no end, wouldn't it, Tamara?"

His aide didn't answer. She was viewing, or reviewing, images transmitted from the scout's helmet.

Farrell gave his orders in a short series. He got a crisp, *"Yes sir,"* from Kristal, who'd be splitting a section of civilians among the strikers guarding the sections ahead and behind; an unenthusiastic *"Yes sir, understood,"* from Gabrilovitch, who had a damned good idea of what it entailed; and from Abbado, *"Roger,"* in a tone of vaguely resentful boredom, as though 3-3 had been ordered to pull a double guard shift.

Blohm didn't make an audible reply. The dot that marked him on Farrell's visor overlay winked twice.

Pretty much as Farrell expected. He'd have been a piss-poor commanding officer if his troops surprised him after this long together.

"The opening was too narrow for the animal's whole body to get through," Lundie said. "How could Striker Blohm be sure of that?"

"I don't know that he was sure," Farrell said. "If

it had come straight out at him, he'd have reacted. He'll react if it comes out another hole. It got in some way."

Most of the time you weren't sure of anything. You usually didn't have a real target, you never had all the information. You played the percentages, you played hunches. You prayed a lot, said the words anyway; or you swore, using a lot of the same words, and you knew it didn't matter a damn either way. If the universe decided this was your time, it was going to nail you whatever you did.

"Six, this is Two-three," said Verushnie from the lead squad. *"The dozers have opened a track. Shall we proceed? Over."*

"Two-three, roger," Farrell said. "Out."

The sound of brush tearing had ended. Metal clanged as a tractor was reattached to the trailers. The tone was off because foliage muted the high frequencies more than it did the low components of the sound.

Farrell nodded to the administrators. He hitched his gear to loosen its grip on his flesh. "I'm moving up with the second section," he said. "We're going to be shorthanded till Three-three gets back, but I don't think we'd be safer to wait."

"Major?" Tamara Lundie said. "According to his personnel records, Sergeant Abbado has had severe discipline problems. But you trust him."

"Ma'am," Farrell said. The conscious part of his mind watched himself and the two administrators from a high vantage. Instinct and emotion controlled everything else. "Since he's served with me, Sergeant Abbado has never had a problem any time that it mattered. If your records say anything else, you can stuff them up your ass."

He strode up the column, nodding to strikers readying themselves to move.

The lead bulldozer shook the striker guarding it worse than the tractor pulling the trailers did; but when you dismounted from the lead dozer you didn't have to run to catch up with the trailers to stow the hard suit. It was a trade-off, and anyway Meyer was too tired to care. After a while you could lose track of what you'd been doing.

She unlatched the gauntlets first. She'd been on the lead. That meant she had a good five minutes to strip before the trailers wobbled by. She wondered if she'd make it.

Somebody sat down beside her. "Can I help you?" he asked.

"Lock?" she said. "You want to throw the catches, you go right ahead. I'm so stiff I'll crack if I try to get the back of the gorget."

Civilians staggered by, too exhausted to notice Lock and Meyer except as obstacles in the trail. Most of them had thrown away all personal belongings except the clothes they wore and a bulging pocket or purse. The strikers were tired too, but they kept their weapons ready.

Lock loosened the catches with the forceful certainty of somebody doing a job for the first time and determined to get it right. Meyer shifted her posture so that the civilian could lift pieces of armor as she loosened them.

When Lock had worked the heaviest piece, the back-and-breast clamshell, over Meyer's right arm, she raised her visor and looked at him. His eyes were a green far more vivid than his chestnut hair.

"What are you after?" Meyer asked bluntly.

"I want you to teach me to shoot," Lock said, just as bluntly.

"Don't be fucking stupid," Meyer snapped. "I'm not training cadre."

"You can teach me the basics, how to load and fire and the theory at least of aiming," Lock said in a tone minutely harder. The iron within was beginning to crush the velvet glove. "I don't expect to become a marksman, but in the event that the savages attack again I can be something more positive than another potential victim whom you need to protect."

"I can't—" Meyer said.

"There are extra weapons now," Lock said, not raising his voice but trampling over the striker's half-formed thought without hesitation. "Those of your dead fellows. I've already spoken to Manager al-Ibrahimi. He's agreed pending approval by the military authorities."

The civilian smiled wryly at his formal phrasing. "I realize you'll have to get permission from Major Farrell," he added. "But there's no reason he shouldn't grant it."

Meyer began stuffing the pieces of armor into the pouch. She shook her head. "You'd blow your foot off or shoot somebody in the back by mistake," she said.

Lock held the mouth of the net bag open. "Not if you do your job, Striker Meyer. I don't have the correct reflexes, I understand. But I don't have the wrong ones either. I don't panic."

The second tractor was getting louder. It must be just around the nearest kink in the trail.

"That savage was *holding* me," Lock said. He

straightened, lifting the pouch himself. "I don't need to be a crack shot to help under those circumstances. I just need a gun and the basics of how to use it."

"The bag goes on the first trailer," Meyer said. The tractor, its huge blade lifted vertically like a second roof over the cab, snarled into view.

"Striker Meyer," Lock said. "They were my wife and my daughter. It was my job to protect them and I couldn't. I should have protected them!"

"You're a fucking civilian!" Meyer said. "It was *my* job to protect you all, you stupid son of a bitch! Do you think I don't know how bad I fucked up?"

Meyer and Lock squeezed close to the edge of the cut as the tractor passed them. The squeal and clanking of the tracks and the high-pitched whine of the generator were overwhelming. The driver and guard were anonymous in their hard suits, but the wounded and infirm looked down from the piled trailer with gray concern.

"Yeah, I'll teach you to use a stinger," Meyer said as the trailer came abreast of them. "If the major okays it. I owe you that much."

"Holy *shit*," Abbado said in relief when he saw the striker waiting for them beneath the trunk of a tree knocked down when the Spook ship crashed. "I didn't think we were going to make it, snake. Even with you coaching us."

"Hey, Sarge," Blohm replied without turning around. "This tree's been dead long enough that it doesn't squirt poison, but don't touch the bark."

The tree was six feet in diameter. The upturned roots kept the bole high enough for the five strikers to walk under, but they all crouched anyway. Abbado'd left

Methie behind for the knee and Glasebrook because, face it, Flea was clumsy.

While 3-3 trekked through the jungle, the scout had carefully circled the Kalendru ship. Abbado studied the fallen vessel. As usual, the first view of the objective thrilled him even though he'd gone over Blohm's images.

"Is there any way in but that crack?" Gabrilovitch asked. He seemed more uncomfortable in the jungle than the strikers of 3-3 were. Greater exposure, Abbado supposed.

Everybody's got a limit to the repetitive stress he can take. Abbado wondered how Blohm was holding up. You couldn't talk about Blohm's mental state in the terms you'd use for most people, even most strikers, of course.

"That's the only opening I've found," Blohm said. Their voices were barely audible. "It's eight feet long and ranges from seven inches to about thirty. The hatches are closed. From the way lichen's started to grow across the metal, they've stayed closed ever since the crash."

"And the critter inside?" Abbado asked.

Blohm shrugged. "He hasn't showed himself again. There may be more than one. It's nothing from the database."

"Naturally," Horgen muttered.

The ruptured seam was eight feet up, running parallel to the ground because of the way the ship lay. Thick vines snaked into the opening, but they didn't affect the wide point in the center. The root ends were lost in the jungle.

Spook ships generally had single-compartment decks. That meant there was plenty of room for the beast inside.

"We haven't seen many animals," Caldwell said.

"There's the wogs," said Matushek. "They're animals. Did you see what they did to the civilians when they attacked?"

"Okay, this is pretty straightforward," Abbado said. "We'll go to intercom on the squad channel. Me and Foley go forward with two fuel-air grenades each. We toss them in. When they blow, we boost Horgen and Matushek to stand at the edge of the hole with rockets. The critter'll be dead but it'll likely still be thrashing around. You guys keep hitting him as long as he's moving, four rockets apiece. Foley, you lift the rest of us to the hole, starting with me. When you've done that, you stay on the ground for rear security with Gabrilovitch and Blohm. Understood?"

Gabrilovitch grimaced. "We're scouts," he said. "You want us on point?"

"This is a standard clearance operation," Abbado said. "Nothing Three-three can't handle. You're way too important to the major for you to get your ass blown away by a ricochet."

"What if the thing sticks its head out when we throw the grenades?" Foley asked.

"Then Ace and me blow it off," said Horgen.

Abbado unhooked a grenade with either hand and thumbed the arming switches live. "Let's do it, people," he said as he rose to his feet.

As Abbado took his first step toward the Kalendru vessel, the creature's head rose snout-first through the crack. The triangular skull was too large to fit the thirty-inch opening any other way. Because the skin lay close over the bone without a layer of muscle between, the beast had the look of a reptile or insect rather than a mammal.

"It can't get—" Abbado said, trying to estimate the risk of tossing his right-hand grenade past the head and neck.

The creature licked out a twenty-foot tongue flaring at the tip into a pair of sucker-tipped mandibles. It gripped Abbado around the waist and snatched him back toward fangs as long as his forearm.

Matushek and Horgen fired rockets simultaneously. The warheads detonated deep in the creature's skull. A fireball of unexpended fuel seared Abbado's bare hands as the double shockwave snatched the grenades away from him.

"Fire in the hole!" he wheezed as he went over in a backward somersault. He'd only been ten feet from the rocket warheads when they went off. The half of the tongue clinging to him flew free and thrashed into the jungle in the same general direction as the live grenades.

What remained of the creature's head flailed the hull in a sleet of stinger pellets until another rocket severed the neck. Abbado's grenades lifted bubbles of seared foliage without harm to the strikers. An instant later, two shooting trees burst with sharp cracks. Their spikes stripped narrow cones of the jungle still farther away.

Foley stepped past the huge head. The lower jaw twitched, but it had no upper surface to close against. He tossed his grenades into the opening, then added another pair to replace Abbado's.

Abbado wobbled to his feet. Orange fire and the stench of burning meat belched from the cracked seam.

"Let's get them," Abbado croaked as he staggered forward.

Waiting for the Axe

In theory Sergeant Guilio Abbado was still in command of 3-3, but none of his strikers had paid the least attention to his wheezing demands to be the first through the opening. The only reason Foley lifted him at all was that Abbado was so obviously incapable of giving Foley a boost instead.

The headless creature thrashing inside weighed at least five tons. The fuel-air explosions hadn't disintegrated or even dismembered the corpse, but they *had* burned every square inch of its hide.

The stench of blackened flesh was overpowering. Abbado switched to his helmet's small air bottle as much for that reason as because the grenades had used a lot of the available oxygen.

He'd set his visor on infrared instead of enhancement, the low-light default setting. Hot gas from the bombs swirled in confusing veils but the figures of the strikers ahead of him were sufficiently sharp. The split seam let a fair amount of light into this compartment, but that wouldn't be true of those further toward the bow.

The vines that entered the ship terminated in bunches of fruit the size of soccer balls, hundreds of them. Grenade blasts had crushed them to reeking pulp against the bulkheads.

The fruit could be of no benefit to the plant, but they'd served as food for the creature. It must have entered through the same opening as the strikers, then grown to its final monstrous size on the diet.

The remains of at least twenty Spooks lay in a fetid mass at the bottom of the compartment. Each body had been bitten in half but not devoured. The creature was a killer without being a carnivore.

The four companionways to the deck above were horizontal tunnels. The interdeck hatches had buckled and couldn't close. Abbado scrambled after Caldwell in the lowest passageway. The steep, narrow treads were vertical obstacles.

The leading strikers hurled half a dozen electrical grenades to clear the third and highest deck. Abbado, panting and dizzy, entered a moment later. There were Kalendru bodies among jumbled gear. The Spooks had been killed in the crash a week or so earlier.

"Nobody left, sarge," Horgen said in faint disappointment. 3-3'd hoped for a fight with something the strikers understood, not leaves and vines. Learning there were no Spooks alive in the ship was like being bilked of a steak dinner after a week of living on lettuce.

The compartment and the one below showed no indication of occupancy following the crash. If Spooks had initially survived, the creature had seen them off. The length of its neck and tongue would have permitted it to scour both levels even though its swollen body couldn't fit through the companionway. There were lasers among the other debris, but ordinary Kalendru troops didn't carry weapons heavy enough to deal with a monster the size of that one.

"You know . . ." Flea said. "I could almost feel sorry for the poor bastard Spooks."

"All right, let's get back," Abbado said. "They'll need us at the column."

The crash had thrown loose personal gear which covered the compartment's lower side like plant debris in a forest swale. It was within the realm of possibility that a Spook was hiding deep enough in it that IR didn't spot him, but it wasn't worth 3-3's time to check out.

"Three-three, this is Administrator Tamara Lundie," said an unfamiliar voice. Because the helmet AIs had to fill gaps caused by signal attenuation through the ship's metal hull, the words were almost toneless. *"Kalendru vessels of this class have a separate control room reached through a hatch here—"*

A deck schematic with a pulsing caret appeared briefly on one quadrant of Abbado's visor.

"—which is at the moment concealed by litter from the crash. Out."

"Who the hell was that?" Caldwell asked.

"The blonde with the broomstick up her ass," Abbado said, straddle-walking forward to keep his balance on the shifting surface. He tossed aside a pile of torn containers, Spook dufflebags or bedrolls, to expose the hatch where Lundie said it would be.

It was locked from the other side, but cloth pinched on the lower side of the hatch showed it'd been open at some point after the crash. Judging from tears and blast patterns, 3-3's grenades had flung the gear that hid it.

Abbado unscrewed the warhead of a rocket, set it for point effect/five second delay, and struck it hard enough against the lock plate to trip the fuze. "Fire in the hole!" he called as he scrambled away.

The blue flash of the electrical warhead lit the

compartment. The shock wave clanged into the hatch like the tip of a three-ton ice-pick, shearing the bolt and flinging the panel open in reaction. Tattered debris flew up in a cloud like dirt tamped around a charge set in an excavation.

"I've got him!" Horgen cried even as she dived through the hatchway. "I've got him and he's alive!"

Caius Blohm watched the foliage react to the single, sharp blast that made the wreck's hull ring. Leaves quivered, pods turned; the whole forest was listening, waiting.

"I've got him! I've got him and he's alive!"

Foley looked at the opening above him, desperate to join the rest of his squad. Sergeant Gabrilovitch nodded to Blohm and muttered, "Great. Now we've got a prisoner to nursemaid back to the column."

"He won't be any more problem than Abbado's lot," Blohm said. And not much more problem than you, Gabe, he thought, but he didn't say.

"C41," broke in the voice that this time didn't bother to identify itself as Tamara Lundie. *"Increased carbon dioxide levels suggest that another party of native humanoids coming from the north is now within a few seconds or minutes of the column. The region between the first and second tractor appears the most likely point of contact. Out."*

Blohm felt his body prickle. He had a vision of Mirica in the grip of a humanoid with a face as remote and remorseless as a storm cloud; of Mirica dead, not on a jungle track but on the threshold of a room filled with the grenade-blasted bodies of other children. He began to shiver.

Gabrilovitch swore softly. "How long do you figure

it'll take us to get back to the column, snake?" he asked.

"Too long," Blohm said. Too long, or I'd be headed back right now even if they hang me for desertion when I get there.

There was less than an hour to sunset. It would arrive like a curtain falling in these latitudes. Besides, even if he tried to make the last of the distance at night—and maybe he could, just maybe—the attack would be over by a few minutes from now.

"Those kid-killing bastards," Blohm said, his lips barely moving. "Those *bastards*."

Sergeant Abbado stuck his head out of the opening in the ship's hull. A moment later he and Matushek thrust a Spook through, dangling him by arms that looked so pale that they were almost transparent. The prisoner was humming loudly, a Kalendru sign of misery and despair.

Foley took the Spook by one leg and reached up to grip him under the arm to lower him to the ground. The Spook seemed catatonic. He was thin even by Kalendru standards; Blohm wondered if there'd been any food in the compartment where he was hiding.

Gabe started forward to give Foley a hand. Matushek boosted Abbado to where he could climb out in turn. Blohm eyed a tree on the other side of the crashed vessel. Its branches were drawing up by minute increments.

Nobody expected a problem: Kalendru stopped fighting as soon as they were captured. Maybe Foley should've been paying more attention to the Spook and less to his sergeant, but any experienced striker was likely to have done the same thing.

The Spook twisted out of Foley's grip with the Kalendru equivalent of hysterical strength and ran toward the jungle, humming even louder. His eyes were open but Blohm didn't think they were focusing.

Gabe shouted and ran to block the prisoner's escape. Foley stumbled as he tried to follow. Blohm knew he couldn't help unless the Spook changed direction, but he sprinted anyway out of the reflex to chase whatever runs away.

The Spook took a gazelle-like leap toward the unbroken forest. Gabe waved his arms, still shouting. Blohm saw what was about to happen and called, "Let him go! Gabe—"

The Spook leaped again. Gabrilovitch dived after him, grabbing the Spook around the shoulders in a high tackle. Together they smashed into a shooting tree about a dozen feet high.

The head of the young tree burst with a vicious crack. Gabe cried out. He and the Spook hit the ground and bounced apart, concerned now with their own wounds rather than each other. The prisoner was clutching his thigh while Gabrilovitch had a hand on his left shoulder. Because they'd been in motion when they touched the trunk, the blast of spikes hadn't caught them squarely.

Blohm reached the victims first. He pried his partner's hand away. There were three closely-spaced puncture wounds; the points of the spikes poked through the back of Gabe's battledress, just below the collarbone. A tree this small didn't fire missiles as heavy and powerful as the adult whose spikes had raked the humans at the crash site.

Blohm took a first aid patch from his medikit and slapped it over the entrance wounds. It closed the holes and leached pain killers through the skin at a rate metered by needs. In a few seconds a color-coded display on the back of the patch would provide a rough diagnosis of the injuries and prognosis.

Foley and Sergeant Abbado joined them. The sergeant looked as grim as a war hammer. He took the Spook by the wrists to anchor him and pull his hands away to expose his wounds. There was only one, a neat hole in the right thigh with no exit.

"Doesn't look too bad," Abbado said. "Guess we got lucky. But this means we've got to carry the sonofabitch back to the column for interro—"

The Kalender's body stiffened. The edges of the wound had darkened. A purple discoloration continued to spread across the gray skin even though the Spook's heart and circulatory system had obviously quit for good. His mouth opened and the tongue thrust out, pink and as stiff as a dog's dong.

"Poison!" Gabrilovitch said. "Oh, Christ, I've been poisoned."

"No," Blohm said, looking at the readout on Gabe's patch: everything well in the green. "You haven't, but the Spook sure as hell was. Their chemistry's different and the trees here aren't targeted for us. Yet."

"I think," said Sergeant Abbado, "that we'll stick here with the ship until daylight instead of starting back right now."

He looked at the sky and the jungle, then added, "God *damn* this place."

"Tell your civilians to lie flat next to the berm!" Farrell ordered as he ran forward. The two satchels of grenades he'd grabbed from the lead trailer swung in his left hand, pulling him off balance with every stride. The stinger wasn't heavy enough to compensate, even though he held it out for leverage. "Squad Two-two come forward, the rest of you hold in place. *All* civilians down, down flat! Over!"

The column moved like an earthworm with arthritis: bunching and spreading at irregular intervals, always moving slowly. Civilians turned and gaped as Farrell ran past, pushing them aside when he had to.

"Down flat!" he shouted. There wasn't fucking time to explain. There was barely time for a wrung-out major with a heavy load to run the hundred yards forward to where the attack was maybe going to come. "Down flat!"

"Down flat!" Sergeant Kristal shouted to the civilians around her. She'd split her six strikers into two groups. When Farrell sent Abbado off, Kristal's weak squad had responsibility for three hundred civilians. The weakest defenses, and the point at which Lundie said to expect the attack.

Farrell didn't assume the natives knew how C41 was deployed. He'd seen enough combat to expect every possible thing to go wrong out of pure cussedness. That's just how life is for a soldier.

There was nothing to the right—north—side of the bulldozer cut except lowering vegetation. A striker got used to his helmet sensors giving him a hundred yards of warning and targeting under any conditions short of a rock wall. Knowing that the natives might appear at spitting distance from the greenery, unseen until that instant, made Farrell feel as though he'd been sent into a battle with his eyes taped shut.

But a striker does what he can, and you don't have to see your target with a grenade.

"Lie fucking down!" Farrell roared to the nearest civilians. "Get your kids down, for Chrissake!"

They were reacting, but not quickly enough. Farrell

was out of sight of the nearest strikers in either direction. Because of large trees and other special circumstances, the trail kinked every ten or twenty yards. This stretch was one of the longer ones, but it seemed to be Art Farrell's alone.

Farrell let his stinger go, dropped one of the satchels, and pulled a fuel-air grenade from the other. He armed the bomb and threw it between the trunks of trees on the edge of the cut. He knew it was going to hit something solid before it travelled more than twenty feet into the tangle; he just hoped that it didn't bounce back among the civilians.

He took the risk because the choice was to leave the initiative with the natives . . . which meant he would die, and that at least the thirty civilians flopping on the ground behind him on his panoramic display would die also.

His own death was one of the things that came with his enlistment oath; theirs wasn't.

Farrell threw a second grenade, then a third. He had a dozen in each satchel. If nothing happened sooner, he'd throw every fucking one of them and throw the three electricals on his belt after that. In these conditions the electrical grenades' fragmentation effect made them both more dangerous to friendlies and less useful against hostiles. The fuel spread and mixed with air pretty much unhindered by treetrunks and ground cover.

"Daddy, what are we—"

A parent's hand clamped hard over the child's mouth. No need for that, but they didn't know. They were civilians, they shouldn't fucking *be* here.

Whoom! and concussion shoved Farrell back like a medicine ball in the chest. Foliage hid the flash of the explosion. The shockwave had a wet, green smell. He took out another grenade.

Whoom! as Farrell threw the grenade, a little higher than he'd intended. His aim was straight enough for safety because he'd allowed for the blast. He was maybe warning the attackers, he knew that, but he was sure-hell putting them off balance and there was never a bad time to do that.

Whoom! as Farrell reached for the next grenade. The torso of a native rode an orange bubble skyward in a sudden clearing thirty feet into the jungle. His limbs were four separated exclamation points at the margins of the flash.

Another native stepped from the undamaged foliage six feet away, his toothed club rising. Farrell threw the 20-ounce grenade into his face, crushing cheekbones and the beaklike jaw.

The native fell into the undergrowth; the grenade bounced back against Farrell's boots. The bomb was harmless; he hadn't thumbed the arming switch.

Farrell armed another grenade without lifting it from the satchel. He threw the satchel as far as he could into the jungle before him. Crouching against the coming blast, he aimed his stinger.

Over my dead body, you baby-killing bastards. And not even then.

Meyer rapped Seligman's shoulder. He was driving the lead bulldozer with her for guard. "Turn us around," she said. The staffer had a helmet as part of the hard suit: he was on the C41 net and knew what was going on. "Drive right into the wogs. They'll run when they see this coming, right?"

The lead squad, five strikers under Jonas as senior

man in lieu of a noncom, was shouting at the nearby cits to lie down. Jonas and two of his people jogged back down the trail to the expected point of contact.

"Are you out of your mind?" Seligman cried. He put the tractor in neutral. "I'm no soldier, honey! You go fight them yourself!"

Matthew Lock clambered onto the tractor's deck. He was awkward because he held a stinger and hadn't rigged the sling over his shoulder to free both hands.

"For God's sake, Seligman!" Meyer shouted. "They need us back there! I can't get there wearing armor myself."

"I'm not going any damn where!" the staffer replied. "You don't have any right—"

Lock tapped the muzzle of his stinger on the helmet at roughly the position of Seligman's right ear. "Do as Striker Meyer orders or I'll kill you," he said in a clear voice. He rapped the helmet again.

"You can't—" Seligman said.

Meyer fired one round into the front mesh. The pellet disintegrated with a *whack* and a red flash that looked brighter because of the cab's dimness. "Turn this son-of-a-bitch!" she shouted.

Seligman thumbed a roller switch on his left handgrip. The blade rose slowly with a whine that made Meyer's armor rattle everywhere it touched the tractor. The seat and controls were insulated from vibration but the rest of the vehicle wasn't; Meyer was familiar with the experience by now. It wasn't the sort of thing you got used to, any more than you'd get used to being punched in the face.

"Don't cut a trail!" Lock shouted in the staffer's ear. He must think the armor deadened hearing; in fact, the receptors were more sensitive than the ears they served, though they clipped loud noises to safe levels with cancellation waves. "Just get us back the fastest way without running anybody over!"

Seligman scissored the left control bar to the rear and the right one forward. The treads ground in opposite directions, turning the bulldozer in its own length. Meyer knew the maneuver stressed the running gear and was likely to throw a track, but it was still the fastest way to change direction. She didn't complain.

If the staffer hoped to disable the vehicle, he failed. He shifted the bulldozer forward, then swung outward to avoid a giant whose spread of buttress roots he'd skirted on the opposite side a few minutes before. The blade continued to rise. For a moment the solid lower portion blocked most of the frontal vision from the cab.

Grenades went off ahead; Meyer felt the shocks despite the racket the tractor made busting brush. She thought she heard the pop of stingers.

"Striker!" Lock said. He held the stinger up to her. "How do I fire this?"

Meyer looked at the civilian's earnest face. You couldn't fault him for lack of balls, anyway. "This is the safety," she said, pushing the button on the receiver over the trigger. A telltale went from green to red. "Now you pull the trigger. But for God's sake watch where you point it!"

A fruit the size of a pumpkin hit the roof of the cab and squashed as enthusiastically as a bomb bursting. Green juice sprayed in all directions and began to drip down. Meyer shoved Lock completely beneath the roof overhang. Her hard suit wasn't affected and the tractor's nickel steel body merely discolored. Chunks of branch and foliage lying in the path of the spreading juice turned black and began to smolder.

Meyer shifted the tank of the flame gun to her left side, taking the nozzle in that hand. She hated flame guns—even more so since she'd seen hers incinerate Top Daye, but it might be the margin of survival.

More grenades boomed. A treetop whipped through the jungle like a barbed-wire flyswatter. It slammed the dozer blade, now held at a forty-five degree angle over the tractor's engine compartment, and bounced back with a crackle of despair.

A humanoid native appeared in a thicket. Stems writhed like an anemone's tentacles but didn't harm him. He squirted caustic toward the tractor and stepped as gracefully as a bullfighter out of the way of the looming vehicle. The flame gun devoured his pelvis in incandescent fury.

Vegetation withered a yard to either side of the brief flame rod. The white glare touched a tree a foot thick. Gluey, blood-red sap gushed from the point of contact. The tree twisted and collapsed around the wound as though only pneumatic pressure had kept it upright.

Lock shouted to Seligman. Meyer had stepped to the right side of the deck; she couldn't hear the words over the sound of the vehicle and nearby grenade blasts. She threw a grenade herself. The orange fireball bloomed almost to the treads as it pulped a hundred square feet of foliage and two humanoids.

Seligman touched a control. The land-clearing blade began to whine slowly down again from its running position.

The tree ahead braced itself against wind forces with flat plates running from the ground high up the trunk.

The tractor smashed through the flanges. Wood shattered like cork, throwing up clouds of fine gray dust. A caret winked on Meyer's visor; Lock was already tugging his neck scarf over his nose and mouth before she could warn him.

Meyer wondered how much good the scarf would do, but she had more immediate problems. She lobbed a grenade over the top of the blade. When it exploded, a jug-shaped tree twenty yards ahead burst into blue flame. It was spurting hydrogen from every pore.

Heat shrivelled the foliage as far as the bulldozer itself. The flames were pale but intensely hot. Lock cried out and ducked despite the gratings in the dozer blade and the cab window. Meyer and Seligman in their hard suits were unaffected.

The driver steered sharply to the right to avoid driving through the center of the blaze. Meyer played her stinger across three natives, then a fourth in the circle the fire had stripped of cover. The humanoids might pass through the jungle unhindered by thorns and poisons, but heat was heat and the laws of physics applied to their flesh as well.

The right blade support arm and that side of the cab twinkled, though Meyer couldn't see the shooter or hear the pellets hitting. Seligman let go of the controls and tried to hunch beneath the level of the window openings. Lock grabbed the staffer's armored shoulder and batted the stinger muzzle against his helmet.

Seligman straightened just as the blade sheared its way back into the trail it had previously cleared. He'd managed to switch on the intercom; Meyer could hear him blubbering. He pulled back slightly on the left control bar. The bulldozer twitched onto a parallel course instead of grinding through the people screaming as they rose in fear of a monster more terrible than the club-swinging humanoids.

Meyer stepped onto the narrow fender covering the right tread. She was afraid to throw grenades while they were so close to the main trail, and the land-clearing blade was too high to shoot over from any distance back.

The blade hit a tree too thick to smash aside. Meyer lurched forward with the shock. She caught herself on the frame that supported the grated upper portion of the blade. Roots pulled out of the soil, releasing the bulldozer as the trunk toppled to the side.

Meyer saw movement beyond a fringe of compound leaves. She hosed it with her flame gun. Humanoids appeared as screening vegetation wilted. The ravening flame converted flesh and bone to gas. There'd been three of them, maybe more. The blade scraped shrunken corpses aside with the trash of undergrowth and topsoil.

The flame died, its fuel exhausted. The ceramic nozzle glowed white/yellow/red back from the tip. Meyer dropped the weapon and reached for the stinger with her right hand.

The left track rocked over a tree which had twisted behind the blade instead of rolling off the side. Meyer fell sideways, awkward in her armor, and over-compensated. The tractor's weight abruptly splintered the bole; she toppled to the left.

Meyer flailed with both hands. They missed their grip on the blade. She began to slide beneath the front of the tread.

Roaring. Blackness. Alone.

Something caught and anchored Meyer's right leg.

Meyer pushed herself back on her armored belly before she dared to stand up again. Matthew Lock, kneeling on the fender, let go of her ankle. "I lost the gun," he said. His whole body was trembling. The scarf still covered his face.

"C41, this is Six," Meyer's helmet ordered. *"Cease fire. We've got this batch too. Good work, people. Six out."*

Strain

There were seven wounded civilians. Four of them had caught grenade fragments; one lost her arm to a stinger pellet because she jumped up screaming when the natives came out of the jungle in front of her. One civilian had died of a stroke.

None of them had been killed by the attack itself. Not one.

Ciler was bent over his diagnostic display. "Doc, I'm getting too damned old for this," Farrell said, his eyes slitted.

Both bulldozers snarled, clearing a campsite. The column hadn't gotten as far as Farrell would have liked, but there were too many injured to treat on the move.

"You're very lucky to be alive," Ciler said. "The spikes on the club passed to either side of a carotid."

He smiled tightly. "Under the present ridiculous circumstances, I have to class the injury as superficial, however."

"I feel like shit," Farrell said as he got to his feet. "That's good, because it reminds me I'm alive."

Massengill took a piece of grenade shrapnel— probably his own grenade—through a femoral artery. What with everything going on at the time, he may not even have realized he was dying before he finished

268

bleeding out. A native chopped Buccolowski in the neck just like Farrell, but Farrell had blown his attacker's chest out while the club was in mid swing. Ski had been a lifetime less quick.

"The one who got me was a tough fucker," Farrell said. "Maybe we ought to recruit here for the Strike Force."

Abdelkader's legs were sprayed with caustic—concentrated potassium hydroxide, not an acid, the brain trust said. If the dickhead had told somebody about it as soon as the shooting stopped so they could flush the goop off him, he'd have been all right. Instead he waited till it really started to hurt.

Ciler said they'd likely save the legs, but Abdelkader was going to be gorked out on pain medication for the next month while he regrew a couple square feet of skin.

Al-Ibrahimi and his aide walked around a crew of citizens laying ground sheeting. There weren't enough staffers in the column to do the heavy work. Farrell noticed that the cits were actually better at the job once they'd learned the basics of what was required.

The project manager nodded to Farrell. "Major," he said, "I regret your casualties, but I congratulate you on your victory. I'm amazed that your troops were able to protect the column with such relatively slight damage. There were ninety-six humanoids in this attack."

"The warning was the difference," Farrell said, nodding in turn to Lundie. "It saved us." He grinned briefly. "Saved you too, I guess."

"But you had only a few seconds of warning," al-Ibrahimi said.

A striker fired a 4-pound rocket. Backblast, transition

to supersonic flight, and warhead detonation merged into a three-note chord: *bam/crack/wham!*

The target was a tree a bulldozer was about to attack. Branches split and fell with creaking objections from the blasted peak. Some striker's helmet had given him a target; he'd taken it.

Farrell lifted his hand from the grip of his stinger and said, "Seconds count," he said. "At the muzzle, a pellet from this thing—"

His finger caressed the weapon's receiver like a cat owner rubbing his pet's jaw.

"—is moving at pretty near twelve kay. Twelve thousand feet per second."

Farrell kicked at bulldozer cleat marks in soil where the sheeting wasn't yet laid. "Ten feet doesn't sound like much, but if you've got to run that far across cleared ground to get to one of my people with a stinger— it's far enough, sir. It's plenty far enough."

"The natives have almost no brain," Dr. Ciler volunteered unexpectedly. "I'm surprised they can even manufacture clubs. It's more like dissecting an insect than even a reptile."

"Sir," said Tamara Lundie to her superior. She nodded to Farrell and the doctor, deliberately keeping them in the conversation. "I believe there's a system in the humanoid attacks."

Farrell's visor displayed a pattern of lines branching downward like a scheme of perspective. Al-Ibrahimi must have been seeing something similar, because his eyes changed focus to a point in what seemed to be empty air.

"Yesterday the humanoids attacked over a narrow front at effectively the same time," Lundie said. Twelve lines, too close to separate at the scale on Farrell's visor, glowed purple for an instant. "If the humanoids came from a common point, it would be in this region, approximately point nine three miles from where the attack occurred."

The wobbling line at the bottom of the display was the column's path through the jungle. A circle glowed around the indicated common point because Lundie was allowing for error. Farrell wondered how she controlled the imagery; her hands were empty.

People were lining up to be fed. The scouts and all strikers in the detached squad had their converters with them so feeding took longer than usual, but the process was entirely orderly. Even the hungriest folks weren't going to fight one another for cups of gray sludge.

Dr. Ciler was excluded from the discussion by his inability to see the display. He nodded and walked to where the wounded lay.

"The second attack was spread over a wider front," Lundie continued. The much larger skein of vectors glowed in turn. "There was a noticeable lag between when the humanoids initially attacked just ahead of the column's center and the attacks continuing in sequence forward along the line."

"Or trying to," Farrell remarked with a smile of grim satisfaction. "Meyer did a hell of a job on the w-w . . . the humanoids. With the dozer. I'll make her a sergeant for that. If we ever get to a place I can put in the paperwork."

Nearby, Mrs. Suares talked soothingly to the train of orphans she'd gathered to fill her own loss. The little dark-haired girl was crying; she refused to take the widow's hand.

Farrell shook his head, thinking about the Spook

tank exploding on Active Cloak. "Meyer's got quite a talent for heavy equipment," he added.

"The time lag would be explained if the humanoids all left a common point in close sequence," Lundie said, "making a straight line through the forest toward the predicted location of the column. Our progress and the consequently changed angle spread the attack over a slightly greater length of time."

The vectors from the two attacks led back to the same point. Because of what she considered to be sufficient data, Lundie didn't bother to circle it this time.

"A village . . ." Farrell said.

"Our information isn't sufficient to judge," Lundie said, answering a question that was really just Farrell thinking aloud. Al-Ibrahimi smiled slightly but gestured his aide to silence while Farrell considered.

From what Ciler said, it was more likely to be a hive. Whatever. Farrell had to do something. Best to deal with a problem at the source.

"Right," Farrell said. "Three-three's more than halfway to the target anyway. I'd like to have more troops. Well, I'd like a lot of things."

He nodded curtly to the administrators and began transmitting his orders to Sergeant Abbado.

The hull of the Kalendru transport was proof against the jungle. Blohm had the first guard shift outside. A single minilight turned the tilted compartment into a volume, not a trap. The smell of dead flesh was the sort of thing you got used to.

The major's transmission ended. "Six, roger," Abbado said. "Three-three out."

"Shit, that's not what I wanted to hear," Matushek

muttered. "How big is this wog village, does anybody know?"

Abbado shook his head. "There's about a hundred fewer warriors in it than there was a couple days ago," he said. "Hell, maybe there won't be anything for us to do but console the grieving widows, you think?"

"If the females look like the males . . ." Caldwell said as she took out her converter to make dinner. "I'd just as soon fight them, all right?"

Horgen looked through the opening to the jungle. She sang softly, *"Let me be your sidetrack till your mainline lover comes . . ."*

Abbado unfastened one bandolier and started checking the pockets. A fungus had begun to grow on the fabric, but the stinger magazines seemed all right. He wondered what he ought to do with the rocket whose warhead he'd expended to blow the cockpit open. It probably wasn't worth the weight of carrying it, but he hated to throw away anything of possible use when the margin was so thin.

Sergeant Gabrilovitch was crying silently.

"Hey Gabe," Abbado said while he continued to examine his ammo with the appearance of total concentration. "How's that shoulder of yours doing?"

"I can't do it," Gabrilovitch said. "I'm just going to die. I know it, I'm going to die."

"Yeah, I know what you mean," Caldwell said. Her powerknife whirred as she sliced off a thick vine stem. "I had a dream as real as could be before Placid Rose. You remember Placid Rose? The place smelled like a bad egg when we landed, but I guess my nose got used to it."

"The Spooks had packed up and gone home before

we got there, right?" Abbado said. Gabe wasn't the first striker to have a bad moment. This was no damn time for it, of course; but tomorrow was likely to be worse. "The place stank like hell, though."

"Yeah, but I was sure, I mean *sure*, I was buying the farm," Caldwell said. "Say, anybody want to try this with me? I set it for beans and franks."

Gabrilovitch began crying openly. "I'm poisoned," he wailed. "The major knows I'll die if I don't get back to the column. I need a *doctor*."

Abbado's lips pursed as if he was sucking a lemon. Gabe wasn't talking, it was the fear.

"*Abbado?*" Caius Blohm asked over a personal channel instead of using intercom or calling through the opening from outside. "*Want somebody to spell me on guard? I'll talk to him. Over.*"

"Hell, Gabe," Abbado said, speaking loudly enough that he was sure Blohm could hear him. "I never thought you could come with us. We're going to have enough trouble with the wogs not to worry about our walking wounded. I figured you'd wait here till we handled things and could come back for you."

Gabe was no damn good to them now, that Abbado could see. The problem wasn't the shoulder wound: a stinger only requires one hand to fire. The jungle had beat Sergeant Gabrilovitch down to his stumps. He might come out of it once things settled down— maybe even if he just got back to the column and was drugged into a night's sleep, something Abbado didn't dare do out here in the boonies.

Everybody's got a redline. It was creepy to be around somebody who'd gone past his, though. Especially if you weren't sure that you hadn't done the same thing yourself and just didn't recognize it.

"I think I better head back at daylight, Abbado," Gabrilovitch said. He hugged himself with his good arm and hunched over as if he had a belly wound.

"You'll be on your own, you know," Abbado warned. "I can't spare somebody to back you up."

And I especially can't spare Blohm, no matter how good buddies the two of you are.

"I'll be okay," Gabrilovitch said with his eyes closed. "I'll get back to the column and the docs 'll fix me up."

"Yeah, that's what I figure too," Abbado lied. "Say Caldwell? Give me a bite of your beanie-weenies, will you? Maybe I'll try a batch myself."

The tank melted around Meyer in the howling darkness. She was dying alone. She would be alone forever. She tried to shout, but her throat was filled with molten steel.

Striker Meyer. Esther.

She came awake flailing her arms. He tried to hold her wrists, but he wasn't nearly strong enough to control her for the first moments. Meyer had his throat in both hands before she returned to full awareness. A rush of white fire prickled across her skin.

She released Matthew Lock and slumped back onto the plastic. The night lived with the sounds of tight-packed sleepers. A few children cried openly. Adult sobs were more likely to be muffled. Snoring, sighing; the creak of plastic as someone rolled over or got up to walk to one of the pit latrines near the perimeter.

"I'm sorry I startled you," Lock said, wheezing slightly. He kept his voice down, though the only privacy in the encampment was that of exhaustion. There were sleepers or would-be sleepers within arm's length of Meyer in all directions. "You were calling out and I was afraid . . ."

"Was I?" Meyer said. "Oh hell. Hell."

Bezant had no moon. Lights in the camp and a few dying fires gave the air a soft presence that didn't really illuminate the occasional standing figure, guards and people picking their way among the sleepers.

Some of the trees were phosphorescent. They stood as pastel ghosts among their night-black fellows, blue and pink and a yellow that was nearly white.

"I'm sorry," Lock repeated. He shifted as if to stand up.

Meyer caught his hand. "I didn't know I was making a racket," she said. She closed her eyes to remind herself. The steel walls of the plenum chamber shrank down on her at once, even though she was awake and knew she lay in a clearing.

She pulled the civilian toward her again. "What?" he said. "What?"

"Don't fucking talk," Meyer said. She slid open her shirt's pressure closure with the side of her hand. "*Don't fucking talk.*"

She kept her eyes open, on his, as she kissed him.

Horgen was on guard. Caius Blohm stood at the edge of the opening where she wouldn't see him if she happened to look back at the ship.

Blohm wasn't at the opening because he didn't trust Horgen's alertness. He just wanted better commo reception than he could get farther within the metal hull.

The humid air blurred the stars. The few bright enough to show through it were smears, not points. There was no breeze, but the forest sighed softly as it grew and planned.

Blohm's visor echoed images from the helmets of strikers with the column. He combed one at a time through the helmets of the camp guards, seeing each remote viewpoint in full fidelity rather than masking it over his own surroundings as a double image.

His fifth try was Dancey watching the east edge and the barricaded inlet track. Mrs. Suares sat nearby, stroking the hair of one of the younger boys. The other children lay around her. Mirica was curled in a fetal ball. Her back trembled as she sobbed.

Blohm continued to watch the distant image until he heard a buzz from within the compartment. Horgen was waking Foley to take over the guard shift.

Blohm switched his visor off remote and lay down. He moved with the silence of a vine growing.

The Axe

The clearing was nearly circular and thirty feet across. Blohm paused. This was the first stretch of forest he'd seen that was naturally open to the sky.

The sky, bright but overcast, wasn't of much interest. The ground cover was something else again. Tawny five-foot swordblades grew as tightly as grass on a putting green.

"I think we better go around," he said. "That stuff's too thick to go through. If the edges aren't sharp, then there's something worse wrong with it."

He didn't have to use intercom or raise his voice. For safety the squad was closed up as much as possible. Abbado's people knew very well that while Blohm's helmet database was copied into theirs, that didn't give them the scout's instinct for aspects of the landscape they glimpsed for the first time.

"Roger," Abbado said. "We're within a hundred yards of the predicted target. I don't see much sign of a village."

Abbado got along better in the forest than Gabrilovitch did. Both sergeants viewed the vegetation as an enemy, but the fact didn't particularly bother Abbado. To him, enemies were something a striker fought or avoided; it didn't matter whether they had bark or pale gray skins.

Gabe found the forest's malevolence unnatural, even supernatural. Imagination made Gabrilovitch a good scout, whereas Abbado's two-valued logic—kill it or run—had struck Blohm as simple-minded during the year and a half he'd known the man.

Close contact under the present circumstances gave Blohm a different view of the line sergeant. Abbado was simple but not stupid. By ignoring questions that couldn't be answered Abbado handled dangerous situations, and he was able to lead strikers with him. Abbado's squad followed not only because of their sergeant's courage but because they accepted his logic.

Blohm checked possible routes around the clearing. He didn't like to be in any one place for longer than five minutes at a time. His rules for surviving in the forest were to touch as little as possible and to keep moving.

"Three-three elements," the helmet warned in the voice of God, the project manager. *"Carbon dioxide levels are rising sharply. A large number of humanoids is approaching your location from the north. Out."*

"Everybody in your null sacks," Blohm ordered. "Fast!"

"Roger," said Abbado, releasing the stinger he'd started to aim. He drew his sack from its pouch.

A line of humanoids came out of the trees on the other side of the clearing and entered it. They parted the grass like rocks dropping through still water.

Blohm took an instant to tack a remote sensor onto a tree, but he was still covered before the leading humanoid was halfway across the clearing. Abbado was almost as quick. The other strikers were a hair slower but still fast enough. Nobody hesitated to obey after Abbado accepted Blohm's instinct over his own.

From the heart of his null sack, Blohm viewed the oncoming humanoids through the sensor above him. He had the momentary sensation of being a ghost watching his own corpse—which was very likely to be the case if he'd guessed wrong. Sacks twisted enough of the optical range that they looked from the outside like lumpy shadows, but they weren't invisible.

The humanoids tramped purposefully through the forest, returning to a compass course whenever they had to skirt a tree. Lesser vegetation eased aside for them. They didn't run but they moved as swiftly as humans striding across a meadow.

Several of them stepped on Blohm in his null sack. Their feet felt soft and unpleasant, like those of slugs with bones.

The humanoids paid no attention to Blohm or the other members of the patrol who happened to be underfoot. The sacks were visible but they had none of the signatures of a life form.

The procession of armed natives continued for five and a half minutes, fanning minutely westward as more and more of the creatures paced from the far side of the clearing. Hundreds had passed before the sequence ended.

Blohm waited another minute, then opened his sack. If it had been his safety alone, he would have stayed under cover for at least five. "Six-six-two to C41," he reported. The other strikers were getting up also. "Two hundred and sixty-four humanoids are moving toward you. Every sixth one squirts acid. The rest have clubs. There are no other weapons, spears or guns. Over."

"*Six-six-two, roger,*" Major Farrell replied. "*We've been echoing your sensor and are reacting accordingly. Break. Three-three, carry on with your mission. Six out.*"

"No rest for the wicked," Abbado said mildly as he restowed his null sack. He glanced at Blohm and added, "How'd you know they'd leave us alone in our sacks, snake?"

"They don't have any more brains than a spider," Blohm said. "Than a tree. They don't think, they react. A sack doesn't give them anything more to react to than the dirt does, so they treat it the same way."

He hadn't known, but he'd been as sure as he was of sunrise. That's what the Unity paid him for—being sure even when he couldn't be.

"Why'd they come right at us, then?" Foley said. There was a little tension in the striker's voice. His fingers were having difficulty rolling his null sack. "They knew we were here, they must have."

Abbado reached over and anchored a corner of Foley's sack with a finger so that the fold didn't slip again like a transient dream.

"They're going from their village toward the column," Horgen said. "We're going the other way because the Spook ship happened to be in the same line. That's why the major sent us. It isn't planning, it's geometry."

"We'll go around the clearing to the right," Blohm said, back to considerations the procession of humanoids had interrupted. "Don't spend any longer than you have to under the tree with the smooth trunk, *mark*, I think the branches can come down like a fish trap."

"Shit," said Sergeant Abbado. "I forgot Gabrilovitch."

So had Blohm. The scout opened his mouth to send a warning, but Abbado was already doing that. "We need to move," Blohm said instead.

It took ten minutes for Blohm to lead the patrol around the margin of the clearing, even though he pulled the others faster than they should have gone. He knew they couldn't afford to stay longer where they'd been, and he didn't dare switch to remote viewing from Gabe's helmet until he'd reached a place to rest.

"Hold here," he ordered beside a tree whose fat trunk had the squishy uncertainty of a water balloon. "And for God's sake don't touch anything."

Gabrilovitch had left the crashed starship at the same time the others did, going in the opposite direction. The location plot showed he hadn't moved far. Abbado'd warned him to set a sensor and get into his null sack. If Gabe had done that, his bead of light would have vanished from the overlay.

"God damn you, Gabe," Blohm whispered as he echoed the panorama from his partner's helmet. "Don't panic and buy the farm!"

Gabrilovitch was running. The forest provided aisles of vision at unexpected angles. A pair of humanoids crossed one of them a hundred feet behind the striker, jogging rather than walking as before. They'd certainly spotted him.

"Six-six-one," Blohm said. "Gabe, fucking listen to me. Get in your sack. It's okay. They'll pass you by, I swear it. Gabe, this is Blohm. Trust me for God's sake, trust—"

Gabrilovitch ran into a dangling web of gossamer-fine air roots. He slashed them with his powerknife. The paired blades hummed and stopped, clogged by fluid showering from the underside of the branch above. Drops ran like clear water down the outside of the roots, but they clouded into glue when they touched the warmth of flesh or a machine.

Gabe began to scream. His arms were caught. His

legs thrashed for some seconds until they too were gummed into the curtain of roots.

The striker's body swayed in vain desperation. The visor protected his face so he could continue to scream.

Five of the expressionless humanoids reached Gabrilovitch. Three raised their clubs. They hacked with smashing, shearing strokes as regular as the beats of a metronome set slow. The other two turned away and thrust their beaklike mouths into the bark of neighboring trees, sucking sap for nourishment. Several club blows struck Gabe's helmet and knocked it askew, but the electronics still transmitted.

Blohm switched back to direct viewing. "Come on," he said. He paused to steady his voice. "This tree's going to burst in a minute or two and I don't want to be around."

The bulldozer snarled against increasing resistance as the blade bit into a trunk crackling like a machine gun. Meyer swayed, gripping the cab with her left gauntlet.

When the first tractor was about to stall and spin its treads against the soil, the second punched its stinger into the same tree at sixty degrees around the trunk. Meyer was braced against the initial shock, but her vehicle's lurch forward as the trunk started to go nearly threw her off the back of the deck.

Both bulldozers halted. The tree fell at an accelerating rate. The trunk's inertia tore the roots out of the ground, jerking the tracks as the vehicles reversed.

The tree tore in a lengthy crash through neighbors still standing. A lesser giant tilted away. As it did, a root uncoiled toward the other tractor. Strikers on the ground shouted warnings to Velasquez, but Meyer had the clear target. She played two seconds of brilliance from her flame gun, carbonizing the root all the way back to the trunk.

Meyer's driver steered the bulldozer carefully, aiming his blade at the next tree. She waved her flame gun to help cool the nozzle.

A rocket went off in the bole of a tree forty feet farther into the jungle, weakening it for the dozer blades in a minute or two. The major had decided to spend ordnance in order to clear an area quicker, both for a killing zone and to hold the civilians in a concentrated group where C41 could at least hope to surround them.

Al-Ibrahimi and his aide picked targets for the rocketeers. Most explosions triggered a result that would have endangered a bulldozer if the warhead hadn't preceded it. The administrators either had instincts equal to Caius Blohm's, or their little headsets had more computing power than a Strike Force helmet.

Meyer's bulldozer started forward. Matthew Lock waddled a minimal twenty feet behind with satchels of grenades. C41 hadn't brought any directional mines along when they left the colony ship, but grenades thrown from the tractor's deck would reach a little farther than they could from ground level. Even when a civilian was throwing them.

Meyer couldn't let herself look back at Lock. If she did that, she might miss a threat that would engulf him. But the movement of the figure at the back of her panoramic display glowed in her mind as if the helmet had careted it.

A drop of rain, scattered and repeatedly recombined by three layers of canopy, landed on Abbado's wrist. The storm had broken minutes before, but this was the first of it to reach ground level.

"There it is," Blohm said.

"That's a village?" Foley whispered.

"That's a hole in a tree," said Abbado, "but it's where the wogs are coming from, right enough."

The tree had begun as at least a dozen separate saplings. They merged as they grew. In combined form the monster covered a ragged circle over a hundred feet in diameter, black-barked and covered with air plants. The neighboring jungle had drawn away so that the swath beneath the spreading branches was clear.

Except for recent wear on the bark covering the lintel, the opening could have passed for a deep fold where two of the trunks joined. A human might have missed the signs, but the helmet AI hadn't.

Abbado scanned for heightened CO_2 levels. The concentration was normal. A breeze drew air into the slot, so there must be a vent at a higher level. The tree's hollow trunk provided a chimney for the humanoids living within.

"Grenades?" said Horgen, taking one in her hand.

"Not till we know what's inside," Abbado said. He loosened his bandoliers. The rain was coming harder, dripping from leaf tips and the underside of branches. Even a downpour couldn't make the air more humid.

"Right," said Blohm, stepping forward.

Abbado touched the scout's arm, drew him back. "My job," he said. "Your job was to get us here."

Abbado released and reextended his stinger to be sure its sling hadn't jammed. He jogged across the ten yards of open space to the tree.

His shoulders didn't quite brush the edges of the hole, but he had to duck his head slightly to clear the top. The opening fitted the humanoid warriors the way the cutter does cookies that come from it. There were two right-angle bends in the passage beyond, a left and a right. The walls were a light trap, dead black and porous.

Abbado stepped around the second bend, expecting darkness and God alone knew what else. He found what else.

The interior was a cavern whose walls glowed like windows of hammered glass. The light baffle was to keep the tree from shining out into the nighted jungle like an advertising sign.

The entire tree was hollow. The floor sloped from the entrance where Abbado stood into a bowl-shaped cavity of even broader dimensions.

He recognized the figures first. Humanoids of slighter build than the warriors crawled over something that looked like a fuel bladder which filled almost half the cavern's volume. The tenders polished the bladder with wads of gray fabric.

A pair of giants detached themselves from nooks in the sidewall and shambled toward Abbado. They were twelve feet tall and carried edged clubs that must have weighed a hundred pounds. Similar monsters stepped into sight farther from the entrance. They shook off coatings of the amber gelatine which had sealed them into individual cells.

Abbado armed a rocket. The nearest giants raised their clubs.

Man-sized capsules clung to the wall of the cavern. There were hundreds in the highest row, forty feet above the ground. Lower down the light of the surface behind the translucent capsules showed the shadows of developing forms. Those at floor level contained fully-formed warriors.

The bladder twitched and deposited another egg high up on the wall. The bladder was alive. Its head and torso were as large as those of the giants but dwarfed by the swollen obscenity of the abdomen to which they attached. Its beak was thrust into the wall of the tree. A line of scarred punctures around the cavern indicated that at intervals the creature changed the point from which it sucked sap.

The mother.

Abbado fired his rocket into the abdomen of the mother in instinctive revulsion instead of killing the right-hand guard as his conscious mind had planned. Backblast reflected from the cavern wall flung him forward. The giants' clubstrokes, scissoring from either side, struck behind him.

The giants stood between Abbado and the entrance. They raised their clubs with the deft ease of elephants lifting their trunks. Abbado dived between them, collided with the first bend in the passage, and pulled a pair of grenades from his belt. He tossed them into the cavern, then tossed two more.

He'd managed to dodge around the second baffle before the bombs went off. The blast spat him like the cork from a champagne bottle instead of smashing him against the dense wood. He sprawled on the bare ground, then rose to all fours with difficulty.

"How many rockets we got?" Abbado asked. His eyes were closed. His back and neck ached, and his calves had a chilly prickle that probably meant they were bleeding. "I want all your rockets."

"Sarge, you can't go back in there," Matushek said.

"We all go back in there," Abbado said. He pushed himself upright and turned around. "The rest of you keep the big fuckers off me. And I take care of that *filthy* thing, I swear I do. Fast! Give me the rockets now."

They only had six including the motor whose warhead Abbado'd used to pop open the bridge hatch. The patrol was heavy on ammo and grenades; Horgen, Foley, and Matushek carried grenade launchers as well as stingers. 3-3'd prepared for a shipload of Spooks without much in the way of rocket targets.

Well, they'd need the grenades. Maybe the stingers too, though Abbado doubted pellets had enough penetration to bring down one of those guards in time to do him any good.

He armed the six rockets. He carried one in each hand; the other four—three and a half—dangled from his belt. Arming the rockets was about the most dangerous thing Guilio Abbado had done since he enlisted, but it wasn't like there was a lot of choice.

"You all saw what's waiting in there," he said to the other strikers. "Blohm and Caldwell, you go as far as the second turn and each throw two grenades into the chamber. Don't waste time getting back. When they blow, I go in and start doing my job. Grenade launchers follow, then Blohm and Caldwell again. Don't know how much good stingers'll do, but it can't hurt."

Abbado smiled. "Watch how you come," he added. "I don't want you all stuck in the doorway while the folks inside are pulling my legs off."

It didn't occur to Abbado that his strikers wouldn't follow. They had to follow. Otherwise the job wouldn't get done.

"Ace, give me an electrical," Blohm said. Matushek

handed him one. The scout carried a pair of fuel-air grenades. Mixing the effects was a good idea.

Blohm thumbed both grenade switches. "Let's do it," Caldwell said as she stepped into the passage.

A thousand one, a thousand two, a thousand three—

Abbado didn't bother to remote the lead team's display. Caldwell wouldn't be going far enough to see anything and Blohm was behind her.

A thousand four—

Blohm reappeared and jumped to the left side of the opening.

A thousand five—

Caldwell, her mouth open to equalize pressure, dodged out and to the right. None of the strikers were in the path of the angled shockwave.

A thousand s—

Red flame belched from the opening. A spurt of acrid black smoke followed.

Abbado stepped into the passage with the grace of a dancer. He held his rockets upright. If he knocked a fuze against passage walls, he'd blow himself and Horgen behind him to hell in little pieces.

Filters clamped his nostrils. The cavern walls glowed through veils of smoke swirling toward the peak of the enormous tree. Three of the giant guards were down near the mouth of the passage. A fourth stood gripping his club, but he'd been blinded by grenade shrapnel. Giants who'd been farther from the entrance lumbered toward the strikers.

Abbado ran ten feet into the cavern and knelt, aiming his rockets at the mother's abdomen again. Green fluid oozed from the previous wound. The creature coiled like a maggot on a spike. Her limbs were too small to touch the ground, but the whole body writhed.

Abbado fired, right and left together. The backblast shoved him like a hot pillow but didn't knock him down this time.

He caught the flicker of a club swinging at him. Five grenades fuzed for point impulse went off in quick succession. The charges shattered the guard's cranial vault just as they would have done body armor or a vehicle's engine. The great arms continued their swing, but the weapon sailed across the cavern instead of driving Abbado into the ground like a tent peg. A bit of grenade casing whacked his helmet.

Launched grenades burst on two other of the shambling guards. The charges were light enough to minimize the risk to the strikers. Using hand grenades in an enclosure, even an enclosure as large as this one, was next to suicidal; though it might come to that.

Abbado sent two more rockets into the mother. He saw the flash of warheads through the creature's skin. Caldwell emptied a stinger magazine into the face of a guard; Blohm raked his across the rows of capsules.

The mother had pulled her beak from the wall. Sap dripped from the tip and from the hole in the wood. Abbado put another rocket into her abdomen. Fluid pooled inches deep on the floor beneath the creature; its bloated flesh sagged like a half-inflated balloon.

Foley dodged a swinging club and slipped. The stroke took his legs off at mid thigh. He was too stunned to scream. He twisted, trying to seat a fresh magazine. The launcher had flown from his other hand when the club hit. Matushek and Horgen fired grenades into the giant's skull. The guard fell forward, crushing Foley beneath it.

Abbado aimed his last rocket at the center of the mother creature's chest. The projectile flew high without the weight of the warhead. The motor was still burning when it punched through the beaked face and into the wall of the cavern.

"Three-three elements disengage!" Abbado shouted through the bedlam as he sighted his stinger. Ten of the troll-like guards were down; one was clubbing the wall thirty feet away and the last kept coming despite what must have been a dozen fatal grenade blasts. "Three-three and scouts, disengage!"

The guard had no more neck than a rhinoceros. Abbado fired at the throat anyway because it was the one part of the creature's kill zone that grenades hadn't cratered. Low flames spread across the fluid leaking from eggs punctured by shrapnel and gunfire. The chamber was becoming noticeably warmer and smokier despite the updraft.

"Get out, for Chrissake!" Abbado said. Using the panoramic display as he backed toward the door, he avoided the guard sprawled behind him.

Three of his strikers were out of the chamber. Horgen reloaded her grenade launcher. Abbado grabbed her by the shoulder and shoved her toward the passage.

The head of the oncoming giant rotated sideways and fell. It continued to roll down the smooth slope toward the burning egg capsules. The body took another step before the weight of the club pulled the decapitated corpse over.

Abbado dodged out of the passage. He dismissed the thought of throwing another grenade behind him. They were likely to need the ordnance on the way back.

And he was so tired. So very tired. The rain-drenched jungle felt unexpectedly cool.

"Good work, people," Abbado whispered. He tried to reload his stinger and found he'd already done that. He couldn't imagine when. "Six, this is Three-three. Mission accomplished. We're heading home. Out."

"Out" rather than "over." That was Abbado's way of saying that nobody was going to task 3-3 for another mission until they'd had time to resupply and recover.

"Three-three, roger," the major's voice replied. *"The drinks are on me. Six out."*

"Sarge, I'm sorry," said Caius Blohm. "You're going to have to make it back without me. There's just a chance I can get to the column in time to help with the wogs we passed going the other way. The rest of you can't."

"Are you out of your fucking *mind*?" Matushek said softly. Ace had taken his helmet off and was massaging his temples. His eyes appeared to have sunk into his skull since the beginning of the mission.

"Maybe," Blohm said. "Move slow, don't touch anything if you can help it, and let your helmets guide you. They know everything I do."

The scout turned away. Horgen raised her stinger.

"Let him go," Abbado said. Blohm vanished into the jungle, moving like a ghost.

"Let him go," Abbado repeated. "I've fought everybody I'm going to fight for the next long while."

Art Farrell stood in the pouring rain on top of a trailer-load of plastic sheets. He wished lightning would hit him, but he knew he'd never be that lucky.

"Carbon dioxide levels to the north are rising," warned Tamara Lundie. She stood beside the project manager at the foot of the trailer. Around them lay the injured and unwell who'd been moved to the

ground till this was over. *"Estimate fifteen seconds."*

"C41, advance party, fall back," Farrell ordered. His fingers probed his stinger's rain-slick receiver, but he didn't eject and reinsert the magazine. "Ten seconds, people. Out."

The bulldozers had stripped a swath of jungle three hundred by fifty feet. Clearance debris including the trunks of full-sized trees lay in a row against the long northern side from where the natives were supposed to attack. Twenty-two strikers waited ten yards back. That was as deep a kill zone as Farrell thought he could afford without pushing the civilians too close to the back edge of the clearing.

Christ, he hoped it was the back edge. All it would take to turn this into a massacre was for twenty or thirty natives to circle the clearing before they attacked.

The advance party of five strikers scampered down from the top of the pile to join the main line. Farrell had placed them there because the location gave Lundie a wider reach on CO_2 levels.

There'd been six in the advance party. Tasman, who had the sweetest voice Farrell ever heard on a person he'd met face to face, stepped on what looked like a solid log and sank in to his crotch. He screamed for several seconds before his torso rolled to the ground. His legs had dissolved.

War has its own system of accounting. In this case, fifteen seconds cost a striker's life. A soldier knows that "want" isn't the same as "need"; and Farrell had needed the fifteen seconds.

Sorry 'bout that. Wish it'd been me.

The civilians, nearly a thousand of them, were behind the main line and not quite crowded into the jungle. Farrell had placed the bulldozers on the flanks. The total guard force for the sides and rear was four strikers and a few who weren't walking but still could pull a trigger.

Farrell would rather have had the civilians in a tight lump instead of being spread out in a line. He'd decided in a heartbeat that it was more important to open the entire front instead of having natives coming straight out of the jungle on top of his strikers.

It rained like a cow pissing on a flat rock. Civilians without light enhancement and commo helmets couldn't see well or talk, so they were that much likelier to panic. Stinger pellets didn't like rain this heavy either, and even a veteran's fingers could slip while changing magazines.

You play the hand you're dealt. Lightning flashed between clouds.

A stinger fired on the right edge of the line. The charge fluoresced from the muzzle like a yellow tulip. Farrell didn't see that target, but three natives appeared over the pile a little farther down. A dozen more stingers lit the firing line. Pellets ripped wood, dirt and the humanoids.

The natives staggered. One of them kept coming even after stingers chewed his arm off. Forty more appeared, all along the line. The berm protected the attackers rather than the defense, but the clearance debris had to go somewhere. Lethal vegetation made the wrack too dangerous to fight from, the way Farrell would have liked to do.

Farrell wasn't shooting. He was C41's entire reserve.

Natives mounted the pile as if it was level ground. They didn't seem organized, but clots of ten or a dozen sometimes converged on a single striker.

Somebody emptied his stinger, then fired his backup grenade launcher instead of trying to reload. The blast five feet from the muzzle blew the humanoid's head and arms in three different directions, but it flung the striker backward into screaming civilians. His helmet fell off and he didn't get up.

Hand grenades went off on both flanks, silhouetting trees against the sullen red glare of fuel-air explosive. Farrell didn't know if the bombers were being attacked or if they were making sure that they weren't.

"Targets, mark," Manager al-Ibrahimi warned on the two-way channel he shared with the major. Four spikes flashed to the rear quadrant of Farrell's lower, panoramic display. He turned, throwing the targets onto his visor's upper register.

They were trees, emergents whose blunt peaks stood two hundred feet above the forest floor and well above the general canopy. They were hundreds of feet distant. Farrell—and al-Ibrahimi, using the major's helmet sensors—wouldn't have been able to see them at all had he not been standing on top of the trailer. The tops of nearer trees screened the emergents from people on the ground.

The crowns of the four trees were swollen. Farrell dialed up his visor's magnification by a thousand, focusing on the nearest. The swelling was a gall, an insect nest, rather than part of the tree proper. Crablike creatures the size of a man's palm crawled on the papery exterior. Others peeped from dozens of entrances to the inside of the nest. Instead of claws, the creatures' mouth parts twitched like long scissorblades.

The tree was wobbling. If it toppled toward the clearing, the swollen peak would land in the middle of the colonists.

Farrell armed a 4-pound rocket, aimed it, and sent it into the center of the nest. The warhead's artificial lightning blew the target to tatters. Shreds of the outer fabric drifted away, burning until the downpour quenched them. The shockwave would kill any of the crabs that the shrapnel didn't get.

Farrell twisted free a second rocket and aimed it. Four rockets, four targets . . . or a lot of people were fucked. Strikers from the rear guard looked back at him. They could echo the major's visor display, but nobody else could hit those treetops.

He fired. In the humid air the rocket motor left a thick white trail before burn-out, then a diminishing thread for the remainder of its course. The second nest disintegrated.

The third tree was swaying in a figure-8 that moved the peak across ten feet from Farrell's left to right; he knew that the long axis of oscillation was dipping toward him. He aimed and fired as coldly as if he were on a weapons qualification course.

Backblast seared the right side of his neck below the visor. The target was a flash and a brief fireball.

The last tree was already falling. It was moving at a slight angle to Farrell, so he had to allow for deflection. As the rocket snarled free, he reached for his stinger though he knew it would be next to useless if those creatures got among the defenseless civilians.

The warhead hit the wood just below the nest, severing the upper ten feet of the crown. It rolled backward from the blast. Crown and main trunk continued to fall. Instead of landing in the midst of the clearing, the top spun into a stand of tall reeds which the dozers had skirted on the south edge.

The reeds flexed around the treetop like water

sloshing in a bucket. The fall would have killed few if any of the crabs. When they came swarming out of the vegetation they'd be impossible to stop before they got among the colonists.

Farrell pulled a fuel-air grenade from his belt. He was close enough to the reeds to throw with the present combination of height and desperate need.

Farrell's thumb froze on the arming switch. If he threw the grenade, the flexible reed stems would fling it back into the civilians before it exploded.

Some of the civilians were trying to get away from the falling tree. Because of the storm and the roaring confusion of the attack most of them hadn't even noticed it.

Flea Glasebrook ran toward the grove holding a fuel-air grenade in either hand. The other strikers at the back of the clearing stopped shooting uselessly into the reeds.

Glasebrook hit with the point of his shoulder as if the grove was a tackling dummy. Mud sprayed as his cleats bit and thrust him through the resistance. Farrell saw the flicker of the precursor charges dispersing the grenade fuel across the interior.

The grenades went off with a huge red flash. The reeds and everything within them disintegrated. The shock wave knocked down people fifty feet away and flung Art Farrell backward from his perch.

If there was a heaven, Glasebrook had just blown his way through the door.

Lessons Learned

A tree twenty feet from Meyer's bulldozer had been smoldering for the five minutes since a grenade went off nearby. Hair-thin spines covering the bark ignited in a gush of white that enveloped the branches a hundred and fifty feet above. As the initial gout died away, the trunk itself burst into vibrant red flame. It pulsed like the muzzle flashes of an automatic weapon.

Meyer tapped Seligman's shoulder. "Let's knock that bastard down," she said. "Otherwise it's going to fall in our direction as sure as it's raining."

The driver probably swore, but he didn't switch on the intercom for Meyer to hear it. He lifted the dozer blade from the ground, then began to back and turn the tractor to line up the target.

A stinger cracked out a single pellet. Somebody was making sure a wog knew that dead meant dead.

The bulldozer started forward. Meyer rocked with a motion become familiar.

She was alone with Seligman on the vehicle. Matt had caught fragments of one of his own grenades in his right cheek and arm. He'd insisted they were just scratches, nothing to worry about, but Meyer wasn't having any of that macho bullshit. He'd been wounded, so he was walking over to the docs and doing whatever they told him to do.

298

She'd been a long time without him, without anybody. She wasn't going to lose him now for a stupid reason.

The tree throbbed before them. Seligman lowered the blade to shave the ground, spilling burning brush to the left.

Meyer checked to be sure the tank of the flame gun was beneath the cab overhang, sheltered from the heat radiating from the trunk. The hard suits protected her and the driver from burning wood, at least for as long as it would take to push the tree over. If the tank cooked off, the metallized fuel could be another thing entirely.

She braced herself. The blade's stinger punched its full length into the fiery tree, just to the right of the trunk's center. The tracks slowed as the cleats bit but continued to work the tractor laboriously forward.

The tree wasn't a particularly big one for this jungle, maybe three feet in diameter. It shook its blazing crown; then the whole trunk started to go.

A branch broke off high overhead and spun toward the clearing, showering sparks through the rain. There was nothing anybody below could do but try to judge its course and run like hell.

Seligman couldn't see the dropping torch; it didn't matter to his job anyway. The bulldozer ground on as deliberately as sand running through an hourglass.

A little child ran past the left side of the tractor, so blind with fear that the heat of the falling tree didn't turn her back. She crossed the ground the trunk would smash and incinerate in a matter of seconds. As she fled she screamed, "Caius! Caius!"

A woman ran twenty feet behind the child, gaining only inches with each stride. She ducked beneath the toppling tree.

The trunk hit with an impact that made the soil ripple. Chunks of burning wood flew to both sides. The woman stumbled but managed not quite to fall. She continued to pursue the child into the unbroken jungle, batting furiously at her coveralls. Though the garment didn't burn, sparks melted into the cloth.

"Did you see that?" Seligman said. He shifted the bulldozer into neutral. "What are they thinking about? Are they out of their goddam minds?"

Meyer sat on the edge of the deck with her legs dangling over, then levered herself off with both hands. She wanted to jump down, but the weight of her equipment was more likely than not to stun her if she got hasty.

The bulldozer backed cautiously. Meyer trotted between the blade and the upturned roots, then into the full glare of the burning trunk. She wished she'd had time to unsling the flame gun before she ran over fiery ground, but there was no time to waste.

If the kid and woman were going to survive more than the next few seconds, Esther Meyer had to get them out of the jungle.

Blohm heard the tree falling—the snap of branches and vines as the trunk tore them away, the sigh of air shoved aside in its passage. Though he knew the tree was so close he could have flipped a pebble against it on an open plain, the only glimpse the scout caught was a wink of bright flame through a gap in the foliage.

It hit. The forest shrugged angrily. Smoke and steam swollen with the odors of life fanned the undergrowth. Blohm opened his mouth to call in his location so that he wasn't shot as he entered the clearing twenty yards distant.

He felt them coming toward him.

Not strikers, because his visor located every member of C41. Humanoids, the survivors of the attack on the column.

He'd moved under branches sturdy enough to stop or at least slow the falling tree's impact. The bark of his shelter oozed sap that vaporized and made his bare skin tingle, but he didn't intend to stay long in its range.

Around the trunk was an open circle three or four feet in diameter; beyond that grew a stand of wire-trunked seedlings that would bind a human. When the attackers came through the screen at him like water through a sieve, Blohm wouldn't be able to drop more than one of them before the rest got him the way they had Gabrilovitch.

He took the last grenade from his belt and cocked his arm for a throw high enough to clear the screen. The fuel would spray down and envelope everything in the thicket when it went off. Do them before they do you.

Just like Active Cloak.

And because he hadn't thrown the grenade at the last possible moment by which it would have saved his life from attacking humanoids, Caius Blohm heard Mirica scream his name as the seedlings grabbed her. He wasted the grenade in the forest behind him as he entered the reeds with his powerknife.

The trunks were rubbery and hard to grip, but the blade sliced through their softness like cobwebs. Blohm could have cut them with the shaft of a spoon if he'd had to at this moment.

He took Mirica in his left arm and hugged her to him as he strode on slashing. He didn't have a plan for how he was going to free Mrs. Suares while holding the child, but in the event he didn't have to. A striker in an ash-smeared hard suit was already pulling the old woman clear.

They were on the other side of the trap. Beyond was a steam-swathed tree trunk and a bulldozer at the edge of the clearing.

The child called, "Caius!" as she clutched his chest and they all four staggered to safety.

Farrell sat cross-legged with his visor down, clicking through alternative arrangements for deploying his strikers on the march. The helmet AI shifted purple dots and the orange masses of civilians with equanimity, but it couldn't tell Art Farrell what the next threat was going to be.

It could have told him that he didn't have enough strikers for the job, but that wouldn't have been news.

"Striker Blohm is here, sir," Kristal said, loud enough to cut through Farrell's concentration.

He raised his visor instead of clearing it. Caius Blohm stood straight, more like a prisoner tied to a stake than as a soldier at attention.

The problem with Blohm wasn't the sort of thing you expected in the Strike Force. Kristal didn't know what facial expression would be appropriate. She was a little too eager for the extra rate than Farrell liked, but no question she was doing a good job filling in as First Sergeant under the worst conditions you could imagine.

Farrell had set a minilight on the sheeting in front of him. He didn't need the illumination, but it showed the civilians that he was present and accessible. Now he turned the light off, then removed his helmet.

"Sit down, Blohm," he said. "Thanks, Sergeant. Tell

God that I'll be unavailable for the next few minutes, all right?"

The present clearing was good-sized, now that there wasn't a battle going on in it. You couldn't call where Farrell sat private, exactly—certainly not from strikers' helmets—but there was a respectful amount of space open around him.

The scout seated himself with cautious grace. He took off his helmet also. Light from the fire crackling twenty yards away accentuated the hollows of Blohm's cheeks and eye sockets, and they were deep enough already.

"I waited till Sergeant Abbado got back to have this conversation, Blohm," Farrell said. "You went out and brought them the last of the way in, I gather?"

"Yessir," Blohm said. "Sir . . ."

He let the word trail off.

"What the *fuck* did you think you were playing at, Blohm?" Farrell said in a voice that never rose above the minimum necessary for the other man to hear him. "You knew it was your responsibility to guide the patrol back. I wouldn't have given even odds of ever seeing Abbado and his people again."

"Yes sir," said Blohm. His body was still, but his palms were flat together and pressing so hard that they trembled. "Sir, I knew it was wrong."

"Do you think we're so short-handed that I can't have you shot for desertion right now, Blohm?" Farrell said. "Is that what you think?"

"No sir," Blohm said. Tears glittered in his eyes; the shiver in his hands had spread to his voice. "I know you can have me shot. I know you can."

"Well, if you know that, you're an even bigger damned fool than I thought you were," Farrell said, relaxing. "Christ, man, you're a lot of what chance we have of surviving this ratfuck. Thing is, I need Three-three just as bad. You lot nailed one set of our problems today, but I've seen enough of this jungle to expect something new in the morning. Were you figuring to guard a thousand civilians all by your lonesome?"

"Sir, I fucked up," Blohm said. He wiped his eyes, angry at his weakness. "I—"

He paused, but this time he finished the sentence: "Sir, I never had anybody give a shit about me before. I can't take care of her alone, I know that. I'll do my job, sir. I'll never not do my job again."

"Go get some dinner, Blohm," Farrell said, rubbing his temples. "We've got a lot of long days ahead of us." If we live that long.

"Yes sir," Blohm said as he rose, lifting his helmet with him. Almost shyly he added, "We're having tapioca pudding again. I told her we would when I came back."

He stepped away briskly. Farrell saw Seraphina Suares and a small child waiting for the scout just beyond the range their presence would be intrusive.

Farrell remained as he was. He told himself he ought get back to fooling with the order of march, but that was a lie. He didn't have enough information to know where he should put his strikers, and he didn't have enough strikers anyway. All he'd really be doing was clutching a security blanket. It wouldn't save one single life tomorrow or in the days to come.

Tamara Lundie sat down beside him in the near darkness. "What I really want to do," he said without raising his head from his hands, "is get drunk. But I can't afford to."

"In celebration of your victory?" Lundie said.

Farrell turned his head. He'd never get used to the blonde's earnestness, not if this damned operation lasted a million years.

"No," he said, careful to keep the disgust out of his voice. She didn't know, she *couldn't* know; and she was trying to learn. "Because I lost people today. I'd like to get drunk enough to forget that, or at least to get some sleep."

"But . . ." Lundie said. He couldn't see any more of her face than a blur as pale as snow. "You've had casualties before. Casualties were very light today in comparison to your achievement."

"Since I took command of C41," Farrell said, feeling his face smile. You had to laugh, or . . . "The company's casualties have been three hundred and fifty percent. The magic of replacements, you see."

"But these were strikers who'd been with you for some time," Lundie said, articulating her understanding in the form of a statement rather than a question.

"I guess they were," Farrell said. "Yeah, I suppose that does make a difference. But I don't take anybody on an operational mission until they've trained with the company long enough that I know them, believe me."

He shook his head. "They all hurt," he said. "Every fucking one of them. I don't remember the names a lot of times, but I see their faces. Every fucking one."

Lundie nodded slowly. "I see," she said.

She stood up. She looked as delicate as a straw doll. "Major Farrell," she said. "I am honored to serve with you and your strikers."

She touched his hand and walked away, toward where her boss was projecting large holographic images for a group of civilians.

In a funny way, Farrell thought, Tamara saying that was better than the usual post-mission quart of cognac.

"Krishna, I'm tired," Caldwell said. "I'm going to treat myself. I'm going to take boots off. I really am."

Abbado snicked closed the latch of the bandolier he'd been about to remove. "What the hell is that?" he said softly. He walked toward the civilians gathered around a huge holographic projection. The sheeting creaked, but his boots and those of his strikers made no sound of their own.

The basis of the display was helmet imagery, mixed from multiple sources and enhanced by a very powerful editing program. You had to have been there to notice the glossy texture that replaced the gritty, vaporous reality.

Abbado had been there, all right. The projection was of the attack on the mother creature and her guards.

"Well, I'll be damned to hell," Matushek said. "How are they doing that, anyway?"

He meant the holograms. Abbado saw God down in front; nothing the manager and his aide came up with was much of a surprise any more. The other question was how 3-3 had managed to survive. That was harder to answer, now that Abbado saw the action as a spectator.

He watched as a figure, Sergeant Guilio Abbado, loosed two rockets at the gravid mother, then stepped forward so that a troll's club smashed the ground behind him. He didn't remember dodging but he must have done. It looked like a ballet pass from the outside, but he didn't remember it at all.

Monsters came from the smoke. Strikers fired point-blank. Caldwell grappled with a guard, sawing at the tendons of the creature's wrist as its other hand closed on her helmet. Grenades flashed on the guard's beaked face. Still it gripped though the club fell from nerveless fingers.

The image faded into pearly radiance, then blacked out. Manager al-Ibrahimi rose to his feet and bowed to the four strikers. Colonists turned, craned their necks and stood for a better view.

There were hundreds of them watching. Hundreds.

"Ah . . ." Abbado said. "Ah, we didn't mean to disturb anybody."

Christ, he didn't know what to say. "Come on," he muttered to Horgen. "Let's get some dinner and I'll check the guard roster with Kristal."

Their billet was nearby, a hundred square feet of sheeting where Kristal had had 3-3's excess gear dumped to await their return from patrol. The plastic heaved. Abbado looked over his shoulder. The crowd of civilians was following them.

"I'll be damned to *hell*," Ace repeated.

Dr. Ciler gripped Abbado's hand and shook it. "I'm so sorry about Striker Glasebrook," he said. "He was a hero. Hundreds would have died. Sergeant, you're all heroes."

"It's not like that," Abbado said, frustrated that he didn't have the words to explain. He saw a civilian give Horgen a drink from a chased silver flask that was certainly older than the Unity. Ethanol was as easy to run from the converters as starch was, but other of the colonists were offering sauces and spices.

Mary, Mother of God. The thought of a meal that didn't taste like refinery sludge . . .

"Doc, it's not like that," he repeated. "We're all in this together."

"Yes," said Ciler. "We are."

Mrs. Florescu was holding Caldwell and crying. The striker looked stunned. When they got someplace he could do it, Abbado'd write Caldwell up for that business with the guard. You couldn't eat a medal, but fuck, the Strike Force usually supplied you with enough to eat.

"I'll be damned to hell!" Matushek said with a bottle in either hand.

No, Ace, Abbado thought. We've been damned to hell. It just might be we'll find a way out after all.

Into the Fire

"The trouble with cayenne pepper," said Matushek as he rigged a pair of 4-pound rockets to balance the pair on the other hip, "is it's just as hot on your asshole as it is in the mouth."

The remainder of C41 had rearmed from the ammo trailer immediately after their battle with the natives. Abbado hadn't had the energy to do that because of the excitement when 3-3 got home. That meant they had to be up ahead of most of the others this morning. They were lead squad again.

A bulldozer started with a squeal of steam and the slowly-building thrum of the turbine flywheel. Meyer stood on the deck, putting her armor on. One of the civilian men was helping her.

Good for Essie.

Horgen was stuffing grenade magazines into the empty pockets of her bandolier. She paused. Nodding across the tailgate she murmured, "Look who's come to visit."

Abbado stepped away from the trailer. He didn't lower his visor. The sky was too dark to distinguish from the canopy, but his eyes had adapted to the light of the few lamps still lit. Caius Blohm walked toward the trailer with a kid hanging onto his pants' leg.

"Hello, Blohm," Abbado said. "Figure you've got something to say to us?"

"Nothing you don't know," Blohm said. "Nothing I haven't said to the major. I screwed up bad. I won't screw up that way again."

"Expect us to kiss you, then?" Matushek said, stepping around the trailer from the other side. His hands weren't any nearer his weapons than any striker's were at any time, but the threat was obvious.

The kid buried her face against Blohm's thigh. He caressed her dark hair. "No," he said. "I don't even expect you to let me buy you a drink when we get out of this. I just came to say it to your faces."

"Ace," Abbado said sharply. "Hop up in the trailer and see if there's another grenade launcher in the front there, will you? I'm thinking of carrying one myself."

Blohm turned. As the scout walked away, he bent and lifted the child to his shoulder. Abbado returned to the tailgate.

"Sorry, Sarge," Matushek muttered.

"No big deal," Abbado said. He had one bandolier pocket empty, so he dragged a case of stinger magazines closer. "Just remember we got a whole jungle out there to fight."

Horgen climbed to the side of the trailer and perched there, reaching into an open box of hand grenades among the jumble of miscellaneous weaponry. "Do you really want a launcher, Sarge?" she asked.

"Naw, I was never much good with one," Abbado said. "I'll take an extra pack of rockets instead."

At least twenty lasers ripped simultaneously into the encampment from the west and south. A stinking black tear zigzagged across the tarpaulin folded over the front of the trailer.

"Contact!" Abbado shouted. He knelt as he armed a rocket, then rose again to launch it into the undergrowth from which the Kalendru fire spat. Backblast whanged the side of the trailer. "Contact!"

Blohm was down but unharmed, raking the jungle with aimed bursts from his stinger. "Medic!" he cried. He hunched to his feet and sprinted for the open south side of the clearing.

Abbado sent his second rocket into a Spook in the direction Blohm was heading. Abbado didn't know what the scout had in mind, but one target was as good at the next in an ambush.

The kid lay twitching on the ground where Blohm had dropped. Her hair smoked. A laser bolt had burned through it and the skull beneath.

The pulsing laser sheared wires from the protective grate on the side window of the bulldozer's cab. "Get down, Matt!" Meyer said as she stepped back and grabbed the grenade launcher slung across her breastplate.

The laser hit the heavy support member at the rear of the cage. A large collop of metal vaporized, then combined with atmospheric oxygen in a secondary flash and a shockwave that flung Lock off the deck.

"Get the kid to a medic!" Meyer said, firing around the cab. She aimed a few feet above the bolts snapping from the jungle. Launched grenades weren't heavy enough to do a lot of damage with tree bursts, but the shrapnel spread over a wide area and suppressed Spook fire better than just killing a couple would do.

Seligman tried to get up from his seat. Meyer pushed him back down. He couldn't get past her out of the cab. "Drive!" she said. "Right into those fuckers in front! Keep the blade up and they can't touch you!"

Not really true, since once the tractor got close the Spooks could shoot from the sides. Either Seligman didn't see that or he figured the bad guys were less likely to kill him than the striker on his deck was. He lifted the blade six inches from the ground and put the tractor in gear.

The land-clearing blade rang as lasers struck it a series of quick hammerblows, marking the surface but doing no appreciable harm. Meyer knew what it felt like to have an unstoppable machine bearing down on you. The Kalendru shooters wouldn't stand long if all they had was anti-personnel weapons.

Meyer switched on the flame gun's pump and pointed the nozzle at the treeline eighty feet away. Her visor was cloudy where redeposited metal vapor plated the outside. The AI corrected, but trees and undergrowth looked as though they were plastic and had been extruded from simplified molds.

She swept her flame rod across the brush to the south a little faster than the tractor's own westward motion would have taken it. The treeline was barely within range. The white glare arched high and started to break up as it fell, spattering rather than sledging the beaten zone.

Light vegetation withered. The bark of giants puffed red and orange fire, but a brief touch of flame didn't ignite the wood itself.

Kalendru ran hooting, then spun and fell in a storm of stinger pellets.

When her thirty seconds of fuel were exhausted, Meyer dropped the flame gun and plucked a grenade from the satchel at her waist. She hadn't attached the hard suit's left thigh piece before the shooting started, so she hoped like hell the hot nozzle didn't twist around that way.

She hoped Matt was okay. The docs probably couldn't do much for a kid who'd been head shot, but if Matt carried her to them they'd take care of his burns.

Meyer threw the grenade over the bulldozer's blade. Rockets and bombs were saturating the jungle from which the Spooks had fired. They'd figured on surprise, but a strike company reacts with no more hesitation than a mousetrap. After the first volley it was a two-way fight and C41 had the firepower.

Meyer hoped a lot of things, but right now what she particularly hoped was that she'd kill the Spook who'd missed Matthew Lock's head by under a centimeter.

The forest was by now Caius Blohm's closest acquaintance. Not a friend, never a friend; but they knew one another. The scout moved as water does on a rough, gently-sloping surface: without haste or certain direction, but inexorably.

Blohm was going to capture a prisoner. They needed a prisoner. And he was going to kill all the other Kalendru he found.

He'd switched off his helmet and stinger. Spook sensors were so discriminating that they could identify even the slight leakage from a stinger's electronics at a hundred yards. It would take thirty seconds to cool the weapon's coils, but Blohm wouldn't need a stinger for what he had in mind.

He didn't think he'd need his helmet sensors, and he didn't want the communications. This was his business alone.

Blohm paused. The roots of forest giants spread as broadly as the branches above, bracing the trunk and sucking nourishment from a wide circuit of the thin soil. A six-foot band of leaf litter lay flat with no striations from surface roots.

He jumped over instead of going around because he was in a hurry. The ground on the other side was firm. If he'd stepped on the open space, a trap would have sprung as sure as the sun rose above the canopy. Blohm neither knew nor cared whether it would have been a pit, a gummy surface, root tentacles or some possibility unguessed.

He hadn't had time to get behind the Spooks before the survivors retreated from C41's storm of fire. He was following a group of six. Paralleling their course, rather, because he'd learned that a moving animal tended to sensitize the vegetation so it reacted instantly to the next one by.

The Kalendru were by their quickness and delicacy better adapted to survive here than humans were, but Blohm didn't have the impression that any of this group understood the forest the way he did. They overcame the forest with speed instead of brute force like the strikers of C41.

Caius Blohm coexisted with the forest, moving through it as a midge does a coarse screen. The forest might resent his presence, but it couldn't touch him while his mind remained one with it.

He hadn't seen the Kalendru since the first exchange of fire. They chittered to one another as they moved, but for the most part Blohm tracked his quarry by the way the forest itself reacted. Leaves turned, branches rustled without wind; even the air pressure shifted. All those things pointed to the Kalendru as surely as a blind man can locate the sun by the touch of light on his bare skin.

The Kalendru moved in quick spurts like mice scurrying from one bit of cover to the next in an open landscape. Blohm's progress was steadier and marginally faster. Eventually the Spooks would stop and Caius Blohm would not.

They were insertion troops, the Kalendru equivalent of the Strike Force. They wore baggy garments that stored body heat electrochemically in tubing along the seams, and they had facial scarves—which they'd pulled down as they ran—that absorbed CO_2 from their breath.

But the Spooks had only personal lasers for armament and their clothing was ragged. Whatever they had been when they arrived on Bezant, these Kalendru were shipwrecked castaways now.

Blohm heard them pause on the other side of a fallen tree eight feet in diameter; its further end was lost in the undergrowth a hundred feet beyond. He moved close, careful not to touch the log. Fungus on the bark formed tiny fairy castles—turret on turret on turret, each sprouting from the top of the one below. Dust motes that drifted onto the amber droplets beading the domes stuck as if to hot tar.

The Kalendru were talking. If Blohm turned on his helmet, the translation program would have told him what they were saying. That didn't matter.

Moving with even greater care than before, Blohm worked around the fallen tree to the opposite side. A tangle of vines as dense and spiky as a crown of thorns now separated him from his prey. Miniature white flowers grew from the vines. Their faces rotated toward the human's warmth. The tips of the vines themselves began to stretch in his direction as slowly as lava oozing from a volcanic fissure.

Blohm smiled at the brambles. Oh, yes, he understood malevolence like theirs.

He took a grenade from his belt and tossed it over the vine thicket with an easy motion.

The morose jabbering became hooting terror. Blohm was moving away with the best speed safety permitted in case one of the Spooks did what Blohm would have done—throw a grenade back the other way.

None of them did. He heard thuds and despairing cries. Limbs thrashed. For ten or fifteen seconds Spook lasers screamed like angry cats on the other side of the brambles.

Blohm switched his stinger on and circled carefully to the opening by which the Spooks had entered the passage between the thicket and the fallen tree. He'd been sure of getting one of them, hoped to bag several. In the event, he heard none of them escape.

They were waiting for him, though only three could turn their heads in Blohm's direction. They'd attempted to climb to safety on the other side of the tree when the grenade landed among them. They stuck like six long-legged flies on a honey-coated rod.

Blohm reached down and dropped the grenade back into a trouser pocket. He hadn't armed it. The Kalendru didn't wear rank insignia any more than strikers did in the field, but one of the silent captives had the prominent facial veins that were signs of nobility among the species.

"You'll do," Blohm said to the officer. He'd switched on his helmet. Its voice synthesizer chittered a translation.

The Spook's torso and both arms were stuck to the

log. He held a laser in his right hand, but it was glued
in the fungus also. Blohm bent, aimed carefully, and
chiseled away the log's surface with a long burst from
his stinger.

The Spook hooted as splinters whacked his belly
at fire-hose velocity. The chunk of bark holding him
pulled loose at the bottom. Blohm grabbed the neck
scarf and tugged hard, half-choking his captive but
freeing him the rest of the way from the tree. The
Kalender's arms were still pinioned like those of a yoked
slave.

Blohm fired a single pellet into the laser. Plastic
disintegrated with a fat purple spark. The captive
flinched away, but he wasn't badly hurt.

"Let's go back to the column, Spook," Blohm said.
He gestured the captive forward with a crook of his
finger. "You know the way. You just came from there.
The major's going to want to talk with you."

They started down the corridor between log and
thicket, the prisoner preceding. Behind them the
remaining Kalendru hooted desperately. The brambles
were easing closer.

Blohm didn't look around.

Abbado's squad had joined Blohm in the jungle, but
they took their positions with most of C41 on the
perimeter and let the scout bring his prisoner the last
of the way to Farrell by himself. At least half the
civilians waited to see what was going to happen,
though only a few dozen at the front of the crowd
would have anything to watch but the backs of their
fellows.

An electronic interrogation was about as boring as
waiting for paint to dry anyway. Unless the interrogator

screwed up, got too deep, and went psychotic, of course. Art Farrell hoped he was too experienced and too careful to let that happen.

"That was a slick a piece of work, Blohm," Farrell said. The interrogation gear was laid out and waiting. He gestured to it and said, "You want to control on the spare set? You've earned it."

Blohm looked more like a corpse than a man; except for his eyes. He shook his head minusculy. "I'll check in with Mirica," he said. "But I did my job first."

"Right," Farrell said. He figured Blohm had to know the score about the kid already. If the scout wanted to hope for a miracle, well, didn't they all? "Kristal, you take—"

"Major Farrell?" said Tamara Lundie. "It might be more efficient if I carried out the interrogation. My equipment includes expert systems for the purpose."

Farrell wondered if he ever in his life had been so earnest. He didn't actually see Manager al-Ibrahimi smile, but he had a feeling God was having similar thoughts.

"Thank you, Administrator," Farrell said, preserving the public formality, "but however expert your systems are, they're not soldiers. I'll handle this one myself."

Kristal and Nessman had laid the prisoner flat on the sheet and taped his ankles. Occasionally the interrogation subject flailed around. The slab of sticky wood pinioned the Kalender's arms so well that they left it. Farrell wasn't sure that the glue could be removed without killing the subject anyway.

"With your permission, Major," al-Ibrahimi said. "I could be of service on the control panel. Not to direct the interrogation, of course; but to support you."

God might not be any smarter than his blonde aide,

but he sure as hell wasn't naive. "Yeah, all right," Farrell said. "Let's do it."

He seated himself beside the quiescent prisoner and fitted the leads from the control box into the socket in his helmet. Kristal had already attached the induction pads to the Kalender's bare scalp. Al-Ibrahimi plugged another set of induction leads into the panel's second output jack and placed the pads at the base of his own skull. Farrell had expected the manager to hook the box to his headset or just to use the control panel's holographic projection.

Farrell closed his eyes and focused on a bead glowing against an azure field; it was the way he always prepared for an interrogation. "Go," he said. Al-Ibrahimi rolled him into the prisoner's mind.

Interrogation by any method is an art. As with all arts, the successful artist has to both know what he wants and be ready to exploit unexpected opportunities.

Some interrogators liked to drug themselves for closer rapport with the subject. That technique provided clearer images, but it increased the danger that the subject's attitudes and perceptions would bleed into the interrogator's unconscious and affect his judgment when he evaluated the data. Even without the risk, Art Farrell wasn't about to *be* another person for the sake of detail he didn't need.

Farrell started with the landing. His will guided the AI in the control box as it furrowed the Kalender's memory the way a plow does a field. The dirt is in no way changed or damaged, but its alignment shifts in accordance with the plowman's desires.

Images appeared in Farrell's mind, flashes of memory:

The Kalendru had made a normal landing, and they'd

been fully prepared for trouble. The prisoner had been an officer with the party of eighty troops who set up perimeter defenses while the main body unloaded aircars. There were three or four hundred Spooks all told; the precise number was deeper in the subject's memory and of no immediate concern to Farrell.

They'd had casualties immediately. The troops hadn't worn body armor even at the beginning. Injuries were more frequent and more serious than those the strikers received from similar dangers. Though the shooting trees were only waist high—they'd sprouted after the asteroid hit to form the landing site—their inch-long spikes punctured limbs and body cavities, killing and maiming.

Memories cascaded into Farrell's awareness faster and more clearly than he had expected. It was more like a training exercise with recorded images than the real interrogation of a non-human subject. The surface of Farrell's mind was aware of Manager al-Ibrahimi seated across from him, smiling like a hatchet-faced Buddha.

"I could be of service on the control panel," he'd said, and that was true with no mistake. Maybe he really was God.

The prisoner watched as troops filed from the ship into the eight large aircars. Farrell caught the subject's unease and regret even though at this stage the interrogation was primarily after data, not reactions to them. The prisoner was very angry at being given the dangerous job of guarding the landing site while others flew to the goal in armored safety.

The cars flipped on their backs and dived into the ground, all of them within a half-second of one another. The subject's eyes stared at a plume of smoke rising

*from the distant jungle and felt a relief as enormous
as the fear and anger of a moment before.*

The fear returned at once. It overlaid every
perception from that point on, though al-Ibrahimi's
hands on the controls shifted it into a thing Farrell
was aware of rather than something he felt personally.

Farrell moved forward, telescoping time:

*The perimeter guards and others from the ship set
out on foot toward their goal. The Kalendru hadn't
brought land-clearing equipment, but they were armed
soldiers without a mass of civilians to protect.*

*Casualties were constant and horrible, though the
Spooks learned the way the strikers had. The rate of
loss slowed. Some of the troops who'd taken off their
helmets ran amok; the unaffected seared swollen insects
off the brain stems of the survivors, but the victims
died immediately in convulsions.*

Thus far everything the subject had experienced
was familiar to Farrell at least in outline. The subject's
hope began to mount; the column was near its goal.
Then—

*The image failed in horror so complete that the
subject's mind could not fix the cause in memory. Farrell
viewed a confused montage of hills, of broad boulevards
cut through the landscape, of running in blind terror.*

*Humans couldn't have survived the panicked dash
through half a mile of this jungle; a surprising number
of the Kalendru did. Their quickness saved them where
the strikers wouldn't have been able to bring their
firepower to bear.*

*The subject didn't see the starship lift off and
immediately crash, though he was aware of the event
when it happened. Farrell couldn't be sure whether
the vessel fled in response to whatever had happened*

to the ground expedition or if the crew was reacting to threats against themselves. It was the wrong decision, but perhaps there was no right one.

The column's forty survivors set off to hike out of the crater. Their only goal now was personal survival. The jungle killed them, but only a few. They were crack troops, experienced in the dangers of their environment and driven by desperate need.

Again Farrell coursed forward in time:

The subject's first sight of the crater's wall brought a glow of elation that forced aside fear's crushing miasma like a bubble forming as water boils. Farrell felt personal joy: the sheer rock wall was the human expedition's goal, too, and this was the first time he'd seen it.

The ground twenty feet back from the edge of the cliffs was almost clear. Vines or roots, yellow-gray and whip thin, ran up the rock at frequent intervals. They had no foliage, but their suckers invaded minute cracks.

Three Kalendru took off their boots and all equipment except a coil of fine cord each. They began to climb while their fellows kept guard on the ground. The climbers studiously avoided the vines. Instead, they found hand and footholds in the slight cracks and knobs present even on a smooth rock face. The Spooks' long limbs were an advantage in a task like this.

The subject stood with his back to the stone, looking up the green wall of jungle rising nearly as high as the cliffs did. He—and Farrell—expected something to come from the trees to attack the climbers.

When the climbers were halfway to the top the rocks supporting their weight crumbled.

The Kalendru plunged a hundred feet straight down in a spattering of gravel. Two died instantly. The third *lay with his eyes open and his lips moving slowly while blood spread in a brown pool beneath the body.*

The subject's slender fingers appeared in memory, lifting one of the pebbles that had dropped with the climbers. Hair-fine rootlets still clung to what had been its inner surface. The roots' hydrostatic expansion had wedged the rock loose; the victim fell with it, unharmed until impact crushed him against the stone beneath.

The subject's memory stared at the cliffs, then covered his face with his hands. His skin puckered and was turning blotchy green in the Kalendru equivalent of weeping. He and his fellows would never be able to climb the rock. To attempt to use the wood of this jungle as building material would be a slower, surer form of suicide.

Something iridescent and sun-bright gleamed in the high sky. A ship was landing in the crater. An enemy ship, but still a vessel which could be captured or at least might supply the weapons and equipment the remnants of the Kalendru expedition lacked.

It was their only chance to escape this crater.

Major Arthur Farrell's body writhed as he came out of the interrogation trance. Kristal and Nessman grabbed him. Even without drugs, the similarity of his situation to that of the subject was so close that he'd been dragged in deeper than he'd expected.

"There's no way out!" Farrell shouted. "There's no way out!"

"They move pretty good," said Caius Blohm. "Now, a lot of it's the way they're built, sure, legs and arms sticking way out like some kind of spider."

The patients lay under the trailers against the likelihood of rain, but a clear tarpaulin sheltered the life support system itself. The lighted control panel gleamed, slightly distorted by folds in the fabric. Dr. Ciler sat sideways to it as he stolidly ate spoonfuls of his dinner. His back was to Blohm.

"It's not just that, though," Blohm said. His left hand cradled Mirica; his right gestured, miming Kalendru limbs. "They really see, sense, things better than we do. Sure, they got great electronics, but that wouldn't do them any good if they couldn't *see* differences that fine, you see?"

The membrane covering Mirica's mouth and nose wicked oxygen in one direction and carbon dioxide in the other. It wasn't quite as efficient as a pressure tent, but it was readily portable. Thin control wires connected the child's upper chest and several sections of her skull to the support system.

"So they should've been able to grease me, right?" Blohm said. "There's six of them besides. But they don't have the instinct for it. Talent, sure, but they don't feel the forest. That was the difference, and that was all the difference in the world."

Mirica's face was waxen. Her chest rose and fell with mechanical efficiency.

"Now, I wanted to get around behind them right at the start," Blohm said with a flick of his free hand. "They ran too fast when we laid fire on them, so that meant I was in for a chase."

Dr. Ciler chewed a gruel that was supposed to taste like chicken and rice. He had no expression at all.

The brain function column on the monitor beside him was as flat as the surface of a pond.

Even without the panoramic display Meyer would have recognized the careful footsteps approaching her from behind. "Go on and lie down, Matt," she said softly. She knew he couldn't get much sleep when he had to keep his arms around her all night or she'd wake up shouting again. "I'm off guard in forty minutes."

"I'm all right," Lock said. He stood close but without touching. Meyer continued to look toward the jungle.

The attorney had lost twenty pounds since the landing; sweated it off, worked it off, worried it off. Like all the rest of them. This operation had been a bitch.

"Esther," Lock said. "Manager al-Ibrahimi and his aide are Category Fours. I watched them with the interrogation equipment. They have to be Category Fours to use it the way they did. Do you think your major knows that?"

Meyer frowned as she tried to assign the words a context from her own experience. "Rejects, you mean?" she asked.

"No, no," the civilian said. By the time the second syllable left his mouth, he'd purged his tone of irritation. "Civil Service Category Four. That's the highest classification there is. They have implanted computers wired to their brains."

Meyer nodded, thinking that she understood. "Oh," she said. "Well, I guess we need all the help we can get, right?"

"Esther," Lock said, frustrated that the only person in the camp he was ready to confide in didn't have the background to understand what he was saying. "I don't think there's a hundred Category Fours in the entire Unity. What are two of them doing here?"

Meyer raised her visor and rubbed her eyes, then lowered it again. The exercise gave her a moment to think.

"I don't know," she said. "Finding us a way out of the worst ratfuck I've ever been dropped into, maybe."

Lock cleared his throat but didn't speak.

Meyer patted his thigh with her free left hand. "Look, Matt," she said, "go get some sleep, okay. And let's not bug the major. He's got enough on his plate with stuff that's likely to get people killed."

Abbado snapped alert when he felt the plastic flex under the weight of someone kneeling beside him. "Hey, Doc," he said to Ciler. "I'd been meaning to look you up."

"I didn't mean to wake you, Guilio," Ciler said. "I had to wait until Dr. Weisshampl took over from me at the medical facility."

"If a striker doesn't learn to take catnaps," the sergeant said, "he doesn't sleep."

He frowned. "There isn't a problem with Methie's leg, is there?"

"No, he's doing as well as one could hope," Ciler said. "Better than I expected, certainly. Ah . . ."

He looked at Matushek, sleeping beside Abbado with both arms over his face. The rest of 3-3 was scattered: Horgen and Methie were on guard, while Caldwell had found a trio of civilian friends and was relaxing in her own fashion.

"Let's go check the perimeter," Abbado said, rising to his feet and snapping his equipment belt around his waist. "About time I did that anyway."

"You're aware that a little girl, a Mirica Laubenthal, was injured in the attack this morning," Ciler said as they picked their way among sleepers to the camp's open border near the berm.

"Yeah, poor kid," Abbado agreed. "Saw it happen. Shot right through the head, right?"

"A through wound, yes," Ciler said. "Not to mince words, Guilio, the child is dead. There's no possibility that she'll ever regain brain function. Eighty percent of the tissue has been destroyed by the trauma."

"Poor kid," Abbado repeated. "Well, that lot won't kill any more. Blohm took care of the ones that broke away and that wasn't very damned many, I promise you."

This close to the berm you could hear the vines move. It was like the sound a cat makes at birds it can't reach through a window: a rapid ticking, not very loud, but thick with frustrated rage.

"It's Striker Blohm who concerns me," the doctor said. "He apparently doesn't realize that the child's condition is irreversible."

Abbado looked at Ciler. "Well, Doc," he said, "A lot of times what a guy knows and what he lets himself know aren't the same thing. Methie'll swear to you that his wife back on Organpipe's got cobwebs growing on her pussy, waiting for him to finish his tour. Don't worry about Blohm."

"Guilio," Ciler said, "we are operating on a shoestring for medical support here. You know how many sick, how many wounded we have. The child is on our only full life-support system, and it's of no *use* to her. You see that, don't you?"

"Ah," said Abbado. "Ah."

He put his hand on Ciler's shoulder and squeezed it. "Look, Doc, sure I see. But I think you'd better keep the kid hooked up anyhow. Like you say, we're short of medical resources."

"I don't understand," Ciler said.

Abbado grimaced. "Doc," he said. "I know Blohm. Now, don't mistake what I'm saying—he may be crazy as a bedbug, but he's okay mostly, you know?"

"Of course I don't want to increase the stress on Striker Blohm," Ciler began. "But—"

"That's not what I mean, Doc," Abbado said. "The thing is, if Blohm ever gets the notion you, you know, finished off his little buddy, he'll wax your ass as sure as I'm standing here. And we can't afford to lose so good a medic, you see?"

"Ah," said Dr. Ciler. "Yes, I suppose I do."

Farrell watched the images al-Ibrahimi and Lundie together had forced from the Kalender in the last instants before the subject died. Jungle lay crushed to either side of a ragged boulevard; then blankness and a kaleidoscope of images—none of them frightening though obviously the cause of the subject's terror.

And death, when the interrogator and controller continued to force the subject's mind toward what it refused to recall.

"It doesn't mean anything to me," Farrell said.

"The last portion isn't really memory," Lundie said. "They're icons for what he wouldn't remember."

Farrell wished that he hadn't been in the Spook's mind himself. These recorded images of the final interrogation were harmless in themselves, but Farrell recalled the fear that suffused the cursory glance he'd had of the same memories. Kalendru psychology differed enough from the human variety that you normally couldn't empathize with the other species; but if you'd been one, this one . . .

"Poor bastard," Farrell muttered. He looked at

al-Ibrahimi and said, "We've got the bulldozers. We can maybe undercut the side of the cliff and make a ramp up."

There were no campfires because of the recent rain. A group of civilians sat around a minilight eating gruel. The pair of strikers with them sang a verse of a cadence song: *"I gotta guy, his hair is red . . ."*

"It appears probable that as soon as a tractor comes within range," Lundie said, "a boulder of size sufficient to destroy the vehicle will drop from the top of the cliff. The only way we can test the theory is to venture a bulldozer, of course."

"Yeah," said Farrell. "Shit. But that's the only choice, isn't it? We get out or we all die—after the ammo runs out if not before."

"—he makes his living by lying on a bed."

The civilians bellowed the chorus, *"Go to your left, your right, your left!"*

"If we can't get out from the rim of the wheel," the project manager said, "and I agree with Tamara that we can't, then the choice is to strike for the hub."

"C41 heads for wherever the Spooks were trying to go, you mean?" Farrell said, thinking of the montage that cloaked the subject's fear.

"I got a girl, her hair is black . . ."

"The entire column," al-Ibrahimi said. "There's no point in separating us civilians from our protection. The known dangers would overwhelm us."

Lundie nodded solemnly. "The Kalendru came here at great risk," she said. "Whatever it was they were looking for may mean our safety."

There was a shout of triumph across the camp. Somebody'd gotten a fire to light.

Al-Ibrahimi smiled. "Or it may mean that I satisfy

my curiosity before I die. Either result is more satisfying than simply being devoured by the vegetation, wouldn't you say?"

Art Farrell started to chuckle. Not because the joke was particularly funny; but because he knew that to the project manager, it wasn't really a joke.

"Go to your left, your right, your left . . ."

Teamwork

The civilians straggled more every day, and there were fewer strikers to guard the lengthening column. Farrell eyed the trees; a striker's job, not a commander's. A job he was more comfortable with, though.

It wasn't anybody's fault. The march was just taking a physical toll of civilians who weren't used to it. Anybody who thought you hardened people by pushing them beyond their limits was a damned fool. What you did was break them.

Manager al-Ibrahimi stood at the right margin of the trail, waiting for Farrell. Farrell crossed the column at a gap but continued to stump forward at his regular pace, a little faster than the line of march.

Farrell was coming from the rear of the column to the front. He planned to talk to the noncom with the lead squad, then start back. Like every day in the past, like every day in the future until he died or they all got where they were going.

Which might mean the same thing.

"Two days ought to get us there," Farrell said to al-Ibrahimi's back. "That's an advantage over going to the rim. That would have been another week."

"Yes," the manager said. He shifted slightly so that he and Farrell stood side by side, watching the jungle and from the corners of their eyes the column marching

331

in the center of the track. "We're wearing down the colonists. At the present rate of collapse, in five days there'll be more people being carried than carrying."

It was a joke of sorts.

"These are good folks," Farrell said, feeling oddly defensive about the civilians. "They don't give up. I'd figured . . . they were drafted, you know. They wouldn't *try*."

"They're intelligent, successful people, Major," al-Ibrahimi said. "They're exactly the sort of people you'd want in any difficult operation. They'd be better for training, of course; but they're getting that, from your strikers and the environment."

A party of five civilians passed, arm in arm. The man in the middle and the young women on the two ends were supporting an aged couple who couldn't otherwise have walked.

"It's a fucking crime to treat people like this," Farrell said in sudden bitterness.

"Not a crime, no," al-Ibrahimi said. "All laws and regulations were complied with. Very likely a sin, though."

He looked more hawk-faced with the diet and labor of each passing day. "Do you believe in Hell, Major?" he asked.

"Not as much as I used to," Farrell said. He laughed wryly. "That's a screwy thing to say, isn't it? But it's the truth."

Nessman marched by cradling a grenade launcher. He was talking to a pair of young women—girls, really. He shut up when he saw Farrell waiting on the trail. The girls didn't understand and continued to chatter merrily.

Farrell turned his head deliberately to follow

Nessman with his eyes, though he didn't say anything aloud. The striker muttered to the girls and lengthened his pace. He nodded awkwardly to the grim-faced major as he passed.

"Tamara doesn't believe in Hell," the manager said. "She believes she has logic on her side, though I think she's wrong."

He smiled very tersely. "She's having difficulties with alkaloids from the vine that attacked her," he added. "I may need to help her walk shortly."

"Is she all right?" Farrell asked, more sharply than he'd intended.

"She has as good a chance as any of the rest of us do," al-Ibrahimi said. "The poisons won't kill her themselves. They affect her mental state, but I don't think she'll do anything unacceptably dangerous."

He glanced directly at Farrell again. "I watch her when I think there might be a problem, Major."

Branches creaked. A tree thirty feet high walked into the cleared track on a tripod of air roots.

Limbs groped for a civilian so tired that he continued to slog toward it with his face to the ground. Nessman fired five times, hitting branches with three of the grenades. Jagged splinters blew out from the flashes. Another branch closed the spray of twigs at its tip on Nessman.

"Down!" Farrell shouted. He backed a step to be sure the jet from the rocket he lifted to his shoulder wouldn't fry a civilian.

The tree wobbled on its long roots like a praying mantis. Two more branches, one of them broken by a grenade, swung toward Nessman. The striker's boots were off the ground.

Farrell aimed at the trunk just below the crown and

fired. As the rocket cracked away, something grabbed him from behind by both elbows.

Farrell's rockets were fuzed for a quarter-second delay because most of the targets were going to be tree trunks. This warhead penetrated to the heartwood and went off, blowing all the limbs away from the bole. Nessman hit the ground hard and rolled clear of the relaxing grip.

The panoramic display showed Farrell what he couldn't turn his head enough to see: a bush with dark green foliage had leaned onto the track to seize him. He'd backed too close to the forest when he launched. He tried to reach the powerknife in his belt; the supple branches bent, but not enough.

The decapitated tree lurched forward with mad purpose. Farrell didn't suppose the blast had affected the controlling intelligence, but the tree's sensory organs must have been in the branch tips. It zigzagged across the trail, folding one root under the trunk and shifting to the new center of gravity with each stride. It disappeared into the unbroken jungle, leaving behind a faint streamer of smoke from its jagged peak.

Leaves closed over Farrell's helmet and began to draw his head back. Through a gap in them he saw Nessman fumbling with a 4-pound rocket. "Your knife!" Farrell shouted. "Cut me loose or it'll break my neck!"

The striker ignored him and extended the blast tube of the rocket. "For Christ's sake, Nessman—" Farrell said.

Nessman fired the rocket into the ground immediately behind Farrell. The warhead, again on a quarter-second fuze, blew both strikers across the track in a shower of dirt and a flare of unburnt fuel.

Farrell tried to sit up. Manager al-Ibrahimi and

several other civilians helped him. The walking tree hadn't left a mark in the walls of vegetation to either side of the trail.

"Christ, Nessman, that was a bit drastic, wasn't it?" Farrell said.

"One good turn deserves another, Major," the striker said with a shaky smile. "There was a spike like a big needle coming out of the middle of that thing. I didn't figure to fuck around hoping I'd get the right spot with my knife."

"Anybody hurt?" Farrell said as he got to his feet. "Are we all okay?"

"Besides," said Nessman, taking the project manager's hand to help stand up. "I never believed there was any such thing as too much force."

"Sarge, my helmet says this branch is moving, mark," Caldwell said. *"Do you—"*

Abbado clicked the image onto the left half of his visor. The tree was thirty feet to the right of the track the bulldozer was cutting immediately ahead of 3-3. Abbado had to shift a few steps sideways to see it directly. The motion of the high branch was minute, but the AI said the tip was pulling away from the column.

Like a striker winding up to throw a grenade, Abbado figured.

"—think—" Caldwell continued.

Abbado raked a burst from his stinger the length of the branch. The pellets had lost some velocity and energy in the hundred feet from the muzzle, but they still chewed wood like the blade of a circle saw.

Bark exploded; the branch shivered like a broken-backed snake. Scores of fist-sized individual pellets, nuts or fruit, flew off the terminal twigs and burst into flame as they fell.

One fireball landed at the edge of the track and splashed clingy droplets across several feet of scraped dirt; the rest smoked and steamed to the jungle floor. None of them did any harm.

The branch dangled from a strand of bark. The stinger pellets hadn't broken it through, but the limb's own snapping release smashed its weakened fibers.

"Josie," Abbado said, "if God hadn't meant us to use reconnaissance by fire, he wouldn't have given us stingers. Break. C41, watch this tree as you pass, *mark*. Some of the other branches may have an idea they want to toss things at us. Out."

"It might've filled you like a pincushion, Sarge," Ace Matushek said. "Remember what happened to Top."

"Hey, it was going to throw something so I broke its throwing arm," Abbado said. "Where's the down side?"

The lead section of civilians had paused while the strikers dealt with the tree. Now they started moving again. Abbado expected them to skirt the sputtering flame as widely as possible, but instead they pretty much ignored it. They'd already learned that worrying about a danger avoided made you more vulnerable to the one on its way toward you.

"Sergeant," a thirtyish woman said to Abbado. "Can you tell me why we've changed direction?"

"Ma'am?" said Abbado. "We're going straight, more or less. As the big trees allow, is all."

"Sergeant," she said, obviously irritated. "I'm Certified Engineer Schwartzchild. I've been mapping the terrain as we proceed. From the point at which we left the landing site we've been marching at a course of two hundred thirty-nine degrees. We've now shifted to a course of two-sixty-eight—with, as you say, corrections for major obstacles."

She waggled a small case covered in gray sharkskin, obviously a navigation and cartographic device of some sort. "I asked do you have an explanation."

"No ma'am," Abbado said. He decided not to reload his stinger. He'd only fired seventy pellets. He shrugged. "You're right, but I hadn't noticed it till you said so. I'm afraid you'll have to check with the major. Or God. Probably God."

He nodded and started forward. Abbado liked to stay about forty feet behind the bulldozer, close enough to judge whatever situation the blade might uncover without being in the middle of it.

Schwartzchild fell into step to his left, a little closer than he liked. "But Sergeant?" she said. "Don't you care? Something must have happened to cause the change, don't you see?"

"Yes ma'am," he said. "But I don't much care, no. Talk to the major about it, why don't you?"

He turned his head. "Hey Ace?"

"That vine up there?" Matushek said, raising his chest-slung grenade launcher.

"Yeah," Abbado agreed. "Pop it, will you?"

You didn't need helmet electronics for communication if you'd worked with people long enough. A vine six inches thick laced through the tops of at least a dozen trees in an arc ahead of the column. It wasn't doing any obvious harm, but Abbado didn't like the look of it.

The dozer poked its blade into the bole of one of the trees. Matushek put a single grenade where the vine spanned the gap between that crown and the next tree.

The tree shivered, starting to go over. Ace fired again, blowing the other half loose. As the tree fell, it carried the vine fragment wrapped in its branches. Broken ends writhed like snakes.

"Ma'am," Abbado said, returning his attention briefly to Schwartzchild. She wasn't bad-looking, not if you liked your women solid. "I trust the major to do the best he can for us. And I trust God to know what he's doing, though that's about all. But even if I didn't trust them, I know I couldn't do a better job of planning myself. Best I leave them do what they do so I can get on with my end. Do you see what I mean?"

The tree hit with the ragged popping of wood fibers stressed beyond their breaking point. The ground gave a hollow boom. The tractor backed slightly to clear the pit the roots had pulled open, then started forward again.

"I don't see how you can live that way," Schwartzchild said. "We could be going into anything and you don't know."

"Ma'am," Abbado said. "Nobody ever tells strikers anything. If they do it's mostly a lie. I'm sorry it's happening to you guys, you don't deserve it. But we're used to it. Go talk to the major, why don't you?"

He noticed a swelling like a giant beehive stuck on the side of a tree ahead. Caldwell was already extending the blast tube of a rocket to deal with it.

"Ma'am," he added to the woman still walking beside him. "You got to keep your mind on your job and hope the people in charge are doing the same."

The bank of clouds to the east was bright with sunlight streaming through a pair of holes in the similar array on the western horizon. The sky above the freshly-cut campsite was as clear as tap water, but it wouldn't be long before the evening rains hit.

Meyer sat leaning back on her hands. Sighing, she reached for the clamps locking her thigh guards onto the torso apron of her hard suit.

"Sit," Lock repeated sharply. "I'll get to them in good time. Just sit."

He lifted away the breastplate. As usual the clearing's humid air felt cool and fresh.

"God damn," Meyer said, closing her eyes. "I think I sweated out ten pounds today. One of these days you're going to open the suit and all that's left of me's going to dribble out onto the ground."

Matt handed her a drinking bottle and started on the leg pieces. "You shouldn't have to wear the suit all day," he said without looking at her. "Another striker could spell you."

"I'm used to the suits," she said. She took a careful swig. She'd drunk some from the condenser in the hard suit, but it was hard to get enough fluid—and food—down while you were *on*. "We're short. It's better not to have people screwing around with their armor if the shit hits the fan."

A tractor was pulling one trailer slowly across the cleared area. Steve Nessman and a pair of girls who'd lost their puppy fat on the march were manhandling rolls of sheeting off the trailer to the teams of civilians waiting to place them on the bulldozed ground.

The whole group sang the "Prisoners' Chorus" from Verdi's *Nabucco*. They were surprisingly good. One of the civilians had been a voice coach.

"I'm learning to drive the bulldozers," Lock said. "Using the blade correctly is surprisingly complex. I hadn't realized that it tilts, it doesn't just push straight ahead."

"What is this?" Meyer asked, lowering the bottle. "Is this converter-run water?"

"There's the usual electrolyte fortification from the converter, yes," Lock said. He began to put the pieces of the hard suit away in the carrying bag. "There's a few drops of lemon syrup also. Mrs. Regley provided it. She had a tree of her own on the roof garden of Horizon Towers. Do you like it?"

"It's good," Meyer said. Really, it was odd; she'd thought somebody'd screwed up the converter setting. She took another swig. The slight tartness did have a cleansing feel if you knew it didn't mean something had gone wrong. "I'll have to thank her."

"You saved her life, you know," Matt said. "The first day. When you saved mine."

"We're all saving each others lives in this ratfuck," Meyer said. She leaned forward and kissed him hungrily. "All of us."

Doctors Parelli and Ciler talked briefly as the latter arrived to take his midnight shift with the wounded. Parelli walked off to join her husband; Ciler sat down beside the monitor.

"Hey, Doc," Caius Blohm said. He smoothed Mirica's hair back from her forehead, then gently placed the child on the nest of bedding where she lay while Blohm was on patrol. "Got time to talk?"

"Yes, ah . . ." Ciler said.

Blohm gestured toward the berm. Ciler thought about his duties and decided that for a few minutes the wounded would be all right by themselves. He followed the striker to the darkness and relative privacy.

"I wanted to ask you about Mirica, Doc," the scout said, facing the forest. "Is she going to get better?"

Ciler considered a number of ways to answer the question. He settled on the truth. "No," he said. "I'm terribly sorry, Striker Blohm. The injury she received is total and irreversible. If we were back on Earth, my answer would have to be the same."

"Yeah, pretty much what I figured," Blohm said. His left hand was gloved. He ran the index finger gently over the surface of a log the dozer blade had wedged into the berm; blue sparks popped nervously from its surface.

"You know," he said, "I thought about maybe bringing ears back to her when I caught the Spooks who did it. There's guys who collect Spook ears. I never got into it, but I thought, you know, for Mirica . . ."

Ciler watched him without speaking. Blohm met his gaze, but the scout's eyes were merely glints reflected from the light beside Major Farrell's hunched form.

"She wouldn't have liked that, Doc," Blohm said earnestly. "She was a great kid, you know? Wouldn't hurt a fly."

A hollow *clock! clock! clock!* rang through the starlit forest, then died away. "I'm glad you came to that decision," Ciler said quietly.

"Yeah," said Blohm. He sounded as though he was discussing a problem with a machine that he couldn't get to run the way it should. "And hell, I couldn't even get pissed at the Spooks. I mean, they didn't mean to shoot her. It was a waste shot, right? They wanted to get me and they fucked up. What am I supposed to do? Hunt down the training cadre that didn't make them better marksmen?"

His gloved hand touched the log three times, each time harder. The last was a full-strength blow with the edge of his fist. Sparks sizzled, outlining his prominent knuckles.

"They just wasted a shot," he repeated. "Everybody does, you know. One time or another, you shoot something you didn't mean to because you didn't have time to think. *Everybody* does."

"Mirica knew you loved her," Ciler said carefully. "I think the part of her that is with God still knows that."

"She was a good kid," Blohm said. "Wish I could've known her longer. What's wired up to the machine now, that's not her, though. I guess you'd like your machine back?"

"There are . . ." Ciler said. "Patients. For whom the use of the life support system would be the difference between life and death, yes."

"I figured that was it," Blohm said. He looked at the forest. "Well, shit. Look, Doc. There's two things. What's left isn't Mirica. But I don't want it to hurt. I don't want it to, you know, suffocate because it just got unplugged. Even though it's just a lump of meat. You understand?"

Ciler thought about the oath he swore when he became a doctor; and he thought about Hell. "I understand," he said softly.

"The other thing is," Blohm said. "I don't want to know about it. Not ever, not in any way."

"I understand," Ciler said.

Caius Blohm strode away without speaking or looking back.

The bulldozer that would be breaking trail the next morning was parked at what would be the head of the line of march. Blohm walked around it and leaned against the curve of the high steel blade. A veil of phosphorescent moss shimmered on the edge of the forest like a magenta dream.

The blade was cool. Blohm took his helmet off and turned to rest his forehead against the metal.

Seraphina Suares appeared at his side. She put an arm around the striker and began to weep quietly.

Blohm hugged the widow close. "There," he said, holding her. "There."

But he didn't shed a tear of his own.

Once More into the Breach

The lead bulldozer cut into the berm and shoved a section of the dirt and debris slantwise into the jungle. Farrell watched Blohm and four strikers under Verushnie step through the gap. The scout vanished into the jungle while the others waited for the bulldozer to begin its advance.

The column was still forming, though it was later in the morning than Farrell would have liked. Manager al-Ibrahimi and his monitors were redistributing loads and help for the injured among those still capable of marching on their own.

"The berm isn't really protection," Tamara Lundie said. Her voice had a distant quality that made Farrell look harder at her. Her face was drawn and her arms trembled even though she clasped them firmly to her abdomen.

"It won't keep the jungle out, that's true," Farrell said. "It's useful as a boundary for the civilians, though. Especially kids."

"We've learned fast," Lundie said. "Even the children. All of us who survived know about dangers we'd never before appreciated."

"Are you all right?" Farrell said abruptly. "Do you have a fever?"

Lundie squatted down, hugging herself harder. She

344

closed, then reopened her eyes but they weren't focusing on her present surroundings. "The poison's affecting me," she said. "I'll be all right in a few minutes. I won't have to be carried if I can wait—"

She wobbled. She would have fallen over except that Farrell dropped into a squat beside her and put an arm around her shoulders. The sheeting was rolled in the first trailer; the bulldozed ground, though bare, wasn't safe to sit on.

"*Six?*" said Kristal's voice. "*We're ready. Over.*"

"Four, start the march any time God gives the word," Farrell ordered. "Out."

He continued to support Tamara Lundie. Her whole body shuddered as if she was in the last stages of a deadly virus.

Nobody gave them more than a glance. Hundreds of civilians were half crippled or wearied to the edge of collapse even now at the start of the day's march. The strikers focused on the things that were likely to cause them problems: the jungle, the health of the colonists in the section they were responsible for today; injuries and sores where load-bearing equipment had worn through their skin in the humid warmth. Two more huddled figures, whatever their rank, were less important than personal survival.

"You were redlined, you know," Lundie said with her face buried against Farrell's shoulder. She wrapped her arms around his stocky torso, holding on like a sailor to a stanchion as a wave surge drags his body toward the great gray ocean. "The whole of Strike Company C41 was redlined."

"I know that," Farrell said. He'd known it even as the boat lifted the screaming, weeping survivors from Active Cloak. Until he got the new orders, he'd hoped the authorities wouldn't look too closely. "They put us on colony security as a stand-down. They didn't know how dangerous Bezant was."

"No," Lundie said. "He chose BZ 459 because it was dangerous. It was his plan to reintegrate you into society by showing civilians what soldiers did for them. Making them understand how helpless they were except for your lives pledged for them. They would see, and you would know they saw."

"*C41,*" Kristal's voice ordered. "*We have clearance from the manager. Lead elements proceed. Remaining personnel follow and keep your sections closed up. Out.*"

"Regiment *planned* this?" Farrell said. The poison was making Lundie hallucinate. 701st Regimental Command was a number of things including uncaring, ponderous and inefficient, but it wasn't crazy; and its power was limited to the Strike Force. This involved civilians. "Can you stand up, Tamara? I see Dr. Ciler over there."

"I'll be all right," she said with a sharpness that meant at least some of her conscious mind was processing data normally. "Just hold me for a minute longer. It wasn't the military that gave the orders, it was us—the Chief Administrator of the Unity and his aide, God and his blonde aide . . . We made a terrible mistake. We didn't know about the Kalendru and we didn't expect the ship to land in the crater. I didn't assemble the necessary information for my chief."

Lundie's body began to shake again. She was crying. "It all went wrong because I didn't do my job."

"You did your job," Farrell said. He patted her shoulder. He felt awkward because his stinger's muzzle prodded Lundie when he leaned. "There's always shit that nobody knew about, always. You did your job just fine."

"I can stand up now," Lundie said in a small voice. She sniffled.

"That's good," Farrell said, rising and helping her up with him. "We're not out of the woods yet."

Lundie turned her back to him. "You're not angry?" she said.

"No, I'm not angry," Farrell said. He looked at the civilians starting another day's journey toward Christ knew what; clinging to one another, dragging the wreck of their possessions. A striker laughed with an old man, then straightened the straps of the almost empty knapsack across the civilian's shoulders. Some of the marchers were even trying to sing. "Maybe those people are, but I'm not even sure of that."

"I'd better see Jafar," Lundie said. She rubbed her cheek with her hand to hide the blush. "He worries about me."

She met Farrell's gaze squarely. Her eyes were a gray purer than anything else in this jungle. "He worries about everyone, you know. Everyone in the Unity. And he came here."

The column filed out of the encampment; worn civilians under the eyes of troops bristling with weapons. The strikers were faceless with their visors locked down, but they were no longer anonymous to those they guarded. Colonists joked nervously; strikers joked back with coarse, grim affection.

"You know, Tamara?" Farrell said. He wasn't sure he'd ever be able to understand what he'd just been told, though he didn't doubt the truth of it. "The hardest thing in the world for strikers to believe is that anybody gives a shit about us. But I guess you've convinced C41, for what that's worth."

"Tractor One," said Esther Meyer's helmet in God's voice, *"this is Admin One. Hold up for stragglers at the next suitable location. Sections One, Two and Three, close gaps and halt in place. Sections Four, Five and Six, continue forward until you've regained your proper interval. Out."*

Seligman immediately took his vehicle out of gear and raised his helmet visor. "This looks pretty damn suitable to me," he said. "Got anything to drink, Councillor Lock?"

"Water for you and me," Matt said. "Try this canteen, Esther."

Meyer walked forward on the deck, swigging through her open visor. The contents were flavored with whiskey, probably the best bourbon she'd ever drunk in her life. Just enough for taste, but it meant a lot more than that.

Twenty feet ahead of the dozer blade nodded huge flowers on twelve-foot stalks. They grew among the roots of a forest giant. The perfume that oozed from the magenta blooms was musky, enticing. The AI didn't find anything dangerous to humans in the complex scent, but Meyer didn't believe the flowers' only purpose in this jungle was to attract pollinating insects. Maybe they were poisonous to Spooks.

She'd clear it with a grenade before the dozer started forward again. Just in case.

"We're heading toward the center of this crater," Matt said in a quiet voice from just behind her. "We aren't trying to get out any more. I think I know why al-Ibrahimi—or Major Farrell?—changed course."

Matt hadn't asked Meyer about the new course of the past two days. She'd have told him. There wasn't anything that she *wouldn't* tell him; but because he was so fucking smart he knew better than to ask her. He was the one to keep, which she'd never be able to do . . .

Meyer put an arm around Matt, careful so that her rigid armor didn't hurt him. "The major doesn't make that kind of decision, love," she said. "Especially now."

"The jungle's artificial," Matt said, lacing his arm over hers. He had a stinger again. He'd never be much good with it, but he was trying. "There's a biological control system here in this crater and it's still operating—look at the way threats have been tailored to human metabolisms since we've been here."

Seligman dumped his hard suit's waste container on the other side of the cab. Privacy for bodily functions had gone out the window since the trek began, though there was an attempt to rig a screen around one or two of the pit latrines each time the column halted in the evening.

"What are we doing here, then?" Meyer said. She grasped the concept but it didn't make any sense. "What are you guys, civilians, doing here anyway? I can see them sending us."

"I don't know," Lock said. "If it weren't for the two Category Fours leading us and the obvious unsuitability of Bezant, any part of Bezant, for colonization, I'd say it was just chance. But the Kalendru were certainly here searching for the biological control, and now we are too."

Meyer turned her head slightly. Her helmet careted a tree in the middle distance that for the moment was only a sliver of gray trunk and a few sprays of leaves with orange veins. A similar tree had flung branch tips like thirty-pound spears to ring and shatter on the tractor's armor.

This specimen was probably safely outside the column's intended course. If not, though, Meyer figured it'd know to choose targets more vulnerable than the bulldozer was. She'd put a rocket into it if God or his aide guided Seligman in that direction.

"The Kalendru are an ancient race," Matt said. His hair was dark and wavy. It'd grown noticeably since they abandoned the ship. "At the height of their expansion half a million years ago, they inhabited a hundred times as many planets as they do now. We humans were still learning to chip flint. Maybe the Kalendru found records, maybe they deciphered a legend. Whyever they came here, they were right. This *is* the weapon that will end the war."

Meyer lowered her arm so that she could turn to face Matt. She could watch him by offsetting her display, but to him it'd seem that she was looking away. "Honey," she said, afraid she was going to sound insulting. "I know these trees are a bitch when it's just an understrength company and small arms. But honey, up against the hardware a line battalion deploys—they're nothing, sweetheart. And a tank wouldn't even slow down for this jungle, trust me."

"Not the vegetation, Esther," Matt said with a quirky smile. "Microorganisms. Disease bacteria and viruses."

Meyer checked her locator grid. Judging from where the striker guards were, Section 4 had closed up to the tractor in the middle of the column and Section 5 wasn't far back from 4. Section 6 was still way behind where it needed to be. It would be several minutes before Seligman got the go-ahead.

"Okay," Meyer said, "that's bad. I guess a lot of people could be killed before everybody in the Unity got immune boosters. But that's what'd happen. It'd cost a bundle, but that's what wars do. They wouldn't beat us that way, Matt."

"We could protect people, Esther," Matt said. He combed the fingers of his left hand through his long, curly hair. "We couldn't protect *all* life forms, though. What if every food crop on every planet died? What if all the algae in every ocean died and rotted, instead of producing oxygen? What if all the animals, wild and domesticated, started attacking people the way those Kalendru attacked us where the ship landed?"

"Oh," said Meyer. "Oh."

"Tractor One, this is Admin One," God's cold voice said. *"Start forward in sixty, that is six-zero, seconds,* count. *Admin One out."*

Meyer took a fuel-air grenade from her equipment belt and armed it. She eyed the giant flowers nodding in the still air.

"I hadn't thought of that," she said as she lobbed the grenade.

Seligman walked around the bulldozer, prodding at the treads to be sure they were locking properly to minimize ground pressure. Abbado moved in front of the vehicle to get a direct view of the terrain. There was no standing water, but his boots squelched with each step.

Horgen sang softly, *"Love is the ring that has no—"*

She felt Abbado's eye on her. "Sorry, Sarge," she said.

Though it wasn't open to the sky, this was the largest clear stretch Abbado'd seen since their column left the landing site. Fat-trunked trees rose from hummocks above the surrounding soil. They stood like pillars set on stone plinths, their branches arched and interlaced a hundred feet in the air. Brush and reeds of varied species covered the ground to a height of ten or twenty feet, but there was none of the intermediate vegetation that screened the canopy from sight throughout most of this jungle.

The major came around the side of the bulldozer with God. Major Farrell looked rock-hard, the way he always did on an operation. Metal can bend and deform, but a rock just wears a little smoother.

The sun would go cold before the major broke.

"We're waiting on the tractor, sir," Abbado explained. "Blohm reported the soil never gets softer than this, but there isn't a way around for at least a quarter mile either way. Seligman says he can make it if his treads work like they ought."

The major lifted his visor to look over the terrain unenhanced, then closed it again. "How do you intend to proceed?" he asked.

"We'll go around the trunks," Abbado said. "Seligman says he can't push trees over here because he'd lose traction, but we don't need to try. The dozer'll take care of the little stuff—it's all got thorns or edges like a razor, but that's no surprise. We've got branches marked to take down with grenades where we need to."

The major didn't speak for a moment as he compared an overlay of Abbado's action plan with the direct view through his faceshield. "Good," he said. "The big mother there, *mark*."

He'd careted a trunk with deep vertical grooves like the flutes of Ionic columns.

"Take the whole top off with a rocket when you're ready to start. It looks too much like the one that came apart into tentacles when we were just starting out."

"This one probably hinges out from root level," Manager al-Ibrahimi said. "The tips of the limbs are armed with spikes, so severing the trunk where it branches should do the job nicely."

God didn't look any different from the first time Abbado had seen him. You could just about shave on the bridge of his nose. He continued, "That tree, *mark*, that tree, *mark*, and that tree, *mark*—those three are designed to topple over. I assume they'll do so if the bulldozer comes within range."

"I'll be a son of a bitch," Abbado said. The noted trees didn't have any mutual similarities the sergeant could see. He'd planned to watch the seed pods dangling from the crown of the one whose bole was as straight as the shaft of a walking stick, but that was all.

"We're over a huge construct extending a square mile below ground," al-Ibrahimi added. "It begins twenty feet beneath the surface, but Tamara and I can't tell from echo shadowings just how far down it extends. Because the soil here is backfill, it's settled to a degree. It doesn't drain as well as the remainder of the forest, so the vegetation is adapted to high water levels."

Major Farrell looked at the manager. "Is this what we're looking for?" he said in a grayer, sharper tone than Abbado normally heard when the major talked to superiors. "Should we be digging instead of cutting through these trees?"

The tractor revved and moved forward ten feet before halting. The staff driver, Seligman, was still on the ground. He resumed his methodical inspection now that a new portion of track had been rotated beneath the road wheels. Essie's lawyer friend Lock was at the controls.

"We can't dig with our present equipment because of the swampy ground," God replied calmly. "There'll be an entrance, probably in the center of the tract. We'll find it, and we'll enter. And we'll find the way to turn off this Hell, Arthur, and escape."

"Sorry, sir," the major muttered. "I—strikers get used to the mushroom treatment. Kept in the dark and fed horseshit."

Seligman awkwardly mounted the bulldozer. Essie gripped the cab frame with one hand and helped pull the driver's armored bulk onto the deck with the other.

"Tamara says she talked with you, Arthur," God said. "Is there anything you want to discuss with me directly?"

The major shook his head. "Nothing that affects the mission, sir," he said. "Hell, nothing at all."

"Sarge, we're ready to go," Essie called from the tractor's deck. She wasn't ignoring the major. By directing the information as she had, she let the brass know the situation without formally breaking in on them.

Abbado extended the tube of a rocket. "Horgen, *mark*," he ordered, "Matushek, *mark*."

He was assigning rocket targets besides the one he was going to handle.

"At the base, three, two, one, fire!"

Abbado squeezed the bar trigger. Exhaust impulse kicked him as his rocket streaked into the trunk a hundred feet away. The warhead penetrated a yard or so before it detonated. The tree's own mass tamped the explosion and sent the bole toppling away from the line of march.

The three giants fell slowly, twisting and groaning like men clutching with angry desperation at a slope too steep to possibly support them. Clouds of varicolored splinters settled around the ragged stumps. Sap flickered into flame from Horgen's tree.

Abbado aimed his stinger at the nearby branch he'd marked for himself. His grenadiers sighted on more distant targets where pellets wouldn't have sufficient kinetic energy to do enough damage. 3-3 had waited to eliminate threats till the last moment so that the jungle wouldn't grow replacements.

"Tractor One, this is Admin One," God ordered. *"Move on!"*

"Now, you see those trees that look like palms there, Mirica?" said Caius Blohm. "The fronds slant up, but look how sharp the tips are. You look at that and you *know* they'll chop you like a meat-axe if you step in range."

The ground here was marginally higher than that of the previous stretch. Instead of semi-swamp, the soil was firm and the forest again displayed full triple-canopy variety.

Blohm moved with easy caution outside the arc through which the fronds could pivot. Separate entities within the forest tended to observe boundaries so they didn't destroy each other. Often the safest passage was just beyond the reach of a particularly dangerous element.

"Now, a lot of the guys," Blohm explained, "they think the helmet can take care of that. Maybe yes, maybe no. The AI catches details, you bet. But you know, sweetheart, the machine doesn't have any feel for this place. This isn't a bunch of things, trees and suchlike. It's *a* thing, a forest."

He saw light through the undergrowth. Ribbon-like leaves hung from vines weaving an arbor through the middle canopy. They were translucent, shimmering in shades of indigo and violet because of the brightness beyond them.

Blohm worked his way around the high curtain instead of passing under it. He stepped through the middle of a clump of saplings that leaned outward. He was at the edge of a track cleared down to the clay and a hundred yards wide.

"Six, this is Six-six-two," he reported. "There's a road cut through the forest here. The only difference between it and what your bulldozer does is this is a hell of a lot wider. Over."

The dirt was dry and cracking, well on the way to becoming crumbly laterite. That didn't take long in this climate. The forest was trying to recolonize the track by means of runners from both edges. The scraped soil was poor in nutrients and couldn't hold water. Swatches of moss and vividly colored lichen looked like chemical spills.

"Six-six-two, this is Six," the major replied as quickly as if he'd been standing beside Blohm. *"Do you think you can cross it safely? Over."*

Blohm looked at Mirica. She nodded solemnly. "Six, yeah," he said aloud. "It's a couple weeks old judging from the regrowth. Do you want me to see where it goes? Over."

"Six-six-two, negative," the major said sharply. *"Get on with your mission. If you find anything that looks like a doorway—anything at all artificial—report ASAP.*

And Blohm? Watch yourself. I'd say that bare ground was a perfect killing zone if we were any damn place but this jungle where every damn thing is. Six out."

"Six, this place isn't so bad when you get used to it," Blohm said cheerfully. "Six-six-two out."

He looked at Mirica. "Now, are you ready, sweetie? We don't want to waste any time crossing this stretch, but I don't want you to run so fast you stumble either. See those two trees that the side's been scraped off halfway up the trunk? We're going to go between them and then wait a minute while we get our bearings."

"I'll be all right, Caius," Mirica said. "You be very careful. There's curled bamboo that'll hurt you."

Blohm dialed up his visor's magnification. Damned if the kid wasn't right. What seemed to be foot-high shoots were the tops of reeds twisted like helical springs. The tips were ice-pick sharp. Blohm didn't doubt the shafts would drive to their full twelve-foot height even if they'd had the opportunity to go through his body first the long way.

"I guess we'd better go to the right of the right-hand tree instead," he said. "Understand? Let's go, then."

Blohm jogged across the cleared track with his faceshield raised, pivoting his head in an effort to look in all directions. The panoramic display would have given him a shrunken vision of reality. He trusted it the way he trusted all aspects of the helmet's sensors and processing algorithms—trusted them to do everything a machine could do. Machines didn't have instincts.

The track was marked by grooves parallel to the axis of movement, each of them a few feet long. They had the appearance of the drag marks made by a harrow lifted into travelling mode but not clearing all the bumps.

Judging from the weathering, the track probably had something to do with the Spook expedition. God would have liked to have a piece of ground-clearing equipment that big, Blohm knew. For his own part . . . well, the forest was no friend of Caius Blohm's, but it played fair. Ramming through it with a blade a hundred yards wide didn't seem right to him.

Blohm skirted the marked tree as he'd planned. The forest beyond the cleared strip was typical of what he'd seen ever since they landed: variations in the form of danger and hostility, but nothing exceptional and nothing that explained the track. The broad pathway meandered through the forest, utterly destroying everything in its path.

Six winged pods a yard across rotated out of the canopy a hundred feet ahead of Blohm. They slanted through the mid-growth toward him. The seeds were pointed and weighed several pounds apiece, but buoyed by their wings they fell too slowly for their effect to be purely kinetic.

"Now what they expect us to do, honey," Blohm said, "is dodge behind a tree. What we're going to do instead is stand right here like we'd froze to the ground. Spinning the way they do, those things can curve around a tree as easy as not and we wouldn't see them coming. Now, you stick with me. When they get a little closer—run!"

With the nearest of the pods ten feet from him in slant distance Blohm sprinted under the spinning missile. Bristles at the seed's tip twisted, tracking his body heat. The pod attempted to reverse its angle of descent.

It wasn't high enough to succeed, though the last of the sheaf of missiles came closer than Blohm had expected. All six hit the ground in close sequence and burst, spraying sticky fluid. The pools self-ignited in yellow-orange pillars which slowly merged in a single inferno.

"Most times running away's near as bad an idea as sitting with your thumb up your ass," Blohm explained with satisfaction to his companion. "You can't run faster than a laser bolt, right? Go toward them and at least you've got a chance to react to whatever they try on."

"Six-six-two, this is Admin Two," said the voice Blohm had learned to identify as Tamara Lundie. *"Initial survey imagery showed a hill or mound in the region you just crossed. Have you noticed any sign of such a feature, over?"*

"Admin Two, that's a negative," Blohm said. He saw a quivering glow through the undergrowth ahead, like an electrical arc softened by a foot of frosted glass. "The Spooks had one hell of a bulldozer to clear the track back there. Maybe they scraped the hill down too. Over."

"Six-six-two," said Lundie's cool voice. *"The Kalendru had no equipment beyond small arms. Admin Two out."*

Blohm used his knife with the power off to very gently pry one of a line of saplings to the side. The sapling's crown suddenly twisted down around the blade like a elephant's trunk coiling.

Blohm withdrew the blade. Savage thorns along the inner surface of the coil squeaked, but they couldn't mark the synthetic diamond. The sapling very slowly began to straighten, recharging the reservoir of hydrostatic energy which it had just emptied. Blohm slipped past while it was still harmless.

He was in a small clearing. A skewed oval door was set in the surface of the ground. Enclosing it, a discontinuity in the air itself like a gigantic soap bubble scintillated across the visual spectrum.

Blohm felt a rhythmic vibration. He wondered if it was an earth tremor. He'd have guessed a starship was landing, except then actinic radiation would have penetrated the layers of foliage above him.

"Six, this is Six-six-two," he reported. "Major, I've found you your door! Over."

Major Farrell didn't respond. After waiting ten seconds, Blohm echoed a remote view from the major's helmet.

He realized why everybody with the column had other things on their mind.

The End

The vibration wasn't initially severe, but the pulses built and formed harmonics. Standing waves humped the swampy soil. An old woman near Farrell at the front of the column fell down.

The thing rose slowly, visible both through the relatively sparse trees and above the spreading canopy. The segmented outer shell was rusty maroon with yellow-gray blotches. It would have passed for a hill of the coarse rain forest limestone.

It *had* passed for a hill when the survey ship orbited Bezant.

"C41 to the front," Farrell ordered as he extended the tube of a 4-pound rocket. It wasn't going to be enough. Heavy Weapons Platoon, full-strength and fully equipped, wouldn't have been enough, but hell, you had to try. "Strikers who pass the trailer, bring all the extra rockets. Admin, get the civilians moving back fast. Throw all your gear away but don't leave people behind. Six out."

The creature advanced like a snail on rhythmic pulsations of its undersurface. Because of its size it moved as fast as a healthy man could walk on smooth ground. The shell slipped down with every forward pulse, then lifted again. The lower edge of each shell segment was pointed the way a snake's scales are. They

361

gouged away everything in the creature's path like the bite of a shark whose teeth were three feet long.

The civilians weren't healthy and the bulldozer's path wasn't smooth. Only a fraction of the Kalendru expeditionary force had escaped the snail's attack, and they were crack troops.

Strikers jogged to the front of the column. Most of them carried rockets. They waited for Farrell's fire command. No point in wasting warheads on branches when you knew the target was going to clear you a field of fire in a moment or two.

"Major," Manager al-Ibrahimi said. "Don't throw away your personnel! You can't stop that creature but you may be able to escape."

"Get your ass out of here, civilian!" Major Arthur Farrell shouted. "This is a tactical decision and I'm in tactical command! Get your people back. We won't be able to hold it long."

We won't be able to hold it at all. But hell, you've got to try.

Seligman was so focused on the ground twenty feet in front of the bulldozer that he didn't notice the creature rising out of the jungle three hundred yards to the side. He increased power to the left tread by minuscule increments to avoid losing traction as he tore the blade through a root.

The ground was shuddering like a lake in an earthquake, but you didn't notice that aboard the tractor. Matt had seen the creature, though. Was it a snail?

Esther Meyer raised her visor's magnification to x64, as high as she could focus on the vibrating deck. The thing's teeth were the plates of its shell. They sawed from side to side as the creature advanced, grinding trees to bits the way a gear train chews twigs that fall in.

The snail must have a mouth on the underside, though, or there'd have been a wrack of destroyed vegetation to the sides of the path through the jungle. Meyer had wondered about that trail when she echoed Blohm's imagery. She'd learned a lot about clearing jungle by riding the dozer.

A rocket skimmed the jungle canopy and struck near the peak of the snail's shell. That wasn't the target Meyer would have chosen for the round she'd started to arm, but the lack of result showed her it didn't make any difference.

The warhead burst with the usual blue-white flash and a spurt of dust blasted from the shell. The dust settled. One of the snail's teeth had shattered. The stump dropped from the socket shielded by the points of overlying denticles.

As the snail throbbed forward to take another bite from the jungle, the segments of its covering shifted and reformed. Meyer couldn't see any change from the normal chewing motion of the teeth, but at the end of it the shell showed no sign of damage. Denticles had moved forward from the back or sides. The creature's ability to shape its body beneath the armor meant that no part of its flesh would be unprotected despite C41's firepower.

Matt fired his stinger. Seligman heard the weapon's snarl and turned to see what Matt was shooting at.

"Holy shit!" the driver cried.

"Aim us at the thing!" Meyer said. "Raise the blade just off the ground. Maybe we can slow it down."

Seligman rotated out of his seat and jumped from

the bulldozer before Meyer could stop him. The driver hit face down, splashing waterlogged dirt to all sides. He lay there while the bulldozer crawled away with no one at the controls.

Matt stepped into the cab. "I'll drive!" he said in a voice as bright and jagged as shards of glass. He adjusted the hand switches. The tractor bucked briefly. Matt had lowered the blade for a deeper bite instead of raising it as he'd intended. He corrected quickly and began swinging the vehicle to the left to face the monster.

There was no way to compare a machine twelve feet high and twenty feet broad with a living creature three hundred feet in either dimension. Driving into the snail wouldn't make any more difference than a fart in a whirlwind, but Meyer didn't know anything else to try.

Matt increased speed. Now the treads didn't need to maintain traction while shoving a load of vegetation and topsoil. The snail was only a hundred yards away. Six rockets hit it simultaneously. An instant later another sheaf hit the same points in the shell. At least some of the latter must have struck temporary gaps in the armor because flesh filtered the warheads' sharp radiance.

The snail continued its advance unaffected. One throbbing pulse after the volleys hit and the frontal armor again was whole. It was like trying to stop a Spook tank with 4-pound rockets.

Just like a tank. Meyer *did* know what to do.

Matt twitched his controls to avoid a hummock supporting a tree ten feet in diameter. That was the last obstacle between them and the snail.

Meyer leaned into the cab. "Matt, bail out!" she said.

He ignored her. The tractor's speed increased to a fast walk. Reeds and thin mud splashed to either side.

Meyer rapped Matt on the side of the head. He rolled from the seat, stunned by the armored gauntlet. Meyer grabbed a double handful of shirt and tossed him as far as she could.

Alone now, Meyer walked onto the left side of the quivering deck. The snail was fifty feet away, too close to see the huge body entire. It was like trying to view the building you stood beside. Rockets smashed against it like hail on a truck's cab, doing damage but no fatal harm. Meyer had armed her four, but it wasn't time to launch them yet.

An instant before she jumped down Meyer threw a fuel-air grenade to the side of the bulldozer. She fell flat, hitting just as hard as she'd known she was going to.

She hugged the ground for the remaining two seconds of the grenade's fuze train. When the bomb went off, the snail was so close that Meyer wasn't able to feel the shockwave. She scrambled to the wide crater and threw herself in. The cavity was already filling with water.

The bulldozer struck the snail head-on. The blade's hard alloy and the harder, more brittle denticles ground together in a curtain of sparks. The tractor's cab lifted. The treads continued to spin while the snail drove the blade into the soil.

The right support arm fractured. Denticles pulled pieces off the blade and ripped away the tractor's hood. Power cables shorted, showering electrical sparks among those of shell on metal. The snail resumed its advance, surging over the bulldozer's demolished remains.

The creature covered Meyer with a crushing darkness she knew would never lift. She shielded the rockets between her crooked arm and torso, letting the soft weight of the snail's foot squeeze her deeper in the swampy soil.

A thousand one, a thousand two—

The foot rippled, driving Meyer into the back of the grenade crater as it propelled the creature forward.

A thousand three, a thousand four—

Meyer couldn't see or hear, but she felt the motion change. She'd reached the mouth. She couldn't even be sure her rockets were still pointed upward, but perhaps the God that brought Matt into her life could take care of that too.

She fired all four rockets. The impulse of the trapped exhaust was an explosion in itself, rending her despite the hard suit.

Esther Meyer felt Matt's warm arms lift her toward the radiance at the end of the tunnel.

"Councillor Lock?" Abbado said. "The major thought we ought to bring you in before dark. He's worried it's still dangerous out here."

The civilian turned and glared at the strikers of 3-3. "It's not dangerous for Esther now, though, is it?" he said in a cold, angry voice.

Abbado grinned. He'd figured Lock was sitting here in quivering terror, afraid even to stand up and walk away. Angry was good. This kind of angry meant the fellow hadn't redlined after all.

"Come on, councillor," Abbado said. "She wouldn't want you to get your ass waxed now. Neither would we."

"Krishna! that was a big fucker," Caldwell said,

looking at the snail's remains. "What's it doing, though? Melting?"

When the creature hunched itself vertical after destroying the bulldozer, Abbado'd thought the damned thing was going to jump right onto the strikers and retreating civilians. Instead it died where it was. It was an hour after things settled down that they'd figured out what Essie Meyer had done. Hell of a good striker, Essie was.

Lock sat fifty feet from where the snail collapsed. The hair on the right side of his head was matted with blood from a pressure cut and there was mud all over his back. He looked at Caldwell and said, "When I saw it swell over the trees I thought it must be pneumatic, a balloon. I even shot at it."

Matushek picked up the stinger lying on the ground near Lock. He began to wipe it down.

"I'll help you up," Abbado said, offering Lock his hand to prod the civilian into motion.

Lock rose to his feet unaided. "It expanded with water like a sponge," he said. "That's how it could lie flat until victims came in range. Now that it's dead, the water leaks out again."

The snail was still a huge mound, but it'd shrunk noticeably since its collapse. Teeth fell out as the flesh pulled away from the roots. Abbado hadn't made the connection with the water deepening into a pond around the corpse, though.

"Wouldn't have been hard to nail it from orbit," Horgen said. "When the Spooks were dropping asteroids, that's sure hell the first place *I'd* have dropped one."

"Wouldn't have worked," Abbado said. He put a hand on Lock's shoulder in a combination of support and guidance. They started walking toward the camp. "Well, it would've smashed our friend there to a grease spot, sure, but the Spooks wanted to get into the control room below. That's why they were here. Anything you could be sure of taking out the snail with, you'd bust up what they were looking for."

"Except what Esther did," Lock said.

Matushek nodded. "She had balls, all right," he agreed.

The sky was turning brilliant crimson. The strikers were going to have to switch to light amplification any minute now, besides having to worry that the civilian would manage to walk into something that hadn't gotten the word about humans being the good guys now.

"A lot of the folks're planning to camp down inside tonight," Abbado said, keeping the civilian focused on something other than what lay in a stinking pool behind him. There was no way in hell they'd be able to recover Essie's body. "There's no showers or anything, but at least it's inside. There's must be miles of corridor."

"Me, I'll stay above ground," Caldwell said. "I always thought the best way to deal with a bunker was fill it full of explosive and blow it inside out."

"Hard it is to find a faithful friend . . ." Horgen sang under her breath. She paused and asked, "Anybody know who built the place to begin with?"

"I asked the major," Abbado said. "He says maybe it was the Spooks themself half a million years ago. The place feels like Spook work, anyway. You know, the way the angles are all off."

It had gone from sunset to full dark in the time they'd been walking. Horgen was in the lead. Lock placed himself directly behind her and followed her steps precisely. A pretty bright guy, Abbado thought.

"What I want to know," Ace Matushek said, "is how we got in. My helmet said that bubble over the trap door would fry my brain if I walked into it. God looks at the thing for a few seconds, steps through, and opens the door to shut it off."

"Manager al-Ibrahimi is a Category Four civil servant," Lock said quietly. There was an undertone to his voice that Abbado couldn't identify. "The bubble would have been a Kalendru mental shield. It interferes with any electrical activity that doesn't match its settings—nerve pulses among them. Manager al-Ibrahimi keyed his brain waves to the requirement, so it passed him."

"Just like that?" Horgen said.

"Under normal circumstances, breaching a shield of that sort would require destruction of the entire base," Lock explained. "Category Fours have cybernetic implants coupled to their nervous systems. The manager—and his aide—could calculate the proper and relative motions of every star in the galaxy if they chose to."

"Jesus Christ," Abbado said.

"Or God, perhaps," Lock said with a slight smile Abbado hadn't expected of him. "I used to think that Category Fours weren't human. Well, I used to believe a lot of things that weren't true."

"We all do, snake," Matushek said, explicitly accepting Councillor Matthew Lock into the company of veterans. Essie would've liked to hear that. Ace chuckled. "That's how we manage to keep on going."

They were nearing the entrance to the ancient bunker. Electrical lights and a few campfires gleamed.

The remaining bulldozer had enlarged the clearing.

"We should've camped back where the snail went through," Abbado joked. "Now, that was land clearing."

"No fucking thank you," Caldwell said.

Lock tensed and stumbled on a clod that'd dropped off the back of a track cleat. Abbado grimaced. "Sorry, councillor," he said.

The civilian looked back at him. "Don't ever be sorry for what you are, any of you," Lock said fiercely. "If you were sensitive gentlemen and ladies, we'd all be dead."

"Hey, we were all in this together," Abbado said, squeezing Lock's shoulder.

Groups of people, colonists and strikers together, were heating dinner. It always seemed to Abbado that the sludge went down better hot. He was sure looking forward to real food, though.

"Was there communications equipment in the base?" Lock asked, nodding toward the encampment. "Or do we still have to reach the intended site to send a message capsule?"

"We got to get to a capsule," Abbado said. "Well, somebody does. Blohm'll take out a team while most folks wait here till the flyers come. God says he turned off the jungle. That's the Category Four stuff you're talking about, I guess."

"You know it's going to be us going out with Blohm, don't you, Sarge?" Matushek said. "And I tell you, I don't trust it's going to be just a hike and a climb."

"Hell, Three-three's the experts, aren't we?" Caldwell said. "I didn't want to sit around twiddling my thumbs anyhow."

Steve Nessman and a group of civilians were lining a bulldozed pit with plastic sheeting. It looked like they were trying to build a bathing pool, though Abbado didn't know how they thought they were going to fill it.

"Hey, councillor?" Abbado said. "Want to eat with us? You spent as much time at the front of the column as we did."

"*. . . if you find one who is true,*" Horgen sang as she unlatched one of her bandoliers. "*Change not the old love for a new . . .*"

Caius Blohm stood at the edge of the bulldozer cut. He pressed the muzzle of his stinger carefully against the resilient bark of a tree that towered almost two hundred feet into the nighted sky.

"Well, I *will* be," he said. "Look at that, sweetheart. Yesterday if I'd done that, a thorn would've stuck out a yard and a half. See the tip right there down in the bark?"

"You wouldn't have touched it, Caius," Mirica said with all a child's certainty. "You know better than that."

"You got that right, honey," the striker said. "But we're going to have to cut down a tree like this to get up the side of the crater. I wanted to make damned sure God was right when he said it'd be safe."

Blohm turned his head. His face grew still when he saw two figures watching him. "Who's your friend, honey?" he asked.

"Her name is Ljesn, Caius," Mirica said.

The children were as like as two peas. Of course Mirica was on the skinny side for a human kid.

At the bonfire twenty feet behind them, Seraphina Suares sat with her contingent of orphans. She saw Blohm and waved. "Come join us, Caius," she called.

"Leesin?" the striker said.

The other child covered her mouth and giggled. "*Ljesn*," Mirica said severely.

"Hey, cut me some slack," Blohm said, starting to relax. "I wasn't some base camp hero, I was a scout. When I needed to talk to a, a Kalender, I let my helmet do it. Leesn?"

"Ljesn," the Spook child said. She was wearing an orange apron like she'd had at Active Cloak, but this one wasn't scorched by the grenade blast.

"You'll have to practice, Caius," Mirica said. "But that's better."

"Guess I will," agreed Caius Blohm. "Now, how do you figure we're going to bring down something this big? Rockets at the base I guess, but I can't figure how we get it to drop in the right direction if we do that. Maybe . . ."

The three of them stood before the giant tree, contemplating the future.

EPILOGUE

The psychology of the Kalendru required them to battle the Unity for primacy where another human society would have been willing to coexist with us. When the Kalendru knew that we had the secret of biological control, they ceded that primacy to us without qualification. A Kalender does not fight when he cannot win; and in that too, they differ from us humans.

The Unity will face more enemies and fight more wars—life itself is a struggle against entropy. But for the time being, the armed forces can be reduced. We will finally release troops whom our need retained though they were worn to shadows of humanity.

I regard my experiment as a success. There will be more colonies sent to dangerous planets and more redliners for their security element. I will lead some of them. Tamara, whom I must again call Miss Chun, believes I am paying debts to men and women whom I used until I had used them up. She is wrong: I can never pay those debts.

But I can do penance.

Miss Chun will return to the Unity administration, as is wholly proper. She had nothing on her conscience to justify what she underwent on BZ 459, though I believe she will be a wiser administrator for the experience.

In thirty years Miss Chun will be ready to retire. The problem of redliners will not have vanished; and perhaps by then Miss Chun will have sins of her own.

My aide when I take out the next colony will be a former attorney named Matthew Lock. I do not see that he has anything to repay. He was a victim, after all; my victim.

But I have learned that we never know what is in a human heart, even our own heart.

For we are all human.